To. Phil

You were a life saver!
Thanks for responding to
our medical emergencies with
your skills and commitment.

Cheryl Peyton

Six Minutes to
Midnight

Six Minutes to
Midnight

Cheryl Peyton

To order additional copies of this book, contact:
Xlibris Corporation
1-888-795-4274
www.Xlibris.com
Orders@Xlibris.com
97570

In memory of my mother,

who told me to write and inspired me

with her poetry.

Prologue

I t was a warm, breezy day in late July, 1939, on the north shore of
Long Island in Peconic, New York. Perfect weather for the favorite
pastime in this resort area: sailing. That was the activity that had
attracted Albert Einstein to this place for a vacation that summer.

But on this day Einstein was in his cabin, awaiting two important
visitors: fellow physicists, Leo Szilard and Edward Teller. They were
bringing a letter that Szilard had drafted, addressed to President
Roosevelt, stating an urgent need for the United States to secure
uranium ore. Szilard was anxious to inform the President that German
and American scientists were in a race to enrich uranium, to develop
an atomic bomb.

The physicist was seeking his old professor's help to rewrite the letter,
and to sign it, adding his validation, in an appeal to the Administration
to take action. The younger physicist felt that the situation was critical,
and, indeed, just one month later, the German army attacked Poland,
igniting World War II.

"Welcome, my friends," the rumpled Einstein greeted his visitors.
"We'll sit out on the back porch. I'm anxious to see the draft of your
letter, Leo."

The younger physicist nodded, indicating the folder in his hand. "Thank you, Albert, for taking time away from your vacation to see me about this for a second time. It's a good thing that you're so close to Manhattan for an easy drive.

"As I told you last time," Leo began, in his heavy German accent, after they were seated on the porch and tea had been served, "when Fermi and I learned of a successful nuclear fission experiment in Germany, we created a nuclear chain reaction using uranium. The few flashes we allowed to go off convinced us that the world was headed for grief if Germany could develop the physics to manufacture such a bomb.

"Here's my latest draft of a letter to the President warning him of the catastrophic consequences to the world if Germany is allowed sole possession of such a destructive power," Szilard explained, handing over the four typewritten pages. "Sachs has promised me that he'll deliver the letter personally, if you've signed it," referring to Roosevelt's economic advisor.

The older physicist frowned as he read through the lengthy letter, and laid it down after he was finished. "It's a good letter, Leo, but I'd like to shorten it; stress only the main points, to convince Roosevelt of the urgency."

On August 2, 1939, Albert Einstein signed the final version, that had been shortened to two pages, and sent it to the economist who, curiously, didn't deliver it to the President until October 11 of that year. After reading the letter, Roosevelt called in his aide, General Edwin "Pa" Watson and exclaimed, "I want you to read this letter, Pa! This requires immediate action!"

The President appointed a "Uranium Committee," but little came of it as the board approved only $6,000 to buy just enough uranium and graphite to conduct a few of the experiments designed by Szilard.

On December 7, 1941, the Japanese attacked Pearl Harbor, and war was declared on Japan by the United States. Research with uranium, now known as the Manhattan Project, became the nation's most urgent mission.

In 1942, the Army Corps of Engineers cleared out three small farming communities in East Tennessee where they erected a complex for the Project known as the "secret city." Large windowless buildings were erected and given code names, like Y-12 and K-25. Eventually 115,000 employees worked in those buildings without knowing the purpose of their labors; only that were working for their government on "something big for the war." Very few people could have imagined that the end goal of their work was uranium enrichment for a weapon capable of unprecedented destruction.

In early August 1945, the people of the secret city learned, along with the rest of the world, that they had produced the world's first atomic bomb when "Little Boy" was dropped on Hiroshima, Japan, killing 200,000 people. Later, a second bomb was dropped on Nagasaki, forcing Japan to surrender days later. "Japs Give Up!" screamed the headline in the *New York Daily News* in their August 15, 1945 edition. The war was over!

Today, the former secret city is the city of Oak Ridge. The Y-12 facility is now the Department of Energy's National Security Complex, which includes a nuclear weapons plant. Over the years, the DOE has secretly transported thousands of nuclear weapons and much enriched uranium in trucks, leaving out of Y-12, that travel over the nation's highways. The shipment is escorted by twenty-seven armed federal agents, riding in nine armored, unmarked vehicles.

The couriers prepare for any level of threat to the nuclear shipment: from sign-waving protesters opposed to the existence of nuclear weapons, to those who would go to any lengths, and use any kind of firepower, to steal a nuclear weapon. An attack could come from a well-organized local group of dissidents, or a world-wide network of jihadists.

In 1947, the board of the Bulletin of the Atomic Scientists at the University of Chicago created the Doomsday Clock, a symbolic clock face, which uses the minute hand to gauge the closeness we are to midnight; the time of a global nuclear disaster. In 1947, the clock was set at seven minutes, and has been changed nineteen times since then: from as near midnight as two minutes, to as far from midnight as seventeen minutes. On January 1, 2010, the Doomsday Clock was reset to six minutes to midnight.

Chapter 1

1999

It had started raining before the first fraternity party of the year. That was one of the factors that led to the outcome of that evening, he concluded, as he looked back on it. Funny how a little water could start a cascade of events that would become a tidal wave that couldn't be stopped; a perfect storm that swirled out of his control. What happened after the party hadn't been planned; and it certainly hadn't been his fault.

He had spotted the tall blonde the moment she walked into his fraternity house, tossing her mane of long blond hair to shake off the raindrops. He knew her name was Catherine Moore, or "Cat," as she was called by her friends. She was the hottest freshman co-ed in a promising crop of nubile, leggy beauties.

The private university in south-western Ohio was known for its attractive female students; a disproportionate number of blondes among them. It was a mystery whether it was the school's reputation for its many social events that attracted only comely young women or, as high school girls visited the campus, only the physically-superior genes felt at home in the gene pool they found here. Either way, it was a bounty to be reveled in by the more average-looking young men who had to use their social skills, and trade on their family's money, to ingratiate themselves into the social circle of the young women and then, hopefully, into their beds.

An hour into the party he saw Cat across the room, coyly seated on one end of a sofa, a beer in her left hand while her right arm was seductively stretched out across the curved back of the couch. Her long tanned legs, nearly fully exposed in a denim mini skirt, were crossed at the ankles for a touch of propriety. Notable in her appearance was her long streaked-blond hair that framed her small oval face and fell in soft curls below her shoulders, teasing her breasts.

But it was the heavy fringe of dark lashes over her brown eyes that she used to the greatest effect, as she slowly fluttered them at her admirers who had flocked around her, practically salivating in anticipation of having a little conversation with her or, hopefully, something far better. To improve their odds for the latter, they were offering her beers to wear down any inhibitions she might have.

When one of her devotees left, presumably for a refill, a little space opened up near her and he quickly made his way across the crowded room to stand in front of her.

"Is it hot in here, or is it just you?" he offered.

Not original, but direct. He had dressed carefully for the party in a well-tailored, gold-buttoned black blazer, beige twill slacks, and an open-necked cream silk shirt. He looked his best but, of course, he couldn't add to his five foot, eight inch stature, or totally disguise his turned-in right foot. He had been born with CTEV, a clubfoot, that hadn't been entirely corrected with surgery.

She barely acknowledged him with a glance. Then she looked around the room. *Looking for someone better looking, or someone taller, someone to rescue her,* he thought. *Bitch.*

"Thanks," she murmured, finally, looking down.

One word. It was faint notice of his interest and a dismissal, at the same time.

The "refill guy" returned and reclaimed his place next to her, and they resumed their conversation as though there had been no interruption. As though there was no one else present. *No one that counted, at any rate.*

He moved on, furious at her snub. *Who does she think she is? I'm the son of a well-known physicist, for Chris' sakes. Her dad probably owns a car dealership in Elyria.*

Toward midnight the party started breaking up; with some couples drifting upstairs to the boy's sleeping rooms, or to the porch, to extend the evening before parting.

Deciding to go out for cigarettes, he left the house by the back door. Finding that the rain was now coming down hard, he ran to his car that was parked in the lot behind the house. His late-model mica gray Mazda Miata looked cool, even in a downpour. The car had been a gift from his father, to ease a guilty conscience for disliking his own son, he had always thought.

Pulling out of the lot, and around to the front of the house, he caught sight of Cat, walking unsteadily, holding her purse uselessly over her head to cover herself from the rain. Pleased to see her distress, he saw an unexpected opportunity to taunt her. Pushing down the button to open the front passenger window, he brashly ordered, "Get in the car and out of the rain, for Chris' sakes! I'll take you to your dorm. You're in Bradley Hall, aren't you?"

He saw her look of pleasure at the sight of the sleek little car. She hadn't even *seen* who was driving it, he could tell. She immediately opened the door, as instructed, and dropped into the bucket seat. Water dripped from her long hair, as it had when he had first seen her.

"Yeah, I'm in Bradley," she cooed. "Thanks. Killer car. I love it. It's a Miata, right?" She gave him a full smile now, and fluttered her long lashes in that patented come-on of hers. Wide-eyed and looking a little-unfocused, she didn't seem to recognize him from their earlier brief encounter at the party. Of course, he looked taller seated in the small car, and it was the car she was really interested in, anyway.

"I want to stop and pick up some cigarettes, okay?" he asked, pleasantly.

"Sure. I'm in no rush," she encouraged him. "I just have to call someone at home tonight. But no bigee if we stop for a few minutes."

So, she's got someone at home. Is that why's she such a tease?

Making conversation, he asked her about herself, like he could give a rat's ass. She prattled on like she was the most interesting person in the universe. What courses she was taking, where she had come from, how much she liked being at college. *Blah, blah, blah.* He was right that she was from Elyria. He found his own insights amusing, at least.

While she was warming up to her subject, going on about her life at college, she had curled her body in the seat to give him what she thought was a tantalizing frontal view of herself; of her full breasts that stretched the ribbing of her sweater and of her long, slim legs. Her knees were pulled up out of her mini skirt with an unspoken invitation. *Amazing what a $26,000 sports car can get you. Too bad she wasn't interested earlier, before she saw my car, when it was just me.* The reaction that he had sought earlier was now a turnoff. The more she offered the less appealing she became.

This would be too easy, he thought. *I'll screw her and that'll be it. She has no real interest in me, except as how I could be useful to her.*

Arriving at the gas station mini mart, the rain had stopped. He got out of the car and walked in front of the low-slung car, into the store, realizing that this was the first time she would see his limping gait.

When he returned to the car he glanced over at her. *Is it my imagination or did she look away with disapproval, again? Yes, that was the same maneuver she pulled at the party. Now she thinks I'm rich, but knows I'm a cripple, so I'm still of no value to her; the car dealer's daughter.*

He turned to her, trying to make his voice sound light and playful. "Hey, since it's stopped raining, let's ride around a little so I can have a cigarette. You want one?" She nodded.

She took one and he lit the two cigarettes, lowering both windows to let in the fresh air and let out the smoke. Then he backed up the little car, swung around and headed out onto the nearly-deserted streets. Glancing at the dashboard clock he saw it was now after midnight.

Smoking her cigarette, she relaxed, took off her shoes and stretched her legs out. He reached over and stroked her hair, always a good move. She responded with a crooked smile. She was still pretty tipsy, he realized.

Turning onto a road that was mostly commercial and dark at this time of night, he pulled the car over onto the verge, braked to a stop, and cut the lights. *Her eyes widened with what, surprise? Fear?*

"Why are we stopping?!" she demanded, more than questioned.

Jesus, could she really be so clueless? Why would any guy stop the car when some bimbo offered herself on a silver platter?

Her ignorance and her rebuff enraged him. He got out of the car, came around to the curb side, opened her door and pulled her out of her seat. The move was sudden and surprised her. She jerked away, but her unsteadiness enabled him to knock her off her feet. She landed hard on her back in a large mud puddle and cried out in pain. "Oww!"

He threw his weight over her, straddling her body and holding down her arms so she couldn't move. "This is where you belong, bitch! In the mud!" Her blond hair disappeared into the dark oily water. She lifted her head up and spat at him, the spittle landing back on her dirt-streaked face. Her ruined appearance both repulsed and empowered him.

"Get off of me, you fucking maniac!" she screamed uselessly, as she could only squirm beneath him.

By way of response, he picked up a nearby heavy branch that had come down in the storm, and pressed it over her throat, causing her to gag and cough violently. She was now wild-eyed; her face darkening as her oxygen was being restricted.

After a minute, she quit resisting, and was quiet. Taking advantage, he reached under her mini skirt, ripped off her panties, unzipped his pants and thrust himself into her, engorged by a feeling of hatred and power he hadn't known before. She continued to be still. She seemed to have passed out. He tossed aside the branch, and exhausted himself on her. She lay there, without moving or making a sound.

He was just considering what to do next, when headlights shone on the back of his car and a male voice called out, "Need any help? Is anyone there?"

He looked down. The blonde was coming around, opening her mouth to scream again. He picked up a large handful of mud in his right hand, shoved it in into her face. She was still again.

Standing up, now visible to the intruder and blinded by his headlights, he waved off the guy, but the car didn't move. Quickly, in the darkness underneath the beam, he stuffed Cat inside the car through her open door, and slammed it closed to hold in her body as it became folded over in half.

He then walked around to the driver's side in front of his darkened car. He smiled back at the headlights. Not seeing anyone, he raised his left thumb high in the air to indicate there weren't any problems. *Move on. Nothing to see here.*

Getting back in the car, he started up the purring engine, motioning out his window for the car behind to move ahead, which it finally did. An older Camry, he thought. *Good. The guy was satisfied that nothing was wrong and was leaving.*

Slowly, he pulled the little Mazda onto the road and drove on. Coming to a darkened strip mall, he turned in and stopped the car. Cat was still doubled-over in her seat. She hadn't moved or made a sound since he had shoved her in the car.

He knew she was dead before he felt for a pulse to confirm it. Pulling her head up, he saw that her eyes had bugged out sightlessly under the dark lashes, accusing him of the ultimate act against her.

"You got just what you deserved!" he chided her. "Don't you see that?! You asked for it, then tried to get me in trouble!" he kept berating the lifeless form. "Now look at the mess you've left me to deal with!" he scolded.

I have to think. This is no time to panic, like when I was lost in the woods at Boy Scout camp. Work out a plan. People had to have seen her get into my car. So what? I dropped her off, and then I don't know what happened to her. There was a missing person's case like this in the news for an entire year. No body was ever found. No charges were ever brought.

Feeling more in control now, he knew what he had to do—to drive out of town and dump the body someplace; hopefully where it wouldn't be found for a long time, if ever. *Okay. Good start. Then I'll figure out the rest. It will be over and done with soon and I can go back to my normal life like nothing has happened.*

Twenty minutes later he had stopped the car in a deserted area, out in the country. No one was around. There were no lights anywhere. *Good.* Opening the passenger door, he dragged the body out by her legs that she had been so proud of. *Well now they were being put to good use. Wait a minute, where are her shoes?* Dropping the body, he leaned over and reached down in front of her seat and picked up the ballet-style flats. Screwing them onto her feet, as best he could, he was ready to proceed.

Pulling the body by her legs through the brush a ways, he dropped the dead weight again, in exhaustion. A better way, he figured, was to hoist her up from under her arms. He then walked backwards and dragged the body for another fifty feet back into the dense woods.

Thankfully, he came upon an indentation in the ground and a fallen tree nearby. Yanking the body into the shallow "grave" he looked over the bedraggled remains of Cat Moore. *But, something was missing. What was it? What am I forgetting?!*

Returning to the car he found the last thing that he had left behind in the car. On the front floor was her little cloth purse. He grabbed it and took it back to where the body reposed. Opening the gold-colored clasp he took out her wallet, holding onto it as he tossed the purse onto the body. *It could have been a robbery gone bad. There's no identification left, either, if she's ever found!*

Next, he rolled the large tree over her, so that no part of her was visible. *I'm damned good at this, for a fucking amateur. You just have to be smart and keep your head.*

Back at the car, thinking through a possible alibi, he got a blanket out of the trunk and laid it on the grass. Picking it up off the ground, he didn't shake it out but put it back in the trunk. *Part of the plan. I'm getting better at this all the time. I almost want to tell someone how clever I've been, but that would be stupid—not to mention ironic.*

Getting back to town, he drove around to the back of a closed supermarket and tossed the wallet into a dumpster. He heard it fall down into the container.

The next day, the entire university, it seemed, was buzzing about the beautiful Cat Moore who had gone missing. She hadn't gotten back to her dorm last night and hadn't stayed over in the fraternity house. Students in his classes were asking, "Didn't anyone at the house know what happened to her after she left the party?"

He heard that her roommate had called the police when she got up in the morning and discovered that Cat had never come back to the dorm. The police had said they couldn't follow up for three days on a missing adult, and besides, she wasn't the first co-ed to not come home after a party.

He had worked out his plan on his drive back to the fraternity house and decided to put it into effect, now. He knew some of the brothers or the girls at the party would have seen Cat getting into his car. He was cool with that.

When he calculated that most everyone had heard the news of the missing freshman, and before the police could start investigating it, he stopped by the district police station and asked to speak to a detective about Catherine Moore, the university freshman he heard had been reported missing.

His performance, in relating to the detective the incidents of the night of the party, struck the perfect note of interest and concern, but not alarm; as he didn't think anything really bad could have happened in this peaceful small town.

He gave details of the time he had spent with "Catherine," telling as much of the truth as he could. *That's where most suspects go wrong; making up everything and then they can't possibly remember the story each time they're asked to repeat it. Too many fabricated details can be easily checked out and found to be untrue. Christ, with all the cop shows on TV everyone should know a little about forensics.*

He admitted offering a ride to Cat (as he called her now, showing a relaxed attitude with the detective). He hadn't seen her leave the party, but after he had gotten his car in back, to run out for cigarettes, he pulled around in front of the house and saw her distress, walking in the rain without an umbrella or any covering. He opened a window and called out to her to offer her a lift. She accepted and was grateful for his thoughtfulness.

He had looked at the dashboard clock and noted it was midnight when they arrived at the late-night market. He went inside alone, bought the cigarettes, and returned to the car where he lit cigarettes for both of them. Then they drove around for a short time, to smoke and talk about how she was settling in to college life.

Feeling like they had become friends, and sensing a mutual desire for a sexual encounter, he had pulled off the road and stopped the car to park. No, he hadn't noticed what road it was, but he could probably find it again. Anyway, they sat in the car for a while, kissing. When things had heated up to a certain point, they both got out of the car, at his suggestion, and he retrieved the blanket out of the trunk. He laid it out on the ground where they then had consensual sex. "Did he mean intercourse?" "Yes," he meant intercourse. He believed the blanket was still in his trunk, if they wanted to see it.

After they got back into the car, her mood changed dramatically. She told him she should never have agreed to have sex with him, that she had a boyfriend at home who was, even then, expecting a call from her. On the drive back towards her dorm, he tried to reassure her that it would be okay, that her boyfriend didn't have to find out, that they had both been drinking and the beer had loosened their inhibitions. She said that she wanted to get out a couple of blocks from her dorm as she didn't want anyone she knew to see her getting out of his car, "putting two and two together," as she had phrased it.

He thought he was doing the right thing by her at the time, but now, hearing that she was missing, he felt guilty that he hadn't delivered her right to her door, like a gentleman. He hadn't any idea where she had walked after getting out of his car, or if she had met up with someone else, as he had driven on to his fraternity house without looking back.

The detective had his statement typed up from the recording that had been made of his statement. He signed it and left the station, visibly upset, but not inconsolable.

I should be an actor. I was Kevin Fucking Spacey in "The Usual Suspects," even down to the gimpy leg; except, I can't walk without a limp when I get down the street, he smiled, ruefully.

Three days later, like clockwork, two detectives came to the fraternity house, investigating the case of the missing co-ed. Foul play was now assumed. They interviewed everyone who had attended the party as well as students from the missing girl's dorm and others on and around the campus who might have seen something.

The detectives advised him that (just as he had thought) several people had reported seeing Cat get into his car. But he remained calm. *Why not? Their statements were not incriminating. Their accounts were consistent with his story, even corroborating it.*

It was obvious that Detective Barnes suspected that he was responsible for Cat's disappearance. The detective, on two different occasions, asked him to come back down to the station where he and his partner, Detective O'Malley, took turns interrogating him or they asked him questions, together.

He was prepared for anything they could ask him. He stayed with his plan of only changing the end of the story, being careful not to say too much. After all, anyone who was innocent wouldn't have noticed every little thing, as though they would have to give a precise account of themselves. There was no evidence. They couldn't charge him with anything, and he knew it.

But the questions continued. How had he and Cat gotten together for consensual sex when no one saw them even talking together at the party? (With the alcohol, the intimacy brought on by closeness in the car and their flirtatious conversation, it was a natural consequence. Besides, why was it so impossible to think that she found him attractive? And everyone knew how sexy Cat was.) *Anyone who was guilty of a criminal act, wouldn't have admitted to having sex with a near stranger, who was now missing.*

What was the exact route they had taken? (He was driven out in the detective's car and declared that scenic Sommerset Drive was the route they had taken.) *There was no way they could ever prove he was lying about that.*

Was there anyone around to see Cat get out of the car near the dormitory? And if not, why not, if it was only twelve-thirty or so? (No one had seen them. A group of people had just walked by, he had noticed. No one else was coming along, just then.)

What time had he gotten back to the fraternity house? (Around one o'clock, maybe earlier. He had had no reason to check his watch.)

Why hadn't anyone seen him come back? Wasn't anyone else still up at one, after a party? (That one was easy. His room was just off the back stairs. He didn't have to walk by someone else's room. The fraternity brothers kept their doors closed at night so wouldn't have heard him, either.)

And on and on. All the questions were asked with obvious skepticism. He kept his cool and showed empathy with the inquiry as he was more concerned *himself,* now that several days had elapsed since Cat went missing, and a worst-case scenario was feared.

He also made a point to talk over the events leading up to Cat's disappearance with his fraternity brothers, and with the girls at the party, when he saw them. He identified himself with them, putting himself on *their* side, questioning and speculating, to throw off suspicion, as everyone knew he was at the center of the mystery.

Posters were put up, a reward was offered for information, vigils were held, and students met with grief counselors. The police led meetings on campus, in several dorms, to discuss how women could stay safe around the campus, as there was fear of a killer being on the loose preying on co-eds. Don't go out alone: travel in groups of three, at least. Walk in lit areas. Don't be out late, unnecessarily. Carry a whistle.

The investigation went into full swing. Registered sex offenders in three counties were all questioned and required to give an account of themselves for the evening that Cat Moore had disappeared. Each statement was checked out and all offenders were cleared. The police were out of ideas. The case went cold.

At the end of the school term, finals were taken and the students went home for the holidays. No one had forgotten the missing Cat, but the subject became one to avoid so as not reopening old wounds that had scabbed over but had not yet healed. At Christmas break, he told his parents about Cat's disappearance after she got out of his car. His father asked him more questions than Detective Barnes ever had, but he never broke. He never would.

He now saw something more than loathing in his father's eyes: he saw fear. *Not a bad thing*, he thought. Maybe his father would no longer bully him. He had been born a cripple, and grew up to be a disappointment to his father, who had hoped that he would become a scientific genius. His father had named him after the most brilliant man in history; a name that had become a cliché, often used as sarcasm, to mean the height of stupidity. For him it had become a curse. He was teased for having a name so similar to the famous scientist. He hated his first name, "Albert," and could barely utter his full name: "Albert Arnstein."

Chapter 2

Dana had looked forward to her day off. She had made plans for a little pampering at the beauty salon in the mall, and a little shopping afterwards. Nothing too exciting. She couldn't have known that before lunch she would become the target of a madman

The day started off like any other day off. Her bedside alarm buzzed, as usual, at eight o'clock. Flinging out her left arm, she hit the button squarely with her balled fist and silenced it. As she became aware of her surroundings, she was relieved to find herself in her own bed under the familiar, squeaky blades of the old ceiling fan.

She always needed a moment to orientate herself to time and place, as there was no certainty where she would find herself. In her job, she woke up someplace else half of the time. If she stayed in the government job until she was eligible for retirement, she would have spent the equivalent of ten years on the road.

At twenty-six years of age, five-foot seven, 130 pounds, slim and attractive, Dana looked like many of the young working women in town; women who had nice safe jobs, who would meet up with one another for lunch and chat about their lives—their husbands or boyfriends, the movies they'd seen, and the books they'd read. But Dana didn't have a nice safe job. She didn't even have any girlfriends to meet for lunch, or a boyfriend to talk about if she did. The few movies she had seen were old releases, on DVD, and the technical material she read wouldn't make for stimulating conversation.

Dana's life wasn't like other women's, as she was the only female nuclear weapons courier ~~who~~ employed by the Department of Energy in Oak Ridge, Tennessee. Her work week consisted of spending long hours and, sometimes, long days and nights in an armored vehicle. Under DOE regulations, the agents were required to drive up to thirty-two hours straight to avoid staying overnight in any unsecured location. To manage the stress, the three couriers in each vehicle rotated drivers every four hours. The only place for rest was a thin cot in the back of each van or truck.

As a Special Response Force courier, Dana's responsibility was to not only guard the shipment, but to pursue any attacker who would be successful in getting away with a nuclear weapon. Despite the near impossibility of such a scenario, couriers had to always be on guard and aware of the people and activities around the convoys. The constant vigilance was tedious. Never having faced any human foes, boredom and physical discomforts had become the enemies.

Dana had just finished her second year in a local junior college in Massachusetts, when she signed up for the Air Force, after being lured by the adventure and opportunity to serve her country at a time of war. In service, she received specialized training in security, and was deployed to the Al Udeid Air Base in Qatar. The base was a major command and logistics hub for United States regional operations, including the wars in Iraq and Afghanistan.

It was while she was stationed there that she had met Jeremy Cooke, a member of the California National Guard, who had been involuntarily deployed there the previous year. Working closely together in the high-pressure job of securing a base where thousands of troops passed through, continuously, she and Jeremy had forged a strong bond of support, appreciation, and affection for each other.

Within a year they had become engaged, and were planning their future together. She hadn't worried *then* that they wouldn't *have* a future together; but when Jeremy was deployed to Iraq, she knew that he faced real danger, euphemistically referred to as being "in harm's way." But he would be okay, she had reasoned, as he was smart and careful.

Six months later, two Casualty Notification Officers had paid her a visit to inform her that Jeremy's truck had rolled over an IED and he had been killed, instantly. Dana had felt that part of her died that day, as well. His death had been a blow to what she had considered their purpose in working in that part of the world.

She heard about the DOE's courier service, on the base, when her contract with the Air Force was about to expire. At the time it seemed to be a godsend that would bring her back to the United Sates and away from war in the Middle East. She applied for the job and was accepted for training as an SRF, the elite unit in the company.

Her parents and her sister wanted her to come back home, to live in the Berkshires, but she knew she didn't want her old life again in small-town New England. Not that she knew what life style she *did* want, or where she wanted to live.

That was two years ago, and over time, she had come to feel unfulfilled, and in conflict. She had thought that she wanted to be in the service of protecting her country, but was in a job where she would never see any action. Not that she *wanted* the convoy to be attacked for some excitement. But she thought of Jeremy, who had sacrificed his life on foreign soil in a war, while she was on a security job for the government in the safe confines of the United States, with only a remote chance of danger.

Of late she had become acutely aware of the deficiencies in her life—few social contacts with other women, little home life; and no relationship with a man that could lead to a future, with the possibility of having children.

As she lay in her bed this morning, she pushed aside her negative thoughts. She would get on with her day and just enjoy it. The sunlight was now penetrating both the blinds and her cream-colored draperies, revealing the slate grey walls, the upholstered mauve chair, framed photos of her family on the light wood contemporary dresser, and the dull black Sig-Sauer P-220 handgun on the night stand.

She settled back into her pillow to luxuriate in a proper bed, for a change, but the room was already getting too warm. She had slept fitfully during the muggy night. She discovered that she had kicked off the top sheet while sleeping, and it was now twisted around her legs, mummifying her lower half. "Damn it!" she cursed, as she unfurled it with one good yank and pulled the sheet up over her head to collect her thoughts before getting up.

She thought first about the weather. Mid-June in East Tennessee was dependably hot and humid. She wondered how hot it would get today. She had accepted the fact that she couldn't have central air in a seventy year-old house, but window units were only really effective if you were sitting in front of them. It seemed unfair that it was so hot at night, too.

She thought of those summers long ago when she lived in western Massachusetts, and an open window was all the "air-conditioning" you needed until Independence Day. The Fourth of July was the start of the "summer season" that ended on Labor Day. Here, summer started in May and the heat lasted until October.

Dana peeked out from under her sheet and checked the clock face. It was time to get up. She had made an appointment for a (much-needed) facial at ten o'clock at the salon in the mall. She rarely indulged herself like that, but the skin care professional had told her it was a necessity for someone who spent most of her life in a van; including eating and sleeping.

After her facial, she needed to find a birthday gift for her sister's girl, Lexy, who was turning eight next week. She hadn't been back to visit her family for over a year. Lexy must have changed a lot since then, she imagined.

Last week, her sister Lauren had sent her a not-so-subtle email with Lexy's sizes; apparently thinking Dana wouldn't remember the date, otherwise. *Lauren was probably right,* she grudgingly admitted to herself. *I'll get her a nice outfit at Belk's.*

After that I'll treat myself to lunch at that place on Melton Hill Lake, she thought. She had eaten most meals out of Styrofoam containers in the van for the past three days. She could take along a book for company. She recalled that mystery she had started last week that she could read for a little excitement.

The sunshine was now drilling into her brain, and demanding that she get out of bed. To limber up a bit, she stretched out full-length under the sheets with her arms up, and held the position for several seconds. Then she brought her arms down, sat up and swung her legs over the side of the bed. Pushing her feet into her white terry slippers she padded off towards the bathroom to take a shower.

After becoming fully awake and refreshed under the cool water, she got out, vigorously toweled off, and pulled on her white cotton underwear. *Not very sexy,* she noted, but then, it wasn't like anyone else saw them. That thought brought to mind Owen Knight, the leader of her SRF group. She was very attracted to him, but had tried not to let it show. She didn't feel available for a romantic relationship, yet. Besides, she could hardly stand herself, in her present state of mind. Why would Owen want a relationship with her, anyway? She was out of sorts, most of the time: *Miss Grouchy Pants,* as she thought of herself.

Right now, she needed to get dressed in *some* pants and get going. Opening her closet doors she reviewed her options. *Pretty boring,* she had to admit. She hadn't had to buy much in Qatar, as she had worn a uniform most of the time. In her present job, she was limited to simple, durable clothing that could withstand charging through brush, or moving along the ground on her stomach; either in exercises, or for real. The couriers didn't wear uniforms, trying to be inconspicuous. They rode in unmarked vehicles, as well, so as not to attract attention.

This morning, as she was going to the mall and out to lunch, she looked for something to wear that was a notch above the rest. Giving up on seeing any clear winners, she shrugged into a simple white short-sleeved shirt and stepped into a pair of olive green linen slacks. *Not that bad,* she decided.

As she stood there she noticed her Louis Vuitton duffel bag on the closet floor. Her parents had splurged on the designer piece of luggage for her birthday, soon after she took the courier job. Her dad had said at the time, that if she had to live out of a suitcase it should be a really nice one. She kept it packed with clothes and toilet articles she needed for her frequent convoy trips.

Having finished dressing, she closed the closet door and made her way to the bathroom to briefly consult the mirror that hung over her pedestal sink. Gazing at her warm, hazel-brown eyes, she only saw evidence that she needed to get more sleep. Her skin looked a little sallow and dull, too, she thought. As she pulled back her long honey blond hair, she expertly caught it up with a rubber band, twisted the hair over the band and pinned it into a casual puff, letting several strands escape.

Similarly, she took few pains with her make-up, only applying a little moisturizer and lip gloss, just enough to get her to the mall for her facial, without looking like she was beyond help. Frankly appraising the final result of her toilette, she twirled her right index finger into the air and rolled her eyes in a cynical assessment. *Elena has her work cut out for her,* she thought.

Walking down the short narrow hallway, she turned right into the kitchen. Pulling out a few things for breakfast, in five minutes the kitchen smelled of savory roasted beans and sweet spice, as she poured a steaming cup of coffee, and buttered her toasted cinnamon raisin bagel. Adding a cold glass of orange juice, she placed everything on a tray to take out to the back deck.

Holding the wooden tray with two hands, she turned the back door knob with just her little finger. The latch was loose in the strike plate of the frame. *I have to get a locksmith to replace that old door handle,* she thought, not for the first time. Then, artfully using her right knee and elbow to keep the door open, she squeezed out through the doorway.

Once outside, she put the tray on the table, and settled in one of the four resin wicker chairs under the yellow-striped umbrella. While munching on her bagel, she flipped through the pages of a life-style magazine she had picked up last week at the check-out counter. *Not my life style,* she thought. "Hosting a Craft Party" was one article. *Yeah, I'll invite the guys over to embroider designs on our tactical vests,* she thought.

Bored with the magazine, she turned her attention to looking out at the yard, where a small bird, whatever it was, had perched on a low branch of her maple tree. *It's nice back here,* she thought. *I should have some people over for dinner. I have to put myself out a little, if I expect to have any friends. Like the Martins, across the street.* She talked to Nancy, regularly, as she'd see her out walking their Norwich terrier, Peanut. Dana enjoyed seeing the little dog, too. She would have liked to have had a dog, herself, but that was impossible, of course, so she bought treats for Peanut. *Pretty pathetic,* she had to admit, *trying to win the affection of someone else's dog, with pieces of dried liver.*

Maybe the Martins would be able to come over tonight, she thought. She hadn't had them over for quite a while, and Nancy watched her house for her, when she was away, so she owed them.

Having finished her bagel and coffee, she checked her watch and saw that it was getting late. Putting the dishes back on her tray, she repeated her door maneuver and went back into the kitchen. Picking up her brown-leather slouch bag off the counter, she looked around, feeling she was forgetting something. *Oh, yeah.* Her Sig wasn't holstered on her waist, she realized. *Obviously, I need a day off when I don't feel dressed without packing a semiautomatic.*

She went out the front door onto the small front porch of her cemestos house, so named for the cement-asbestos siding used in most of the structures built in the forties, like hers, for the "secret city." They were all very similar on the exterior, only differing in size and floor plans. Even natives could hardly tell one style from another. Turning, she saw Nancy and Peanut, halfway down the block, coming towards her. Dana waved and came down the stairs to meet them at the end of the sidewalk.

Nancy was a chatterbox who regularly talked to all the neighbors in the four-block area where she walked the dog. Dana wondered if that was the reason Nancy *had* a dog. He was the perfect pretext to get in a conversation and check up on everyone. As the twosome arrived, Dana knelt down and petted the little tan-colored dog who looked at her expectantly. "I don't have a treat right now, you little bugger," she smiled, standing up again.

"Nan. I'm running late for an appointment, but I'm off today and I'd like you and Tom to come over for dinner tonight, if you don't have plans. Say at 6:00. Just casual, on the deck. Jamie too, if she can make it," she said, referring to the couple's teenage daughter.

"Jamie's away for a couple of days, staying with her grandparents in Chattanooga, but we've love to come. Six o'clock would work. Tom usually gets home a little after 5:30, and I'm not at the shop today. It'd be nice to be on your shaded porch. Feels like it's going to be a scorcher today, doesn't it?"

"Yeah, it's *always* hot now," Dana commented. "It kills me that the weather girl comes on everyday, chirping, 'another beautiful hot and sunny day,' all smiles, when it's *too hot* and *too sunny* and everything is half dead. And then, if there's a rare chance of rain in the forecast, she refers to it as a 'threat' of rain. What's *threatening* about rain in the middle of a drought, for heaven's sake?"

"You have a point there, Dana," Nancy agreed, smiling. "We're used to the hot dry weather here, but there's a lot of rain expected next week. They'll have to change their script. Anyway, we'll see you later. Looking forward to it."

"Yeah, later," Dana said, waving and walking over to get into her metallic green Ford Escape, parked on the curb. *There I was, all grouchy again,* she thought, as she drove off. *I can't even talk about the weather without sounding off.*

At the end of her street, she turned left off onto New York Avenue, and soon came to the main thoroughfare with the overblown designation of "turnpike." Turning right at that light, she headed towards the mall.

In the mall's parking lot, she was fortunate to find one space in the third row from the entrance, considering how crowded the place was. There were many people walking toward the entrance, she saw. She got out and joined them.

Pulling open the heavy plate glass door, she strode into the mall and her senses were assaulted with cool perfumed air, piped-in music, and a chorus of voices in conversation. Walking to the right at the main concourse, she soon came upon the salon and walked inside the bustling place.

The receptionist directed her over to Elena, who was waiting for her, hands on hips, looking annoyed. She quickly slid into the black vinyl chair, as a pink nylon cape was thrown over her. She felt a little tension, which was only heightened when Elena shone a blinding light on her face and peered down at her, still frowning.

"Vat haf you been doink vit your skeen, dahling?!" Elena demanded, in her Hungarian accent. "You haven't been vashing your face vit soap again, haf you?"

I'm lucky if I can even vash with soap, she thought, acidly, but said, "I'm on the road so much, Elena, that it's hard to take care of my skin. I'll buy some products to take home."

I'm trained to kill terrorists, but I'm totally intimidated by a beauty consultant, she thought, dismally.

Chapter 3

Albert followed her from the parking lot into the mall. He knew her type the moment he saw her step out of her green Ford, sling her purse over her shoulder, take long strides towards the entrance, and click the remote car lock behind her: *emasculating bitch.*

He could follow her all day and she'd never notice him. If he crossed in front of her, she'd look away so as not to spoil her view by glancing at his slight physique and limping gait. She wouldn't think he was much of a man. *That's all right. I could show her how wrong she is and it wouldn't be the first time I taught a little bitch like her a lesson,* he smiled to himself.

Annoyed by the blonde's self confidence and air of superiority, he followed her into the mall concourse. After she walked around the first corner, he saw her abruptly turn into a beauty salon. *Damn.* He couldn't follow her in there, but he wasn't done with her, he decided. *She reminded him of Cat Moore; same cool blond looks, long legs, and sense of power over men. Cat thought she had power over men, too; but not this man.*

Looking around, to wait for her, he took a seat on a nearby bench in the pseudo-park at the center of the mall. Teenagers were standing

34

around, talking loudly and laughing. Older people had sat down to rest. Nearby kiosks were busy, taking advantage of the doubling of foot traffic where two concourses crossed.

Sitting there, with this as entertainment, Albert wondered, not for the first time, what he was even doing here, in East Tennessee. He thought back to eight years ago when his father had uprooted the family from Chicago when the old man had taken the position of head physicist in a Y-12 laboratory.

Prior to the move, his father had been a professor of nuclear physics at the University of Chicago. And before that, he had been a senior scientist with the Argonne National Laboratory. His professional stature had made him egotistical enough to compare himself, intellectually, to the likes of Robert Oppenheimer, Edward Teller or, even, Albert Einstein. *Jesus Christ, how his father had made him live with* that *illusion every day,* he thought.

Maybe the old man had wanted to move to Oak Ridge because the city had been built to enrich uranium for nuclear energy; his love. He wasn't sure that was the reason, as his father hadn't discussed the move with him, in advance. His father had simply asked him to have his personal items packed by a certain time, if he chose to move with his them; and there was an unmistakable lack of encouragement in the request. Albert would have stayed behind, if he could have supported himself. He had already been subjected to his father's disapproval, and his mother's disinterest, for twenty-one years, at the time.

His earliest memory of his father's disapproval occurred when he was just six years old and was still occasionally wetting his bed. When his father discovered this one morning, he came into his room that night and poured cold water on his sheet as a reminder of the discomfort of such disgusting, infantile behavior.

From that time on, Albert learned how to hide his bed-wetting, a problem that plagued him for years, afterwards. He would always awaken early and change his sheet, if necessary, hiding the soiled one until he could launder it in secret and return it to the linen closet, without being observed.

His parents ignored him most of the time, anyway. They were unaware of much that he did. They rarely spent time together as a family; almost never took a family vacation in the summers, as his parents preferred to travel with their friends. Albert would be sent off to specialty camps to learn skills, like playing the oboe or how to survive in the wilderness.

One summer his parents didn't attend the concert on the final night of music camp, missing his solos in "Peter and the Wolf." He had to stay over in a closed camp, with just another counselor, as the other campers had gone home with their families after the concert.

The following afternoon, his parents drove up and found him, with his head down, waiting on the porch of his now-empty cabin. In the car, his parents seemed not to notice the boy's sullenness. "Did he practice hard during camp?" they wondered. "Did he learn a lot?" And, by the way, "How was the concert?" The boy mumbled one word answers to questions, for fear that if he talked too much, he would start to cry.

Even worse was his one time at Boy Scout camp. The week had been marred by his inability to keep up with all the physical activities, due to his limp, and his embarrassment the one morning that he had to rinse out a sheet.

But the final humiliation had occurred towards the end of the two weeks when, on an all-day hike in the hills, he had gotten separated from the group. He became panicked when he found himself alone in a silent, unfamiliar and frightening wilderness.

After two hours he had spotted the scouts on the path far below him, and screamed for help. The scout leader hiked back up the trail to get the trembling boy, and brought him back to the troop, that had been held up waiting for them. Albert had seen both the smirks and disgusted looks on the boys' faces. Their taunts were even sharper.

"What a baby! Why don't you go home to your mommy?!" And, as tears stung his eyes, they sang out, "There's no crying in Boy Scouts!"

His mother often heard his father ridiculing him and would say, "Go easy on the boy, Harold. He has enough problems." He didn't think she was any too fond of him, either.

Shaking him out of his reverie, she reappeared; 'Ms. Green Ford,' as he thought of her. Walking along, carrying a plastic bag of purchases from the salon, her head was held high. With her blond hair pulled back and twisted on top of her head, he could get a good look at her face. *There was that same attitude of self-importance that Cat had. Like, I'm too good for you.* He wanted to bring her down a peg or two. He would enjoy that.

Ms. Ford continued on her way without looking around, apparently sure of her destination. She walked by kiosks selling enticing items like jewelry and hair accessories, without taking any notice. As she passed by him, he got up and followed her. He knew he could get her name if she stopped to buy anything; she would be asked for identification. In the broad concourse, he could keep her in view at a distance, so he stayed back in the foot traffic; patient to wait for the perfect opportunity.

As she turned into Belk's, a popular department store, he followed her in, hoping she wouldn't end up in the lingerie section that would call attention to his presence; but she didn't. She walked into the girl's clothing department. He walked into the adjoining boy's department and started looking through the racks of kids' clothes, waiting for her to decide on something and make a purchase.

Finally, she picked up some clothes and walked over to the cashier between the two departments. He picked up a boy's t-shirt and moved over to stand right behind her to purchase it. He was about her same height; not noticeably shorter, at least. He stared at the nape of her neck, revealed by her swept-up blond hair. Wisps of hair on her neck were sexy. She smelled good, too. Firm body. Not bad. He felt his palms getting sweaty. *With desire? With the reminder of Cat Moore?*

Ms. Ford handed a couple of clothing items to the clerk and said she'd like a box for them, and she'd like to charge them. Her voice was a little husky. A hint of an accent—maybe east coast? Not a native Tennessean. That's for sure.

The clerk asked her for her area code and phone number, just as he had thought. Ms. Ford spoke just loudly enough that he could catch it. He repeated it to himself to remember it. But when she was asked for her license, she cupped it in her hands so only the clerk could see. When the clerk swiped the charge card, she said, "Thank you, Ms. Knowles."

When "Ms. Knowles" turned and glanced at him, he was shocked to see a flash of recognition in her eyes. *How does she know me?! Did she see me sitting on the bench? Or following her on the concourse? I could have been going anywhere! Who was she, anyway? Not some kind of cop, I hope.*

He'd have to be careful that she didn't see him again today. The next time he saw her he'd have a better plan than sneaking around display cases like some goddamn floorwalker spying on a shoplifter. *I can match wits with her. She shouldn't try anything foolish with me. Hell, I can get away with murder.*

He didn't look after her as she walked away. He just stood there with the stupid t-shirt in his hands. Noticing that the clerk had reached out for his purchase, to ring it up, he said, "I've decided I want something else. But thanks for your help," he said, with a smile.

Chapter 4

A s Dana walked out of the department store, she felt a sense of accomplishment to have found something for her niece. It was a cute outfit, and Lauren would give her credit for buying something generously-sized, to withstand a little growth spurt. *I can even get it there on time,* she thought.

But something about the transaction gave her pause. She thought back to when she turned around after making her purchase. She had recognized the man standing behind her as being the same guy who had been walking behind her as she entered the mall this morning. She noticed his limp, as she watched his reflection in the glass doors, at the entrance. Of course, there wasn't anything particularly suspicious about crossing paths with someone twice in the same shopping mall, but coincidences had to be noted.

She got a good look at him when she passed by him at the cashier's table. He was about her age, slender build, longish brown hair, with feminine, almost pretty features, on a smooth, thin face. He was better dressed than most men walking around the mall. He was wearing an open-necked white linen shirt and well-cut khaki slacks. Not a bad looking guy, really, but he was strange—weird. *Maybe, it was that he didn't smile when our eyes met,* she thought. *His eyes were cold and dead.*

Back in her car, twenty minutes later, she pulled up to the sleek sculptural exterior of the restaurant. After parking the car, she strolled into the glass-walled interior. The restaurant had a contemporary vibe, with the generously-spaced tables set with crisp white linens, on a stained-concrete floor. Looking around, she wondered, illogically, if the creepy guy from the mall might be there. *Get a grip. Jeez.*

Although the place was crowded, within a few minutes the hostess showed Dana to a choice table next to the window, where she had a long view of the water. The restaurant was situated on a small peninsula that protruded into a fifty-mile long reservoir that fed the Clinch River, so the view was of water from both directions, backed by the greenish-blue Cumberland Mountains in the distance.

A young waitress approached and introduced herself as Lindsay and promised to "take good care" of her. Dana ordered a glass of chardonnay and a mesclun salad, which arrived shortly afterwards. *This is more like it,* she thought. *Sitting at table,—with a view, no less—and taking my time to eat a meal on china, while sipping a glass of wine.*

Picking up her book, and reading a few pages, she put it down, again, drawn to the view of the water. Off to the left, was a long boat (scull?) with a crew of eight rowers. Sitting with their backs to the bow of the narrow craft, the crew rhythmically pulled back the oars in unison, dipping them in and out of the water, with ease and precision. Each stroke left the smallest ripple on the surface of the water. Dana was mesmerized by the repeated movements for several minutes, as the boat glided down the lake.

She had heard that the reservoir was well known in the rowing world, and was the site of many regattas during the year. This scull was probably a crew in training for the USRowing Club Nationals that would be held on the lake the following month.

She could appreciate the rigorous conditioning of the rowers, as she was always working out to stay in top physical condition, to maintain the skills required for her job. Several days a week she did her routine of weight lifting, repetitions on resistance equipment, and running on the treadmill.

Three times a year the agents had to pass a stringent physical fitness recheck of strength, speed, endurance, balance and agility. In addition, once a year they were required to pass an annual physical exam, given by one of the DOE physicians.

They were regularly tested on marksmanship, and had to shoot with a minimum of 80% accuracy. Dana often took target practice at the courier's live-fire shooting range, which was a modern, well-equipped facility with a full-time staff. Her scores for shooting with accuracy and speed were among the highest of the group.

One last annual performance test was a check-ride on one of the big rigs, to remain certified as commercial drivers. Usually, all the SRF members were needed for their specially-equipped vehicles, but occasionally, there were extra SRF who could take a rotation in driving one of the trucks.

Next week, as scheduled once or twice a year, the couriers and their staff, would fly out to Fort Smith, Arkansas, to the DOE Academy and Training Facility at nearby Fort Chaffee, for a full-week of simulated terrorist attacks on convoy vehicles like the ones they they rode in every day.

Having enjoyed her leisurely lunch, Dana left the restaurant, to head over to the nearby supermarket. She had planned to do spinach pasta with pesto chicken, a simple green salad, and crusty French bread, with a prepared dessert. *Not too taxing.*

Maybe when she got home she'd call Owen to see if he was free. He wasn't on a shipment trip, she knew. He had been over many times for casual get-togethers with other agents, but this invitation would be more personal. The whole idea made her a little anxious; uncertain of the significance, or his response, come to that. *It was just a casual dinner with the neighbors, for Pete's sake. Don't make too much of it.*

An hour later, after getting home with her groceries and putting them away, she screwed up her courage and called him. He picked up on the second ring with the casual, "'lo."

Hanging up the phone, after her conversation, she sighed with relief. *Well, at least he's coming. That wasn't so hard.*

A little after six, Dana answered the door wearing a belted ruffled white blouse over turquoise pants, she had miraculously unearthed in her closet. Owen just stood there for a moment, looking surprised. Coming in, he gave her a kiss on the cheek. "Hey, Dana. I like your hair down. It looks great. I mean, you always look good, but—oh, hell. I can't get out of this one. Who are these people who are coming over, again—Ron and Francie?"

"*Tom* and *Nancy*," she chuckled. "You look good, too. And thanks for the bottle of gamay" she said, taking the bottle and reading the label. "I'm not familiar with it, but I'm sure it's a good choice. I mean, you would know, so—I'm not winning this one, either. Come on in."

Owen looked a little different, himself, wearing a collared shirt and slacks, instead of his usual polo shirt and cargo shorts. Evidently fresh from a shower, his dark hair was still damp. Handsome, in a rugged way, he had deep-set brown eyes under full brows on a smooth forehead, high cheek color and a slightly crooked nose, having broken it in the boxing ring years earlier. He was tall and well-built, like most of the male couriers. *A real hunk,* she thought, appraising him.

Hearing conversation outside, they both looked through the screen door to see Nancy and Tom, with the dog leading the way, walking up the front steps. Dana went to the door and opened it. "Come on in. You have good timing. Owen just got here."

As the couple came in, Dana said, simply, "Nancy and Tom Martin. Owen Knight." The men shook hands, while the women told each other how nice they looked.

Nancy was wearing a white embroidered tunic, that obscured her rounded figure, and set off her tan. She was the epitome of the Southern matron: feminine, but sturdy, with a forceful personality. Plain spoken and direct, she seemed natural and well-intentioned; never rude.

"Dana, I love your blouse!" Nancy drawled. "That's a new look for you, isn't it? You know what?" she asked, as though a thought just occurred to her, "you should come in to the shop one day when I'm working, and you're off, and try on some of the new things we've been getting in."

"I think that's a good idea, actually," Dana agreed. She imagined, given her total lack of style, that she had been a target for one of Nancy's makeovers, for some time. *I could really use some help*, she admitted to herself.

Tom looked like his usual self tonight: a polo shirt worn over pleated slacks with canvas slip-on shoes. The ubiquitous sunglasses on top of his head seemed permanently attached. With his casual look and easy-going personality, he had been successful as a sales manager for an area boat dealer.

"Well, let's go out back and sit down," Dana suggested, "and I'll bring out the appetizers. Come on, Peanut. I've got something for you, too."

As Nancy and Tom sat down and Peanut curled up under the table, Owen went into the house and came back with a bottle of chilled chardonnay, which he uncorked and poured into the four glasses. A minute later Dana brought out a tray with cheese and crackers, some red grapes, and thin slices of cantaloupe.

Sitting down, Dana mentioned that Owen had grown up in Chicago, knowing Tom had visited there a few times.

"Oh, yeah? I was there a couple of months ago for the boat show at McCormick Place. We all stayed at the Ambassador Hotel which is a pretty classy place, right there across from the park and the lake front.

It was my third visit to Chicago. The place is easy to get around for a visitor. I think it's a great city."

"Yeah, it is, but it's changed a lot since I was a kid, growing up on the north side," Owen said. "My parents still live in the same bungalow where I was born—on Wilson Avenue. It was one of the mean streets back then, but now it's considered a hot area. When I was a kid, the only things that were hot in the neighborhood were the TV sets that Big Eddie sold out of a panel truck near the 'el' stop. My parents couldn't afford to buy their house, today, if they had to.

"Don't get me wrong, though. I like that so many of the old neighborhoods have been 'gentrified,' as they call it. When they tear up the sidewalks and put down bricks you can expect your house to appreciate thirty percent."

Everyone laughed, and, as Dana went back into the kitchen, she heard more laughter at something Owen had said. She came back out with another bottle of chardonnay, their salads and a loaf of crusty bread.

As they were finishing their salads, Dana returned to the kitchen to put the last touches on the entrée. She was surprised by Owen, coming in soon after, with everyone's salad plate. *My God, this guy is unreal*, she thought. After putting the entrée servings together, they each carried two plates out to the porch, and rejoined the guests.

The sun had now sunk low above the horizon, so that the air appeared to thicken and obscure the trees and shrubbery in the small back yard. Dana lit citronella candles for the light, mostly. She had sprayed the yard just before everyone arrived and luckily, she hadn't noticed any mosquitoes since then.

"Are you planning any trips this summer?" Dana inquired of Nancy and Tom, pouring the gamay in their glasses.

"We're all going to Hilton Head the first week in July, which sounds like we need a new travel agent, don't you think?" Nancy laughed. "Not that we have one. Anyway, we're renting a two-bedroom condo, a short walk from the water. At the end of the week, we're going to drive over to Savannah for a couple of days. Jamie hasn't been there and she'll love the romantic charm of the place. I do, too. Being close to the water at Hilton Head, it should be cooler than here, and we'll be in swimming a lot. That's a good place to go in the ocean. The water's very warm, and shallow quite a ways out."

"We got a good deal on the villa as it doesn't have its own pool," Tom added. "We can use a pool shared by two or three other renters, which is fine. And, like Nancy said, we're right near the ocean."

"That reminds me, Nancy. I'll be gone all next week for field training. I'll set the lights, as usual, but would you just keep an eye on the place as you come and go? I know you always do, but I wanted to let you know it'll be a longer trip than usual."

"Sure. No problem. Between my walks with the dog and your being right across the street, I see your house all the time, anyway."

Nancy was aware that Dana did some kind of security work for the DOE at Y-12, but she knew not to bring up the subject with her. Many people in Oak Ridge had sensitive jobs with the DOE, and it was understood by their friends and neighbors to not ask too many questions. It was still a "secret city" in many ways.

As it became dark, Dana brought out hot cherry turnovers and ice cream for dessert. The Martins lingered a while after eating; talking over brandied coffees. When Peanut had to go "out" for the third time, they decided it was time to go home. At the front door, they both thanked Dana for a very enjoyable evening.

"Hey, that was fun. Good job!" Owen said, after closing the door behind them.

"You're the one who did a good job. Smooth host, entertainer, waiter, bus boy—you'll be invited back, mister. Do you want to go back outside for a drink—a Bailey's or wine?"

"Sure, why not?" he answered, easily.

When they got to the back porch with their coffees and the liqueur bottle, Dana relit the citronella candles, for a little mood lighting, this time. *Owen seems very much at home here,* she thought. *Maybe . . .* her thoughts trailed off.

After sitting outside, drinking, for a few minutes, Dana was feeling a little buzzed on the liqueur and the earlier wine. So when Owen queried, "Well, shall we?" cocking his head towards the house, she flushed and gave a little shrug, before she realized he wanted to help clean up the kitchen. "Oh, sure!" she said, recovering. "Let's go in. But you don't have to worry about this. I can take care of it."

After the dishes were rinsed, put in the dishwasher and the kitchen cleaned up, Owen looked over at Dana, hanging up a dishtowel and said, "Well, I guess I'd better go, huh?" sounding not really convinced.

"Yeah, I guess so," Dana replied, "but this was really nice. And thank you. We'll have to do it again, some time, as they say."

Chapter 5

Albert left the department store and started heading down the concourse back towards the entrance, without looking around, for fear she might still be in the vicinity. He didn't want to risk locking eyes with her again, today. She had freaked him out. *Who was she, anyway, and how did she know him?*

Mentally, he went over every moment from the first time he had seen her in the parking lot to when she turned around to look at him standing behind her at the clerk's station in the kid's departments. *She was aware of who I was. I saw that in her eyes.*

It's not logical. I've got to be logical, rational. Why she recognized me, must be significant. We must have a connection, somehow.

He went over the scene where he had followed her from the parking lot into the mall. There were other people walking from their cars at the same time. After he spotted her and decided to follow her, he had been discreet. *I was always behind her, where she couldn't see me, and she never turned around. I watched her as she walked down the concourse and turned into that beauty shop. She never turned around.*

The next time she could have seen me, I was sitting on the bench by the fountain. I was surrounded by people doing every damn thing, while I just sat there. *So why should she have noticed me? I nearly missed seeing her walk by, for Chris' sakes, and I was waiting for her.*

What other possible explanations were there? I'm sure I saw recognition in her eyes.

Then it came to him. *She didn't recognize who he was. She recognized what he was.* She knew he was someone to fear. He had recognized that in himself the night of Cat Moore's disappearance. That night he had seen himself as a phoenix rising from the ashes of his own damaged psyche. He had seen himself as a superior man with special powers and had proven himself in the investigation afterwards.

Several months after the incident, he had graduated from the university with a major in computer science and a minor in chemistry, but he had never found a career equal to his qualifications. He continued to live in his parent's home, now in Oak Ridge, until last year when his father insisted he leave. It was after his firing.

He had been employed as a member of the "Brain Train," in a large electronics store, riding around in a little car, making service calls at customers' homes and businesses, to fix or install equipment. Programmers had made the technology so user-friendly it baffled him how people could screw it up so badly.

Nevertheless, with each call, he summoned up his impersonation of charm: a half-smile, nodding in assent; or a serious expression, while investigating the trouble with the equipment. Customers were always so grateful for his understanding. It amused him how easily he could fool people.

The company called the computer technicians, "agents," and gave them some of the same titles used by intelligence agencies. He had been promoted from Counter Intelligence agent, working in the store, to Deputy Field Marshal, always on the road. He preferred being out on the road, alone. He hadn't made friends among the other agents. It was exhausting enough being personable with the customers. When he got off work he wanted to be alone, as well. He didn't usually eat at his parents', preferring to take most of his meals out. Sometimes he'd pick up a prostitute at one of the clubs. It was something to do.

On calls, he had amused himself, as the other Brains did, by downloading pornography from customers' computers onto discs. He never watched it at the store, but it was common knowledge that a lot of the managers and the other agent Brains did.

But one day, his manager had called him into the office, and informed him that they had become aware of his illegal activity in stealing porn, and that he was being terminated, immediately. No notice. No severance pay. *Who was the shit head who turned him in? he had wondered.* It must have been one of his dumb-ass customers. The job was beneath him, anyway, so it wasn't worth his time to even find out. He'd move on to something better.

When his father learned that he had been fired, he told Albert he had to leave the house, too. He found a furnished apartment in town that his father was willing to pay for to have him gone, and he moved out within two weeks. His mother hadn't protested. She had cried that he had brought shame on the family: she was more worried about what her friends thought than what would happen to him, out on the streets.

Since then he had barely sustained himself through part-time work in an auto garage restoring vintage cars. Three years ago, he had traded in his college Miata for a classic sports car, a white 1965 Mercedes 230 SL Roadster with a black rag top: a rare 4-speed manual.

He had rebuilt its engine, restored its interior and had it repainted and re-chromed. The painstaking work gave him a new skill. Showing off his car, he landed a job as a mechanic in a specialty garage, saving the fine-tuned vintage automobiles from ending up in the bone yard.

When he got to his car in the mall parking lot, he sank down into the driver's seat and rested his head on the steering wheel, exhausted and frustrated from thinking through the strange encounter with that Knowles broad. Taking a piece of paper out of the small glove compartment, he jotted down the memorized phone number.

Using his smart phone, he got her address from reverse-listing. She had a gender-neutral listing under "D. Knowles," and probably lived alone. Diane, Denise, Deborah, Darla or Dinah. He couldn't think of any other "D" names for girls. It had to be one of these. *Somehow I don't think she's Darla or Dinah.*

He'd take a drive past her house, tonight, he decided and see where she lived. Whatever else he could find out about her. Did she live alone? He hadn't seen a ring on her hand; a good sign. He'd wait until after dark, when he wouldn't be seen, but he could see inside a lighted house. Her address was in the older part of town, within ten minutes from his place.

Driving up to his apartment building, he looked up to the third floor, to his apartment. He saw his neighbor, out on the little balcony, like his own. Henry de Salvo was a weirdo who had moved in next door, as his only neighbor, about a year ago.

He was a nervous, bouncy little man given to excitably quoting Bible verses that he sprinkled in his conversation. Physically, he was short, with a puffy middle and skinny legs and arms. He had a receding hairline with dark cottony tufts of hair covering the rest of his head. His constant wide-eyed expression, under his dark-rimmed round, thick glasses, in combination with his hair, made him look like the stereotypical mad scientist.

When Henry had knocked on his door, last fall, to ask for his help to move a couple pieces of furniture, he had obliged, mostly out of curiosity. After they were finished, Henry asked him to sit and rest, and offered him a soft drink. He was dying for a cold beer, but before he could get away, Henry had to tell him his life story.

He had been born in Pasaic, New Jersey, as the only child of immigrant parents, and had moved moved down here with his family when he was a teenager. Feeling uprooted and out of place, he had taken up with a wild crowd; kids that weren't fitting in with society, either. He started drinking at the age of fourteen; using drugs shortly thereafter, until he had a cocaine habit and was stealing money from his parents. Dropping out of school at sixteen, his parents had despaired and sought spiritual guidance at a nearby church, the Temple of Bountiful Salvation, or the Temple of B.S., as it was usually abbreviated.

His parents had convinced him, at one point, when he was clear-headed and remorseful, to come to church with them. In that first service, his demons were exorcized by the pastor, Brother Bob, and his life had been changed. The pastor had called him up to the front of the storefront church and had grabbed him, and started shaking him back and forth, screaming at Beelzebub to come out of him. Henry said he then felt the turmoil of a struggle within him, which he identified as the Devil, refusing to come out. "Out! Out! I command you! In the name of the Almighty One, I charge you to come out!" Henry had quoted the minister's rant.

Then, according to Henry, a miracle happened. He had felt the movement of the Spirit inside him, and he fell to the floor, unable to stand. It was as if a strong wind had knocked him off his feet. Brother Bob then raised up his hands, swaying with emotion, sweating with the strain, and offered up the soul of Henry to the Lord, where the Devil could never claim ownership again.

The congregation, which had witnessed all this, started speaking in strange tongues. Henry did too. He didn't know what he was saying, himself, but he was powerless to hold back the message he was imparting from the Holy Spirit, now within him.

Henry then heard the voice of God from above, who told him to change his ways and follow the teachings in his Holy Word. Henry's body was now the temple of the Holy Spirit and he must no longer consume harmful substances.

More people started coming forward, rushing Brother Bob for his touch to cast out their own devils, in case they had any they hadn't noticed. Some writhed on the floor, overcome with emotion. Brother Bob kept exhorting the Devil to come out of them, too.

All the while, the choir had been singing about the land of Glory, swaying and clapping hands. As the small electric organ swelled to its fullest sound, some of the congregation formed a conga line and snaked around the rented hall, singing along with the choir. Others just stood and shouted, "Amen! Amen!" Eventually, they all became exhausted and the exorcism was over. Brother Bob collected an offering before sending everyone home. It had been a profitable evening for him.

Henry told him that, after that first service, he gave up all his previous vices. He no longer smoked dope, used hard drugs, drank or even went out at night. He had renounced all his sins, and turned against his former friends. He was now on a mission to defeat the Devil on earth and to thwart those who practiced evil. Christ would be coming to earth again, soon, to set up his kingdom and Henry was going to be ready. "I am the Alpha and the Omega, says the Lord God, who is and who was and who is to come, the Almighty—Revelations 1:8." Henry quoted. Henry quoted a Bible verse every time Albert saw him, after that.

The month before, Henry had lost his job as a machinist working in the Y-12 weapons plant, and had become deeply depressed. Henry had told him he started going to the Temple of B.S. three times a week seeking the Lord's blessing. His pastor, Brother Bob, told him he needed to read his Bible more and to pray more. He must not have been vigilant enough to hold off the Devil from making his boss let him go. Henry was now spending almost all of his time reading scripture and praying. He was waiting for the Spirit to send him another job.

As Albert looked up, he saw that Henry was now on his knees, apparently in prayer. Good. He thought he could get up to his apartment without a Bible lesson or sermon on changing his evil ways. Henry always preached at him to quit smoking. It was from the Devil. *Yeah, that was his worst sin.*

Walking up the three flights of stairs in the old building, he cringed at the sight of the peeling paint on the walls and ceiling, and the scuffed wood stairs. He tried not to breathe in the rancid odors of old cooking oil and the stench of the lack of hygiene. No wonder Henry was depressed. So was he, living here. The only up-side of the offending smells, for him, was that smoking was allowed anywhere. No one cared about cigarette smoke in the air when the hallways smelled like the inside of a Mongolian tent; no offense to Mongolians.

He thought about the exterior of the building that was built of asbestos, and the interior that was last painted when lead paint was in general use. The place would become a death-trap if the materials were ever disturbed in renovation, not that he had to worry about that happening any time soon.

Reaching the third floor and his apartment, he opened the warped flimsy door and looked around at the impersonal shabbiness of the place.

The small, square living room was furnished with three upholstered pieces: two dark green tufted-back chairs and a sofa that had been beige sometime in its youth. The carpet was a nylon multi-toned loop in brown and beige, not lending any color to the apartment.

A battered mahogany coffee table, with a milky leatherette top, sat in front of the sofa. On each end of the sofa, was a forties-era table holding a lamp with a fringed shade. A metal stand in the corner held a small television set. Opposite that was a small desk with his computer and printer.

The saving grace for the apartment, if any, was the tiny balcony on the other side of the French doors on the south wall of the living room, where it was sunny most of the day. It was just big enough for a bistro table and two chairs, but, at least he could get out of the dreary apartment. *He deserved better than this.*

The narrow kitchenette, open to the living room, had one wall of cabinets that were covered in an oak-grained vinyl. One end wall was fitted with a two-burner electric stove and a small refrigerator stood against the other end wall. A counter with two stools in front of the kitchen was the only dining space.

The bedroom, down a short hallway to the left, was crowded with a queen-sized bed. A small dresser, with a book supporting one broken leg, sagged against the wall opposite the bed, taking up most of the walkway space. Only one of two folding doors of the closet, next to the bed, could be opened for access to his clothes, in which he took his greatest pride. He felt that good clothes, appropriately, represented his superior presence.

In the kitchen he put together a ham sandwich and poured himself a beer. Sitting on one of the stools at his counter he quickly ate a sandwich, swilled the beer, and headed over to the computer. Pulling up a map of Oak Ridge, he searched areas of the old section to locate N. Knowles' street. *I think it's somewhere up on the Ridge,* he thought. Locating her street coming off New York Avenue in the upper Ridge area, he felt a small chill at his prospects. He still had to wait until dark, though. Maybe he'd play his new porn movie, "Peter Pain."

At nine o'clock, dressed in dark clothing that covered him completely, despite the heat, he tiptoed down the stairs and around to the back of the apartment building to get his Mercedes. Seated in his bucket seat, low in the car, he took a moment to think through his plan. Taking a deep breath, he jabbed the key in the ignition, and started up the car, accelerating a little too much. *Game time.*

It took less than ten minutes to drive from his apartment building to New York Avenue and up to her street. As soon as he turned the corner, he braked, looked down the street and opened the window to listen for any sounds of people being outside. He didn't hear anything.

Cautiously, he inched the car forward, looking at addresses. Then he spotted her car, the metallic green Escape parked in the carport. *There was some irony.* The last thing he d in mind for her was *escape.* He double-checked the address. *This was it.* He felt a wave of excitement.

Slowing almost to a stop he could see some lights were on inside. *I'll just pass by this time, go around the block and park close by, but not too close.*

Two blocks over he parked in front of two darkened houses. Walking the two blocks back, he still hadn't seen anyone out on the streets. It was totally dark now out now with few street lights. When he got to her block he slowed his steps when he was two houses away and he heard the murmur of voices, up ahead. The voices were behind *her* house.

Taking one last look around, and not seeing anyone, he slipped between a couple of bushes between her house and the neighbor's, and started creeping slowly towards the back of her house. He could hear men and women talking, but he couldn't make out the words. He crept closer until he was at the corner of the back of her house, just a few feet away from her patio? Or deck? He couldn't see. It sounded like maybe four people were talking. He identified her voice and three others, he thought. Someone said, "Dana" and she was the next person to speak. *D. Knowles. Dana Knowles. That was her full name. Much better than Darla.*

Just then, one of the men said in a voice loud enough for him to hear, easily, "Jeez, I don't know what's up with this dog—he's asking to go out again, to the yard. Maybe he saw a rabbit or something. I'll make sure and take him again. I'll be right back. And, yes, I'd like another cup of coffee."

Shit. What's a stupid mutt doing here? It's not even her dog. Albert quickly moved back the way he had come. When he got to the sidewalk, he looked around. No one was there. He stood up and started walking back towards his car. *I didn't plan on her having company, for Chris' sakes. Wait. What did that guy say? He wanted a second cup of coffee. Maybe they'll be leaving soon. If I can find a place nearby to watch when the one couple with the mutt leaves, she might stay outside with the other guy, and I can find out who he is.*

Getting to his car, he got in and pulled out of his parking space and drove around the block, turning onto her street. He again parked the car; this time, just a few houses away from her hers. He couldn't see her front door, but he could see her front yard and that would be good enough. He had the lights turned off. He sank low in his seat. He waited. Twenty minutes went by.

Suddenly, her porch light came on which illuminated the front lawn. He heard voices coming from the front of her house. Within moments, a woman dressed all in white, a tall guy, and a small orange dog came into view, crossing the street and walking into the house directly across from Dana's. He waited. *The other guy hadn't left.*

He waited ten more minutes. No one came out. He decided to risk it. He got out of his car, walked down to her house, checked the street, and snuck back into the bushes between the houses. He quickly made his way back to the rear corner of the house, again.

This time the voices he heard were very low. He couldn't make out anything being said. The back porch light was off now, darkening the back yard. He didn't dare slip around the corner, did he? No. He couldn't afford to be discovered, and for what? He could tell that this guy was some boyfriend. As he couldn't make out any words, he decided there was nothing more to be learned from this evening.

Sneaking back through the bushes, he checked out the house to try to figure out the floor plan. It seemed that the kitchen was in the back and there was a door in the kitchen opening up to the deck. Getting to the sidewalk again, looking down the quiet street, he quickly walked back to his car.

He'd come back before he arranged a little meeting with her. He'd have to learn her schedule: when she left for work and where she worked. He'd had a good day, and it would get much better than this. *Good night, Dana. I'll be back.*

Chapter 6

O n Sunday afternoon, two days after her dinner party, Dana
drove the twenty miles southeast, to the McGhee-Tyson
Airport of Knoxville. Nearing the airport, she followed signs
to Cherokee Aviation, a fixed-base operator that had its own terminal,
runways and parking area. Earlier in the day the DOE had flown in
one of their DC-9s from the fleet kept at headquarters in Albuquerque.
The plane was now parked on the tarmac, baking in the late-afternoon
sun, as it was being readied for the 6:00 p.m. flight to Fort Smith,
Arkansas.

When Dana arrived at the lot designated for Cherokee Departures,
she found spaces close to the small contemporary terminal, and neatly
swung the little car into a spot.

Getting out of the car, she slung her purse over her shoulder.
Opening the car's hatch, she lifted out her large brown ballistic nylon
suitcase, heavy with clothes and personal essentials. She needed
several changes of clothes, including a lot of old clothes for the tactical
exercises staged each day on the dirt roads and in the brush, and in
the high heat and humidity of an Arkansas summer. *A week in the sun,
without the fun.*

Lastly, she pulled out the commodious black canvas bag, standard-issue to all of the couriers for the transport of their tactical vest and their combat, anti-ballistic vest. Both vests were kept handy on racks in the rear sleeper compartment of all escort vehicles, to be ready for combat.

The tactical vest had several pockets with the equipment for paramilitary operations: ammunition magazines, smoke grenades, metal and flexible plastic handcuffs, chemical lights, first-aid kit, portable radio and the ear microphone, all together referred to as the "kit."

Piling the bag on her suitcase, she pulled the wheeled-luggage behind her for the short walk to the Cherokee terminal. When she went into the glass-walled building, she heard the hum of conversation of the earlier arrivals. There would be approximately forty couriers, along with their commanders and trainers on the flight to Fort Smith. Most of the plane's passenger seats would be occupied, with the balance of the reconfigured plane utilized for the storage of their tactical gear.

Walking to the service counter, Dana passed over her suitcase and canvas bag, with its orange ribbon for easy recognition in the baggage claim area after they landed. Displaying her badge and photo ID, she handed over her paperwork to the bright-eyed young female agent, who pounced on it with zeal, thumbing through the pages, tearing off a couple, banging the stamp, then pounding the stapler, and ending the mutilation with a mad scribble on the top ticket. "You're good to go!" she proclaimed. *Jeez. I'm glad she doesn't work with museum documents.*

The flight to the Fort Smith Regional Airport would take just under two hours. The city of 80,000 was located just east of the Oklahoma state line at the confluence of the Arkansas and Poteau rivers. When they landed, DOE Academy training staff would meet the group and drive them, in retired escort vehicles, to the Fort Chaffee Maneuver Training Center, just one mile southeast of the airport.

The Fort still looked as it did in 1941when it was an army camp training soldiers for inevitable combat in World War II. Hundreds of uniform, low-rise, framed rectangular barracks and administrative buildings were laid out on the flat land in straight-lined military formation, creating a grim and austere presence, bordering on threatening. The feeling was underscored by the sign posted on its perimeter: "Dangerous, Hazardous Material—Do Not Enter." Many of the buildings stood empty while waiting for the costly dismantling of lead-painted walls and asbestos-containing materials prior to their being torn down. Many more had burned down in a spectacular fire several years earlier.

In the late 1950s Elvis Presley had arrived there for basic training. In the 1970s it had temporarily housed Vietnamese and Cuban refugees who had sought asylum, and after August 2005, it had accommodated thousands of Katrina evacuees.

Since 2000, the DOE's National Nuclear Security Administration's Office of Secure Transportation had made it their permanent facility for the Academy, training new federal agent recruits. Only 140 people remained to staff the facility as trainers, administrators and support staff.

The courier training would be conducted on the one hundred square miles of DOE land surrounding the huge quadrennial of buildings. The convoy would travel on thirty-five miles of curving, narrow roads, through mostly flat terrain, bordered by brush and deep woods, passing over the occasional river and in sight of a few small ponds. There were no buildings, signs or scenic vistas en route for interest. All interest was focused on the surprise attack on the trucks, which would be followed by combat between the attackers and the couriers.

For the past several days, in the courier rooms back at Y-12, there had been talk about the combat exercises from the previous year, and curiosity about how the maneuvers might be different this year. To get ready for the training, many couriers had taken their tactical vests and other gear home to clean, or to make any necessary repairs. Agents got together in small groups, to make arrangements to stay at the same

Fort Smith hotel and share a rental car for the week. The DOE had reserved blocks of rooms in three different hotels.

In the early years of the department, due to budget constraints, agents were made to share a room during the in-service training week at Fort Chaffee. The policy had been changed when outraged agents successfully argued that the policy created a hardship; a total lack of privacy. Their work already required that the three-agent teams be confined together, for long hours, inside the escort vehicles.

Not all of the couriers would be involved in each training exercise. Those who would not be in exercises would meet in the training compound and listen to the VHF radio transmissions of the action. Like an old-time radio show, they would hear a narrative of when and where the attack occurred, the sound of the explosions, who went down and who was left standing.

Some evening exercises would also be scheduled starting at dusk and going until dark, using night goggles for visibility. Couriers had to rely primarily on their short-distance radio receivers and mics for communication on their tactical advances.

As Dana entered the waiting room of the airport, she looked around for people she knew. In a far corner she spotted Owen waving her over. He was talking to John McGinnis, a fellow Chicagoan, though John was from a suburb. They had a friendly rivalry, often seen between people from different parts of the same large city.

"Hey, Dana," Owen greeted her. "Thank God, you're here. John, here, was just driving me crazy with his talk about his tough times growing up."

"Hey, Knowles." John greeted her. He had been her team leader last year, during training week. "So you think you can keep from being taken out this year?"

"Well, if you recall, Captain Marvel, the guy who attacked me didn't go down after he had received a direct hit, and he gave cover to the other guy who jumped out and hit me."

"That's right!". I remember, now. It wasn't caught during the action, but Special Ops had seen the kill, and it was straightened out later with the CC. That dumb bastard who had been hit still stood there, shooting off his M-4 after he had been zapped with the laser."

"Yeah," Dana agreed, "it confusing when the "dead" guys keep firing and coming after you like zombies from *Night of the Living Dead*. Another hit was my own stupid fault, though. Hey, who do we have for the OPFOR this year? Green Berets or some trainers from Albuquerque?" she asked, referring to the combatant that would stage the attack as the Opposing Force.

"I heard Green Berets," John, answered.

"Good," Dana said. "They're cool. Very serious. I like going up against them. They're the best in the world. Let's you know how good you are. Or aren't," she added.

"Just make sure you don't get hit," John said. "I hate to see you in the loser's circle again, after the exercise."

"I wouldn't worry about Dana, John," Owen countered. "She's a better shot than you are. Better looking, too, I might add."

Just then, Ronnie Bateman, one of Commander's Rocko's staff, picked up a microphone and asked for silence to take the roll call. The voices quieted as he called out each courier's and staff member's name, alphabetically, getting a response of "here" after each name. After the roll call, Ronnie announced, "Everyone's present and accounted for. Boarding will begin momentarily, following instructions to be given by the Cherokee gate crew."

A couple of minutes later, one of the female gate attendants announced, "DOE flight 256, non-stop to Fort Smith, Arkansas is now ready for boarding. Please take your seat and allow everyone to board before attempting to store your carry-on pieces in the above compartments." *Yeah, right. That'll happen,* Dana thought. *This is such a courteous bunch.*

Twenty minutes later, the fully-loaded DC-9, with sixty-five passengers aboard, started rolling through the heat waves on the tarmac. When the pilot intermittently applied the brakes, the plane was slow to pick up speed, rumbling and shaking from side to side, without lift-off, until the pilot released the brakes allowing the plane to sprint ahead. The force threw the passengers backwards against their seats as the clumsy aircraft left the runway. Once airborne, the big plane turned so its wingtips caught the last golden rays of sun, and pointed its nose southwest towards its destination.

Chapter 7

On Sunday, Albert sat on his stained, lumpy sofa, and brooded, trying to sort things out.

In the afternoon, the sunlight crept in like an unwelcome busybody prying into every corner, not illuminating, but taking away the comfort of darkness and solitude. He remained still as a statue, sitting with unfocused eyes facing the wall where the print of a cottage garden hung; not seeing its blue-toned sun damage, or seeing it at all. He was looking at his past, his present and his future.

I need to show all of the people who have rejected me, just who I am, and what I'm capable of. I realized that the other day when I followed Dana Knowles. She recognized the power I have, and showed fear, in spite of her smug self-assurance. I need to get to her and bring her under my control and show her the full extent of my powers.

That thought took him back to a couple of nights ago when she was a few feet away. He had promised then that he'd be back. He'd go over there tonight, after dark, and see if her lights were on, and if her car was in the carport. If they weren't, he'd be able to park on the next street, walk back to the house and sneak through the bushes to the porch; maybe even get a look inside.

There was a knock at the door. Yanking the stuck door open, with a curse, he was alarmed to see Henry standing there wearing a white robe with a large silver cross around his neck and an open Bible in his hand. Walking in the apartment, Henry jabbed a finger at one page, shouting, "'I will take vengeance on my adversaries, and will requite those who hate me! I will make my arrows drunk with blood, and my sword shall devour flesh!' That's in Deuteronomy, my friend!

"I told Brother Bob that I hadn't been led to a job by the Spirit. No one had called me. He told me to open the Bible, randomly, and without looking, put my finger down on the page. Wherever my finger landed, that would be the Spirit's message. And this is exactly where my finger landed today. It is perfectly clear, my brother. The Spirit entreats me to seek revenge on those who hate me; those carnal manifestations of the devil who did the Evil one's bidding, to retaliate against me, for choosing the Spirit.

"Those demons at Y-12, who were responsible for my termination, must be punished in the name of the Spirit. They have put me into reduced circumstances, not befitting a man who has the Spirit within him. I have been humbled by poverty, obliging me to accept charitable contributions offered to me from godly men moved by the Spirit. From them, and from the State of Tennessee."

"You're starting to make some sense, Henry, and that's scary. I was just thinking, myself, that I have the power to defeat evil people who have persecuted me, and I haven't yet done anything to them. Don't worry; we'll both get our revenge."

"Thank you, brother," Henry said. "I think the Spirit must have led me to you, too."

After Henry left, Albert returned to the kitchen for another beer, with a sense of satisfaction. Henry's madness had uncovered a basic truth: "An eye for an eye." He knew that much from the Bible.

He hastily ate a cheese sandwich, with another beer, anxious to get on with his mission. He really hoped that she would not be at home, so he could gain entrance to the house. Those cemestos houses had been around since the early forties. The doors had undoubtedly warped over time, and the locks were outdated and worn, as well, he was sure.

He decided to take a few basic tools with him; a couple of screwdrivers, a putty knife, and a small flashlight. Hopefully, he could get in without leaving any evidence behind. He didn't want to arouse her suspicions to make her watchful. *She can't sense my presence. Not now. I'm not ready to reveal myself.*

Two hours later, he had dressed completely in dark clothing. He stepped into the hallway to avoid attracting Henry's attention and quietly went down the stairs and out the building.

Taking the same route as Friday night, in ten minutes' time he turned onto her street. Driving very slowly, he looked at each house until he got to hers. When he saw it, he stopped short and stared, open-mouthed. *There were at least two lights on in her house.* He was so sure of his mission, he had been certain the house would be dark. But there was no car in the carport. *She couldn't be home if there was no car in the carport.* He looked down the street in both directions to see if she had parked at the curb, for some reason. No.

Okay. What were the possibilities? The lights were on at both ends of the house. *Either she had left lamps on knowing she would be home well after dark, or she had lamps on timers, as she was out of town.* In either event, he felt he could continue his investigation, taking it slowly; one step at a time.

Driving down the block and making turns onto other streets, he ended up on a dead-end lane with parking spaces at the terminus. There were no other cars. He parked there, picked up the small box holding his tools and the small halogen flashlight, and got out of the car. There was a new moon out tonight, shedding very little light, but he could see where he was walking from the few lit porch and yard lights.

Up high on the Ridge, where Dana lived, only the main streets were lit in the evening. The narrow curving streets that branched off the through-streets were shrouded in darkness, each house isolated by large trees, many of them planted when the city was just a government complex in the nineteen-forties.

In his dark clothing on the deserted streets, he was able to move, unobserved. Quickly covering the two blocks back around to her street, and onto her block, he soon found himself standing in front of her house. Looking around, he was assured that there was no one about the area. He checked out her friends' house across the street and saw that they appeared to be home, as several lights were on and the draperies were drawn.

Dana's porch light was off so he could safely move into the deeper shadows of the bushes without being seen.

With care, he moved through the shrubbery on the left side of the house to the back corner, where he had hidden the other night. There was total silence. He stepped into her backyard. Typically, for the houses on the Ridge, it was a small lot, but it was privatized by lush greenery all around the perimeter. As he now stood directly behind her house, all that he could see outside of her yard, were the flickering lights of a few neighboring houses, as they sparkled through the trees.

There was no light coming from the kitchen. The light appeared to originate from the front of the house, the living room. He suspected the other light would be in her bedroom.

He stealthily climbed the three steps onto her raised deck; careful not to dislodge pots of geraniums he had brushed by as he was finding his way, walking around her table and chairs. He was pleased to discover that there was glass in the upper half of her old back door. He could see through the kitchen to the lighted living room. The house appeared to be unoccupied. Looking at the door knob, he saw it was weathered and rust-pitted. Boldly turning it he was almost surprised to find that the door didn't swing open.

Pulling a chair up to the door, and using it as a table, he put down his box. He pulled out his small halogen flashlight, which provided a pinhole of bright blue light, enough to see the lock. Taking out a screwdriver from his bag, he jimmied it in between the door and the strike plate. It was almost too simple. He wedged the screwdriver behind the latch, turned the handle again, opened the door and stepped inside.

He paused and took in a breath to quiet himself. He was standing in her kitchen. It gave him a rush. He extinguished the flashlight, as there was adequate light from the front of the house to make out objects in the room. There were cabinets on three walls with a table and a couple of chairs on the wall opposite the window. He checked the sink and found it completely dry, so he knew that the faucet hadn't been turned on for several hours.

The countertops held very little clutter; a toaster, a coffee pot, the usual. At the end of the counter by the door was a letter holder. *Bonanza.* But there wasn't much there that revealed anything personal: an electric bill, a credit card offer, a coupon for a big box store. All were addressed only to Ms. Dana Knowles.

Opening the refrigerator door, he found surprisingly little food. No short-term perishables like fruits or vegetables, or fresh meat; just bacon, packages of ham, some cheese. *Christ, it's less stocked than my refrigerator.* She looked like someone who would eat fruit and vegetables. If he was right, she could be out of town. Probably, but he couldn't be sure.

Finding nothing else of interest in the kitchen, he crouched down low and moved on to a small dining room behind the Kitchen, which then opened on to the living room. The cord on a lighted lamp on an end table confirmed what he had hoped: the light had gone on with a timer.

Looking around, he took in the comfortable-looking upholstery, dark wood tables and the mellow hardwood floors. *I should be living in a place at least as nice as this.*

Coming to the hallway, he could straighten up and walk normally down to the bedroom where the nightstand lamp was on but the draperies were drawn closed, giving him privacy. *Another indication that she was out of town.*

He moved over to the dresser to inspect the several framed photographs displayed there. He recognized Dana in one photo with a young woman, who bore a resemblance to her. *Must be her sister.* There was an apparently older photograph of a couple standing outside, under a rose arbor. *Parents?* Finally, a professional family portrait of the woman he had identified as Dana's sister, seated with a small, curly-haired child on her lap while her husband stood behind them, beaming. *It was all just so sweet, it made him gag.*

In her nightstand, he wasn't surprised to find a gun safe in the bottom storage area. He left it alone. The drawers held the usual feminine articles and a couple of manuals. There was a memo, with a Y-12 heading, from a commander to couriers. *She works at Y-12 as some kind of courier? Was she away on her job, then? Maybe. Or she could be on vacation. I can't remember the last time I took a fucking vacation.*

Opening her closet door, he appraised her clothing: plain things. *Nothing special,* he thought. Then he saw something interesting; something that didn't seem to fit. On the floor of the closet was one of those Louis Vuitton duffel bags with the designer's initials, L.V., all over it. He was familiar with the costly barrel-shaped canvas bag. Bending down to examine the workmanship he was certain that it was a genuine Vuitton and not an inexpensive knock-off. *Pretty pricey for the shit in her wardrobe. I should have luggage like this.*

As he picked it up, he was startled to find it was packed. Had she forgotten it when she left on her trip? He opened it up and pawed though the contents. It appeared to be things for a short trip. There were a few pieces of under and outer clothing, shoes, and a small bag with toiletries and cosmetics. *She keeps this packed because she often goes away on short trips.*

He had a thought. He'd check back next Sunday night; just drive by. As she was gone today, Sunday, and she had left her short-trip bag behind, she most likely would be away for at least a week. And if she were back by next Sunday, she'd be returning to work on Monday. He could be waiting nearby and follow her to her workplace.

Right now, he'd better get out of the house. Looking at his watch he saw that had been there about twenty minutes. He had been discreet, keeping low in the lighted rooms with uncovered windows, but he couldn't be sure he wasn't seen. Particularly if someone had come by checking on the place.

He moved back through the house down the hall to the living room where he crawled through the dining room and into the kitchen. Now what? He had to lock the door or she would know someone had broken in. He locked it turning the button. He walked back to the dining room and lifted up the old double-hung window, part-way. Squeezing through the opening, he was able to lower himself full-length before he had to drop the last couple of feet to the ground.

Going around to the deck, he retrieved one of the chairs, carried it back and placed it under the window. Standing on the seat of the chair he was able to just reach the sash of the window with his fingertips and pull it back down in place.

Carrying the chair back up to the deck, he put it, and the other chair, under the table. Picking up his box of tools, he placed his flashlight inside, and looked around to make sure nothing looked disturbed. Satisfied, he went back down the stairs.

Hidden by bushes, he crept back along the side of the house. As he peered through the shrubbery, he caught sight of someone walking a small dog. *The neighbor and the mutt are back.* He waited a few minutes until they had passed by before he came out of the side yard onto the street. *I have a perfect right to be walking on a public street.*

He continued walking at a normal pace. No sense drawing attention to himself by running. He was just a law-abiding citizen out for a stroll.

In the corner of his eye he observed the nosy neighbor and the dog coming back on the other side of the street. He didn't turn his head. Moments later he was at the corner and turned left, towards where he had parked his car.

Driving back to his apartment building he smiled and congratulated himself on getting into her house so easily. *So, Dana works for the DOE at Y-12,* he thought. *Maybe she knows Henry. Maybe she knows my father. Hell, maybe we can all be one big happy family.*

Chapter 8

O n the first morning at Fort Chaffee, there was the usual one-hour briefing session, with instructions for the exercise.

The commander reminded everyone to check that their MILES units were operational, referring to the Multi-Laser Equipment System. All combatants would wear the infra-red sensitive target vests that registered hits from the agents' rifles that fired blanks that had a small charge, and gun powder, but without a projectile. Firing the guns, created the same sounds and recoil, but the discharged gun powder would set off a laser beam where a bullet would have traveled.

The MILES vest sensors would signal an indirect hit, by a broken beeping sound, or a fatal hit, by one long beeping sound. In the heat of battle, the beeps couldn't always be distinguished by the combatants, so the Exercise Controller closest, would listen for the beeps and make sure the "fatally" hit agent, or OPFOR, would drop out of the action.

The Commander then told the convoy teams that for the first exercise, the nuclear shipload would be W-62 MIRVed Warheads. These mock-ups would be readily identifiable by the agents, if the OPFOR was able to steal one, during the attack.

After the briefing session, the couriers checked their assignments on the white boards outside the meeting room, and left to find their assigned vehicles. They were all retired armored cars and vans, in order to give the agents practice maneuvering the clumsy vehicles while under attack.

Dana and her team leader, Rob Woods, and team member, Dave Witkowski, lugged their canvas bags, stuffed with their vests, to their Econoline van. The teams' Special Ops soldier and their Exercise Controller were already at the van, waiting for them, wearing their orange vests to be easily seen during the exercises.

"Okay, let's stow our gear and get on our way," Rob ordered. "This is Mike, from Special Ops, and Kevin, from the OST in Albuquerque. Dave and Dana," Rob said, nodding to each one named, by way of making introductions.

"Dave, you'll take shotgun and Dana will be in the sleeper. Let's make our rally point four o'clock at 20 yards. Be ready to exit as soon as the Klaxon goes off.

"It's already about 90 degrees, so stay hydrated," he added. "I put a cooler with bottled water in the back. Dana can hand them out."

Like all the armored vehicles, the Econoline van had sides and the cab clad with $\frac{1}{4}$ inch ballistic steel with 39 millimeter glass for the windows. Both the fuel tank and battery are encased in bullet-proof steel, as well, bringing the vans in at a hefty 8,000 pounds, each, without passengers and equipment, making it cumbersome to maneuver.

Dana, sitting on the thin mattress in the sleeper, looked though the parted Kevlar curtain, in front of her, to take stock of their preparations. The console HF and VHF radios were lighted and operational. The dark-red unlit Klaxon hemisphere sat silent on the dashboard. It would make an ear-splitting scream when activated.

Across from her on the racks were the modified M-4s and their vests. There was a little more floor space in back, than usual, as they weren't storing the munitions they would have on a regular convoy.

From her position, she was only able to see outside through the back window, as there were no side windows.

Looking at her team members and the controllers, she thought about how the unit would work together when they were under attack.

Rob was always cool and in control, which made him a natural leader. Physically, he stood out, being over six feet tall, with an olive complexion, dark hair and deep-set eyes. His training in jujitsu was evidenced in his smooth and rapid movements in the field, even when he was weighted down with a tactical vest full of heavy equipment and carrying an assault rifle. While his deep voice was commanding, once out of the vehicle, the team leaders gave directions only with hand gestures.

Dave Witkowski, at age fifty, was the oldest courier, having been a nuclear escort for over fifteen years. He was a couple years away from military retirement. While having to maintain his physical abilities and marksmanship, he grunted through the more arduous physical exercises. At five foot nine, and over two hundred pounds, he was beefy, but had not yet surrendered to corpulence.

His hair color had lightened to gray, almost without notice, as it had been shaved to within an inch of his head since his army days. His coarse, simple features, inherited from many generations of Eastern-Europeans, gave him a weathered, dependable look.

Consistent with his physical appearance, he was candid and plain-spoken, when speech was necessary. He preferred to be quiet, only offering his opinion when asked, and then giving it, without any room for misunderstandings. Although gruff, he was not unlikable, as he was known to be honest and hard-working. *The Lou Grant of couriers,* Dana thought.

Roused from her musings, she heard Rob on the VHF radio receiving instructions from the Operations Commander. "Let's roll," he said to his team.

Chapter 9

After the conclusion of the morning briefing, Owen Knight, as SRF leader, met with his team members, John McGinnis and Danny Greco, for their pre-exercise briefing outside their grey Econoline van. Meeting up with them were Scott Wilson, a trainer from Albuquerque and Joe King, from Special Ops.

"I'm pumped, with this team!" John said to his fellow couriers. "Three hard asses that came up from the streets. We'll give 'em hell."

"I hate to remind you, John," Owen cut in, "but the streets you came up on were planted with shade trees. Danny and I didn't see a tree before we were twelve, and could take the bus to another neighborhood."

"Whatever," John responded. "Concrete don't make you tough."

"Anyway, let's get down to business." Owen went on. "We've all been here before. Special Ops knows what they're doing and so do we. I want us to be confident in our skills. We've all worked hard, trained hard. We're prepared and capable of putting down the attack that will be launched against the shipment, and to go after the stolen weapon, if necessary.

"Make sure you de-ass the vehicle in a hurry when the Klaxton goes off. Grab your M-4s and vests and go to the rally point, which will be five o'clock at twenty yards, right off the back of the van. If you have to, put on your vest after you get there, so you don't lose time.

"John, you'll be riding shot gun, and Danny, you're in the sleeper. Oh, sorry, I almost forgot. This is Joe, from Special Ops, and this is Scott, from Albuquerque. This here is John, and he's Danny. So, where was I? I think you all know the drill. Put your gear in the back and let's get in."

When the group had stowed their gear in the van and were in their seats, Owen picked up the VHF radio, "Roger, Commander. We're on our way."

Owen pulled out of the lot, turning right. At this point, they could see Rob's van and the trucks. As they traveled on several roads, they wouldn't keep a visual on the shipment, or, on other vans.

"Hey, did you get a chance to see the paper this morning, John?" Owen asked. "The Cubs are playing the Mets today in New York. They'll start Lilly. He's looking good."

"No, I didn't see the paper, and I haven't seen Lilly, but the Cubs are all fuckin' lilies. What kind of a baseball player is named 'Lilly?' 'Fisk.' 'Ordonez.' Those are baseball names. Remember that old joke, 'Name eleven baseball players named for body parts. Answer: Rollie Fingers, Barrie Foote, and the nine assholes that play for the Cubs.'"

"What about the 'Putz' on the Sox roster?" Owen asked. "I mean the one with a capital 'P,' not all the other ones. A reliever, right? When Guillen calls for Putz to warm up, three pitchers start out of the dugout.

"But I can't argue that the Cubs have been a good team, lately, but it's a great franchise. Show me a better park. No comparison with Comiskey, oh excuse me, *U.S. Cellular Field*. Wrigley has ivy growing on the wall, instead of signs, and the park's right in the heart of the city, surrounded by great bars. You know how many great bars there are right around the park, John?"

"Yeah. Not enough. Not for fans of those pathetic losers."

"Ha, ha. That's what makes the Cubs' fans so great. We always look forward to next year. We're tough. It's too easy to be a Yankee's fan. Or sit inside some glass-covered atrium ballpark to watch baseball like you're a fucking potted plant, like at Target Field in Minneapolis.

"Did you see the pictures of the Cubs' opening day this year, the first week of April? What asshole schedules baseball in Chicago for early April, anyway? Some guys in the bleachers had on ear muffs. Ear muffs, for Chris'sakes. Watching baseball. Those are real fans.

"Hey, Greco. Did you fucking die back there?" John called back to the sleeper.

"Nah, you guys are just too damn entertaining. I didn't want to interrupt. I might have pointed out that, if you were Phillies' fans, you'd have something to talk about with guys your age. You two should hang out at some nursing home where people would know what you're talking about. By the way, the Phillies' have a new pitcher named Bastardo. You think the fans'll do anything with that name?"

The Phillies had been Danny's team all his life as he had grown up in Philadelphia. Not the Main Line area. Actually, where he grew up it was never called anything other than South Philly; so far south in the city its northern border was South Street. The other borders of the triangular neighborhood were the Delaware and Schuylkill Rivers. No uncertainties about the boundaries of the community or the ethnicity of the residents. Most surnames ended with an "o" and most boys were called "Tony," or "Frankie," usually preceded by 'yo.'"

It was the kind of neighborhood where no one knew they were poor because everybody was poor. If you really needed something, a relative would get it for you; maybe not from a retail store. You didn't ask a lot of questions. You didn't want guilty knowledge.

Danny didn't have many relatives. Until he was eight years old, it was just he and his Mom, Angela, living in a tenement on 23rd near Broad Street. When he was old enough to understand, Angela told him that he had an older sister, somewhere. She had been forced to give up the baby for adoption, by her own parents, as children born out of wedlock in the late-fifties brought shame to their families. When Danny was born five years later, Angela had insisted on keeping him, despite her parents' objections.

Not having the means to take Danny's father to court to try to establish paternity, she struggled to support the two of them without help from anyone else. She took classes to learn the retail clothing business and worked as a salesperson and later, as a buyer for an upscale dress shop in the city.

When Danny was seven, she married a part-time musician. Long work hours and late weekend gigs contributed little to the family's finances, but much to the family's woes as the hard life made the relationship more and more volatile. The marriage ended in divorce after nine years. Danny still had only his mother's love and support.

But, when Danny was twenty-four years old, working as a Security Specialist in the Air Force, his long-lost sister, Maria, located the family with the help of a child welfare agency, and soon came to town to reunite with her birth mother and half-brother.

Maria made the effort to be part of their lives, which was gratifying to Angela and rewarding for Danny. Months after their first meeting, Maria traveled to South Philly for Danny's twenty-fifth birthday. She brought with her twenty-five birthday presents: an age-appropriate gift for each of his birthdays up to that day. Danny, picking up on the spirit of the gesture, impersonated all the younger versions of himself as he opened each present. The excessive and funny gesture succeeded in breaking tensions and created a new family bond.

For the past five years as a SRF courier, Danny had been respected as a tough, reliable and skilled agent. Standing over six feet tall, with a powerful physique, a deep baritone voice, and a commanding presence, he looked the part. He still talked to his sister nearly every week, by phone.

"I said, Yo, Danny!" John's voice broke through Flogging Molly's 'If I Leave This World Alive,' playing on the FM radio. "I just got a call from Commander Rocko. He said the trucks are stopped for the guys to kick a tire," referring to the trucker's expression for answering nature's call.

Owen steered to the right to pull the heavy van off the paved road onto a dirt road and slowed the vehicle to a near stop. Just then the Klaxon light blazed red and the instrument roared into life with a bleating electronic scream and all hell broke loose.

Chapter 10

For the first two hours, Rob's team traveled across barren scrubland as the white sun climbed higher in the clear blue sky, slashing inside the van on the left side, piercing through their light-weight clothing. The heat, permeating the windows, overwhelmed the air conditioning, causing the occupants to sink down heavily into their seats in discomfort. Dana, in the sleeper compartment, had already handed out water bottles to everyone, once.

During the morning, all of the nine convoy vehicles radioed their positions to one another with regularity. The scout car was traveling a few miles ahead of the trucks. The trail car, with the Tactical Commander, was about the same distance behind the trucks. The SRF vans had changed positions, one in front and one behind the trucks, both out of view of the shipment. Only the two Quick Response Teams kept the shipment in view, behind and in front of the trucks.

The agents continuously kept a lookout on the road to spot anything unusual. All seemed well, but as time went on, the suspense built.

Dana, looking through the curtain noticed, with relief, that they would soon be passing into woods on both sides of the road, the trees shading the dusty road. As the van entered under the leafy canopies, the inside temperature immediately cooled when the darkened interior shut out the heated light.

As Dana momentarily relaxed, feeling the cooling shade, she was alerted to the squawking sound of the VHF radio and heard Rob respond, "10-4. Tango 8," telling the caller he received and understood the message, and identified their vehicle. "We'll slow down," he said, over the mic.

"That was Commander Rocko in the trail car. He said that the three trucks have pulled over to kick tires." With that, Rob swung the wheel of the big van to the right to pull off the road and onto rutted dirt tracks, and slowed the van down to a crawl. The woods were close here, muffling the sound of the tires on the soft earth underneath. After a minute, Rob braked and brought the vehicle to a stop in a small clearing behind the cover of high brush adjacent to the woods. "We'll sit tight here, until they call back."

Then all was quiet; strangely quiet. No one spoke. There was an air of expectation; a feeling of something coming.

And then, there it was. A commotion outside, up ahead of them. As Rob opened his window to hear better, they heard explosives in the distance, as the mock AT-4s were being launched.

Unknown to them, a hundred yards ahead of Rob's team, a silver minivan, coming out of nowhere, had crashed through the brush onto the road, and screeched to a stop between the second and third tractor-trailers. Three dark-clothed assailants jumped out of the minivan, armed with shoulder-mounted AT-4 rockets. One assailant ran back, past the last truck, to the Convoy Commander's vehicle and launched his armor-piercing rocket, aiming dead center at the windshield, eliminating the vehicle, the Commander and the two other agents from the exercise.

Only the driver of the last truck had witnessed the flames sending laser beams to the target, in his side view mirror. He set off his Klaxon alarm to bring reinforcements. The Exercise Controller threw out a small amount of explosives, as an alert of the strike, to all combatants.

In Rob's van, the Klaxon alarm let out a high-pitched scream and flashed a red light to mobilize the team into action.

Dana quickly pulled out the vests and M-4s, handing them off to Dave and Rob, even as she took her own and opened the back door to exit. Dave jumped out of his door and joined Dana, who was already moving quickly to the agreed-upon rally point at four o'clock at twenty yards.

Rob jammed the van's gear shift into park, pulled out the keys, and dropped them under the seat, leaving the van prepared for quick re-entry and getaway. Taking a moment, he retransmitted the Klaxon for other escort vehicles that may have been out of the two-mile range for the first signal. Then, grabbing his vest and M-4, he exited the van through Dave's door, as the passenger's side provided more cover.

Rob joined Dave and Dana at the rally point, as Dana was on her portable radio calling John. "Tango 8, Mike," she said, identifying their team and "Mike" as code for being on foot and on the move towards the trucks. She heard back from John that they were waiting for Owen at the rally point.

Back at the trucks, another assailant from the silver minivan fired an AT-4 into the driver's side window of the cab of the last truck, instantly taking out all three agents before they had had a chance to react. The cab was wreathed in white smoke from the explosions, as the assailant ran back to his van.

Seconds later, a white minivan jumped forward out of the brush, charged toward the first truck, and came to a spinning stop just in front of that tractor-trailer, sending up a cloud of dust and pebbles. The driver got out of the van, fired his AT-4 at the windshield of the cab, blasting it and setting off an explosion that instantly took out the three agents, leaving the cab covered in the white smoke.

Another of the assailants jumped out of the white van. He ran forward to the first Quick Reaction Team vehicle. The agents hadn't been aware of the attacks on the third truck and the Commander's car. The assailant leveled his AT-4 at the QRT vehicle, launched it broadside creating another burst of explosives and eruption of smoke, taking out the three agents.

The two assailants moved on to the second truck, shooting out the cab's windows. One agent was taken down. A second agent had a chance to react to the mayhem by stepping out of the passenger side of the cab, firing off two rounds at an attacker, bringing him down. The accomplice, having seen the hit, took out the agent with his AKM before the agent had a chance to get back into the cab. During the exchanges of gunfire, the third agent in the sleeper compartment of the cab, was able to grab his rifle and vest, jump out of the cab and escape through the brush to the trees.

During the firefight, the Controllers had been setting off quarter sticks of dynamite with strings attached. In pulling the strings, a whistle would sound, with a five-second delay, and then they'd throw real explosives nearby, in a safe place. White smoke rose above the explosions.

Back at the rally point, Rob had taken charge of the team's maneuvers. With his M-4 in his right hand, Rob gestured to Dana and Dave, touching his nose with this index finger and bringing his flattened left hand forward, he pointed in the direction he wanted the team to move toward the trucks. As Rob directed, Dave led the way as point man.

The team quickly moved uphill through the woods in a triangular formation, about four yards apart, the detonation distance of a hand grenade. The air crackled with the sound of discharged explosives that were getting louder and coming closer together.

As they moved forward Rob, in the middle, looked to the left while Dana, as trail man, looked to the right and behind. Dana, in her position, also functioned as radio operator. She had not yet heard that the other SRF team had started moving towards the trucks. She wondered if Owen had not met up with his team at the rally point.

Rob's team neared the top of the hill where the trees had thinned out, and Rob slowed the team's pace in anticipation of a shooter at this position, watching over the attack site. He crouched and paused momentarily to signal to Dave that they had approached a dangerous area by holding his left hand, palm down in front of his throat, and moving it back and forth a few times. Dave acknowledged, and then turned to Dana to relay the message.

Back at the trucks, the three remaining assailants moved to the back of the silver minivan and lifted the back gate, quickly removing several explosives and equipment. They worked silently and capably, assembling explosive charges to attach to the side of the disabled, smoking third tractor-trailer.

One assailant grabbed an explosive plate where the charges would terminate, took it under the trailer to the other side where he attached it. Running back to the minivan, an accomplice held a large reel of wire and handed him the two wire ends. The first assailant then rolled back under the trailer with the wires and twisted them onto the plate.

The assailant at the minivan moved quickly up towards the tree line, unwinding the wire from the reel, while his accomplice under the truck plugged his ends of the wires into the receptacles on the plate.

The third assailant searched for a place for the three of them to be sheltered from flying shrapnel after the explosive was detonated. He was also on the look-out for any surviving agents that may have maneuvered through the woods, to interrupt them. A minute later his two accomplices joined him in a thicket behind several trees.

Seconds after that, the dynamite on the plate detonated in a deafening explosion, and the two-man "blow team" ran safely from their shelter back to the trailer, leaving the third assailant at the tree line.

Getting to the blasted-out side of the truck, the blow team stepped inside the side panel of the specially-equipped exercise truck, through a man-sized opening. Inside, the team found the air thick with smoke that filled their lungs, choking them, preventing them from working on unlatching the bombs until the air would be breathable. They needed to stay near the opening to take in fresh air until the smoke was exhausted.

As they stood near the opening, the two assailants, looked out to check on any possible activity around the trailer. Seeing none, they were assured that they had done a good job at the start of the attack, neutralizing the agents in the trucks, and the command vehicle. Then they heard disturbing gunfire in the distance.

A few minutes earlier, TC Rocko, in the trail vehicle, about two miles behind the trucks when they stopped, made radio contact with the scout vehicle. Rocko advised the agents that he had been unable to reestablish contact with anyone from the trucks, or the Command vehicle, for several minutes; not since they had radioed that they were pulling over. As he hadn't heard from the QRT in the CC's vehicle, he had to assume that they were dead or fatally injured.

"Get back to the trucks to check things out," the Commander ordered the agent. "There could be shit going down, there! I'm calling the SRF to get them on the scene and report their visuals."

Immediately after the radio contact, the agent driving the scout vehicle, turned it around and headed back to the trucks' last known location, about two miles behind him where he stopped.

Dana received the call from Commander Rocko informing the team of the urgent situation concerning the trucks, with orders to respond to the location immediately. Rob heard the transmission through his ear mic and motioned in the affirmative to Dana, who, in turn, acknowledged the request for assistance from the TC. "Ten-four, Rocko."

As Rob reached the crest of the hill, he hit the ground and crawled to the edge where he could look over and be unobserved. Down below he was sickened to see the ravages of the assaults on the two QRTs and the trucks. Smoke was everywhere, pouring out of the empty fronts of the vehicles and the trucks' cabs where the windshields had been, out of the sides of the trucks, and rising above the destruction.

No one was moving. Wait. Smoke was clearing out of the large opening in the side of the third truck, revealing two men looking out. They weren't agents. Scanning across the scene and up into the woods Rob saw a third man in dark clothes facing the bombed truck and away from him. Rob gestured behind him to Dana and Dave that he had the OPFOR in his sights and to come forward and stay low.

The two team members read the signs and joined Rob at the look-out and took in the scene below. Dana radioed the Commander with their visuals.

As she did, she spotted a thicket down and over from their position which would give her a better shot at the OPFOR, at the edge of the woods. She indicated the place, and her intent, to Rob. He acknowledged and waved her ahead. He and Dave would give her cover.

Stealthily, she got up on her haunches and moved quickly and silently, not taking her eyes off her target that hadn't moved. She was still about a hundred yards away but had the advantage of higher ground to get off a good shot. Behind the thicket she could set up without being observed. Looking through the telescope sight installed over the rail of her assault rifle, she measured her target for a dead-center hit. Drawing in her breath to steady the weapon and her nerves, she pulled the trigger. Bulls-eye.

As Rob and Dave saw the hit, more shots rang out some distance away. *Who was that?* Just then, an agent stepped out from the brush in front of the woods to show himself to his reinforcements. Evidently he had escaped from one of the trucks and had waited for back-up against the three OPFOR. Dana's shot had brought him out. Rob gestured to him to keep an eye out; that they would soon be moving.

Rob and Dave were devising their plan to circle around to approach the third truck from two sides. When Dana took out the enemy standing at the edge of the woods, the two accomplices in the truck looked up. The OPFOR knew they had to act fast. So did Rob and Dave.

Rob signaled for Dana to give them cover while they went down the hill and across to where the third truck was parked. Both men got up and ran, then hit the ground, firing off a round towards the direction of the disabled truck, and then got up and ran again.

As they approached some trees, Rob stood up and moved into the woods while Dave crawled through weeds down the hill towards the road. Rob got off another round past a tree to cover Dave, who was now exposed. The agent nearer the trucks was firing at the center of the third truck keeping the OPFOR away from the opening.

The OPFOR in the truck were getting off a few wild shots from the edge of the hole, shooting blindly into the woods and up the hill. Dana fired back but didn't hit her target as the OPFOR ducked their heads back in, again.

Dave had gotten to the road, down fifty yards from the truck, when he took cover behind one of the bombed QRT vehicles. Rob, seeing Dave in position, whistled to get his attention, then gestured to move out together towards the truck. With that, the two agents stood up with their assault rifles blazing as they rapidly moved forward. Rob was able to make several direct hits on the opening in the truck.

The air became filled with the repeated reports of the gunfire, mostly from the agents, including the isolated agent who had come down from the woods and had joined the fight, overwhelming the men in the truck. After a couple of minutes, the OPFOR emerged through the opening in the side of the truck with their hands up and their heads down.

It was over. The good guys had won, and the nuclear cargo was safe. But it had been a costly battle. One SRF team hadn't reported for action. Fourteen agents had been taken out: three agents in each of the QRT vehicles, and eight agents from the trucks. Only two of the OPFOR had been taken out, and two had surrendered. The OPFOR had controlled the attack with the element of surprise, and the fire-power of anti-tank rockets, to quickly take out their quarry and the first responders. It was a winning strategy, but in the end they lost; this time. It was only a simulated battle and no one was really killed; this time.

.

Chapter 11

Owen found himself alone, disoriented. He was sweating, feverish, crawling up a steep incline through weeds, saplings and broken branches. His face was getting scratched and his arms were being bitten by buzzing insects. Thistles stuck to the mesh of his vest. His eyes were bleary. His holstered Sig dug into his hip as he pulled his weight over its hard contour. To propel himself forward on his knees, he stabbed the butt of the M-4 rifle into the ground. *What the fuck had happened to him? How had he lost his way?* He couldn't see the others. Any others. *Where was he?*

He felt a pain in his left ankle like he had sprained it. It hurt like hell. He glanced down. His ankle was swollen up like a horned toad. He couldn't see any blood. It wasn't broken, so he had to keep going.

He remembered the Klaxon alarm blaring on the console, in the van, and some music about "leaving the world." *Had he left the world?* He had pulled over and set the gear to park and then jumped out on the opposite side from John. The rally point was to be at five o'clock at 20 yards. He'd gone at least 30 yards. He wasn't at five o'clock. *Where was five o'clock from here?*

He knew this was just a training exercise, but he was the SRF leader and had gotten separated from those under his command. There would be hell to pay. As it was just an exercise, he would only be called out for screwing up, but, next time it could be a real attack and a mistake could result in a disaster.

Just then he heard distant explosions. Muffled, really. *How far had his van been ahead of the shipment?* He knew the blasts meant that the tractor-trailers had been hit dead-on. He had to move towards the trucks with his team, John and Danny. *Where were John and Danny?*

He remembered that John had been driving and he had to set the shift in park to hold it. John should be coming along behind him. But John wasn't anywhere around. *Because John was at the fucking five o'clock position where he should be,* to rendezvous with the team and decide on their next move.

He couldn't stand up if he couldn't see, and didn't know what was around him. The OPFOR could be there in the area and take him out. That didn't happen to him. He was the one to score the "kills."

Never, since he was a young boy, had he backed down from a fight, or not been equal to, or better than, an opponent.

The thought took him back to when he was a kid in Chicago, living on Wilson Avenue, attending P.S. 406. He had been small then, smaller than his classmates, especially Rudy Duncan who taunted him, smelling his fear. Rudy would wait for him in the gangway between the Green's and the Murphy's and knock his book bag off his back, sending his books and papers flying. He would reach out to gather up the dirty wet papers, tears staining his cheeks, and Rudy would then step on his hand. He was ashamed of his own cowardice, and his submission to the brutality.

Then one day, as the familiar scene was repeated, his older brother Pete came around the corner into the gangway. Immediately sizing up the situation, Pete swooped down, and in one fluid slow motion, grabbed Rudy, tossing him into the air, as he squealed like a pig, before he landed in the mud next to the Murphy's two-flat.

He and Pete never spoke of that incident, and he knew Pete had never told their dad, a brawny Irishman who managed a large meat-packing plant down by the Chicago River. His brother had protected his ego as much as he had protected his body.

Pete offered him a practical course of action by taking him to the old gym over the body shop on Ashland Avenue. There, on the cupped and yellowed varnished wood floor, they began what would become their regular Saturday morning workouts, which consisted of lifting weights, jumping rope and shooting some hoops.

Then, one day, Pete tied a pair of boxing gloves on him, and they changed everything. The feel of the gloves was transforming. His small hands were now cocooned in the big leather mitts with the thick foam-padded protection. No one could step on his hands and hurt them anymore. Now, his hands were weapons that could fly through the air and land with precision, if not power.

Even with his newly-developed muscles and recent growth spurt, he wasn't big; but he discovered that the fighter with speed and balance had the advantage in boxing, that weight was handicapped, to equalize opponents. He wasn't even fly weight yet, more like gnat weight, but he circled his opponent with feet dancing over the canvas like fingers flying over a keyboard.

He spent hours pummeling the bejeezes out of the speed bag, blurring it with lightning jabs delivered in rhythm one after another, after another, mesmerizing himself. But sparing on the heavy bag was a reminder that he lacked power as the big bag absorbed his blows with fixed solidity.

Outside the ring, he walked with an air of confidence, never swagger; but no longer with the stooped posture of a victim. As he grew in size and in strength, he developed his athletic skills in other sports. By his junior year in high school he was on the varsity football squad as a running back making the big plays.

Following graduation, he accepted a football scholarship to the University of Illinois. After two years, with the country at war, he joined the Air Force, with his parent's approval and Pete's encouragement.

In the service, he was attracted to security work. After basic training, he became a Security Specialist, guarding nuclear weaponry at European and American Air Force Bases.

When a DOE convoy made a delivery at his Air Force base in California, he learned of the courier service, and contacted the Department. That was four years ago.

Now, unable to rise off the ground, he heard the sounds of so many explosions he knew that the QRTs, including the CC, must have been taken out by the OPFOR. He hoped the SRF teams had maneuvered their way close to the trucks to pursue the attackers. He wanted to help them.

Just then he heard the thunderous explosion of a simulated AT-4 rocket launcher detonated on one of the trucks, allowing the OPFOR access to the shipment through the special pop-out panels in the exercise trucks. *Oh, shit. He had to get moving.*

Now, breathing hard, he felt for his portable radio to press to transmit and call for help. No luck. Taking stock, he quickly assessed his situation: he was out of the action, out of communication, out of sight, out of breath and, apparently, out of commission; he couldn't walk.

It made him think of the old joke about the guy on his first day in paratrooper school who was taken up in the plane and given the same instructions, repeatedly: jump out of the plane and then pull one cord and then another and, if neither of them work, pull the last cord and when you land, the truck will be on the ground to take you back to camp.

Then the guy finally builds up his courage and jumps out of the plane; pulls one cord that doesn't work, and then another cord that doesn't work, and when he pulls the final cord, it doesn't work, either. The guy says to himself, "Great. I bet now they won't even have the truck there on the ground to take me back to camp."

It was silly, but it cheered him up even as he was feeling more pain and finding it hard to breathe.

He thought again, "I have to get up. I have to get up."

"Owen! Owen! It's all right. Can you hear me, can you see me? It's Dana, Owen. How do you feel? We've all been worried about you." He recognized her voice, but it was small and distant.

"Owen, can you hear me?" He heard her closer, now.

"Dana? Wha?" his voice trailed off, straining to rise up on his elbows under the restraints of some kind of covering around him. His right hand was tied to some cords. The blurry green room was unfamiliar, and there was a TV floating up in the air. "Where am I?"

"Oh, Thank God, Owen, you're coming around. Don't try to move. You need to stay still. You're in the hospital. You were taken by ambulance from the exercises yesterday, to the emergency room. You got a nasty bite from a copperhead, just when you got out of the van, apparently. Danny went looking for you when you didn't arrive at the rally point, while John held the position. You were delirious when Danny found you, and in respiratory distress. You were lying face down about fifty yards in the opposite direction from the rally point.

"Danny was a hero. He saw your swollen, red ankle right away, and found the bite marks and figured out what had happened. He put pressure above the bite, to hold the poison, and called for help. He knew you had to get to the emergency room as soon as possible.

"John came over, notified the CC and drove you, himself. It was the fastest way to get you to the infirmary at the Fort where you were stabilized and transferred to the hospital. John called Rob after you got to the emergency room and the SRF have been taking turns visiting you. You've been in pretty bad shape.

"I've talked to the doctor and took down some notes." She picked up a sheet of paper, and read from it. "You had an anaphylactic reaction to the venom. Your blood pressure fell off a cliff, which is why you were so weak. Your throat had swelled making it hard for you to breathe, so they gave you a good jolt of antihistamines to open your airways. If that hadn't worked, they would have done a tracheotomy. Finally, they gave you a horse serum antivenin, as an antidote to copperhead poison. They've been watching you very carefully, as some snakebite victims have an anaphylactic reaction to the serum."

"Jeez, Dana. I can't believe this. A copperhead. I don't even remember seeing a snake. How does the doctor know it was a copperhead, when I don't even know? Maybe he's treating me for a bite from the wrong kind of snake.

"The last thing I remember is a horrible pain in my lower leg. Then I have images of growing up on Wilson Avenue, and my brother, Pete rescued me from a bully. And I think I was hearing some of the exercise. I heard a lot of explosions going off, unless I was dreaming about that, too."

"There were a lot of explosions. You dreamt about Pete helping you out, because you were in trouble, again. That makes sense. Anyway, the doctor was pretty sure it was a copperhead, from the bite marks, and the fact that the copperhead is the most common poisonous snake in the area. He didn't say that there are antidotes for different poisonous snakes."

"I can't see my ankle. What does it look like?"

"The swelling has started to go down, and it's not nearly so dark," she said, cautiously.

"Going down. Not so dark," Owen said. "Interesting way to put it."

"I thought I'd put a positive spin on it," she smiled back at him.

"You said I came here yesterday. I can't remember anything after getting out of the van. What happened in the exercise while I was laying down on the job?"

"I'll tell you all about it," she answered, sitting back in the chair. "One thing you should know. I haven't been killed off, yet."

"Oh, yeah? Well, I'm really glad to hear that. I want you to stay around for a while."

Chapter 12

"You should have been there, Knight," Danny was saying. "It was pretty cool. We had a nighttime exercise when you were in the hospital. It was almost dark when John and I were hunkered down on the hill above the trucks, surrounded by the OPFOR who were all over in the woods, around and behind us. We couldn't get a visual on anything. We didn't know how many were still out there, how close they were, or if they had us in their sights. Nothing. We knew they couldn't see well, either, as it was getting dark, but it was so still, so quiet, we couldn't even disturb the high grass for fear we'd be heard. Nothing was moving. Stalemate.

"Then, out of nowhere, we heard a distant whirring sound, which grew louder and louder until we could see double rotors coming into view over the trees, and made out these two Chinooks. Two fucking Chinooks! As they got closer, the noise from their motors and blades was ear-splitting. They were flying low, churning up brush and grass and dirt like crazy. As they came overhead their lights shone down onto the road and picked up the trucks in their beams.

"John and I took off running down the hill like we were trying to catch a bus. Under the cover of the Chinook noise, but out of their light, we headed straight for the trucks before anyone knew what was happening. It was beautiful. We joined up with the QRT that was there and that was all she wrote."

It was Saturday night at Victor Charlie's, a local bar in Fort Smith, where the couriers had gotten together on the last night of in-service training to have a few beers, socialize with their friends, boast about their successes, and gripe about some of the action and the outcomes. Exhaustion had been replaced with relief at having gotten through the brutal schedule and the physical demands.

This was the time when they relaxed and had some fun sharing their experiences and the lessons they had learned. It had been a significant week, as all their training was put to the test; realistic attacks had to be suppressed while minimizing the loss of agents. It brought into focus the importance of their job, the dangers they could face and the teamwork that was necessary for their efforts to succeed.

Over the course of the week there had been thirteen simulated-attack exercises; ten daytime and three after dark. Agents had been taken out in eleven of them. Terrorists had been taken out in all thirteen, but had gotten access to the shipment in eight. In the end, the terrorists had been defeated every time in reaching their objective of stealing nuclear weapons.

"Sounds great, Danny," Owen said. "I would have liked to have been there. I had some pretty exciting adventures of my own, of course. But I'm sorry I let you guys down in the first exercise. It wouldn't have gone so badly if our team had been in on the action."

"Hey, you're not some fucking Steve Irwin hunting snakes," John put in.

"No, I guess not," Owen replied. "Since he's *dead*."

"What did you guys think about that Wednesday morning exercise, with the OPFOR that stood there like they were dummies? Dave asked. "We picked them off like we were a freaking firing squad. What did that take, like ten minutes?"

"I don't know. I kinda liked that one," Rob replied. "I thought they were playing *really stupid* suicide bombers who didn't realize you have to throw a bomb first, and *then* you get killed. There are probably some of them like that. We got an early lunch and it made us look pretty good, I might add."

"Well, I have another question," Dana said. "Getting back to Owen's problem. Why don't we have an EMT on the convoys? On the job we've been a half day away from any medical center. Like when we're doing a run out to the Pantex plant in Amarillo. You'd be in trouble getting really sick after leaving Oklahoma City.

"I didn't know how to treat a snake bite, for instance. To tell you the truth, I thought you were still supposed to cut an "x" and suck out the poison. Good thing Danny knew better than that. But I've heard talk that the DOE is planning on initiating an EMT program for the convoys. I guess, for now, be very careful."

"They stopped that business with the cutting and sucking out the poison the first time a guy got bitten, with only another guy there to help. I guess before that, women were always around," John suggested.

"John, speaking of women being around, which is always a good thing, by the way, did you hear about that female Air Force sniper in Iraq last month, who took out the guy with the backpack?" Owen asked.

"No, what's that about?"

"Well, the way I just heard it, some snipers were with a U.S. convoy watching for any signs of trouble. An Iraqi guy with a backpack was just walking along, nearby. But this female sniper got suspicious, and radioed her commander. He gave her the green light and she picked off the guy with her M-16, at a couple hundred yards; the bullet going through his chest and into his backpack which instantly detonated into a huge explosion. He was a suicide bomber, and she took him out with no one else getting hurt. The story's making the rounds."

"Hey, that's pretty good. John has a story about a couple of women we saw the other night who weren't great shots. How about it, John?" Dave asked, nudging his friend.

"What? Oh, you mean when you and I stopped by that bar, The Bitter End, really late? Yeah, that was pretty good. We had both been out on a night exercise that went long. We were really dragging tail when we decided to stop in that bar for a beer. We hadn't been back to the hotel since the morning exercise, so we were pretty dirty and grubby and beat up from fighting in the thick brush for about eight hours. We really needed to get back to our rooms, shower and hit the sack but, we figured, let's just have one beer.

"Anyway, we walked in about 2:00 in the morning and couldn't believe our eyes. Guys were watching two broads in the back playing strip pool with each other. Unbelievable. And lucky for us, neither one of them was very good with the cue stick, apparently, and were down to the bare essentials.

"It really made us feel a lot better. We weren't even tired after that. We stayed for a couple of beers, talking to the girls. Nice girls, really."

"I'm sure they were, John," commented Rob. "Anyway, I think it was a pretty good week. Most of the exercises ran pretty long with everyone getting in the mix. Dana did some pretty good shooting, herself. If she draws a bead on you, say good night."

"I think that's what I should say, now," Dana added. "It's pretty late, for me, anyway."

"I'll go back to the hotel with you," Owen said, "if that's okay."

Chapter 13

Monday morning's gray skies hung low over streets dark and shiny from the pre-dawn rain. Raindrops, trapped in the leaves, continued to drip off the canopies of the trees as Dana split the blinds open to take a first look at the day, on her way to her shower.

Is it possible it finally rained? From the drops still coming off the leaves, it looked like it had just stopped. It might rain again, even, from the look of the gloomy sky. It would be good for her lawn and her flower box plantings that were at the mercy of the elements.

A half-hour later, coming into the kitchen, it was still dark enough out that she had to switch on the overhead fixtures. The light instantly warmed the white walls and brightened the red-checked curtains and honey-maple cabinets. After getting her breakfast together on a tray, she carried her coffee, cantaloupe chunks and a slice of toast into the dining room, setting the tray on the round cherry table.

Switching on the living room television set to a local channel for the news and weather, her attention was drawn to the anchorwoman, when she said, "The DOE is considering a plan to convert plutonium from abandoned weapons into a reactor fuel called MOX to help power TVA plants." She went on to explain that warheads could be transported by truck to the DOE's Savannah River plant in South Carolina, converted to the oxide-mixed fuel, which would then be trucked to Soddy-Daisy or Athens, Tennessee. She stated that the plan was controversial, as the transport of weapons-grade plutonium across miles of open country exposed the material to terrorist attack. The DOE and TVA officials answered the criticism by arguing that specially-licensed shippers would safely transport the spent fuel and other radioactive shipments, just as other nuclear material has been shipped for years.

Dana thought back to the in-service training exercises of the previous week. *Safely transported? Well, not exactly.* In the simulated attacks on the nuclear shipment, many agents had been taken out by the OPFOR. But the would-be attackers were Army Green Berets, not terrorists. They were highly-trained in tactical guerilla warfare.

A terrorist group wouldn't have the same proficiency in combat. Besides, even if they were able to steal a bomb, they would need to be able to crack the codes and the self-disabling devices to detonate a nuclear weapon. Maybe stolen weapons-grade material could be stolen from a shipment. It could then be either used to fabricate a crude nuclear weapon, or create a dirty bomb made from as little as a stick of dynamite and enough radioactive material to fill a shoebox.

If a terrorist could get his hands on even a cup of plutonium, he could manufacture a bomb as powerful as the one that was dropped on Nagasaki. He would need a lot more of enriched uranium, about thirty-five pounds, to make a working bomb. But *that's* not a lot, either, she was thinking.

The sudden ringing of the doorbell startled her out of her musings. Going to the living room window to check on who it was, she saw Nancy, and imagined Peanut was next to her, although the small dog wasn't visible.

Opening the door, Nancy smiled. "Hey, Dana, I was just out walking the dog and saw your car. I wanted to tell you something that happened last week when you were gone. Do you have a minute now?"

"Yeah, sure. I was just watching the news with my breakfast. You and Peanut come on in. It looks like it's just about to rain again."

"Okay, he seems to be desperate to come in," Nancy replied, as Peanut pulled her into the living room.

"You can take him off the leash, Nancy, as far as I'm concerned. He usually just sits."

Freed from his tether, the little terrier, nose down to the floor, intently sniffed along an invisible trail leading out of the living room. Quickly he continued his tracking through the dining room into the kitchen, and back to the dining room. Rounding the corner, he pattered down the hall into the bedroom and came back to the dining room. Finally, he went over to the dining room window and jumped up against it.

"Peanut, what on earth? Nancy asked. "I don't know why he's acting like this. Did you just polish the floors, or something?"

"No, it wouldn't be cleaning products he smells, I can assure you. He usually goes over to the cabinet where I keep his treats. I'm always amazed he can smell those. I can't imagine what scent he's picking up now. No other dog has been here. Maybe there's a lingering scent from last weekend when you all and Owen were here."

"I don't know," Nancy said, unconvinced. "I wonder. Anyway, I don't know if it's related, but I stopped by to tell you about something I saw that concerned me. When you were gone last week and I kept an eye on the house."

"Oh, really? What was that?"

"Well, one night, right after you left, I think it was Sunday night, I was walking across the street with Peanut when I saw a guy in front of your house. It seemed as though he had come from your back yard, as suddenly as he had appeared. It was dark out and I might have missed him coming from down the street from the other direction, but I don't think so."

"What did he look like? Had you seen him before or since?" Dana queried.

"Well, he had longish hair and was kinda puny, you know what I mean? He had on dark clothing, long-sleeved shirt and pants. And it was really hot out that night. That didn't seem right, either. As I walked down the street, he was just about across from me, but didn't look over. He walked with a hitch in his steps, too. And, no, I didn't know him from the neighborhood and I haven't seen him since that night. But I think I'd know him if I saw him again. Don't worry. I'll keep an eye out."

"Yeah, thanks Nan. It was probably totally innocent: Someone cutting through from the street behind us or someone's relative or visitor who got turned around because all the houses look the same. There was no sign of anyone having broken into the house when I got home yesterday. The doors were still locked. Everything was in order. But thanks for telling me. Hold on just a sec and let me get a treat for Peanut, the great hunter."

After Nancy left, Dana was left with something nagging her at the back of her mind. Something in what Nancy had said had triggered a memory of something she had seen. What was it? She couldn't get jumpy because an unfamiliar man was walking on the sidewalk one night when she was out of town. Still, there was something unsettling about Nancy's report. *Hmmm.*

Walking back to the bedroom, Dana picked up her Sig and holster, and came back to the living room. *I don't think anyone wants to mess with me.* Making a mental check of what she needed for work, she pinned on her federal agent badge, and pulled the leather belt through her pants loops and in and out of the gun holster slits, pushed the prong of the buckle through the leather and guided the belt end through the keeper.

Then, picking up her Sig, she moved the slide back and rotated the gun while cupping the ejection port to determine that it was empty, inserted a loaded magazine, chambered a round, and slid the gun into the holster. It fell close and heavy against her right hip. She then loosely tied a light rain jacket over the belt and weapon. *No sense showing my piece to the entire neighborhood.*

Getting into her car, she headed out in the rain, on the familiar route to the Y-12 National Security Complex. Turning on the radio she heard the British rock band, the Cure, singing "Friday, I'm in Love." *Maybe it's an omen. Of course, this is the same group that did the music to "He's Just Not That Into You," so don't get carried away.*

Crossing over the Turnpike a few minutes later, she was approaching the complex surrounded by signs forbidding access to other than "badged personnel." *Is "badged" even an adjective?* Driving up to the gate nearest the courier building, she handed over her NNSA ID card to the guard she had seen a hundred times who, without her proper ID, wouldn't have let her in through the gates. "Hi, Frank," she said, without expecting a reply. Frank gave his mouth a slight pull, in response, and put up the gate.

Driving past the guard house, she turned into the lot for the 2356 building where the couriers had their lockers, meeting room and administrative offices. It had stopped raining. Picking up her purse, off the seat, but leaving her rain coat in the car, she slid out and hit the button on her handle to lock the car. *Like someone could get past security, or even want to steal her car,* she thought as she walked inside to get the day's assignment.

Chapter 14

At seven-thirty in the morning he sat there slumped in the driver's seat in his classic car, its showy looks made nearly inconspicuous by the dullness of the day. He had been there, staring out the windshield, since the pre-dawn darkness, chilled by the rain and his blackened mood.

He was parked around the corner and halfway down the block from *her* house, and was half-hidden by shrubbery planted close to the street. This was the second time he'd been back since he'd "visited" last Sunday night. He had driven by the house late last night to be sure that the metallic green hatchback was back, parked in the carport. That was a good thing about the cemestos houses for surveillance purposes: no one had a garage.

He had been proven right about her length of absence—one week. She should be going back to work this morning, which was why he was here to follow her; to fill in some of the blanks on what he knew about her.

Following her this morning, he'd possibly learn her occupation. He knew that she worked somewhere in the Y-12 complex, but that covered hundreds of acres.

He was enjoying this project, shadowing Dana Knowles; although he hadn't yet decided on an end game. His intrigue with her was based on her resemblance to Cat, and her recognition of his special powers. He wanted to dominate her. Maybe he'd grab her and hold her some place, where she would service him for her survival, he fantasized.

But right now he was feeling very sorry for himself, that he had to sit outside in the rain like some sleazy private dick. *She might have even forgotten about me since that day in the mall when I saw fear in her eyes. It was humiliating to be putting himself out for her, but that would soon change.*

He could confront her anytime—today, if he wanted. He could surprise her in her own home, with that shit lock she had on the back door. That wouldn't keep out a coked-up teenager looking for drug money. She seemed smarter than to not have security in her own home.

Of course, people in these quiet neighborhoods probably felt very safe in their houses, knowing all the people around them, maybe for years. Strangers had no cause to go down their short streets that didn't lead anywhere. The houses stood in close proximity to one another so neighbors could observe most of what went on with the people next door, anyway.

This was the kind of place where, after some husband is arrested for butchering his wife with a meat cleaver, the neighbors tell the reporters, "He was such a nice, quiet man. A very good neighbor who always kept the place neat and grew tomatoes in the back yard in the summer."

Most people could be easily duped. *I've been able to fool people my whole life. I can appear to be anything it's in my interest to be: the sensitive man back in college, the concerned and helpful technician on the job. Before I arrange a meeting with this broad, I'll know what role I should play to lure her in.*

So where the hell is she?! I've been sitting out here in the rain and gloom for nearly two hours. I might have caught my death of pneumonia, thanks to her.

Just then, an old woman in a white fuzzy bathrobe came out of her house across the street. Eyeing him and the car, she stared, her forehead furrowed in a frown, craning her neck to get a better look. Bending over to pick up her newspaper that had been folded into a plastic sleeve, she kept an eye on him and hesitated before turning around and heading back into the house.

Great. Now I'll be the talk of the neighborhood. The old bat is probably still looking at me out her window. I should look back at her with the binoculars I brought with me. That would give her pause. Why can't people just mind their own business? I'm not bothering anyone, now. I'm just planning on bothering someone, later. He smiled to himself at his own humor.

Caught up in his thoughts, he almost missed the green Escape as it turned right at the corner, driving away from where he had parked, heading towards town. He started up his motor and slowly pulled away from the curb staying a block behind her. He didn't have to stay close. He knew where she was going, in general, just not which entrance. She would never be aware he was there. He waited to turn left at New York Avenue while a couple of cars passed, and then he pulled out behind them. He was three cars back at the light at the Turnpike. She couldn't even see him in her rear view mirror.

There was heavy traffic now funneling into the area from all directions. Most of it would be moving towards the Y-12 Complex. Crossing the Turnpike he caught only glimpses of her car in the two-lane flow of cars and trucks. As he neared the facility, a few vehicles had dropped out of the line turning into other businesses.

Finally, he saw her car turn into the restricted area closed off to public traffic. He pulled off the road onto the shoulder and stopped the car. Picking up the binoculars from the passenger seat, he could follow her movements as she approached a guard house. As her car was stopped, he saw her arm reach out holding her pass, presumably. The guard didn't say anything to her but tacitly accepted her security clearance and pushed the button to lift the gate for her to drive through.

He saw the parking lot she turned into at Building 2356. He could still see the driver's side of the car as she parked. As he watched her getting out of the car, she was facing him. When she moved her purse up over her left shoulder exposing her right side, he let out a gasp. *Holy shit! She was wearing a gun!* Not one of those cute little snub-nosed Colts, either. This was a service semi-automatic that meant business. She didn't wear it back on her hip on a loose belt like a cop or a security guard. It was in a holster right at her waist; ready-access for quick draw and discharge. *What does she need the gun for? She's not an office worker, that's for sure.*

The woman he had thought would be an easy target, he now had to consider capable of blowing him away. *Okay. Don't panic.* He thought of his Glock at home in a drawer. *I have a gun, too, and I'm not afraid to use it.*

One part of his plan was already taking shape. He would meet up with her on one of her days' off. That was obvious, anyway. She wouldn't be wearing her artillery walking around town. On the other hand, she would have a carry-permit and would probably keep a small gun in her purse.

He had to go home and do some research on Building 2356, to see what he was getting into. He remembered the memo to "couriers." What kind of courier was she? He'd find out. He could find out what he needed to know and then it would be easy. Knowledge was power.

By the time that he had turned the car around and was heading home, he was feeling resolute. *So what if she had a gun?* He had a gun, and a brain to go with it.

A half hour later he was pouring over a map of the Y-12 National Security Complex, slowly tracing across the small print with his right index finger. *Building 2356, Building 2356. Here it is.* Offices of the National Nuclear Security Administration, Office of Secure Transportation. *What the hell?* Nuclear Materials Courier Offices. The light came on. *Nuclear Materials Courier. Courier.*

She's a federal agent who escorts shipments of nuclear weapons. He sat back in his chair to take it all in. *Well, that explains the big gun. Probably carries some C-4 in her purse.*

He needed to do research into the work done at Y-12, and to learn how the Office of Secure Transportation operated. A lot of information was sure to be classified, which would complicate things. Henry could help him out with what work was being done on weaponry that was being transported. He'd been a machinist in the weapons plant. Of course, it would be hard to keep him on the subject for any useful information. Henry was still enraged that he had been let go and was acting more and more deranged.

How ironic that he was the son of a nuclear physicist who, up to this point, had ignored this birth-right connection to the source of the greatest power on the planet; and now his life was becoming more involved in that world, through his chance meeting with a that woman.

So many coincidences were swirling around in his head. He didn't believe in fate or predestination. He controlled his own destiny. But it was hard to ignore the collision of the events that led him to this precise moment in time: his family's move to Oak Ridge, the very place where American scientists had created the material for the first atomic bomb. *What was that called? Oh, yeah, The Manhattan Project.*

Even Henry figured into this, in a way. His neighbor had worked on the weapon parts that carried that nuclear power. Of course, he was nuts. But he had been inspiring; Henry was a reminder that there are people in the world who need to be punished.

And now, he had crossed paths with this woman, who was one of the few people who was a guardian of the power the scientists had developed for the Manhattan Project.

Maybe he was the heir to that quest for power, in some twisted way. Not exactly the *Manhattan* Project. He was more like the "Mad

Hatter," Batman's enemy in the comic books, who was the brilliant neuro-technician with knowledge about how to control and dominate another's mind through technological means.

Maybe he was a Mad Hatter working on his own Project. Close enough. It all fit. It must be additional evidence that he was on the right path to find his true worth and dominance over others. He'd think of it as: *The Madhatter Project.*

Chapter 15

Coming home from work, Monday night, and entering the house, Dana was reminded of Nancy's visit with Peanut that morning. Looking around, she smiled as she recalled how the little dog had evidently picked up on some scent or odor? That he had tracked it from room to room.

When a dog follows smells through your house, it's time to clean up a little. I guess I'm lucky he didn't try to roll in something on the rug. Nancy had suggested his behavior might be related to that man she saw outside the house, but I've seen no evidence of anything missing or even out of place since I came home from Ft. Chaffee. No one would break into someone's house and not take anything. That would be insane. Of course, I really haven't carefully looked around as I never suspected a burglar had been in the house until Nancy suggested the possibility.

Armed with vacuum cleaner, rags and polishes, she went through the house, going over all the surfaces and checking inside drawers and closets. Her few pieces of good jewelry were in their place, as was the gun she kept in her bedroom safe; even the dusty surface of the box showed no recent fingerprints. Now, come on. Any self-respecting burglar would surely take a gun.

Moving into the closet she scanned her few belongings, quickly. *That reminds me. I have tomorrow off, which would be a good time to visit Nancy's shop, as she suggested, to buy some new clothes. It's her usual work schedule, but I'll give her a call to be sure she'll be there.*

Going over the rest of the closet one thing caught her attention. *Funny that I put my duffel bag on top of my shoes. Oh, jeez, now I'm thinking like a CSI detective. Maybe I should swab it for discarded skin cells while I'm at it.* Just to be sure, she sheepishly unzipped the bag and rifled through the contents. *Yup—pants, t-shirts, jacket, underwear and a toiletry bag. All accounted for. What a surprise.*

Scrutinizing the dining room window where Peanut had jumped up, she didn't see any dirty fingerprints, but noticed the lock was turned to the open position. *I really should be more careful to keep that locked. But someone would have to bring a ladder with him to get in through the window. Now that would be noticed.* Just in case, she looked out onto the ground under the window to see if there were any ladder feet impressions. *None.*

I think Nancy might be getting carried away with her self-appointment as the Neighborhood Watch captain. Strangers better beware. Don't walk down our streets without an invitation in your hand. And, definitely, not with a ladder.

Thinking about Nancy, she recalled that the family was going away for the Fourth of July, next week. She punched in Nancy's number on her phone, to report on her home inspection, and to make an appointment with her to try on some clothes the following morning.

Chapter 16

After following Dana to work, Albert got on his computer and compiled several pages of useful information on the nuclear couriers. There were few specifics on on their duties and their cargo, however. Reading through the material, he felt confident in his choice of quarry. She would be a challenge.

So what if the couriers were an elite paramilitary group, selected among the best candidates from the military and law enforcement, or that recruits went through a punishing physical program?

These people put emphasis on their physical accomplishments, he thought. They were like all his tormentors in his life: the star athletes, who could run with a ball, while he was on the chess team and in the orchestra; and attractive girls who used their sexuality to give them power over their admirers, and then dumped them for being suckers.

These people were superficial, who didn't know that real power belonged to those who had the real instruments of power: intellect and wealth. These were long-lasting. These were the attributes that could control those who had short-lived beauty and physical ability.

He saw himself as being in the former group, while Dana was obviously in the latter. He would undoubtedly prevail with his greater intelligence and resolution of will.

He couldn't wait to meet up with her. She would be off for a day or two next week for the Fourth of July, but would probably be with her boyfriend, whoever he was.

He still needed a lot of information that would be hard to get. He saw that the timetables for shipments as well as the destinations were kept secret. That wasn't important except that he needed to know Dana's days off as she didn't have a regular work schedule. He had to install a GPS tracker on her car that would send a signal to report the exact location of her car, in real time, to his phone with internet access. He had installed many of them when he worked as a Field Marshal for the Brain Train.

He was adept at finding places to hide trackers, and keep the driver unaware of them, while the trackers could still get good reception. Metal interfered with the transmittal of the tracking devices, but they could be placed under a plastic bumper, or wheel well. The smallest GPS trackers were less than three inches long and weighed two and a half ounces. He'd need to make another trip over to her house.

After midnight, he drove by her house, which was dark, like most of her neighborhood. Her car was parked in the carport. Continuing down her street, he turned right at the next corner, drove another block and then turned right, again, to park behind the bushes where he had waited this morning in the rain.

Dressed again in all dark clothing with his small box of tools, he stealthily walked in his quiet crepe-soled shoes, towards the corner of her block. Earlier that day he had installed the necessary cell phone software and registered an account for the tracking device he brought with him to install.

Walking past three houses that were all dark, he moved back into the shadows of the bushes in her neighbor's yard. Getting down low he inched towards the carport, careful to not make a sound.

Looking around, squatting on the driveway just inside the carport, he stopped and listened. The sound of a night bird startled him, but that was all there was. He moved around the car to the front that was parked facing inside the carport, so that he was hidden from view.

In the darkness he shone the pinpoint beam of his flashlight onto the front passenger wheel well, and then stooped down under it. Taking out the magnet and the device, he placed it in the well where it couldn't be seen. Satisfied with the placement and solidity of the installation, he turned off the flashlight. *Nothing to it.*

Minutes later he was back inside the Mercedes, starting up the big motor and turning on the headlights. Putting the car in drive, he eased away from the curb and into the night. He didn't notice the curtain being pulled back in the front window of the house across the street.

Chapter 17

The next morning, Dana entered the colorful, well-stocked boutique, where her neighbor worked. A couple other women were going through the racks and one woman was paying for her purchases at the cash register.

"Hi, Dana!" Nancy said. "We've been busy, but I've just finished up with one customer and Joan, here, is taking care of the others,so I'm free to devote myself to you," Nancy effused without taking a breath. "I've put aside just a couple of things for you to get started with."

"Hold on, Nancy," Dana cut in, making a referee's time-out sign with her hands, and smiling at her neighbor. "You'll have to go a little slow. One step at a time. I don't know just what I want. I guess one new outfit that's a little dressy, but still relaxed, you know?

"Sure. How about a few pieces that you can mix and match, that'll stretch your wardrobe a little. Very versatile. How does that sound?"

"That sounds good," Dana responded, doubtfully. "Just don't get carried away."

An hour later, Dana had a pile of clothes, from which she selected a few pieces. "Good job, Nancy. I'm sure I'll be happy with them. Do you have time to go to lunch with me?"

"Yeah, this would be a good time to go out. Oh, my gosh. That reminds me. Back to our conversation yesterday morning, about the strange guy who was walking by your house, you know?"

"Nancy. He was a guy who was a *stranger*, not a *strange guy*, right?" Dana clarified.

"Yeah, whatever. He seemed a little strange, the more I thought about him. Anyway, now there may be something else about him."

"Something *else* about him? We don't know *anything* about him. We don't even know who he *is*. How can there be *something else*?" Dana asked incredulously.

"Well, give me a chance and I'll tell you. I was out early this morning, with Peanut, walking around the block. As we were walking by the Elwoods place, you know Gladys, don't you? They've been here since the year one."

"Yes, I know who Gladys is, but I don't really know her," Dana again clarified.

"Well, anyway. Gladys was out this morning picking up her paper when we walked by and she called me over to talk. She said she wanted to tell me something because I know everyone in the neighborhood and I talk to a lot of people."

"She's got *that* right," Dana offered.

Ignoring the thinly-veiled sarcasm, Nancy continued, "So Gladys said that yesterday morning, when it was raining, she went out to pick up her paper and there was a strange, excuse me, *unfamiliar* small white convertible sports car with a black top, parked across the street from her house. She wasn't sure what make of car it was. It was an older car, she said. Like a vintage car. But it was in really good shape. She couldn't see the driver, clearly, because there was rainwater on the windows, but she was pretty sure that it was a *man*."

"That's shocking," Dana mocked.

"No, listen. *That* isn't what she had to tell me. What she really wanted to tell me is that late last night, well after midnight, *the same car was back, parked in the same place.* This time she caught a glimpse of the driver. She looked out when she heard the sound of a motor start up. The car's interior light stayed on for a few seconds. Apparently the driver had just gotten into the car. She saw a young man, between twenty-five and thirty-five, Caucasian with long brown hair. She didn't get a look at his face, because he was looking straight ahead, but it sounds like the same guy I saw in front of your house last week."

"Okay, I'll admit that it's odd for the same car to be parked there twice in one day, but we need to check it out for an explanation. Did Gladys notice a light on in any houses where he might have been visiting? We may be able to ask a neighbor who knows him what he was doing there."

"No, it was dark all around. That surprised her. She said she had gotten out of bed to take a pill. I know she takes several pills, at different times. She has high blood pressure—"

"Nancy, Nancy," Dana, interrupted, "she had gotten out of bed to take a pill and—what?"

"Oh, yeah. She got out of bed to take a pill after she had fallen asleep. She thinks she subconsciously remembered she hadn't taken her nighttime pill. When she saw that the whole neighborhood was dark, she realized how late it must be. Even the Goodman's house was dark, and they have a teenager. She was just about to make her way back to bed when she heard the car motor. She looked at the kitchen clock after he pulled away. It was ten minutes to one."

"Well, I think as you walk around the neighborhood you should advise other people to be on the lookout for a car of that description," Dana suggested. "Too bad we don't know the make of car, or the year. I don't suppose she got a license plate number."

"No, it was parked so she could only see the front of the car, not the back. When he pulled away, it was too quick, and too dark for her to make out a number," Nancy responded.

"That's understandable," Dana agree, slowly nodding. "We'll ask the neighbors, if anyone sees it, to try to get the plate number. Then we can run down the owner and investigate further. But I really can't see taking any action, other than alerting the neighbors to watch for the car as being possibly suspect. It's a unique car so, probably, that description is enough to identify it.

"So far, it's really a stretch to make much more out of it. You can't possibly know if it was the same man in the car who you saw a week ago, and we don't even know that *he* was a suspicious person. There are no reports about break-ins in the neighborhood. So all we're left with, is that someone from outside our area, parked a car twice in the same place. I don't see that that's cause for alarm. We should all just be vigilant.

"I think it's time I told you, Nancy," Dana continued, lowering her voice, "that I'm a federal agent. I've had extensive paramilitary training and carry a gun. I work as a courier, protecting classified cargo out of Y-12. That's why I'm away so much."

Nancy had gone a bit pale and lost her natural composure for a moment, blinking her eyes in surprise. "I knew you were a little different," she finally said, shakily. "But you're so pretty to be a federal agent," she added, lamely.

"You're my friend and confidante and I want you to know that I can take care of myself. I've always appreciated that you keep an eye on my house when I'm gone, but you shouldn't worry about me. I'm glad you're so observant and recognize anything out of the usual. And I think you're right to pass along Gladys' information. But I don't think there's a reason for people to be fearful. In fact, we need to be careful *not* to frighten people. Just tell them to be on the lookout for this particular car.

If I see this guy doing anything suspicious, I'll take care of him. If he's planning on causing any trouble, he's the one who has something to fear. He doesn't know who he's dealing with. Come on, let's go eat."

Chapter 18

There was a knock at the door, just as Albert was stubbing out his third cigarette and finishing his second cup of morning coffee. *Who the hell is that?* Going to the door and yanking it open he found Henry standing there looking like he had been in a near-fatal accident: His head was shaved bald, and his scalp was white under the glare of the overhead bare bulb. The shadows on his face were darkened with grey streaks across his forehead. His old blue bathrobe was hanging in strips like it had been attacked with garden shears. In his outstretched hands he was holding his ever-present Bible, now fringed with yellow post-it notes coming out of it from all sides.

"Henry, what the hell has happened to *you?*"

"I found a new revelation, my brother, and I had to tell you! Please forgive the intrusion. I know now who I am from the Great I Am!" Henry exclaimed, stretching his arms out from his sides.

"Yeah? Well, that's good because *I* can hardly tell who you are. Come on in. I was just having a cup of coffee. You want some? I mean, coffee's okay, right? I know it's not in the Old Testament, but I'm all out of nectar of ambrosia. Have a seat at the counter and pour yourself a cup. And keep your robe together, for God's sake."

"Smells like the devil's weed in here," Henry said, audibly sniffing at the air, as he walked over to the counter and sat down. "I see you're still smoking tobacco; defiling your body."

"Yeah, well, I don't have any pot, so it's the best I can do. Why don't we talk about what you've done to your body? What's with the shaved head, for instance?"

"That's what I wanted to tell you. I've been reading the Old Testament, as that's where the Spirit has been leading me to place my finger when I open the Bible randomly." Henry held up the book. "See, I stick on a post-it note in every passage I've found, to refer back to. Anyway, yesterday I was definitely led to Job, the book, and the person. My finger went to the first chapter, verse 20. Let me read it."

Holding up the tabbed book, Henry cleared his throat and read with dramatic emphasis, "'Then Job arose, and rent his robe, and shaved his head, and fell upon the ground, and worshiped.' And, in the next verse it says 'the Lord gave and the Lord has taken away.' And that's what's happened to me," Henry said, putting the Bible down on the counter.

"Obviously, the Spirit is telling me that I must endure tribulations, like Job," Henry argued. "Maybe I shouldn't seek vengeance against those people who have done me wrong."

"Hold on Henry! Get a grip, okay? You're a good guy, right?" Henry pursed his lips and nodded. "Evil people shouldn't be allowed to get away with pushing you around. I don't think you've read far enough. Give me that book!"

Albert grabbed the Bible from Henry and scanned down, turning to the next page. "Look! On the next page, see what it says? 'Does God pervert justice? Or does the Almighty pervert the right? If your children have sinned against him, he has delivered them into the power of their transgression.' And down a couple of lines, 'if you are pure and upright, surely then, he will rouse himself for you and reward you with a rightful habitation, and though your beginning was small, your latter days will be very great.'

"See? Those people at Y-12 are the children, and you need to deliver them right into the power of their transgressions. That means they have to be punished. Shit, you're the 'pure and upright!' Do you think that you have a 'rightful habitation?' Of course not! You live in a shit hole! Where do you suppose your former boss lives? I bet he's all comfortable in a nice big house. What was your job, anyway? I'd like to know more about that. What did you do, exactly?"

"Hah! That's right! What I did—I did *exactly*. I made component parts for nuclear weapons using five-axis computer numerically controlled machine tools, called CNCs. It was very delicate work. After making the parts, I would have to fit them together by hand. This had to be done with absolute precision, being careful to have extremely accurate dimensions and thicknesses, as the motions of the various axes had to be simultaneously and continually coordinated to maintain a predetermined path. How can you do something like that and be unstable, like they said? Huh? I ask you."

"That's right. You're not unstable. You're a goddamn genius! They fired you because you were a threat. You knew more than they did about nuclear weapons."

"Well, I know how they work," Henry said, sheepishly, "what they're made of: fissile material of uranium-235 or plutonium-239. Those elements can sustain a fission chain reaction. If you wanted to make a bomb, you'd need only like 35 pounds of uranium-235 or nine pounds of plutonium-239.

"But *you* can't *make* fissile material," Henry explained. "It would cost like a billion dollars and take about ten years of intensive work. The United States stopped making fissile material for nuclear weapons years ago. We have it stored at Y-12. Terrorists have tried to obtain components parts of weapons elsewhere in the world but haven't succeeded yet, but about forty other countries, including North Korea, have the material."

"Do you know anything about the DOE program of moving the nuclear materials? I've heard they're moved in convoys with armed federal agents riding along."

"Yeah, that's right. I know that our weapon parts and material are regularly loaded into trucks at Building 52B and driven to military bases and weapons plants, like Savannah River in South Carolina and the Pentax Plant in Amarillo. It's a pretty secretive operation, so they keep the schedule under wraps. I just knew when it was time for a shipment to go out.

"Why are you asking? What do you want to do? *Steal a bomb?* That would be crazy!" Henry snickered. "You'd have no way to deliver it. I don't mean to move it. I mean the delivery for detonation; in a missile or as a projectile in a gun-type system. Of course, it would be easy enough to make a dirty bomb with a little plutonium or enriched uranium mixed with some dynamite, to spread the radiation. *But you're not crazy, are you?*"

"No, I'm just curious," Albert said, defensively. "Don't you think there's a message in the fact that we have access to the weapons that could bring about Armageddon, the battle between good and evil that would occur at the end of the world? That's the Biblical prophecy, isn't it?"

"Yeah, I guess so," Henry answered, uncertainly. "But I haven't been led to the book of Revelation, yet. That's pretty scary stuff. I have to get back and read more about Job.

Hey, do you think it's just a coincidence that Job, in the Bible, and the word 'job' have the same spelling? I don't think so. That's the Spirit at work. But maybe you're right about reading further. I'm led to one place but I should keep reading for the complete message."

With that, Henry turned and walked out the door, with strips of fabric flapping over his white scrawny arms and legs as he clutched his book to his chest.

After Henry left, Albert sat in thought for a few minutes. Things were getting interesting, no doubt about it. Henry was the Mad Hatter. Yes, it was all fitting together perfectly.

Picking up his cell phone, he dialed up the GPS tracker's modem and received the SMS message and map location on the phone's screen. *Well, look what we have here. Miss Dana didn't go to work today. She's at that historical square where there are retail shops and restaurants. Maybe she would like some company.*

Making a hasty decision, he dressed quickly in good slacks and a silk shirt. He felt energized with the anticipation of a personal meeting. He ran through a few scenarios in his mind; then decided he'd trust his instincts when the time came.

A few minutes later he was in his sports car driving over to the shopping district. As he neared the square he thought better of parking his car in the parking lot in front of the buildings that were laid out in a u-shape. He didn't want to attract any attention while he was on surveillance and uncertain of his plan. Parking the car two blocks away, he walked back to the square and rechecked his phone. He saw he was at the right location when he spotted her car parked in the lot.

He couldn't just stand there without having anything to do. Luckily, there was a coffee shop where he could go across the street, and watch the shops' entrances.

Taking a seat near the front window, with a cup of coffee, he felt more comfortable. He knew that when he would see Dana come out of one of the half-dozen shops he could get across the street to the parking lot in seconds. *Then what?* He would engage her in conversation, pretend to be looking for a car, whatever. She'd want to get to know him, sensing his intellect and power.

As he pondered his move, he saw her in front of a dress shop carrying a couple of bags. *But she wasn't alone. Who the hell was that with her?* She looked familiar, actually. *Why did she have to hook up with some broad to go out and buy a fucking dress now, for Chris' sakes?*

He certainly wasn't going to make his move today. He'd have to wait until Dana's next day off, after the Fourth. It would give him more time to work out a plan. With the tracker installed, he would know her every movement. She couldn't get away from him. It was just a matter of time.

As he thought about it, he smiled to himself. *If she causes me any trouble, she's the one who has something to fear. She doesn't know who she's dealing with.*

Chapter 19

The morning haze was a portent of the high heat and humidity that would arrive by the afternoon: The kind of weather so typical of the Fourth of July in most places in the country, but no more so than in East Tennessee. It was a holiday when the temperature was specially noticed, and often even remembered, as people spent most of the day and evening out of doors, attending the morning parades, the mid-day picnics and the evening band concerts followed by fireworks.

Dana had gotten up early, as she needed to allow enough time before the activities started, to go out and pick up a chocolate sheet cake for the afternoon couriers' picnic, to be held at a local park. Both groups of agents, their commanders and staff, along with everyone's spouses and children were invited to the annual get-together.

The event was one of the infrequent occasions when all the agents of the Oak Ridge Section had an opportunity to get together socially, along with their families. Everyone who attended had to help out; bringing food, setting up games, and cleaning up. Each agent would sign up to bring a dish to share for the picnic. Volleyball games would be set up for adults, and egg-tosses and three-legged races were on the program for the kids. Some people would be content to just sit in the shade and watch.

Dana was expecting Owen to drop by in the afternoon so that they could drive together to the picnic; and he had suggested driving downtown, afterwards, to see the fireworks.

She'd better get going. She had thought about making a cake until she figured out it was a doomed plan. She could have complete confidence in a store-bought cake, and had a reasonable doubt about one of her own making. Besides, no one in her group would appreciate the effort that would go into a homemade cake, anyway.

*   *   *

Owen stopped by about two o'clock, having picked up his contributions for the picnic: buns for hamburgers and hot dogs, potato chips, a case of beer and a bottle of Yeagermeister.

"John, Rob, Dave and Danny are bringing the hot dogs and hamburgers and condiments for about twenty people," he commented, standing in her kitchen. "Are we forgetting anything?"

"Plates, napkins, and plastic silverware? Actually, I've got a lot of those things. I'll get them together. You want a beer? We can go out on the deck."

"Sure. That's just what I want, actually. I'm hot from running around picking up all this stuff for the picnic.

Dana grabbed a bag of pretzels, and a couple of beers out of the refrigerator, as Owen held open the back door. "That cake looks good, Dana," he said, looking over at the box.

"It should be fine. It's chocolate, and most people like that. I know you do. I was thinking of making one and then I got a reality check, and remembered that I don't make cakes. Here, you want some pretzels?" she said, pouring some into a bowl at the table.

"Sure," he said, picking up a few, and taking a swig of beer. "So, did you notice that George Newsome signed up for the picnic?

"Yeah, I did, as a matter of fact. I noticed, because he doesn't usually come. We'll get to meet his wife and son," Dana added.

"Yeah. Should be a treat. By his accounts she should look like Scarlett Johansson and, if his son is anything like George, the kid will explain to us how to play volleyball, including the physics on how the angle of contact and speed affect the ball's trajectory.

"George is so full of it," Owen continued, shaking his head. "He knows *everything;* and he's done *everything,* according to him. Of course, just hope that you don't have to depend on him knowing anything.

"The last time we had an exercise in clearing a building, Rob and I were supposed to do a button hook maneuver with him. Instead of George going left, like he was supposed to, he turned right, colliding into Rob like he was tackling him. 'Oh, I didn't see him,' George whined. Yeah. Rob is only six foot two, and it was broad daylight. You can't believe anything he says, can you? I hope he doesn't hang around us. Why do you think he's coming this year?"

"I guess he needs to find new people to impress," Dana responded. "He's run thorough our crowd. Anyway, he couldn't be excluded, you know. They couldn't post an invitation, 'Everyone Welcome, except George.'

"He is obnoxious with all his made-up stories," she agreed. "I mean, did he ever tell you about the time he dove into the ocean and saved a woman who was drowning? He said that she got caught in an undertow, and was thrashing in the water, waving her arms in the air. He jumped in, pulled her out, dragged her up on the beach and gave her artificial respiration, bringing her back to life.

"Right," she said, scornfully. "You can't have your arms up in the air when you're caught in an undertow! It drags you *under.* That's why they call it an *undertow.*"

"Ha! That's a good one," Owen chuckled. "He told me another version of his heroics in saving someone who was drowning. He said he was poolside at a ritzy resort, (which I don't believe, either,) when a large woman who was in the pool sank down to the bottom, and didn't come back up for long enough that other people yelled for help.

"George got off his chaise lounge, jumped in and pulled her to the surface. Then, holding her up, he swam over to the side and pulled her up the ladder, laid her out on the pool deck, gave her mouth to mouth resuscitation, and saved her life!

"Sound familiar? A large woman, as dead weight, was lifted up a ladder? You know the size of George. He's not large. Although he is dead weight," Owen concluded, smiling.

"Makes you wonder if the guy can ever go swimming without saving someone's life," Owen offered. "And don't get me *started* on what he did in the Gulf War."

"Okay, I won't," Dana smiled. "But wait! I almost forgot to tell you that your absolute favorite guy is coming, who also never comes to these things: *Ernest.*"

"Oh, God, no. Not 'In' Ernest!" Owen groaned, as though in pain. "How's he going to play volleyball with a rule book in his hands? Wait! What am I saying?! He'll make a big stink that we're even playing volleyball; or, jungle ball, as we call our version. He'll say, 'That's not SOP,' Owen intoned in a sing-song voice, mocking his co-worker. "Seriously, he'll spoil it for everybody.

"You know our rules, Dana. A serve is made by the guy in the back right corner. There are no more than three touches on each side. But staying on your own side of the net? No way. The ball is up for grabs, anyway you can get it.

"For us, it's a gladiator sport, to see if we can overpower the guy on the other side of the net. The ball is almost incidental. It'll come down on one side or the other—eventually. Of course, the net usually comes down, too, with maybe a couple of guys on top of it, but that's within the rules; the 'laws of the jungle.'

"You watch, Dana. 'In' Ernest will have a copy of the Rules of Volleyball with him. He'll lecture us on how sacred the net is. It can't be touched. Even the invisible line *under the net* can't be crossed. He'll read the rules aloud to all of us.

"You know what a piss-head he is in the vehicle. His stuff can't be touched. The invisible line *around his stuff* can't be *crossed*. He's called the Commander to report me for *moving* his *stuff*, which is against SOP, I guess, somewhere in the fine print. I *had* to move his stupid rifle, once, so I had a prayer of getting to *mine* in case I needed it. You know, like, *if we were being fired on?*"

"I know," agreed Dana. "He's so smug, I'd just like to smack him! What I can't stand about him is his self-righteous attitude. I don't know how such a short man can always be looking down his nose, but he seems to be. He's always lecturing."

"Jeez. Are you sure we even want to go this picnic? It doesn't sound like much of a picnic with these crazy people."

"We have our friends, too, who'll be there," Owen reminded her.

"I know. They'll be our human shields. John won't put up with George's bullshit. And if Ernest objects to how we play, John will tell him to go toss an egg with the kids. Or worse."

*   *   *

That afternoon, the courier families, numbering about a hundred and twenty, gathered at Staunton Park, a historic Civil War battle site memorializing the heroism of Captain Cyril Staunton, who died there saving other Union soldiers. It was now a large public park on the northeast side of city, with different areas for relaxation and recreation.

Commanding the center of the park was a rampant, two-front-feet-in-the-air equestrian statue, with the mounted Staunton, with sword drawn, charging into battle. Although it was a myth that two steed's legs lifted in front indicated that the rider died in battle, it meant that to most people. Besides, it was the case with Captain Staunton.

The great oak trees in the back area of the park provided cooling shade during warm weather, and visitors liked to sit on the wrought-iron benches under the trees' canopies. There, residents could peacefully reflect, read, or just be entertained by the squirrels gathering acorns, when available, or, otherwise, asking to be fed.

Another area of the park was clear of trees, and devoted to baseball and other team sports and games. While the baseball "diamond" was rudimentary, it did have a dirt infield with square rubber bases that had been put in place, roughly equidistant from one another. Base lines were nonexistent and outfield boundaries varied with those who were playing at any given time. But the field had functioned well for the level of play it had hosted over the years.

The grassy area next to the baseball field was well-suited for easy setups of games like badminton, volleyball, or the newer, bag toss. All of these required only simple equipment, which was easily transported and supplied by those who came early to stake out the area for play; or reserved it, in the case of a large group.

Adjacent to the fields, was a playground with slides, a jungle jim, a swing set with six belt swings, an old-fashioned see-saw, sand boxes and plastic spring-bottomed horses.

Completing the facilities of the park, was a cinder jogging path, which meandered through most of the front area of the park, skirting the play areas, terminating at the walkway to the public restrooms and water fountains.

The DOE had a permit reserving the large grassy field for the games, as well as the surrounding wooded area for the picnic. Of course, individuals in the group could use the rest of the park's facilities, depending on the amount of public use there was at the time.

By three o'clock, most of the courier group had arrived, and families were occupied with setting up their folding tables and chairs, or spreading blankets in preparation for the picnic. Teams of agents were performing their assigned duties of heating up the grills, setting up the buffet tables, staking the volleyball net, and marking boundaries and placing equipment for various games.

As the adults took charge of arranging the numerous heaping bowls and platters, the kids ran around to scout out the play possibilities. In this pursuit, they hooked up with other kids close to their own ages, and became instant friends and partners for the afternoon's contests.

Wives knew one another from previous get-togethers and found plenty to talk about. In addition to the topics of the day, they could compare notes on coping with the long and frequent absences of their husbands, while trying to maintain their homes and family life.

By four o'clock the party was in full swing. The hotdogs and hamburgers had been grilled and served alongside such traditional picnic fare as potato salad, watermelon, and baked beans. As the plates were filled, everyone settled down in their small groups to eat.

Dana and Owen were joined at their table by Danny, John and Rob. Owen mentioned Dana's chocolate sheet cake on the dessert table that they wouldn't want to miss. John said he'd go get a few pieces for the table, and maybe several of those chocolate chip cookies, while he was at it.

George stopped by the table to introduce his family to his "very good friends." His wife, Ginny, turned out to be a slightly plump, pleasant-looking woman; not likely to be mistaken for a movie star. His ten year old son, Donald, said he was pleased to meet the people who were helping his dad protect the convoy from a terrorist attack to steal nuclear bombs. George, flushing a little, said that they had to hurry off to eat before their food got cold.

Second servings, dessert and beer drinking extended the picnicking into the late afternoon.

The remainder of the day would be spent playing games, the highlight being the annual brutal athletic contest known to the agents as jungle ball. The teams were the same as at work, intensifying the competition of the event. The number of players was not limited, except that the two teams had to be equal.

After everyone got lined up, there were fifteen agents on each side, three rows of five players each. John was the captain of one team and Fred Wilson was the captain of the other. After John and Fred conferred privately, John laid out the very basic rules to everyone. As expected, Ernest, who was on John's team, protested that the net was not protected, according to the official regulations.

"Ernest," John said through his teeth, "This is a game. Our game. We made the rules. If you don't want to play against the net, don't. Just be prepared to get creamed, and that might be *after* the game, too, if you fuck it up for the rest of us."

"Fine," Ernest pouted. "We'll play it your way. But it's not volleyball," he had to add, peevishly.

The game was as hotly contested as ever with bodies crashing against each other on either side of the net with the ball squirting out erratically, without being under anyone's control. Most points were made or lost at the net where there was little finessing. When John's team had twenty-five points, they were declared the winner, without rancor, by most. Everyone agreed that it had been a hard-fought match.

It was nearly time to head out to watch fireworks by the time that the couriers' group broke up, and people started making their way to their cars. Parents called to their children, who reluctantly came out from their hiding places, ending their game of Hide and Seek. Everyone left feeling tired, well-fed and contented.

The clean-up committee stayed behind to pick up the inevitable litter left behind after so large a party. Owen and Dana had volunteered for this duty, along with several others. Fanning out with large heavy-duty plastic bags, the group moved through the two main areas, efficiently covering the space and quickly finishing the chore.

Much later that evening, after the spectacular fireworks downtown, Dana and Owen drove back to her house on the ridge. Neither one having much energy left, they both just collapsed on the sofa for a few minutes, to have a glass of wine. Turning around to look out the front window Dana remarked, "I almost forgot that I need to check on Nancy's house. You know they're on vacation for the next few days, yet."

"Oh, yeah, that's right. Hilton Head and Savannah," Owen replied. "I've never heard of any burglaries around here, but people feel better if they think someone is checking on their house when they're away."

"Nancy had gotten a little nervous over an incident last week. Gladys Elwood, who lives around the corner, told her that a white vintage sports car had been parked across from her house; in the early morning and again after midnight. Nancy made a connection between the guy in that car and some guy she saw in front of my house when we were at Ft. Chaffee. I finally told Nancy that I'm a federal agent, so she wouldn't worry about me."

"I don't worry about you, Dana, but do you think some guy is stalking you? Have you seen any guy following you?"

"No, no one that I've noticed. When Nancy told me about the 'strange' guy in front of my house, I checked to see if anything was missing, but nothing was. I pretty much dismissed the whole incident as Nancy letting her imagination run away with her. She's told all the neighbors to be on the lookout for this particular car, and get the license plate number. If someone does, I'll check out the owner, and look into it."

"There are some nut cases out there. I hope you're not a target of one of them. Call me if you 'make' someone following you, okay? You might need some help."

"Sure, but I haven't had any encounters with a strange guy, so it doesn't seem very likely. Since the whole neighborhood is looking out for his car, I think we're covered. You're on a three-day trip this week, so you won't be around, anyway, but don't worry. I'll be on my guard.

"Oh, that reminds me. Too bad that you'll be away next week. The USRowing Club nationals will be at Melton Lake. I'm going to stop by and watch them on my day off. I saw them practice a while back, but I've never seen a race. You might've liked to have seen that, too."

"Yeah, I haven't seen one, but there'll be other regattas. If you like it, we'll go together another time, okay? Anyway, it's late and I think you'd like to get to bed." He stood up and moved to the door. "You know, it was a really good day. The picnic was much more fun with you there. Thanks." He bent down and kissed her cheek.

"It was good for me, too. Take care on your trip this week. I'll talk to you when you get back, and tell you about the regatta."

He likes me! she thought, after closing the door. He *likes* me? Who am I—Sally Fields?

Chapter 20

"Attention!" the Starter's cry crackled over the loudspeaker, as he raised a bright red flag straight up and high into the air. Then, pausing as though frozen, the tension became palpable in the air as expectancy grew in the prolonged silence.

The spectators were hushed, as the young female rowers in their bright-colored spandex shorts outfits, sat taut and alert, holding their oars up above the water; four women facing the sterns in each of seven sculls that had been pulled up in alignment at the starting dock. They all took a deep breath and held it as everyone in the stands seemed to take in a deep breath, along with them. "Go!" the judge finally ordered as he swung down the red flag in a flourish to emphasize his command.

The narrow boats coursed rapidly ahead. The rowers coiled forward with their arms outstretched, brought the oars straight down into the water, catching it to power the sculls ahead. Quickly pulling the oars through the water, their bodies moved into a slight lay-back position, as the exertion burned their abdominal muscles.

As the oar handles were moved down, the athletes drew the oar blades straight up out of the water and then turned the handles from vertical to horizontal. Then, moving their hands away from their bodies, past their knees, they came forward in the sliding seats until, recoiled and knees bent, the rowers were ready for the next catch of water.

The movements were repeated in unison, in cadence, as the skinny boats skimmed across the smooth water. The long thin oars, anchored to riggers that acted as fulcrums for the levering action, rose and fell rhythmically, their "hatchet" blades plowing against the strong counter-force under the surface. Each time the oars came out of the water, they remained horizontal as they were evenly pulled back to submerge again to propel the crafts forward.

A motor boat purred behind the rowers, moving slowly from side to side inside the width of the seven-lane course, avoiding the buoys along the way. The boat was steered by one man as another man stood and intently watched the movement of the sculls.

At one point, the motor boat speeded up to pull alongside one of the sculls, as the man standing called out the sculling team. He raised a white flag and brought it down across himself, pointing the tip towards his right, to indicate that they were out of their lane and needed to move over to the right. The four rowers nodded and kept pulling the oars, without breaking their rhythm, as their scull drifted over, back in their lane. There was no penalty for this, as the rowers faced the stern of the boat, and couldn't move forward in a nearly-straight line throughout the course of a race.

Other heats would have sculls with a coxswain, the only team member who could face toward the bow of the boat. A coxswain did not oar, but acted as coach and could steer the boat. The coxswain, according to the rules, had a qualifying weight minimum to meet in order not to give an advantage to one team over another. For men, the coxswain had to weigh at least one hundred and twenty pounds, and the minimum weight for a woman was one hundred and ten. They were weighed just prior to the races, like jockeys, and were required to wear "dead-weight" sand bags, if needed, to come up to the minimum weight.

The race had continued along the course without incident and was nearing the end, when one of the sculls moved noticeably ahead of the others, bringing cheers from the crowd to encourage the nearly-exhausted "green" team in their final push.

As that scull's "bow ball" crossed the finish line, an air horn erupted, signaling the victory. The finish judge, clicking on his split-time stop watch, called out "One!" and quickly raised and lowered a red flag. As the other boats reached the finish line, the judge continued to record their time, called out their positions, "two," "three," and so on, raising and lowering a red flag for each arrival which added to the pageantry and celebration of the race. The winning team had come in at 6:08.85, a fast time for a four-rower team over the one-and-a-quarter-mile course.

Dana, seated alone up in the stands, had cheered on the winning green team, along with the crowd. She had arrived in time to watch many of the first-run women's races. Climbing up to the top bench on the temporary bleachers that had been erected at the midpoint of the race course, she was able to get a good view of the entire run.

The program had noted that there were over 1,400 rowers for the event, which included junior, intermediate and senior level competition. Races would be held over four days, from nine o'clock in the morning until eight o'clock in the evening. Each race listed the level for men and women, the type of boat, and the number of crew members. The presence of a coxswain with a crew was indicated on the program with a plus sign, following the number of rowers.

Reading up on sculling in preparation for her first regatta, Dana had learned that there was a comprehensive vernacular in the sport that had a name for every movement, and every doodad or piece of equipment. She had read through the many terms such as: "sweep boats," "scull boats," "coxswain," and "boots, sleeves and "buttons," that had nothing to do with clothing, and "catching a crab," which had nothing to do with seafood. Fortunately she found a website for spectators, who just wanted to follow the action.

There she read that the best crews were the ones who made it look easy. Optimum sculling was described as a the oars having a fluid motion, without a beginning or an end, in synch and without splashing when they went in and came out of the water. The scull's speed should be consistent and the look should be graceful, and elegant.

She had been surprised to read that rowers were considered by many experts as the world's most physically-fit athletes, as all the muscles of the body were involved in oaring, with the most strength required from the legs. The rowers' pace was 45-50 strokes a minute at both the beginning and ends of races. After the exhaustion of the race, the crew would need to row more slowly for five to ten minutes in order to cool down.

Dana had decided to stay on into the afternoon to watch some of the men's events. The races had many variables, to make them more interesting. The rowing style differed whether it was a scull, where the crew each had two oars, or a sweep boat, where the crew each had one oar. The boat lengths varied with the crew size, from a one-person, twenty-seven foot skiff, up to a sixty foot scull for an eight-person crew with a coxswain. The distances varied between 500-meter "sprints" up to the full length of 2,000 meters.

By noon, the stands had filled up with spectators. Some people appeared to be coming from work during their lunch hour, while most of the others had brought tote bags filled with supplies to spend the day. The whole area was taking on the atmosphere of a fair, with white tents sprouting up all over. The vendors inside were selling all manner of sculling equipment, accessories, related and unrelated products.

This was only the third time this national championship had been held at the Melton Lake facility. It was a special honor to host such a regatta, which brought additional prestige to the venue, already considered one of the best in the country. One of the reasons that the Rowing Club brought the championship regatta to Oak Ridge was that the city's leaders encouraged community support of the competition.

Dana thought back to when she had first seen the scullers the day she had lunch at the nearby restaurant. She wouldn't eat there today, as it would take too much time away from the races, and there were vendors selling food and soft drinks close by and in the boathouse.

At one o'clock, she made her way down the stands and walked over to one of the vendors and got a hot dog and soda. Finding a temporarily-vacant picnic table, she sat down to eat it while gazing out at the dock areas where sculls were being readied for later races. There were now crowds of people milling around the tents and lining up at the food vendors' stalls and carts.

Most had come to be in time for the men's competition which would be starting soon. As it was summer, there were many young people in the crowd, joking and laughing together in groups. But also, many adults had made time to attend the biggest regatta of the season.

Dana walked away from the crowd to look across the lake at the picturesque wooded hills. Even on her side of the waterway, there were no buildings, other than the boathouse where there was the one parking lot. Most people had parked along the road that was at the base of a steep wooded hillside. At the top of a were a few large homes that took advantage of the broad vista of water where the lake connected with the river. The Cumberland Mountains served as a stunning backdrop.

After walking around after her lunch, Dana returned to the stands that were now so crowded she had to climb up several rows before finding a space, next to a family with young children. As she took her seat, a man right behind her sidled past, on his way up. *Something familiar about him. Had she seen him before?* She didn't want to turn around and stare at him. But there *was something* that evoked a memory.

The spectators were just quieting down as the Starter picked up the loudspeaker and shouted "Attention!" He then paused for several seconds, before he released the racers with "Go!" and another heat was off. As Dana looked at the boats, she mentally identified them: Coxed Eights [8+], 65 foot-long sweep boats with eight-man crews, each with a coxswain. *Hah. I'm getting pretty good at this,* she thought. She couldn't resist turning to the woman next to her, to say something to pronounce the word coxswains, correctly, as "cox-ens."

It was a close race which was decided *after* the heat, with the aid of the finish-line photo. The white bow ball at the very front of each boat was to better identify the first hull that crossed the finish line but, sometimes, a race involving several boats was too close to call.

The winners, after rowing to cool off, rowed over to the floating Winner's Dock, stepped out of their sweep boat, and accepted their ribbon for winning the heat. After pulling the boat to the shore, all eight men picked it up and carried it back to the rack, as was the rule.

As Dana sat through two more races, she couldn't shake her feeling of discomfort about the man who had been behind her on the steps. *I don't know him, but still* . . . She thought of a maneuver to get another look at him. Taking a lipstick out of her purse and a small mirror, she adjusted the mirror to look behind her, over her right shoulder. As she covertly looked at the reflections of people in the next row up, she caught one image which brought back a clear memory. She had remembered that day when she had gone to the mall, and walking in she had noticed *that same man* as she was seeing him now, as *his reflection had been in the glass door* then, as he had walked in behind her. Now *his reflection was in her mirror,* as he was sitting behind her.

He had been *behind her* at the cashier, at Belks, too. She had dismissed that as coincidence that day. So what was this? A lot of people were here, but this didn't *feel* like a coincidence. It was just a hunch, but that was enough to act on. She'd test her theory by making a show of gathering up her things and leaving the regatta, being sure she had gotten his attention. *I'll wait one more race, in case he noticed me flashing the mirror around. I don't want him to suspect that I'm aware of him.*

The regatta had attracted a large crowd so it was likely that he had come here on his own and hadn't followed her here. But seeing her here, he seemed to be following her. Maybe he just found her attractive and was checking her out. *Not impossible.*

As the next race got underway, it didn't hold her attention as her mind was running through the possibilities. He didn't *look* threatening, she had to admit. He wasn't a big guy. She wouldn't have any problem subduing him in a physical altercation. Of course, she was probably getting ahead of herself in that scenario.

If he just wanted to hit on her, she would just tell him to get lost, and that would be the end of it. If he was asking for trouble, she was prepared to give it to him.

The third race ended in a clear victory. This time Dana was so preoccupied she hadn't even noticed if the winner was a scull or a sweep boat. Picking up her purse and her program, she turned to the woman next to her, again, "Well, I can't stay for any more races. I really need to be going, now. Enjoy the other races."

"Uh, yeah, thanks," the woman said, again startled by Dana's words.

Dana stood up and carefully stepped down the bleachers to avoid anyone's belongings. As she got down to the ground, she stopped momentarily and stretched her arms and pulled her shoulders back. She had been sitting on a hard, backless bench for a few hours and was a little stiff, anyway.

Then she turned and started walking away from the stands, towards her car that had been parked on the other side of the street, close to the woods. As she moved onto the gravel path that turned into the trees, she heard voices behind her. But they came from a couple of teenagers.

As Dana crossed the street, she heard uneven footfalls behind her and discretely glanced around. This time it was the creep. There he was, walking along with one foot turned in, dragging it a little. Nancy's words came back to her—'He walked with a sort of a hitch in his step,' describing the man in front of her house. This must be the guy! *This is getting too weird.*

Walking past a row of portable toilets, she saw her opportunity, and turned the corner behind the last one and waited. Moments later he came around the same corner and stopped short, a look in his eyes of panic and confusion. She just stood there, calmly facing him, arms folded. "You're following me," she said, evenly. "What do you want?"

"Wha-what are you talking about?" He stammered. He then pulled himself up and took a deep breath to regain his composure, and countered, "I've been at the regatta, and I was just walking back to my car."

"Oh?" Dana asked, wide-eyed, "Did you park your car behind the toilets? I've seen you *before today*; twice on the same day at the shopping center in town. You walked into the mall behind me, and hours later you were right behind me again when I bought something at Belks. I hadn't thought much about it at the time. But today, I saw that you were sitting behind me up on the bleachers. And now, *here you are again*, I've run out of any reasonable explanations, so I'm asking again, *why are you following me?*

"Okay, you're partly right," he admitted, sounding agreeable. "I saw you outside the mall as you were walking in, and I thought you were very attractive, but I didn't *follow* you anywhere. Later, I just happened to be shopping in the same place you were. I didn't *follow* you then, either. Today, when I saw you going up in the stands, I thought I'd sit by you, see if I could start up a conversation; get to know you. I had felt there was a connection between us. I thought you felt it, too."

"A connection? Why would I think *that*? Why would I think *anything* about you? Sorry, but I have no interest in getting to know you. If it's all just innocent, as you claim, let's just leave it at that, but I don't want you following me again. You got that?! I don't want to have to deal with this again."

Facing him as she finished speaking and was about to leave, something over his left shoulder caught her attention and she let out an involuntary gasp. "Your car," she breathed.

Parked across the street in the boathouse parking lot sat a vintage white Mercedes sports car with a black convertible top. He turned to follow her eyes.

"Is that your sports car?!" she asked, pointing over at the little car.

"Yeah. What about it?" He scoffed. "You have a problem with that, too?"

"I'll *tell* you why I have a problem with that!" Dana flashed. "Your car was seen parked in my neighborhood! You frightened an elderly woman who lives near me when you were parked across the street from her home early and late. You must have followed me home from the mall, that day, and you've been back since then at least twice, that I *know* of. I think that's *stalking*. How would you like to discuss this with the *police*?"

She watched as his face became contorted with rage; his mouth twisted into an ugly snarl. His ice-blue eyes narrowed, glaring at her with cold hatred.

"Who do you think you *are*, bitch?" he bleated. "You think you can make trouble for *me*? You can't prove anything. I'm sure I'm not the only guy in the area who owns a white Mercedes. Why would I want to follow *you* all over town, anyway? You're nothing to me! I *use* sluts like you for my own pleasure. I can control you with special powers. You knew that when you saw me in the mall. You *want* me to control you. Don't try to tell me you haven't *thought* about me!"

"What I *think* about you is that you're crazy!" she shot back. "And I can make *plenty* of trouble for you. I'm warning you, don't push me any further. I *know* that you've been stalking me. I *know* that you were skulking around my house doing God knows what when I was out of town. I *know* that you were sitting around in your fancy car, scaring innocent people, while you tried to spy on me. Don't even *try* to *deny* it."

"You want to see my car?" he snarled, moving towards her. "Let's go for a little ride! I'll show you what I can do to little sluts like you!" He leapt forward, punching her with his right fist, connecting with the end of her nose. Dana was momentarily thrown off balance. As she shook off the sting, blinking her tearing eyes to clear them, he kicked her in the shins.

"How do you like that, bitch?" he taunted with a sneer.

Dana, now oriented, again, reacted with lightning speed. Bringing up her elbow she cracked him across the ridge of his nose.

"Ow!" he yelped. "What the hell?! Oh, my God!" he gasped as he saw blood spurting out of his nose. "I'll kill you, you fucking whore!"

Facing him now, she put her full weight and force behind her fist, punching him in the solar plexus, knocking the breath out of his lungs.

"Ugh!" he buckled forward from the force and loss of air. As he sagged weakly, Dana followed up by striking him in the groin with the side of her hand. Now bent over double, he howled in anguish, crossing his arms and holding himself to try to ward off another blow and to try to alleviate the pain searing through him.

"You won't get away with this, cunt!" he squeaked, still doubled over.

"This is a warning," she said, poking him, to get his attention. "Stay away from me. Far away. I don't want to ever see you again."

"I'll go wherever I please! You don't scare me! I have great powers!" he cried, as he bulled his way forward with his head down. Dana neatly stepped aside and grabbed him from behind wrapping her right arm around his neck, bending her elbow in to apply pressure. He started choking and gasping for air. His bloodied nose was dripping onto her arm.

He was now uselessly flailing around, trying to kick her, and trying to free himself from her choke hold; unable to do either. Finally, holding his hands up in surrender, in a hoarse voice thickened with pain, he croaked, "Stop! Stop! I give up! You're going to kill me!"

"I'm not going to kill you, but you should know that I could really hurt you, and I will, if you should ever threaten me again. By the way, you don't have 'special powers.' You're just a sick bastard. Get some help. What's your name, anyway? I don't believe we've been properly introduced."

"I don't think I have to answer that. Someday you'll find out," he growled, spitting blood.

Dana turned her back and walked away leaving him sitting on the ground next to the portable toilet groaning, with his head back now, as his broken nose was copiously bleeding. *If I went to the police, they'd probably arrest me for assault. I think I adequately handled the situation. Besides, I can't believe he'll ever bother me again. He can't be that crazy.*

Chapter 21

He sat there, leaning against the portable toilet for several minutes, trying to think straight. How badly was he injured? She had tried to kill him! He hated her enough to almost get past his physical pain. Almost, but not quite. There would be time for him to exact his revenge; and it would be on a monumental scale. That had been decided the moment the beast from hell had laid her filthy hands on him.

Right now, before he even tried to move, he needed to figure out the extent of the damage. He felt achy all over. As his brain continued to register all the pain he was feeling, he realized that his whole body had been traumatized. *For her sake, she should have finished me off. I survived to destroy everything in her world.*

His head was aching and throbbing so much that he could feel pulsing in his temples, pounding against the side of his head. His ears didn't seem to be registering external sounds. He only heard chaos inside his brain, silencing everything else. *Jesus Christ. I could have a concussion. I could have brain damage. I might be deaf.*

His eyes were stinging from sweat running down his forehead. When he brought his eyelids down they scraped against his eyeballs like sandpaper. As he looked around him he couldn't focus beyond his own hand. Gingerly touching the bones around his eyes he could feel the bruising and tenderness around the eye sockets. *I'm practically blind.*

As he concentrated on each area of pain he realized that it was his nose that had suffered the greatest injury. His nose was the *center* of his pain. As he looked down he could see how it had already swelled. The pain radiated out from under his eyes as though on hot wires that connected to every point on his face. And he couldn't stanch the bleeding coming from high up inside. He kept his head back and put pressure under his nose, in a vain effort, as there was still fresh blood coming and dripping into his mouth. The strong taste of iron was making him gag. *My fucking nose is broken and I could be bleeding to death!*

As he drew in a deep breath, to test his lungs, he felt a sharp twinge. *I might have a broken rib. I don't know if I can even stand!*

He still felt the searing pain in his groin from when she had hit him in his manhood. Her hand had felt like a club whacking him. The pain had blinded him and was still burned like molten metal. *I could have been made permanently impotent by that banshee!*

He was getting the picture. She had planned the whole thing, that day in the mall. He had to hand it to her. She was good. First, she had flaunted her sexuality, daring him to take the bait and show an interest in her so she could set her trap.

He had been right that she had recognized him for what he was, an *omnipotent force* in the universe. She had admitted that she had noticed him in the mall. *Yeah, I would say she* noticed *me. She noticed my superiority. She noticed my power. She noticed that I could have her for the asking. She noticed that she had something to fear from me if she didn't cooperate.*

Today, she tried to deny that she felt any connection with me and that she hadn't thought about me since that day at the mall. What a liar!

Why would she entice me away from the races to attack me if I wasn't on her mind?

She accused me of following her. She knows what a damned lie that is! I haven't been following her. I've been duped by her to catch me off-guard. She has plotted to defeat me by weaving her evil web to entangle me in a trap so that my powers were temporarily diminished.

The mistake I made was that I underestimated her. I didn't realize what a vile, evil bitch she is. She has toyed with me, mocking me. She had to lie in wait to sucker punch me, to be able to disarm me with dirty blows to sensitive body parts. I allowed her to take me down today, but it's a long season.

I've given her too much credit, that she was intelligent enough to be aware of my superiority. She should have been much more fearful. Apparently she doesn't realize the retribution I will bring down on her or she would never have gotten me so angry.

She all but told me that she would kill me. Does she possibly think that she is capable of killing me? Or that I won't act on that threat by killing her before she makes another feeble attempt on my life? Killing her is now my mission: But not my only mission. Oh, no. I'm not just going to snuff out her life. She is just one insignificant target of the vengeance I will wreak on her and all those who have wronged me. She's not the first villain in my life. She's only the last villain in a long string.

I've suffered at the hands of others long enough: bullies, employers, parents, and that stupid whore from college who made a mess out of things.

When I was younger, there was no one who would save m from the abuse. No one. Now they'll pay for it and I won't save anyone, either. No one.

I'm going to use this slut as an example, to show the world what happens when evil is allowed to take charge; when the exceptional are put down by the unworthy by the use of lies and trickery. I'll show her *and the world what they have to fear. She and her people will know the extent of my fury—a fury that will reach well beyond her.*

I know just how I'm going to do it. She guards the most powerful force on earth: nuclear weapons. Whoever possesses those can rule the world. I could be the one to take that power away from her. That will terrify her and everyone else who's evil like her.

It's the right time and the right place, and I'll have the means for my perfect revenge. I can create terror. Do they think only Muslim extremists can do that? I have more to prove than they do, and I don't plan to leave this world for thirty virgins, either. I'll be around to enjoy my success.

He felt empowered and self-righteous. Using the portable toilet as counterbalance, he hoisted himself up, standing uncertainly. *I'll heal and use this experience to be stronger. She might have injured my eyes but my mind has a clear vision*

Walking slowly across the street to his car, he opened his door and sank gratefully into his seat. *Dana Knowles drove off in her Escape. How ironic. That bitch will never again be able to get away from me. She has signed her own death warrant and the death warrant of countless others.*

But right now he had to take care of himself. He needed to get home and heal his wounds before he could formulate a plan to take out his enemies.

Back at his building, he had to pull himself up each step slowly by holding onto the sticky banister, and pitching forward to propel himself onto the next step, he managed to get to the top of the stairs.

In the hallway, now out of breath from the exertion, and feeling woozy, he careened over to Henry's door, and leaned against the door jamb. He blinked to make out the words crudely-printed on yellow-ruled paper, taped on the dark varnished surface:

"Let him hear what the Spirit says . . . He who conquers shall not be hurt by the second death." Rev. 2:11

He pounded on the door with all the strength he had left. Henry soon swung it open for him, screaming in horror at the sight of his neighbor who stood there with bleary eyes glowering out of a swollen, bruised and bloodied face, wearing dirty, blood-soaked clothes, with his hair matted with leaves.

"Just let me in, Henry!" Reaching out to Henry for support, he nearly fell inside, and lurching over to a torn-up old chair, he collapsed into it.

"What happened to you?!" Henry shrieked. "You look like you've been stoned by the Philistines! Who did this to you, my brother?"

"You want to know what happened to me? You want to know who did this to me? You want to know?" A thought suddenly came to him. "I'll tell you who did this. The most diabolical woman in the world—a modern-day Jezebel, that's who!" He was becoming more animated with the sudden inspiration of a biblical reference, for Henry. "Wasn't Jezebel the most evil woman back there, in the Old Testament? Didn't Jezebel use her sexual powers against men, to trick them to their deaths? That's what this woman did to me, except she couldn't quite kill me. She lured me into a trap and tried to kill me, though."

"Jezebel was married to Ahab, the King of Judah," Henry said in a stentorian voice, now on a familiar subject. "She worshipped Baal and talked her husband, Ahab, into worshipping Baal. That angered the God of Israel, who cursed the land with a famine. During the famine, to get a man's vineyard, Jezebel lied about him, so that others would stone him to death. They did a lot of stoning in those days, apparently. The God of Israel then put a curse on Jezebel, saying that dogs would eat the flesh off her bones.

"When she painted her face, to save herself from a man named Jehu, who came to avenge the death of the vineyard owner, it didn't work. He had her killed and the dogs ate her flesh and chewed her bones, so that there was nothing to bury, as prophesied. Jehu then had all the people killed in Judah, who worshipped Baal. There was a lot of killing in those days. That all happened because of Jezebel who had lied and used her feminine wiles."

"That's exactly what we're up against, here, Henry! This evil woman, Dana, who works at Y-12, has used her sexuality, like Jezebel, to try to kill others. She has connived to destroy me through her trickery. She wasn't able to achieve her goal today, but she has sworn to kill me in the future.

"Today, she ambushed me, and broke my nose and clubbed me in the crotch. She has to be taken out, Henry. She, and the others who do the evil bidding of the government, for the Department of Energy at Y-12.

"These are the same people who destroyed you, Henry. They lied, by saying that you were unstable, so they could take away your livelihood, to condemn you to a life of constant want and misery. They're like the worshippers of Baal who stoned the poor guy with the vineyard, but these people have nuclear weapons that are more powerful than any other force on earth. And these weapons are in the wrong hands!

"We have to find a way to take some of these weapons to use the weapons against them to retaliate for the evil they've already done to us.

"Henry, I can see it now. We're in the most important struggle ever. It's the final battle of good over evil. It's like the Battle of Armageddon!"

Chapter 22

I n the afternoon, Dana was sitting in her living room reading, when she heard a car drive up. Looking out she saw Nancy, and Tom, and their daughter, Jamie, arrive home from their vacation. As she watched, Jamie was the first one to get out of the car, jumping out of the backseat, ponytail flying, disappearing into the house through the carport. Tom then opened the trunk and he and Nancy started pulling out suitcases and bags.

Dana walked out of her house and down her stairs, waving to her neighbors when they saw her. "Hey, Nancy! Tom! Glad you're back!" Dana crossed the street, joining them by the open trunk. "Here, let me carry something in for you."

"Hi, Dana. It's good to be home, and I'm not kidding." Nancy smiled. Picking up a few bags she said, "Uh, why don't you take that lavender-colored bag there, and you can carry it home, 'cause it's for you. A little souvenir from Savannah; some salted and chocolate-covered pecans, and some peanut brittle. I guess that last item is a gift for your dentist. And there's some peach salsa, too. You know—Georgia."

"Thanks. Let's try some of it, together. I came over to welcome you back and ask if you could both stop over at my place when you finish getting unpacked. Just for a drink."

"Thanks, Dana. But we're kinda tired, traveling all day. I don't think we'd be good company." Nancy said.

"I won't keep you, I promise. I just have an incident to tell you about. Nothing serious, but something I wanted you to know. I'd like to hear a little of your vacation, too. Whenever you're ready, just come over, okay?"

"Oh, okay. I'll just unpack the suitcases. Pretty much everything is going into the laundry so it shouldn't take too long."

About an hour later, the doorbell rang, and Dana opened the door to both Tom and Nancy.

"Hi! Come on in. Let's sit in the living room, okay? It's like 109 degrees out there. The air conditioner in the window is helping some. I'll get the snacks. What would you both like to drink?"

"I'll have iced tea, if you have it," Tom requested.

"I do have some in the refrigerator. With lots of ice for you, I know."

"I'd like a glass of wine," Nancy put in. "Anything white and chilled. I need to relax. We've been driving since nine this morning—it's over four hundred miles from Savannah to home."

"Yeah, Nancy needs to relax." Tom agreed. "Of course, I did all the driving."

Dana smiled at the tease. "Okay. You just take it easy, Nancy. I'll join you in a glass of wine. I didn't do any driving today, either."

Having returned with a tray of snacks and beverages, Dana sat and took a sip of her wine. "First, tell me, how was your vacation?"

"Well, for openers, I got stung by a jelly fish," Nancy began. "I thought it was a great white when it struck! Unbelievable pain! Some man at the beach suggested tomato juice to take out the sting."

"So Nancy went back to the condo and fixed herself a Bloody Mary," Tom interjected.

"Ha! That's right! Actually, I did, after the tomato juice had no affect on the burn."

"Let's see, what else?" Nancy continued. "Well, we had a lot of family time, which was a little dicey at first. We had told Jamie, there would be *no texting or calls* to friends for the week. She sulked for a day or two and then she figured that she had to talk to *us*. Turned out, she liked to talk to us. We all had some good times together, just hanging out."

"We did," agreed Tom. "Turns out, Jamie talks almost as much as her mother. Now that we're home, I expect things will return to normal."

"I saw Jamie when you drove up," Dana interjected. "She jumped out of the car and dashed into the house, not to be seen again."

"Yeah, I know," Tom said, shaking his head. "She couldn't wait to get inside to check in with a friend, to let her know the big news that she's back. Really, she's a good kid; just becoming more independent, and sometimes trying too hard to make the transition. Right now she's somewhere between being an adult and just a pain in the ass."

"So tell us, Dana, not to change the subject," Nancy inserted, "but what was the incident that you wanted to tell about?"

"Well it's nothing too terrible," Dana responded. "Nancy, you remember when I was out of town for training, and one night you saw that man walking in front of my house who seemed to have come out of my back yard?"

"Yes, of course. Was he here again?" Nancy asked, with alarm.

"No, not *here*," Dana assured her. "Let me tell you from the beginning. I went to the USRowing Championship regatta at Melton Hill Lake last Thursday."

"Oh, yeah?" Nancy queried, a little confused. "And something happened there?"

"Yes, actually; something did." Dana answered. "I was sitting up in the stands by myself when I recognized this guy who I had seen before at the mall, a couple of weeks ago. He had been behind me when I walked into the mall and then, much later, he was behind me again in Belk's when I was buying something. The had noticed the two sightings as I'm trained to be aware of what's going on around me.

"Anyway, at the regatta, who shows up again?—the same guy. He was sitting right behind me, in the stands, having walked up behind me as I climbed up to my seat. That couldn't be another coincidence, I thought. To be sure, I made a big show of leaving early, to see if he would follow me. I wanted to let him know that his attentions were unwanted.

"As I walked toward my car, he was following me. Then I noticed that he walked with a limp, that he had a turned-in foot. I remembered that I had noticed his club foot when I saw him in the mall. Then I remembered what you said. That the guy you saw in front of my house walked with a 'hitch in his step,' as you put it. At the time that description brought back a dim memory for me, but I couldn't make the connection with the guy in the mall, who I had forgotten, until he was walking behind me at the regatta."

"Oh, yeah, I remember how he walked." Nancy nodded, listening intently to the story. "That was one of the things that drew my attention. So then what happened?"

"I turned a corner to catch him in the act. At first he denied it, and then I saw a vintage white Mercedes convertible that was parked nearby. He admitted that it was his car and that was the clincher. You know, what Gladys said. That's when I told him that I knew he was stalking me; that he had been seen in our neighborhood on several occasions and I was ready to turn the matter over to the police."

"Oh, boy!" Nancy exclaimed. "Then, what?"

"Well, then it got ugly and he took a swing at me," Dana went on. "I had to get rough with him. I ended up breaking his nose and gave him a pretty good going over, before he got religion. I told him I never wanted to see him again; that it would only get worse. I think he got the message and I'll never see him again.

"But I wanted *you* to know that you were right, and he was spying on me, or whatever. I have no idea why. Tell the neighbors again, that if they see his car, to let you or me know. As I said, I really doubt that we'll ever see him again, but I thought you should know what happened. I told Owen, too, and he'll be on the lookout."

"I can't believe that I was right!" Nancy said. "Sure, I'll let everyone know that it's for real, that he was up to no good. But I won't alarm anyone. It sounds like you took care of the situation. It's just a shock that he actually was an intruder who was trying to cause trouble! I was going by the instincts that we all have when something doesn't feel right."

"Give yourself more credit," Tom spoke up. "You're more observant than most people to spot anything out of place, especially in our neighborhood. That was good work. It was your reporting about this guy and his car that allowed Dana to put it all together."

"That's true," Dana agreed. "But, anyway, it's most likely a dead issue. We should all stay alert, for a little while. He's a real jerk and he might try to retaliate against me or someone else. You never know what someone else is thinking. He could still surprise us—or me."

Chapter 23

"**A**re you crazy?" his father chided him. "Why would you want to work in the courier motor pool? I thought you already had a flunky job in some grease pit."

Albert had been at his parents' home all afternoon; in his father's study for the last hour, keeping his anger in check, as he was assaulted by the older man's rebukes. It sickened him that he had to come here and ask for help to get a job. Of course, he would deliver the ultimate insult, and that irony sustained him through these indignities.

His father had kept his distance, assuming the authoritative position, seated behind the large oak desk, holding "court." He noted that his father's hair had now gone completely grey, lighter at the temples, but remained thick and wavy. The dark eyes, under bushy brows, still bore through him as he peered over silver-framed reading glasses which sat low on his patrician nose.

Albert had telephoned early in the day and spoke to his mother, who registered more surprise than pleasure at his request to stop by, though she had invited him to stay for dinner. There must have been a lull in her social calendar, as well as a need to get rid of some leftovers, he had concluded. She had met him at the door and her light blue eyes had widened at the sight of his battered appearance. Her own appearance had been as well-groomed and coiffed as usual: Highlighted brown hair swept back framing her perfectly made up oval face.

"I'm a *Master Technician*," he sniffed, in answer to his father's latest barb, "certified to work on foreign and domestic cars that are vintage, customized, and high-performance. I'm not a grease monkey. And I don't work in a grease pit. I work at an automobile restoration facility."

"Okay. Okay, Albert. I stand corrected. It's an *elitist* car repair shop with an attitude. I'll restate my original question. Why do you want to leave your present employer, offering highly-skilled technical work, as you say, to work for a government motor pool where you'd top off fluids on tanks and trucks? Isn't that beneath you?"

"Tanks? I'm not planning on shipping out," he said, dryly. "The fact is that the courier division of Y-12 owns highly-customized armored vehicles equipped with state-of-the-art technology for security and communication. I'm ideally suited to maintain everything on the vehicles. I'm an electronic technician and a certified mechanic."

"But I thought you were a classic car enthusiast who wanted to preserve the few-remaining quality automobiles of another era?" his father persisted.

"I'm just trying to be more realistic, like you, Father. There aren't enough people around here who appreciate appointments like Connelly leather upholstery, and birds-eye maple dashboards. How many touring cars with running boards have you seen parked outside Wal-Mart's? he asked, oozing sarcasm.

"Working for the government would pay better and offer me job security," he continued, resuming a more reasoned tone. "If that means sacrificing my artistic principles for commercial gain, I'm willing to make that sacrifice. Do you think I can possibly continue to live on the meager stipend I get from you?" he asked, raising his voice. "And some day I'd like to live in a place that isn't carcinogenic. The rat hole I'm forced to live in now should be condemned by the EPA!"

"You little ingrate!" his father shouted back. "You're lucky to have a roof over your head, considering the shenanigans you pulled on your previous job! Or have you forgotten how you got fired and embarrassed your poor mother and me? Don't blame me for your troubles. You brought yourself down to your present circumstances, which are far better than you deserve, I might add.

"I always provided for you in grand style," his father continued, now gripping the edge of the desk. "You went to the best schools, to camp every summer when you were a kid, music lessons; the works. You've had every opportunity, but so far you've been nothing but a screw-up." The older man exhaled, and put his face in his hands for a moment. Then putting his elbows on the desk, and his hands together in a steeple, he puckered his lips in thought, mouth and peered over at his son. After a few seconds he sighed, and said, resignedly, "But all right. I'm willing to accept, for now, that you've had an epiphany and you want to turn your life around.

"In fact, I'm glad to hear you finally making sense about finding work that will pay you a living wage. I think you'd be far better off pursuing a career in your major—chemistry—schooling that I paid for, I might add. But I'm not going to raise objections to your self-improvement at this point. It's possible that I've been too negative towards your efforts in the past.

"When we started this conversation," his father reminded him, "you said you needed my help in your securing a job in the motor pool. What did you want me to do? I don't know anything about their job requirements or your qualifications.

"On the one hand, you tell me that you're a Master Technician, uniquely qualified to work on finely-tuned engines and electronics. But when you showed up here today you're your face all bruised and swollen, you told us that you broke your own nose by dropping a heavy wrench on yourself while you were under a car. My God, you could have dropped it on your eyes and blinded yourself! You don't sound very competent to me."

"I can prove myself on the job," Albert scoffed. "I just need an 'in' and some references, so they can trust me with the security clearance you need to work there. You're in a position to help me as the head of a nuclear research laboratory at Y-12. You do this for me, and I'll be able to support myself and save you some money."

"I hate to point out the obvious," his father said, pronouncing each word slowly and distinctly, as though speaking to someone feeble-minded, "but I don't have to help support you in either case. Anyway, I have heard that any of the positions that need high security, such as that job, requires clearance from the FBI, and their investigation takes over a year. Besides that, you would need several references from non-relatives. A parent's referral wouldn't make a difference. Your biggest hurdle would be the scrutiny of the investigation. I'm sorry. I wish I could help you out here, but I can't."

"I'm not concerned about a background check. I'm totally clean with the law," Albert answered back defensively. "I don't have any kind of record. I've never had so much as a speeding ticket," he argued.

"I'm sorry," his father said again, with resignation, "but you can't use me this time. You'll have to go through normal channels and procedures."

"I can't fucking believe you're turning down your own son for a small favor!" he shouted, again jumping to his feet.

"I don't appreciate your language, or your tone," his father responded, coldly. "I'm sure I gave you a referral for your job at the electronics store and look what you did with that opportunity. You acted like a sex pervert, downloading stolen pornography. You got yourself fired. Furthermore, it was a reflection on your family and was a disgrace. I can't believe that you expect me to put my reputation on the line for you after what you did."

"Why don't you admit it? You wouldn't help me get a job to pick up shit in the park!" he exclaimed.

"I think you should clean up your mouth and your attitude," his father advised, tersely, now opening a file in front of him, concluding the discussion. "Let me hear from you when you have a valid plan. That probably won't be anytime soon."

"Oh, I have a valid plan, and you'll be hearing about it soon," Albert said, swinging out of his chair and making for the door, "but probably not from me."

Chapter 24

"I have just come from the Temple, brother!" Henry announced, bursting into Albert's apartment. He was wrapped in voluminous yards of white fabric that were gathered around his girth by a clothesline knotted in front. The long folds of material dragged on the floor picking up dirt and bits of debris as he swung the skirt around his sandals, with each step, to avoid tripping.

"Okay, okay. Damn it, Henry! Calm down. And knock first, next time. You scared the shit out of me. And is that a sheet you're wearing, for Chris' sakes.?

"I would normally object to your language, brother, but in this instance it happens to be accurate. I opened the book of the Revelation and landed on a passage about the twenty-four elders seated around the throne in heaven. They were all in the Spirit and they all wore white garments with golden crowns. The bed sheet sufficed as a robe but I need to find something suitable for a headpiece. I thought a gold crown was a bit much."

"You could say that," Albert agreed, rolling his eyes. "By the way, I see your hair is growing back, but let's hope it comes in a little faster. That fuzz cover you've got makes you look like a Chia Pet."

"Never mind about appearances. I am of the Spirit! What I came here to tell you is that I have just recruited three more soldiers who are joining our army against the modern-day Babylonians who have usurped the ultimate power that belongs only to the Great One and his disciples."

"What?! Henry, who have you been talking to? I told you it's our secret! One word said to the wrong person could be the end of our plans. Shit, it could be the end of us. We're surrounded by the enemy just waiting to destroy us. You *know* that."

"Do not fear any indiscretion, my friend," Henry countered, reasonably. "I have only confided in these brothers of the faith who have spoken the Truth as you have revealed it to me. I overheard these three enlightened brothers at the Temple. They have formed a group called DOWN, their acronym for Destroy Our World's Nukes. I approached them cautiously to get a better understanding of their message. At first, they were very suspicious of me, and didn't want to tell me anything. I *suggested* to them that I may have a friend who had been personally threatened with annihilation by one in possession of these terrible weapons."

"God-damn it, Henry! You shouldn't talk to anyone about *my* situation without *my* approval. Those pacifists sound like a bunch of weak-minded faggots. I want to use these weapons to destroy others; not *destroy* the weapons, for Chris' sakes. And I don't need any help. I want to get revenge against those evil people who have tried to get rid of me—and you! Don't you get it?"

"I *do* understand," Henry asserted. "These brothers share your commitment to take away nuclear weapons from the godless government that is armed against all the rest of us. The brothers wish to meet you. That's all, I swear, in the name of Yahweh."

"In the name of who?" he interjected.

"The Hebrew God of the Old Testament. Don't worry about it.

"You can decide whether you want to include them in our plans, but keep in mind their resources to fortify us in the final battle. Let me tell you about them, before they arrive"

"Before they arrive?! You invited them over *here* without my permission? I swear, by Yahweh and every other God, Henry, if you fuck this up for me—"

"Pul-ease! Just hear me out. The founder of DOWN is Gray Fordham. He led a holy militia in Michigan to arm the Lord's children and to protect the Second-Amendment. He's not a pacifist. He understands the struggle between good and evil and believes that the citizenry in this country should be an armed force to suppress the tyranny of the government. His group had been harassed by the local gendarmes who had located their cache of weapons when they were preparing to do battle with the Antichrist; the government.

"Gray decided that was a good time to leave Michigan. He moved down here to Oak Ridge to mobilize protesters against the nuclear weaponry stockpiled at the government's DOE facility. He's a skilled mechanic and got a job with the motor pool for the nuclear couriers. He now thinks the birthplace of the atomic bomb is where the battle will take place and he's doing his own stockpiling."

"He has an arsenal of rifles, assault weapons, rocket and grenades, dynamite, and other explosives and he knows how to use them. We need him for combat."

"He works in the motor pool?!" Albert asked, incredulously. "I can't believe he escaped the scrutiny of the FBI, Henry. What do you know about him? If this guy and his friends are legit, they could be just what we need to help us, but the story doesn't make any sense. And who are the others? They're not going to show up in sheets, too, are they?"

"One question at a time. I understand Gray comes from a wealthy family in Michigan who has disowned him for his activities with the militia. They don't understand his passions for individual rights and for the power of the Spirit. They worship only mammon. They, too, are idolaters. Gray has been looking for a worthy accomplice to do something 'big' to attract attention to his cause. You're a godsend to him.

"Another brother is Dirk Black. He's had an unfortunate life. He's been persecuted by society and the authorities. I understand when he was a teenager he was arrested unjustly for concocted charges. He served time in a juvenile facility. No prison time. His mother was an addict who couldn't take care of him, so he's been on his own since he was thirteen. He was rescued off the streets by Brother Bob a couple of years ago. The Brother got Dirk a job as a janitor at Oak Ridge National Laboratories. Dirk cleans the church for his supper on Sundays. He's been real close to Gay since they met at the Temple when Gray showed up a year ago.

"The last brother is Hubie Strange. He's devoted to Gray. He'd felt like an outsider all his life until he met up with Gray at the Temple. Gray took him under his wing, accepted him into the family with Dirk. Some people thought that Hubie wasn't right in the head. I guess he used to kill little animals and skin them to see how they were made inside. He was just curious. As you can imagine, everyone in town called him 'Strange Hubie.' He does seem a little slow. But Gray is beautiful with him. Gives him time to get his thoughts out. If Hubie gets frustrated he can get pretty violent, I understand.

"Gray has a couple of mobile homes out in the country, off marked roads. He has an apartment in town, too, but the three of them spend a lot of time out in Gray's trailers. Hubie and Dirk live in the mobile homes. They all train there, dressed in camouflage. The fire high-powered rifles at squirrels and birds and tin cans they've set up on fence posts.

"Gray calls them all Christian Soldiers; each man certain of the Spirit moving within him directing him to keep the testimony of Jesus Christ alive, ready to lay down their lives for the cause, to keep men free."

"Yeah. Well, I'm no damn Christian Soldier. But we all want to destroy those who have nuclear weapons and an artificial authority against us.

"You shouldn't have told them to meet here, though. I want to protect the secrecy of the operation, but I've had a setback, thanks to my goddamn father. It looks like I need some help. What did you tell them about me?"

"Nothing, I swear. I knew that you were touchy about anyone else being a part of this. I only told them what I already said—that I may have a friend whose life has been threatened by a government agent."

"From now on, just keep your mouth shut, okay? As long as they're coming, I'll talk to them to see what they're all about. I'm not about to include them in my plans without investigating them. I would rather work alone, but my father saw to it that that's impossible."

With these words there was a knock at the door. He motioned for Henry to answer the knock. Henry wrenched open the door and admitted the three men. Two of them were scruffy-looking in dirty jeans, with long hair, and tattoos. The third man was tall and muscular, in his mid-thirties, dressed neatly and clean-shaven with very short brown hair.

This third man walked in first and extended his right hand to Henry. The other two men followed and stood behind him. "Henry, good to see you, my brother," the leader said, shaking hands.

"Gray. Thank you for coming," Henry replied.

While his toned body and grooming gave an overall impression of discipline, and self-control, the man's appearance was not that of good health and well-being. His handsome countenance was shadowed by a haunted look in his dark eyes as he slowly scanned the entire room before coming back to gaze at Henry.

Then, looking back over to the counter he took a step forward, extending his hand, saying, "And you must be Albert. Uh, I'm Gray Fordham." As there was no hand extended back to him, he maintained composure and gestured behind him towards his two companions, "And this is Dirk Black, with the mustache, and the guy with the long beard is Hubie Strange. Thanks for meeting with us," he finished.

"Yeah. Okay, Gray," Albert responded. "Actually, this is not my idea. Henry took a few liberties in inviting you over without checking with me first. But I'm willing to at least talk with you to see if we might be able to work together for everyone's benefit.

"But I want to get a few things straight, right off. This is *my* operation. If we have any discussion about the plan, I have the last word. I'm the one who has come under attack. I've had my life threatened by a federal agent, a she-devil who would gun me down in the street if she got the chance. Therefore, it's personal for me. I need to retaliate in my own way, and I have the most to lose.

"I understand," Gray said. "Our purpose in coming here today is to share what I believe to be our common ideas about the threat we all feel, coming from the government, particularly as they control nuclear weaponry, and want to take away our weapons away."

"From what I hear, Gray, you're employed at the nuclear courier's motor pool, which means that you survived an FBI investigation for your security clearance. Is that right?"

"Yeah, and I've just passed probation. I went after the position to get access to information and the equipment," Gray answered. "I've been there just over a year waiting for the right opportunity. You seem to be it."

"Henry tells me how you got here from Michigan, and you brought with you an arsenal. Is that right?"

"We have some weapons, yeah," Gray responded, more warily.

"That's good," Albert said, reassuringly. "We might be able to work together. I've drawn up some plans in the bedroom. Why don't you come with me, Gray, and I'll show you what I have in mind."

He led Gray into the short hallway and around the corner to the bedroom as the others stood waiting by the door. Walking over to his dresser, he opened a drawer, took out a cloth-wrapped item, turned around revealing a Glock semi-automatic in his outstretched right hand, he chambered a round and leveled the weapon at Gray's forehead.

"Close the door."

Gray complied and turned back to his captor. "What's this all about? What do you want?" he asked, obviously confused by the turn of events.

"What do I want?" Albert asked, his eyes becoming slits. "How about the *truth* for a change!" he hissed, keeping his voice low. "Who do you think you're dealing with? We're not all morons, here, you know. I didn't believe that load of crap you peddled for a second. You led a religious militia in Michigan, got caught with illegal weapons, came down here to lead a Holy War with the likes of Henry, Dirk and Hubie; and got cleared by the FBI to work in the nuclear courier's motor pool?" he asked, incredulously.

Gray nodded, slowly, opening his mouth to speak.

"I don't think so!" Albert snarled, in response to his own litany. "Now why don't you tell me who you *really* are and what you *really* want? And stop playing me for a fool. Are you a federal agent? No, I don't suppose you're stupid enough to answer that,—and keep your hands up where I can see them!"

"I can explain," Gray said quietly. "There's no reason for you to hold me at gunpoint."

"I'll decide that," he sneered. He walked over to his prisoner and patted down his chest, felt around his waist and continued patting down each leg. "No wire and no weapons."

"I told you there's no need for this. I'll show you my identification that's in my wallet in my back pocket. My real name is Mark. Mark Hunter. I'm really from Michigan, but I wasn't the leader of a religious militia. Let me show you my ID." With that, he removed his wallet, and keeping his hands up, he threw it onto the bed.

"The truth is I've spent most of my adult life as a soldier. I did five tours in the army; in Iraq before the draw-down, and then Afghanistan before I was sent home last year. In the beginning of my time in Afghanistan, I worked on the trucks as a mechanic, which I had been back in the states. Then, because of my mechanical abilities, I was trained as an EOD specialist. Explosive Ordinance Disposal. It was my job to dispose of or safely detonate IEDs.

"You've probably never seen your friends blown to bits as I have. There were times when troops in my own truck, sitting a few feet away from me, were blown up by undetected IEDs.

"It became a scavenger hunt, a contest between the Taliban and us as to who could bribe the Afghans more. The Taliban paid them to place the IEDs and we paid them to show us where they were buried. I was no hero. I just tried to stay alive and get out of that fucking hellhole.

"After my last tour I couldn't take it anymore. I was given some assistance to find a government job stateside and ended up at Y-12. Now I'm helping to transport weapons of mass destruction. That's what's been festering in me. They should be done away with.

"I can't sleep at night. I continually hear explosions and see chaos in my mind. I can't walk anywhere without imagining an IED under my next footstep. I want to show the government what has happened to me! My objective is to take one of their goddamn weapons and get their attention to show them that the weapons aren't safe!

"I had known about the religious militias in Michigan, and knew that those people are convinced the government is the agent of the Anti-Christ and must be defeated. They're the most fervent believers that the government wants to take away their weapons so they won't be able to win the Final Battle of Armageddon. Then I heard about the Temple of the Bountiful Salvation and their beliefs about the end times and I paid them a visit. I met Dirk and Hubie and realized their potential as recruits for action against the DOE and the nuclear weapons.

"They'd been badly mistreated by authorities and were looking for a champion. They had a cause and needed a friend, and so did I. I don't know anything about an Anti-Christ, but we have the same objective of creating civil disobedience and taking away the bombs. I made up a name to set-up a completely separate life and background story for them and to evade the FBI investigation. I used my knowledge of real Michigan militias to gain their confidence and support. Everything I feel about our mission is true. My ideology is real.

"So now you know everything you need to know about me, and I don't know anything about you. And you're still holding a Glock on me."

"Yeah, and we're going to keep it that way for now. This could be just another cover story you're telling me. I don't really trust you and you have no reason to trust me either, so that's protection for both of us. We could be very useful for each other with our special skills. With your inside position, you could be the most critical one to execute my plan.

"Looks like we're all in this for different reasons, but we're using the same means to the same end. I think we can form an alliance, with me in charge. Hubie and Dirk look to you as their leader, so that has to change. We'll go back in the other room and finish this meeting with the others. I'm keeping the gun with me." He re-wrapped the firearm. "All right? Let's go."

Entering the room, "Gray" took a seat at the counter and awaited further instructions.

"I've worked out our arrangement with your friend, Gray," he explained to the other three men still standing back by the door, "and he's agreed that I'll be in charge and you'll be informed of the plans on a need to know basis. This is a strictly business relationship. The less you know about me, the better. All you need to know now is that we share a belief that the government threatens our lives. As your leader, I will demand your allegiance, and your obedience to make the plan successful.

"I'm not ready to get into the specifics right now about the plan. As Gray knows, nuclear weapons are being shipped by semi tractor-trailers out of Y-12 at least once a week and are delivered to military installations, and military bases, around the country. A convoy of armed agents, traveling in armored vans, escort the shipments. Our target will be a trailer on one of these convoys. I have to figure out a way to get into one of the shipment trucks and we'll need to take out the agents.

"Our goal is to defeat the evil military complex and to take power, ourselves. My own goal is to take out the agent who has tried to kill me once, and has threatened to shoot me, if she ever see me again.

"I want to meet next time at your camp, Gray, where we won't be bothered by anyone. Remember: Nothing that was said here today or will be said in the future is to be repeated to anyone outside this room. Got that? We'll set up a covert system to communicate between meetings to circumvent the use of traceable cell phone calls, as much as possible.

"That's it for now. What I want to know is, are all of you in on this?"

"I'm in," Gray asserted, staring at Albert, unsmiling.' "How about you, Dirk? And you, Hubie?" Gray asked, looking at each of them, in turn.

Dirk, Hubie and Henry had remained silent as Albert was speaking. All three looked at one another, quizzically, uncertain of what had transpired. They had all heard the confrontational tone of the bedroom discussion, but hadn't made out the words.

Dirk was standing with his hands on his hips, and his feet spread apart in an aggressive posture. His dark hair was cut in a long mullet style, signaling a disinterest in convention. His rough look was that of a renegade; from his hostile black eyes under his heavy brow, his wiry mustache to his thick studded leather belt over dusty jeans. Tattoos on his muscled arms were evidence that he was a fighter and a believer.

"I reckon I'm okay if you are, Boss," Dirk slowly drawled, in his raspy smoker's voice, speaking to Gray. "As long as I'm with you in the field, I got no beef."

Hubie, meanwhile, was nervously shifting his feet, wringing his hands, and pulling on his beard as he warily eyed his new leader. He was scrawny with the bad complexion of a teenager, belying his thirty years. His greasy dark blond hair was pulled back in a ponytail that hung halfway down his back. His visible tattoos were all religious: Jesus with a halo, a white cross and the words, 'Onward, Christian Soldier,' in Old English script on his right forearm.

"I dint unnerstan' some of the words what Albet said," Hubie stammered, stroking his long scraggly beard, "but I know how the govermint wants to take our guns and here dey haf bombs to throw at us. I kin shoot purty good an I wanna kill the bad guys and take their bombs."

"Okay, good, Hubie," Gray said kindly. "You said it all. I guess that's it. We're all in. What's the next step, Albert?"

"Next Sunday, at the Temple, Henry will pass along my next instructions. Prepare for war."

Chapter 25

After they left, Albert sat with his head in his hands, his fists pressing up against his cheekbones squeezing his eyes closed, while he listened to his long, slow breaths. Then, sitting up he lit a cigarette and inhaled deeply to fill his lungs. Slowly he expelled the acrid smoke and leaned back against the counter to mentally review the last hour and a half.

As he thought back on the scenes in his apartment, he tried to make sense of the newly-formed alliance with the men he had now included in his plans for retribution against Dana Knowles. Following her attack and threat to his life, he had allowed her to live and walk away, only after he figured out that her punishment would be all the sweeter if carefully planned and expanded beyond her, to teach all oppressors a lesson.

Now he had the opportunity to wield more power than even he had originally envisioned. Thanks to his father, he had to work with a delusional religious fanatic, a feeble-minded hick, a savage ex-con and a self-acclaimed imposter, suffering from Post Traumatic Stress Disorder. Not exactly a hand-picked crew. But, they were a specialized team of technicians with knowledge, skill and commitment. Even their madness would give them an edge, as their belief in their divine righteousness made them fearless.

These men were now his soldiers for his incubating plan to launch an unprecedented attack against the government of the United States which, in the end, was the source of the group's grievances.

He and his motley band would pull off a feat that had been feared as only even possible by the most cunning and murderous jihadists: the seizure and detonation of the most powerful force on earth, a nuclear weapon.

And, if his group were successful, the authority of the world's greatest armed forces would forever be compromised. Hard-won treaties, that had balanced nuclear threats among the super powers, would be violated. The breadth of destruction on American soil would be unprecedented.

There would no more homeland security in the United States. After the detonation, there would be chaos in the streets for weeks; maybe for months or years. As the mastermind of the organization, he would be the most notorious person in the history of mankind to many and the most brilliant hero and liberator of all time, to many more. It wouldn't be long now. The time was near.

Right now he had a lot of work ahead of him to ensure the success of the mission. He felt the sudden rush of adrenaline, preparing him for action. He would spend the week crystallizing the scheme before meeting again with Henry, and Grayson and his flunkies, weaving together their skills and the use of highly-technical equipment in his plan.

Gray had a stockpile of weapons in a hideaway, was a mechanic, had extensive experience with explosives and, as an insider, had access to information and to the targets. Crazy Henry was easily manipulated and was a genius with nuclear weapons. Hubie and Dirk had knowledge and skill with firearms and had access. Along with Henry, they were devoted to Gray and believed in his concocted Battle of Armageddon, against the evil government of the United States.

And, of course, he was the brains of the outfit. He was always the smartest guy in the room. He had shone brilliance in all his endeavors: in music, chemistry, electronics, and auto mechanics. He had even been brilliant in committing murder. He thought of a fantasy resume listing Detective Barnes from Ohio as a reference who would describe him as "innovative, results-oriented, with a proven track record." Yeah. He was the right one for this job.

And for the next few hours he worked out the perfect strategy for the greatest heist of all time.

In the morning, setting the first piece of his plan in motion, he visited a competitor of his former employer, where he purchased two real-time GPS trackers with receivers and cellular phone modems that would send a signal to his phone at set intervals. The current models no longer required sky-view placement which would simplify the unseen installations he had planned.

He was relieved to see that the modems on the trackers could be programmed with their own mobile number and had SMS, or text messaging, which was capable of being contacted to send a brief text message with the co-ordinates of its position, all without the requirement of a service contract to covertly use the system, without leaving a paper trail. Translating the co-ordinates onto a map would not be too difficult in a targeted area.

His next stop was at a fabric store where he purchased a spool of fine dark brown thread, proud of himself that he had accurately remembered the right shade so that the completed job would escape detection.

Back in his car he pulled up the internet from his phone to check on Dana's car location. He was pleasantly surprised to find that it was parked in a neighborhood a couple of miles from her home. That was significant. That meant that Dana was visiting someone on her day off. Hopefully she was at her boyfriend's house and would be gone for hours, but this couldn't be checked out as he didn't know Owen's last name. Still, this could be his best opportunity this week to gain access to her home. He'd better do it this evening and right after it was dark, in case she'd still be returning home yet tonight.

Back at his building, he knocked on Henry's door. Henry answered wearing his usual white sheeting, but what attracted his attention was the writing of words up and down his arms and across his forehead.

"Henry. Don't tell me. You're out of paper."

"Hey, neighbor, I get it! You're making a joke, but this is serious. This morning I opened to the book of the Revelation again, and found a passage that spoke to me even as we plan our great retribution against the persecutors of the godly. The scripture reads, 'He who conquers, I will make him a pillar in the temple of my God . . . and I will write on him the name of my God, and the name of the city of my God, the New Jerusalem.' I wrote down several names to be sure to get the right one for the name of God."

"Okay, Henry. That's fine. I'm glad to see that you're preparing for a victory. What I need right now is to use your car this evening for a special errand. Is that beater of yours, parked out back, still driveable?"

"It's becoming a vintage vehicle, like yours," Henry sniffed. "Maybe you don't like the powdered finish. It still runs, though. And yes, you're welcome to use it for the cause. This is getting very exciting! I knew we were on a righteous course of action when I found the verse this morning. And to think I was helpful in introducing you to Gray and the others!"

"Just remember that I'm the one in charge. And be careful with Gray and his followers. We don't really know them so we don't completely trust them. You can only completely trust me and do what I say. Is that understood?"

"Yes, of course. Just tell me what you want me to do and I'll do it."

"Okay, that's what I want to hear. Give me your car keys, okay? I'll return them later tonight."

Right after dusk, and before all the porch lights came on, he drove the short distance over to the Ridge and up to the street a block away from Dana's house. He had checked the GPS tracker to make sure that her car was still at the same address where she was visiting. Now he felt sure that she was with her boyfriend and might stay overnight, or at least would be gone through the evening. As he was driving a car that had not been seen in the neighborhood before, he was confident that he didn't draw any attention and had a measure of safety. He was just a "friend" visiting in the area.

He parked at the end of the dead-end street where he had parked when he had entered her house before. This time his "tools" were secreted in his pocket. He walked along cautiously, looking left and right without turning his head much, to avoid suspicion. He came around the corner onto her block as the darkness was descending. No one was around.

Approaching her house, he slipped back into the shadows of the bushes and eased his way around to the back of her house. Again, he mounted her deck stairs, walked to the back door and found the same loose, wobbly lock which he easily picked with his screwdriver. *It's almost like a key in this fucking lock.*

The whole house was dark now. It wasn't late enough for the timers to come on, he supposed; unless they weren't set as she was expected home soon. He would have to complete his task quickly.

He made his way down the hallway and into her bedroom. His destination was her closet which he entered, momentarily, and flicked on the light. And there it was. What he had come to find. Her Louis Vuitton duffel bag was on the floor under her hanging clothes where it was always kept when she wasn't on a convoy trip.

Getting down on his knees he gathered up everything that was packed in the carry-all into both hands, and laid the whole pile on the floor next to him. Then, taking the small seam-ripper out of his pocket, he expertly insinuated the sharp tip into the seam and carefully ripped a couple of inches of the dark brown lining. He then inserted the programmed GPS tracker into the opening. Satisfied that the shape and size of the 1½ inch by 3 inch device was not noticeable at the bottom of the valise, he took out his already-threaded needle, that he had stuck into a cotton ball, and sewed up the seam again with tiny stitches to match the rest of the tailoring. The thread color was indistinguishable from the original thread. *He was truly gifted,* he thought, not for the first time.

Replacing the pile of clothes and toiletries in the duffel bag, he switched off the closet light and made for the bedroom door. As he came back down the hallway, he saw the arc of headlights swinging across the front of the house and into the driveway. *Are you shitting me?!*

Scrambling down the hallway, now, he turned the corner, skidding across the kitchen floor, to the back door and turned the lock. Coming back around the corner to the dining room, he pulled up the sash partway and squeezed out the window, on his stomach, clinging to the sill by the fingertips of his left hand while he pulled the window back down with his right hand, without closing it on his fingers. He then slid down the outside wall of the side of house hoping to break his fall enough that he wouldn't be injured. Fortunately the ground was soft and padded with vegetation and he landed like a cat, on his feet.

Son of a bitch. That was close, but he was safe. He saw lights go on in the house as he slinked away into the darkness of the backyard and onto the rear neighbor's property. His mission had been accomplished. It had been a narrow escape but he had the nerves for it. He was prepared for anything.

He would soon be the most infamous man in the world.

Chapter 26

On Sunday evening, Henry and Albert drove out into the country in Henry's dilapidated car, following the directions given to them by Gray Fordham. There weren't many street names; mostly it was a list of landmarks, like trees with crooked trunks and a collapsed shed, along with the approximate number of miles between each one. Fifteen minutes past the last marked county road they came to the final landmark, a tall pine tree split by lightning. They turned left onto yet another narrow rutted trail that had been created solely by use and not a whole lot of that.

A minute later they saw two trailers with nearly-flat roofs and tiny windows. They were surrounded by high weeds, like the fields surrounding them. One trailer had been white, but was now streaked with orange rust. Its front door was at the top of a pile of cinder blocks. The other trailer, that had peeling beige paint, boasted concrete steps up to the door with a stoop at the top allowing room for a bent aluminum folding chair, its torn webbing discouraging anyone from sitting.

"They don't look too bad," Henry commented as they neared the two trailers.

"Compared to what?" Albert responded, sourly.

Gray's truck, parked in front, was the first familiar object they had seen on the whole trip. The truck, along with the two trailer homes were the only evidence of any human presence for miles. No mailboxes had been seen, either, to allow for any outside communication.

As they drove up, Gray came out of the rusted trailer with a rifle in his hand. Turning off the engine, Albert cautiously got out of the car with his hands up. Henry waited in his seat.

"Hey," Gray flatly intoned, recognizing the visitors. "Sorry about the rifle. I didn't know the car. Any trouble finding the place?"

"No, but if one of those fucking trees falls down I won't be able to find it again," Albert replied. "The good news is that no one else will be able to find it, either. We might need a place like this to disappear for a while. This is Henry's car, just so you know. It seems my vintage sports car is too conspicuous for me to use anymore. That federal agent told me if she ever saw it again, she'd shoot to kill."

"Well, you're safe here, Albert," Gray assured him.

Henry teetered on the unstable cinder blocks, having to pull his robe up to his knees to get his footing. At the top he gingerly hopped off through the open door to the trailer, as Albert and Gray followed.

The interior was roomier than appeared possible from the outside. The "front room," while not showing any evidence of a decorator's visit, did contain a comfortable-looking sofa and a few chairs, giving some sense of welcome to the space.

The kitchen was open to the living room. Its cabinets and appliances, as well as a small table and two chairs, appeared to be able to function as a place to prepare and eat meals. Hubie and Dirk were seated on the kitchen chairs, each with a can of beer in his hand. They both nodded in recognition of the arrival of the newcomers.

"Hubie, Dirk." Albert murmured, in response, glancing their way. Then turning to Gray said, "I'll have a beer, and then we need to get this meeting underway."

With his beer in hand, Albert sat in the largest upholstered front room chair while Henry and Gray sat at each end of the sofa. Leaning back and taking a swig of his beer, Albert looked pleased as he glanced around. "This is one mother-fucking day. We're going to be the first ones in history to actually steal and detonate a nuclear bomb. It's never been done before! Do you get that?" He challenged them.

"We're number one!" Henry sang out.

Albert shot Henry a look of disdain, as Hubie giggled. Albert went on. "The Russians have reported the attempted smuggling of nukes from their huge stockpile. But no one ever got away with one! The geniuses in the U.S. military have *misplaced* quite a few weapons but none has turned up yet."

He allowed a cheerless smile to cross his face. "We are going to plan a *fail-safe* attack on the devil oppressor, the government of the United States. The whole world will hear about this. We're the first ones in history with the fucking brains and balls to carry this off."

He narrowed his eyes to slits, as he sized up the other three men. "At least I *think* you ass-holes are prepared to do this. If you're not, say so now, because I'm putting everything on the line here. If you follow my instructions, *to the letter,* we can do this. And our ace in the hole is our inside man, here, who's right in the middle of the fucking enemy." He cocked his head towards Gray.

"Hell, I'm pumped!" Dirk blurted out, with uncharacteristic intensity. "And I'm ready. I've taken shit from everybody my whole life. Now my job is cleaning other people's toilets. Getting even will be sweet, but hell, I'm no fool. I know I could get myself killed, but at least I'm going down by getting back at them."

"The spirit is here in this place!" Henry chimed in, out of sync with the last speaker. "I can feel it. And my verse this morning was from Thessalonians. 'Since indeed God deems it just to repay with affliction those who afflict you . . .' And then later, that 'they shall suffer the punishment of eternal destruction.' Every time I open the good book I read about evil and how we must do battle against it." Henry gestured with his arms thrashing through the air to imitate combat, and then re-wrapped his robe.

"I'm wit' you guys, too," Hubie added. "Gray has taken gud keer of me and I owe him to do what he says. It's only right and proper."

"Thanks, Hubie," Gray responded. "You're a good man. We're all good men who have just had some bad breaks. It's not us. It's them. We have to stop their madness. People of wealth and influence control everything. They've assumed authority over all of us, making us fight their wars, to be blown to bits in some fucking desert on the other side of the world, while they argue high-sounding ideologies from cushy government chambers. They threaten other nations with extinction with nuclear weapons that can destroy everyone on the earth several times over. We can take away their arrogant little game plan and teach them a lesson they'll never forget."

"Good speech, Fordham," Albert said. "But what we need from you right now is some inside information. We *know* about the weekly shipments of nuclear weapons loaded onto armored trucks equipped with special access controls as deterrents. We know the trucks are escorted by armed federal agents traveling in armored vans and other vehicles. What we *don't* know is their schedule, and their routes. These are kept secret, even from the agents, until the briefing before each trip."

"I've gotten wind of some info lately," Gray responded. "The word in the motor pool is that there's a lot of activity going down for the next month or two coming out of Kings Bay, Georgia, the naval submarine base there. What I hear is that the base is expecting an Ohio-class submarine coming into port, loaded with nuclear warheads that need to be retrofitted at the Pantex Plant in Amarillo. There'll be a lot of fucking movement between Oak Ridge and Kings Bay and Kings Bay and Amarillo, and back again to Oak Ridge."

"What kind of warheads? What size? What weight?" Albert broke in.

"I know that some of the warheads are W-88s. About so high," Gray said, holding his hand flat, about three feet off the floor. I've never loaded them, so I don't know what they weigh. I know they're the most efficient warhead in the U.S. arsenal," he added.

"I think I can supply some information, here," Henry spoke up. "I've refitted some of them. There are about 400 W-88s deployed and the Ohio-class is the largest type of submarine that carries the warheads. They haven't been produced since 1991, so they're regularly refitted. There's been talk about a new composite warhead based on the earlier W-78, which is 100 kiloton less yield than the W-88, but it'll take years before the adoption and production of such a warhead, so they'll be refitting the W-88s for some time."

"Henry, you're a fucking genius," Albert said, shaking his head. "Do you know about the size and shit of W-88s?"

"Yes, "Henry answered. "The warheads are cone-shaped, about three feet long, like Gray said, and weigh 800 pounds each. They're designed to be launched from SLBMs, or Sea-Launched Ballistic Missiles. But they can also be detonated without launch, I believe, by decoding the PAL—Permissive Action Link—the special access controls on all nuclear bombs. But that will be a major hurdle. However, if detonated, at 45 megatons, the W-88 is many times the yield of the bombs dropped on Hiroshima and Nagasaki."

"What?" Hubie gasped. "We're going to steal one of those and set it off?"

"We're not the first ones to think about it." Henry said. "The Navy even has their own name for a stolen nuclear weapons or parts—they call them 'Broken Arrows.' The Navy is probably more concerned with a component part being stolen as they wouldn't think anyone would be able to carry off an entire bomb."

"But that's *exactly* what I want to do," Albert said. "We just need to have the right equipment at the right place at the right time. We can do that. We could have a fucking tractor with a utility attachment ready to off-load a warhead from the semi-trailer and set it right on a pick-up truck.

"First, we need intelligence about the routing and the stops. What do you know about those, Gray?"

"Well, I know that all the vehicles and the trucks travel up to 1,800 miles, or thirty-two hours on the road, without stopping for an overnight. The couriers take turns driving. They take brief stops for refueling, get take-out food they eat in the vehicles, and stop to kick the tires along the roadside, when necessary. I think at least one courier remains in each vehicle at all times until they reach the destination or a secured stop. The vehicles don't all stay together, but I'm sure the trucks stay close with each other and at least one or two vehicles would keep the shipment in view.

"It's a nine-hour drive from Oak Ridge to St. Marys, Georgia, which is right near Jacksonville, Florida. The usual route is I-40 to 26 to I-95 then, most of the way, taking the exit a few miles from the naval base. So that would be a straight shot, obviously.

"From St. Marys to Amarillo you're talking almost 1,400 miles, or a little over twenty-three hours on the road. They would most likely hook up with I-40 west most of the way. The southern route would be taking I-10 west to I-20 west. But I think they'd take I-40 as they're so familiar with that route and with its exits for fuel and food.

"So, what I'm saying, is that the convoy would be on the road from point to point. They'd be leaving Oak Ridge, empty, and pick up the shipment off the sub, and stay overnight on the Naval base. The next day they'd take off for Amarillo, loaded with the warheads. We'd have to hit them at some stop between St. Marys and Amarillo. You're talking about a lot of miles and hours to follow them without being detected."

"That's right. It *would* be hard to follow them all that way without being detected," Albert said, with a smug smile. "And that's why we're not going to *physically* follow them." The four other men turned towards him now and watched him reaching into his pocket as he pulled out a small black case that appeared to be a cell phone.

Holding up the object he said, "This is the latest model of a real-time GPS tracker. It sends a signal when you call its programmed phone modem and it texts its co-ordinates. All we have to do is locate the coordinates on a map. Of course we'll need to be in the area but we won't have to be visible to make a surgical strike at the right time."

"At the risk of stating the obvious," Gray, ventured, "even if we're right on the scene with our tractor and warhead transportation, we'll be left with a keypad-locked truck and twenty-seven armed federal agents to deal with."

"Oh, *that*," Albert again smiled and took a long drink from his can, taking his time before continuing. Putting a hand on his knee he leaned forward. "Well, that's where you come in, Gray. You're the one who has access to the vehicles. You're responsible to check them out, and to service them prior to every trip, right?" Gray nodded, hesitantly. "You maintain every one of their electronic, mechanical and fluid systems and then turn them over to the s.o.b.s who operate them, right?"

Gray nodded, again, and said, "But I'm not the only one and I'm not even in charge. We work off a detailed check list, which is gone over by the Service Manager of the motor pool, before and after we service each vehicle. And he's constantly observing our work. Both the Manager and the mechanic have to sign off on the service report."

"Well, we wouldn't want you to sign off on anything that wasn't true, or get you in trouble!" Albert mocked in a sing-song voice. For emphasis, he crushed his empty beer can on the floor with the heel of his shoe, and threw it across the room. "Fuck the Service Manager! We have more important things to worry about, wouldn't you say?

"What we have to worry about is getting the combinations of the keypad so we don't have to blow a fucking hole in the fucking armored truck. We need to find a way to sabotage the vehicles to incapacitate or kill the fucking agents. Am I going too fast, here? Do you follow me?"

"Yeah, I can follow you," Gray answered with disgust. "Just what's your fucking plan? I don't need a lecture. I'm quite capable of handling whatever you have in mind. So quit the cute stuff. We're all dead serious here."

"Okay. Fine. What do you know about the keypad? How is it set and who sets it?"

"There's a keypad on the back of each trailer. The code is entered by the agents who have the responsibility for that trip, while the trailers are still empty in the service center."

"Before the weapons are loaded?" Albert interjected.

"Yeah, they set the locks in the service center to make sure that everything is working, and they won't have to change trailers. Only those two agents know the trip code."

"Okay, You'll be able to make good use of this," Albert said, taking a small pair of binoculars out of another pocket. "These are 7x magnification, which is what the military uses to allow optimum light, enlargement and minimal distortion of movement. You could be fifty feet away, on the other side of a window and take down the code for the keypad. Can you handle this?"

"Look, I told you, cut the crap. I don't need to be told what the military uses. And, yeah, I think I can find a place where I'd be unobserved and still get a sightline to the keypad when the code is punched in. Next?" he challenged.

"The armed agents," Albert responded. "We need to take out as many as we can at one time because there are twenty-seven of them and only five of us. To be realistic, that t pretty much leaves out firearms, at least at first. And as you said, they're not all in the same place at one time. So that means that we have to bring something lethal to many different places all at once.

"You have access to the vehicles and can set controls in them before the agents get them. The most obvious choice would be poisonous gas released into the vans and trucks, but the timing is critical. We need to have the gas released when we can take advantage of a temporary stop. Of course, with our trackers we'll know where they are at all times.

"I'd like to use carbon monoxide which is already present *outside* the vehicles. It's non-irritating, odorless, and colorless and is deadly in great enough quantities. If one survives a higher level it will at least cause confusion and collapse. What you have to do is create a leak into the vehicles from the exhaust manifolds. We'll need a blast of over 800 ppm to take them out in just a few minutes. The trick is to create the leak when we're ready for our assault.

"Another possibility is placing a canister of poison gas like a nerve gas like Tabun, Sarin or Soman. The victims would die a few minutes after they're inhaled or taken in through the skin, but that's more complicated and the timing is still the problem. I think we need to work out the delivery system of the CO. That's your job, Gray."

Gray took a moment to respond. "It's possible I could cause leaks in the exhaust manifolds. The trucks are no problem. They can't operate the windows. I'll need a few days to come up with something. Maybe, more to the point, you should talk about the payoff of the whole plan: detonating the bomb."

"Like Henry said, we have to get around the fucking PAL box that contains cryptographic mechanisms that need to be decoded to set off the firing sequence. I've done some encrypting. They're all the same. It doesn't matter what the application is. Any encryption involves simply changing and reordering data multiple times in multiple ways. As long as I have a little time I can decode it. I know they use several groups of numbers, but they're only numbers. No words, as I understand it. I've got encryption software which should make it easier, yet.

"What I need is a secure building where we can take the bomb where no one will come nosing around. The agents will either be dead or in no condition to follow us from the place of the attack. If any one has survived the gas, we'll pick them off with our firepower. We have all the advantages—the element of surprise and inside information. They aren't prepared for us. We'll be prepared for them down to the last detail.

"This week I want you to install the GPS tracker in one of the trucks and check out the exhaust manifolds. Also, find a secure place to see the keypad code with the binoculars and make sure you can get it from that place every time, no matter where the agent stands to punch in the numbers, or who is around.

"Hopefully, they'll make a run to Kings Bay, and I'll get the coordinates on all their stops. I don't know if they stop at the same place every trip. I would think that there's more security in using the familiar, where they can more easily spot anything that's out of place.

"We'll meet here again next Sunday at the same time. Gray will report on the motor pool operation and I'll have the route and the stops made by the convoy. Then we'll be ready to work out all the particulars.

Chapter 27

Wayne Miller knelt on the ground to closely examine the end of the dislodged rail in the section of his fence that ran along the woods. It was a mystery why the board had come down, but the opening seemed to explain how two Guernsey cows and one calf were missing. The absence of the three animals was discovered at dusk yesterday when the herd had returned to the barn for milking. After taking a second count this morning, Wayne explored the property and had just come upon what appeared to be their escape route. He'd have to search the woods to find them. A daunting task, considering how dense it was. He hadn't walked through the woods since he was a boy.

While Wayne's attention was focused on the fence rail, his border collie, Shep, was impatiently running in circles, and sniffing the ground; probably picking up the scent of the truant animals.

Not seeing any break in the wood piece itself, he stepped through the opening with Shep and lifted the rail back into place behind them. Patting the eager dog's head he urged him on by saying, "Okay, boy, let's go find them!" Wayne was well aware that he was giving permission, rather than giving a command. The dog was acting on the instincts that were imprinted on his DNA passed down from his ancestors who were first bred to herd and tend livestock hundreds of years ago.

Shep bounded ahead into the woods, all but disappearing from sight except for the white tip of his black plumed tail. The snowy little "flag" continued to be visible bobbing up and down in the darkness as the dog athletically maneuvered through the heavy brush and trees. Wayne did his best to keep up with the tracking dog following him into the shadows. He hoped they would soon come upon the errant cattle peacefully munching on wildflowers, unaware of their owner's distress at their absence from the farm and his concern for their welfare.

Wayne had grown up on this dairy farm in south-central Ohio, but it was only last year, after the death of his father, that he and his wife, Belinda, had inherited the farm and, with it, the responsibility of running the operation. Wayne and Belinda moved back into his boyhood home soon after the funeral. At the young couple's insistence, Wayne's mother, Esther, continued to live in the spacious Georgian-style farmhouse with them. She enjoyed staying close with her family and kept a hand in the business, as well, by capably taking care of the books.

The farmland consisted of a hundred and twenty-five acres of rich Ohio River Valley loam which the Miller family planted in hay, soybeans and alfalfa for the main diet of the grazing herd. The dense woods on either side of the property afforded the farmhouse privacy, while the location of the property was convenient, being only a half hour outside of town.

As Wayne and Shep moved deeper into the woods, there was still no sign of the beige-colored heifers and calf that should have easily been spotted if they were there. After several minutes, the collie changed directions and more and more light came through the trees until Wayne realized they were getting close to the road.

Suddenly the dog became excited, barking sharply and jumping up against a fallen tree. As Wayne approached, the collie was pawing at some kind of dark fabric under the base of the dead tree. When the dog pulled out a small scrap of material, Wayne took it from him to take a closer look at it. It appeared to be a scrap of decayed denim.

"What the heck? What have you found there, Shep?" The dog continued frantically trying to dig under the old tree as Wayne held him back. "Sit, Shep. Let me move this tree away and we'll take a look." As the dog obediently sat, wiggling with anticipation, Wayne was able to carefully roll the large fallen tree over enough to expose more denim and other material (clothes?) underneath the old wood.

At first he couldn't identify what he was looking at: scraps of cloth, an old purse, maybe, and a woman's flat-heeled shoe. Leaves were obscuring a mound that appeared to be related to the items. Visible in the mound were grey sticks or branches poking out of the pile.

Then he saw one item that took his breath away. At the far end of the pile was an object he recognized, even as it was turned on its side and partially covered with dirt and leaves: it was most definitely a human skull. "Holy shit!" he said aloud.

Wayne rocked back on his haunches, with his hands on the ground behind him supporting him, as he absorbed the shock. He could now identify all that he had been looking at, and the realization made him feel sick. This wasn't just a pile of rags and sticks. It was the skeletal remains of a human being, probably a female. This person had evidently met with a violent death: she had most likely been murdered. *Right next to his farm.*

Taking a few seconds to recover his composure, he stood up and carefully turned the dead tree back over to where it had been positioned when Shep had alerted to it. Fortunately, the dog had only gotten hold of the one piece of cloth. He himself hadn't touched anything. He knew that much about forensics. *Don't disturb a crime scene.*

Pulling the still curious Shep away from the remains, Wayne led the dog towards the road. Taking a white handkerchief out of his back pocket, he tied it onto a low branch of a tree, satisfied that it could be seen from the road if one were looking for it. Not finding anything else he could do at the moment, Wayne told the disappointed dog to heel and the two walked out onto the country road and started making their way back to the farmhouse.

The phone call was transferred back to Detective Larry Barnes, Homicide Unit. A Butler County resident, Wayne Ian Miller, was calling to give a report of finding the skeletal remains of what appeared to be a female. The skeleton and some clothes were found under a fallen tree in the woods adjacent to his dairy farm. The caller had been checking the woods with his dog for some lost cattle and the dog had alerted to the scene. Mr. Miller gave directions to his farmhouse where the responders could meet and the farmer would lead them to his discovery.

From the caller's description, it was apparent to Barnes that it was a crime scene requiring the attendance of the Medical Examiner, the Mobile Crime Scene Investigation unit, as well as a couple of uniforms in a black and white to protect the area while the scene was being processed.

After he hung up the phone, Detective Barnes shook his head in amazement at the report. He'd worked on dozens of murder cases over his thirty years as a detective, but this would be his first investigation into the identification and circumstances surrounding the death of a human being with only skeletal remains. Looking around the detective's room, he signaled his young partner, Peter Enright, to put down his filing and come over.

The older detective relayed the caller's information to the stunned young man who had made detective last year, after eight years on the police force. He was a bright, energetic, detective who had scored very high on the exam. Barnes felt lucky to have him as his partner. Their age difference served them well as they both were willing to learn from each other's perspective.

The two detectives quickly divided up the list of the forensic professionals and police to call, and proceeded to phone to make immediate arrangements to visit the scene.

A half-hour later, en route to the dairy farm, the two detectives had a chance to catch their breath and think through their initial impressions and avenues of investigation they would pursue.

"It's not the first time we haven't had an I.D. on the vic, but it will be our most challenging, for sure," Barnes opined to his partner. "Mr. Miller thought that it was a female, which makes sense, based on the discovery of a purse and woman's shoe at the scene. The ME can determine the sex of the vic on sight, if we have enough bones. The caller thought the skeleton was pretty much intact as the scene appeared to be undisturbed. He said he was careful not to touch anything. His dog had scratched at the tree and had pulled out a scrap of denim material but then he moved the dog away."

"We can't be sure that the clothing items belonged to the vic," Enright offered. "They could have been left as subterfuge as the perp didn't expect the body to be discovered for a long time after he hid it. It's suspicious that a purse was at the scene unless the perp intentionally left I.D. to influence the investigation. Either he wanted an easy I.D. of the vic to send a message or he left a false I.D. as a red herring. Hard to say at this point," he concluded. "We'll have to have this Wayne Miller come in for prints. What do we know about him?"

"He mentioned that it's been his family's dairy farm for years but he just moved back with his wife a year ago after his dad died," Barnes responded. "Seemed legit and shocked to have made the discovery, but you never know. We'll thoroughly check him out."

An hour after Wayne had notified the police, he was standing on his front porch giving them general directions on where he would be driving; for them to follow and park nearby. The detectives asked that he not park too close to the scene as there may be some evidence to collect near the remains. After the amount of time that had passed since the body had been left it was unlikely, but police work had to be meticulous.

With Wayne leading the way, the detective's sedan, two squad cars, the CSI Mobile Unit and the ME's van drove about a mile down the country lane and parked in a line on the roadway as there was no shoulder. The uniforms quickly set up barricades for both directions and prepared to re-direct what little traffic could be expected.

The group of investigators carefully picked their way along, walking towards the tree with the white handkerchief tied on a branch. The detectives were searching the ground for anything unusual. Not surprisingly, they didn't find anything noteworthy.

The two detectives were the first ones to look at the scene, as was customary. Barnes and Enright carefully lifted the fallen tree off the spot Wayne had indicated. Nothing could be seen without removing the tree. With the tree off to one side they could observe the mound of dirty fabric and the ends of a few grey bones of a human being. Being careful not to touch anything prior to CSI doing their work, the two men just looked, making copious notes in small books they carried with them for that purpose.

"Judging from the small amount of denim, it would appear to be a skirt or jacket rather than jeans," Detective Barnes said to his partner. "If it's a skirt belonging to the vic that could indicate that it is a *young woman* that we have here. I know Mary would never wear a skirt that small," he said, referring to his wife of thirty-five years. "The ME will be able to test for age, anyway. I'm just trying to get a sense of the vic while we're right here at the scene.

"Janey," Barnes turned to address the head of the CSI Unit, "I know I don't really have to tell you, but be sure you don't put even a gloved hand on the metal clasp of the purse. It's possible we might have a latent there. Who knows? We could get lucky."

"I've got tweezers here, Larry. Why don't I pry the purse open right now, in case there's some identification in it?" Janey suggested.

"Sure, go ahead, Janey. That's where we have to start," agreed Barnes.

As everyone stood still, barely breathing, the CSI chief gently pried open the small brown leather purse and, as carefully, tweezed out the contents, placing them on a metal tray. There was no wallet. Only a tube of lipstick and a brush remained that were still somewhat intact.

"A brush, rather than a comb?" Detective Barnes asked out loud. "If it belonged to the vic, possibly she had long hair."

"Janey, after you take all your pictures and start bagging everything, be sure you keep the purse separate. I'm still hoping we might get some kind of print off the clasp. I don't think our Jane Doe, if this belonged to the vic, was holding her purse when she met with her demise. Even if it's her print, and not the perp's, that could take us a long way to id-ing the remains."

For the next two hours the professionals went about their procedures methodically, the CSI taking photos of the scene from every angle and then close-ups of every item as they were found in place. Notes were also taken by the CSI team to describe the items: where they were in relation to each other, how they appeared, whether or not they were ripped, or folded, whether or not there was dirt underneath the clothing. These observations were not as informative as they would have been at a fresh crime scene, as the extensive deterioration negated much of the evidence.

The ME collected the bones and skull to take back for his examination, which would be exhaustive, as it was an unknown victim. Dr. Johnson would be able to extract more information to describe the individual than would be thought possible, the detectives knew from experience.

The one shoe was bagged separately, and a note was made to powder for a latent print, or to test with chemicals that might reveal a print of the victim or her assailant.

"I wonder where the other shoe was dropped?" Detective Barnes asked, cynically, of no one in particular. "If it's not here, that would indicate that the vic didn't die here."

Finally, all the items were bagged and tagged and carried to the mobile lab unit. In this case, as so much time had lapsed since the deceased was placed at the scene; all testing would be done back at the laboratory. Depending on the results, some items would possibly be sent to a larger facility, or even the FBI lab in Cincinnati.

The Medical Examiner, as a forensic pathologist, would attempt to determine the cause of death and the manner of death as well as the sex, age and as many physical characteristics of the victim as possible. The professionals had worked the scene as though it were a homicide. At the very least, the death was witnessed by another. People don't end up lying under fallen trees when they die from natural causes. Someone else was present at the time of death and had taken pains to hide the body.

In the days following the discovery of the skeleton, the two detectives awaited the findings from the ME on the forensic testing and from the CSI on the results of their evidence testing.

The ME's report arrived first and advised that the skeleton was definitely that of a Caucasian female, of western European ancestry. The examination of the teeth and the bones and the measurements taken of the later told a story of the deceased: she approximately five foot eight inches in height and between fifteen and twenty-five years of age at the time of her death. She had been well-nourished, probably athletic, based on her body type as having proportionately long legs, and elongated tapered fingers and toes with high arches in her feet. Her spine was straight and strong and there was no indication of disease that could be discerned from the bones.

The cause of death was indeterminate from the bones as no trauma could be detected. The manner of death was indeterminate, as well, as the soft tissue had long since been decomposed. Similarly, the time of death could not be determined as there was no longer any insect activity. The body had most certainly been at its discovered location for a minimum of three years.

"Well, this narrows it down to just a few thousand missing Jane Does," Detective Barnes sourly observed to his partner after they both had perused the Medical Examiner's report. It may be really helpful that we know she was Caucasian. We could get lucky and she was pretty and from a wealthy family. That's the only type of missing person that the media and the public are interested in. We could get some help from that, if we can put together some more clues about her looks.

"We'll have to wait for the CSI's report and see if we can fill in a few blanks. I mean, *almost all* females who are reported missing are between fifteen and twenty-five years of age. And there are what, three hundred to five hundred women who are reported missing in the United States every year? At just three years, and it looks like a lot longer to me, that could be fifteen hundred possibilities, if the vic is from some other part of the country. Of course, we'll proceed on the theory that she's a local woman.

"Just out of curiosity I pulled up the current NAM US Missing Person's report this morning to see what the outside number could be, man or woman. Right now there are 4,912 persons reported missing in the United States. Most of those are probably still alive, out on the streets, out of touch with any friends or family."

"Having the complete skeleton was helpful in eliminating in terms of race and height," Detective Enright added, on a positive note. "We have the complete dental and DNA, of course, if we come up with a probable ID, but useless at this point."

"Anyway, I saw Janey this morning, Larry. She thought they'd have something by this afternoon. She didn't volunteer anything, of course. These scientists aren't about to speculate or share any information until all their tests are completed."

Good to her word, Janey Lawson, Chief of the CSI Unit, hand-delivered the unit's preliminary report a few minutes after three that afternoon. Barnes read through the relatively slim report first and handed it over to Enright, without comment.

After a couple of minutes Barnes asked, "Did you see it? Page four?"

"Jesus H. Christ!" Enright swore, uncharacteristically. "A partial print was lifted off the purse's metal clasp!"

"Incredible!" Barnes agreed. "It's a good thing that purse had a metal clasp. That's the only surface where a print could have survived this long. It has to be the vic's or the perp's. Either way, that's about all we could have hoped for from such a cold scene. I can't believe we got a print at a scene with a pile of bones. I'll run the print through IAFIS right now," he continued. "They have 47 million prints on record, when you add in all the government employees, other civilians, criminals and whatever. If we get a hit, I'm giving Janey a big kiss, I swear to God!"

"I'm sure she'll be thrilled," his partner drolly observed. "I'm going to have Wayne Miller to come in for questioning and exemplar prints. After that, I'm going to get him to bring that dog of his back to the scene, with me, for a second look. I'd lay more odds on that dog finding something relevant than we have. If he does, I'll give him a kiss," he said, smirking at his partner.

"Wisenheimer," countered Barnes, lamely. "I know we're looking for miracles here. But, you know what? I think we're going to crack this one and nail someone's ass in the process."

Chapter 28

Monday morning Albert sat at his kitchen counter, impatiently stubbing out one half-smoked cigarette after another, waiting for a call or text from Gray, as had been arranged for yesterday. He was waiting to hear that Gray had been able to place the GPS tracker in one of the three semi-trailer trucks that transported the nuclear weapons.

Finally, his phone signaled that a text message was coming in. He looked down at the display. "The bird is in the nest," it read. *Good. Gray had installed the tracker on a truck and had the fucking brains to be a little obtuse with the message; although it stood out like a sore thumb as a code phrase.*

He hoped Gray also had the brains to place it some place where it couldn't be found. The device was marketed and sold as spy ware so was designed to be undetectable when installed: no visible or audible signal to indicate a call coming in to its modem, and small enough to be placed most anywhere in a vehicle. This latest model didn't even need a sky-view. It transmitted its location data in real time so that there was never a break in information.

Now that the devise was installed, they could track the shipment of nuclear weapons anywhere on the planet, without the risk of their being discovered, if they stayed within eyesight of the truck.

Next, he had to punch in the number of the tracker to make sure that it was connected and was operative. On his cell phone, he entered the modem's number that he had committed to memory: 621-6179. He waited for a visual signal that the tracker was on line. There it was. *Beautiful.*

The modem on the tracker instantly texted its coordinates to his cell phone. Looking down at the screen, the geocode appeared: +32.01453 -84.25638. Mentally he translated the numbers into the more familiar form: 32 degrees, 14 minutes and 53 seconds North (of the equator) by a Longitude of 84 degrees, 25 minutes and 65 seconds, West (of the meridian passing through Greenwich, England.) Last night he had looked up and memorized the geocode of the address of the motor pool at Y-12, as a reference for "home" and to check the accuracy of the tracker. *Fucking perfect.*

While he had his cell phone in his hands, he punched in another memorized modem number. The screen displayed the geocode of Dana's home address. That was good. What he wanted to see. As this was just a dry run, he didn't care that she was not in the convoy. The fact that she wasn't on this trip, increased the odds that she would be on the next trip. The one that mattered. The last trip of her life.

He needed to wait around a little while to see if Gray would text him again. The plan was that he would send a text if the trucks left the service area so Albert would know when to begin to monitor the movement of the shipment. He had decided he would follow the convoy by traveling on either a parallel route or a few miles behind the truck. As he could remain out of sight, he planned to drive his own car for this initial surveillance and had filled the tank last night.

Looking at his watch, he noticed that it was a quarter after ten. It didn't appear that there would be a trip today. Yesterday Gray had told him that if the trucks were still parked in the Secure Transportation building after ten o'clock in the morning, it was probable that they wouldn't be leaving on a trip that day. He'd wait another half hour, to be safe, before he left to take care of the next item on his list.

After drinking another cup of coffee and smoking another cigarette, he re-checked his watch. Five minutes to go. Just then, his phone signaled that a text message was coming in. "The bird is flying away." *Fucking Gray. He must love this secret code shit.* Now, thanks to Gray's misinformation about departure times he was going to have to really get a move on.

Against his better judgment, he had told Henry to be prepared to go with him; warning him that he would only be allowed to go on the trip if he wore conventional clothing. Albert had explained to him that he didn't want them to arouse suspicion, or be remembered, wherever they would stop to eat, take a break, or stay overnight. Henry had assured him that he still had normal clothes that were never described in the Bible. He wouldn't be noticed.

Albert couldn't imagine that Henry could do or wear anything that wouldn't attract attention or be remembered. Henry was certifiable, but Henry knew a hell of a lot more about nuclear weapons and the nuclear transport operation than he did. Besides, he needed someone to act as navigator; to read the road maps and the latitude and longitude maps of the southeast that he had bought at a book store yesterday. Earlier this morning, he had supplemented the purchased maps with routing options that he had pulled up from the Internet and printed.

Before he got packed, he walked out into the hallway and knocked on Henry's door. He wondered what Henry would even look like in regular clothes. He didn't have to wonder long. Henry soon opened the door, standing there dressed from head to foot in the bright orange team color of the University of Tennessee: baseball cap, t-shirt, and sweat pants.

"Henry, what the hell is the matter with you!? Do you think those are normal clothes that won't attract attention?"

"I thought it was a good disguise to look like a sports fan," Henry whined. "It wouldn't attract any attention around *here*," Henry protested, clearly disappointed in his neighbor's reaction.

"Just go put on something that isn't a costume, for God's sake. Khaki wash pants, dark t-shirt, that kind of thing. We've got to get going—the truck's on its way out to Kings Bay, we presume. Gray's put the tracker on one of the trucks. You're going to be the navigator for our route and to keep track of the shipment. I'm going to drive—my car—so we know we'll get there. I'll be back for you in fifteen minutes and stop fucking around, for Chris' sakes."

Back in his apartment, he thought a minute about what he needed for the trip. The convoy leaving today had taken him by surprise. He had figured on them going tomorrow, allowing more time for their preparations, as this was such a big operation. He had to be more alert. Not take anything for granted.

In his bedroom, it took him less than ten minutes to pack what he needed into a small duffel bag for their short road trip. He just had to collect some equipment; like his laptop, camera, and binoculars, and he would be ready to walk out the door.

Two minutes later, he was at Henry's door again. This time he was gratified to see Henry wearing a pair of standard beige cotton pants and a light blue short-sleeved shirt. Nothing could be done with his patchy hair growth, he supposed. Henry's hair had always looked strange.

"Okay. That's much better, Henry. Do you have everything ready?"

"I've got a couple changes of clothes. Very boring clothes. Don't worry."

"Good. We don't need much. It'll just be one or two nights on the road. We'll take the Interstate east going out of town and be well behind the convoy. We'll just keep their location monitored. I don't really give a fuck where they stop on the way down to the submarine base.

"After they pick up the shipment, we're going to have to stay close but still out of sight. We need to get a visual on them at their stops and scope out the surrounding areas, until we find the stop that's right for us. Of course, Gray might have fucked up on everything and they're not even going to Kings Bay. Then all bets are off. Okay. Enough chatter. Are you ready? Let's go."

Sitting low in the sports cars' bucket seats, Henry had soon disappeared behind full-size maps that he was holding up and trying to examine at close range.

"Just unfold one section at a time!" Albert snapped at his trip mate. "Jesus Christ! I can't even see the fucking road! I can't have *any* distractions. We don't want to get stopped, you know."

An hour out of Oak Ridge, traveling on the Interstate, Albert said, more calmly, "Okay, Henry. Call the modem and get the latitude and longitude coordinates. We need to know if they're still heading east for us to continue this trip."

Henry called the modem and looked at the screen, uncomprehendingly, and read the numbers to Albert who briefly explained the system of latitudes and longitudes. "But you don't even have to worry about translating the numbers. Here, take this slip of paper. See the site I wrote down? You've got the laptop. Pull up this site and you'll get a map where you'll see a space where you can enter the numerical series. The plus sign preceding a number is the longitude, and the minus sign is for the latitude. The first eight numerals are enough to put in. Then look up at the map and you'll see a blue pointer someplace and that's where the shipment is."

Henry found the site and put in the digits and said, in amazement, "They're on I-40 east not far from the junction with I-81 north!"

"Good, so far. Check it again in half an hour and see if they've stayed on I-40 east. Your job for the trip will be calling the modem, getting the geocode numbers and locating the truck on the map. Now don't fuck it up, okay? I'm counting on you."

"Okay. I've got it under control, Colonel."

"And don't call me Colonel! Especially when we're in a public place. That's what I mean when I say we don't want to attract attention. Just call me Al. Yeah, that's it. Al."

Forty minutes later Henry redialed the modem and got the coordinates. Entering the strange long numbers, he announced, "The truck has passed 81 north and has continued on I-40 east!"

"Son of a bitch, Henry," Albert said, smiling now. "I think we're really on our way to Kings Bay. The bird is migrating south."

Chapter 29

" I can't help but be discouraged, Pete. I swear to God I thought we'd get a hit on the latent. I mean, it was a *miracle* the print was even *there*," Detective Barnes exclaimed as he looked at the report back from the CSI. "There are 47 million prints on file with the FBI. You'd think we could get a hit on one of them. Jesus."

"There are over 300 million Americans and that doesn't even count the people not known to the census," Detective Enright countered, not unsympathetically. "Don't worry. After we get some more information about the vic, and we can possibly ID her, we'll come up with some persons of interest and get their prints. One of them will match. I don't think it was a stranger. Too much effort was made to hide the crime. That indicates someone could be linked to her. Hell, you were brilliant in making sure that print was protected and having it run. I can't believe it's going to go to waste, my friend.

"The dairy farmer, Wayne Miller, is coming in to the station to have his print exemplars taken and to give his statement," the younger detective, continued. "He'll be here in an hour, after lunch. You want to talk to him or you want me to handle it? I can't believe it will be anything but a formality. I'd like to talk to him, actually. I still want to arrange to revisit the scene with him and his border collie. Those dogs are the smartest breed there is and that dog of his got the scent of the vic. Maybe there's some other clue around. If there is, you can bet that dog will alert to it."

"Sure, go ahead," Detective Barnes agreed. "That's your call. You should follow up. I'm going to pull up the profiles of females that have been reported missing from our county and the surrounding counties. I can start eliminating based on our vic's height, age, race and 'Northern European' ancestry. I love that one. That'll keep me busy for the rest of the day and then some. Good luck with Miller. I agree with you that he's got nothing to do with this. He didn't live there when she was left in the woods. And even if he did, why would he leave a body in the property next to his own, and then find it for us?"

At exactly one-thirty in the afternoon Wayne Miller walked into the station and asked to see Detective Enright. He was shown into an interview room, where he was seated a minute or two before the detective came in, and greeted him and shook his hand. *No trembling,* the detective noted.

"Okay, just relax, Mr. Miller. If you don't mind, I'm going to start the tape recorder so we can get your entire statement about how you came upon the skeletal remains of the unknown victim. Then we'll have it typed up and you can sign it. While it's being typed, we want to take your fingerprints for what we call 'exemplars.' These are fingerprints that we could legitimately find at the scene. We always have some footprints and fingerprints of our forensic investigators and others at the crime scene that we need to take for exclusions."

"Sure. No problem. Whatever you need. I want to cooperate to help you possibly track down the monster that's responsible for this. I mean, my God, the poor soul was left under a tree to rot!"

"Okay, fine," Detective Enright said, soothingly. "I appreciate that. Let's get started. Just tell me the date and time and the circumstances that made you walk into the woods and how you discovered the skeleton under the tree."

Over the next half hour, Wayne Miller gave a detailed account of how he found the bits of fabric and pile of bones that had once been a healthy young woman. He spoke slowly and carefully to be sure to include everything that could be important for the investigation. There were no differences in his formal statement from his original call to the station, or in any other informal statements he had made to the investigators since he found the human remains.

After he was finished Detective Enright said, "Thank you. That was very good. Now, I just want to ask you a few questions to finish our investigation as it concerns you.

"Could you tell me, for the record, when you lived in the farmhouse where you currently reside with your wife and mother? I understand you grew up in the home."

"Yes, sure. I lived there from 1967, when I was born, to 1988 when I moved out and lived on my own for a time, and then got married, in 1991. Between 1985-1988 I was away at college for most of each year. I moved back into the home with my wife, after my father's death last year. I was on the property during the day after 1985 to the present as I worked the farm, helping my mother and father to run the place, when my father was alive."

"Had you ever heard at any time, over the years, any commotion or cries coming from the woods, particularly where you located the skeleton?" Detective Enright queried.

"No, I never heard any noise coming from the woods. I wasn't *near* the woods very often, and unaccustomed to walking in the woods. Frankly, I think I accepted what my mother told me as a child—that the woods were dangerous. As a teenager I explored them some, of course, but I hadn't walked through them as an adult until the other day when I made the discovery with my dog, Shep."

"In conjunction with my last question, had you ever noticed an unfamiliar car stop near that place in the woods, over the last several years. I realize that we can't be very specific, but just tell me, of any occurrences of unusual activity near the place you marked with a white handkerchief the other day, that you can recall."

'I'm sorry, Detective Enright. I never noticed anything unusual around our property. I've asked my wife and mother as well. We're a good bit away and far back from the road, as you know. The nearest neighbor toward that direction is a half-mile away, but you could ask the Bensons if they ever saw anything. They're good people and they've been there since I was a boy."

"Okay, that's fine. Maybe we'll do that. Those are all the questions I have for you, now, Mr. Miller. Excuse me for a moment, and I'll give the recording to a secretary to type up for your signature."

Returning a minute later, Detective Enright sat down and smiled at the farmer. "You know what I'd really like to do?" the detective asked rhetorically. "I'd like for you and your dog, Shep?—is it?—to accompany me to walk around that area in the woods, again. It's possible that there is another piece of evidence on the ground somewhere nearby that we couldn't see. Would you be willing to do that? We've got a canine unit in Cincinnati, but your dog has already alerted to the victim's remains and the articles at the scene. He's got that scent."

"Sure. No problem, at all. I can vouch for Shep being able to track down the same scent, if something's there. He found my missing cattle later that day I called you people. There was no catching sight of them, either. They were over a hill, some ways off. The dog headed in the right direction all the way until I could see them."

"I know those dogs are really something. After you sign your statement, and we take your prints, I'm going to sign out a piece of evidence that's been processed, and follow you home to pick up Shep."

An hour later the young detective, the dairy farmer and the herding dog were back in the woods near the scene of the discovery. Shep had sniffed the one shoe that had been found with the body that Detective Enright had brought with him in an evidence bag. The two men stood back away from the fallen tree as the dog made circles in the brush. He seemed to have a system as the circles barely overlapped as he moved ever closer to the road. Suddenly the dog stopped, put his nose down into the undergrowth, stepped backwards and barked sharply, as he had done when he came upon the tree.

Both men, reacting to the excited dog, approached and, as they came closer, the detective motioned for the farmer to stay where he was. The detective, nearing the barking dog, said, "Miller. Call Shep." The dog obeyed and went to his master, as the detective reached down with his gloved hand, where the dog's nose had been.

Under twigs, heavy grasses and weeds in the ditch, the detective's hand came up holding onto a woman's ballet-style flat-heeled shoe. The detective now had a pair. He carefully bagged the newest piece of evidence in the case.

Back at headquarters, Detective Enright described the scene of finding the second shoe with his partner. "I just had a feeling," the younger man said. "The scene was so intact it really bothered me that the second shoe was missing. It should have been there. You commented on that, yourself, Larry."

"Yeah. But you went out and found it. Great work. As far as I'm concerned, this means that she died, or was killed elsewhere, and her body was dragged to the location by the tree. That's the most logical explanation of how one shoe was in the ditch."

"I agree. It was at the bottom of the ditch where the pulled body would have been its heaviest as dead weight. The perp probably stopped and as he started up again, maybe changing positions, the shoe caught on something and came off without his knowledge. Probably means the body was hidden at nighttime, which is also logical.

"Of course, none of this is helpful, so far, in identifying the vic," Detective Barnes complained. "I spent the afternoon going through the local missing persons. I was able to eliminate quite a few, but there were still over a hundred missing women in the age group going back over ten years. And I don't even know if that covers the time period. It's unbelievable how many young women have gone missing in a nice quiet area like ours. It's shocking, really. Even a tough old cop like me can't help but be affected."

"Anytime a young person dies, it's tough to accept. A life snuffed out well before it's time," Detective Enright agreed.

"There has been an exciting development I want to tell you about, Pete. I got a call from Shirley Johnson, at the bureau, in Cincy. You know her, I think. She's their forensic artist. We've used her several times over the years when there's been some decomposition to a corpse, and we don't have an ID."

"Yeah, I know who you mean. She did a sculpture to reconstruct the features of the skull from the accident victim last year in Cincinnati. That poor kid had gone off a bridge in his car and had drowned in the Ohio River. His body wasn't found for months and there was no ID there, either. It was all over TV and in the papers when they found the body. But no one came forward until Shirley's sculpture was photographed. The boy's aunt was the first one to recognize him from the reconstruction. It was sad, but at least it brought some closure for the family."

"She's going to try and do a sculpture reconstruction of our vic?" Enright asked.

"She could," Barnes answered, but that would take a few weeks the way it's done by adding successive layers of clay and waiting for each layer to dry. It's quite complicated, adding tissue depths according to averages with age, gender, and ethnic origin. The artificial eyes are then put in, guessing at color. Hair, too.

"As we talked, she said she'd like to try this new computer program they have, that can build not just the three-dimensional representation of the face, but can also add expression. Oftentimes, a person's identity is difficult to determine without any animation to the face. This new method of recreating a face includes adding the simulations of the 24 muscles of facial expressions. With the computer images, she can change the hairstyle and color easily, to offer a variety of looks for the individual, as well."

"That sounds great, Larry. I never heard anything about this new forensic method of recreating the image of a deceased."

"I've set up an appointment for tomorrow, Pete, for both of us to transport the skull down to Cincy to meet with Shirley. She thinks she can come up with a result while we wait. She's been using the program on some skulls of known individuals and claims the results are very true to life."

The next day the two detectives drove the fifty miles to the FBI offices in Cincinnati with the evidence that could unlock the identity of the victim and lead to the solution of her demise.

Shirley Johnson, in her white lab coat, met them in the anteroom of the forensic laboratories and respectfully received the square metal box containing the cushioned skull. She advised the detectives that both the CSI and the Medical Examiner's office had faxed their full reports to aide in her reconstruction efforts. Also, she said, one of the bureau's top computer imaging specialists would be assisting her to insure that they got the best result possible.

Taking down Detective Barnes' cell phone number, she promised to call as soon as they had a good image, and then they'd see how to proceed, at that point.

"Let's go get something to eat, Pete," Barnes suggested. "It'll take at least an hour. Shirley told me that they first scan the skull, and then they input all the tissue depth information from her genetic tables, based on the ME's profiling. Apparently facial tissue is different thicknesses all over the face depending on ethnic heritage. The data input will take the most amount of time and then the rest is done by the computer program. Pretty amazing.

An hour and a half later, the two detectives were back in the forensics' laboratory waiting room like two expectant fathers. They weren't there long when Shirley came out, a smile on her face, as though she were the obstetrician bringing them good news.

"We have a fine, realistic image. Come back and see for yourselves."

Both men followed her through the labyrinth of rooms to a room that was darkened to dramatize a single lit-up computer screen. Taking two seats in front of it, the detectives stared, transfixed, as the three-dimensional image of a beautiful young woman with long blond hair, spun on an axis on the screen in front of them. Her face was enlivened with the expression of pleasure as though posing for a photographer.

"I gave her long hair, as CSI said that a brush was found in her purse," Shirley Johnson explained. I made her blond, based on the ME's report that she was of northern European descent. Whoever she was, she was lovely," Shirley said, wistfully. "Do you think it's lifelike enough that someone could identify her?" She asked, anxiously.

Detective Barnes didn't immediately respond, but kept staring at the screen. Finally, in a flat-toned voice as though in a daze, he said, softly, "I can identify her. It's been maybe ten years, but I couldn't forget her. I never knew her when she was alive. But you've brought to life the exact photograph of her that I was given when she was reported missing after the fraternity party at the university. Her name is Cat Moore. Great job, Shirley. Really great.

"And I think I know the son of a bitch who killed her and put her under that tree," Barnes said, in a stronger voice and with conviction. "I could never lay a finger on him, before. But just maybe he's laid his own finger down where it didn't belong, and I can get him now. I couldn't forget his name, either. Albert Arnstein.

"Let's get out of here, Pete. We've got work to do."

Chapter 30

At seven o'clock that evening, Albert took the exit off I-95 that was eleven miles north of St. Marys, Georgia. Turning onto a frontage road, they came to a franchised motel that advertised bargain rates and Albert pulled into the parking lot.

"The sign says they have a pool, Al," Henry said, brightly. "That would be nice."

"Jesus Christ, Henry! We're not here on a fucking vacation! Have you forgotten that we're here to set up an assault on a convoy of armed federal agents; to steal a nuclear bomb?!"

"No, I didn't forget," Henry replied, haughtily. "I just thought we could take a little swim. It would be refreshing. We're only a few miles from Florida, and it's hot out," he argued, but without confidence, sensing a backlash coming from his travel companion.

"Don't even tell me you brought your swim trunks!" Albert shrieked. "We are not on our way to Disney World. This is the *real* world and we have an important job to do. And you have to help me see it through, god-damn it. Now, let's get our bags out of the trunk. We'll go register, drop off our luggage in the room and then get something to eat.

"I hope this flop house takes credit cards. They may operate a cash-only business, from the looks of the place. I can't wait to see the fucking room we have to share. And, by the way, Henry, we're going over some rules at dinner so I can get some sleep tonight."

Albert got out of bed before seven o'clock the next morning and redialed the tracker's modem. He had memorized the latitude and longitude of the base as they verified the convoy was there last night. Not surprisingly, the geocode of the submarine base appeared on the cell phone screen. Of course the truck was still there. *Where else would it be at seven o'clock in the morning? Jesus.* He had to relax.

He felt that his nerves were on edge, and that wasn't good. He needed to be calm and methodical. That's what had worked in the past. But he needed some answers. There were too many unknowns at this point. Like, when do they load the truck? How long does it take? Gray had said it takes only about an hour to load up the trucks at the Y-12 facility, using the heavy equipment they have available. Of course, they do this all the time, follow the same procedures, and load up the same or similar parts and weapons that are stored at the same building at the complex.

Gray didn't know the procedures on the submarine base to off-load missiles from a submarine and load them onto the trucks, but he felt certain that all three of the trucks would be loaded, given the number of missiles that were being shipped to Amarillo.

Albert dressed to go out and get coffee. There wasn't any complimentary breakfast in this joint. Not that he minded, given the general lack of cleanliness in the establishment.

Coming back with a couple of take-out coffees and some rolls, he found that Henry had gotten up and was dressed, as well, in khaki shorts and a black t-shirt, thank God. That was a good sign, anyway.

Albert had to admit that Henry had proved himself capable of reading the coordinates, yesterday, and kept him informed of the shipment's location. He needed to encourage Henry to stay focused on the mission as he needed his assistance.

For his part, he would try and be more patient with the guy. It was too easy to go off on him when he acted crazy, and that didn't help things. Besides, Henry was as close to being a friend as anyone had been in his life. Not that he was going to start getting sentimental. This was only business.

"Here, Henry. I brought back some decent coffee for us and a couple of rolls, each."

"Hey, thanks for the breakfast. I figured you went out for coffee. You're so good to me. Did you sleep all right? I didn't blow my shofar, or ram's horn, to summon Yahweh last night, so it wouldn't disturb you. You said I should be quiet after ten o'clock."

"Yeah. You were a fucking barbiturate. Listen, Henry. This is serious. You're going to have to be on top of things today. Tracking the shipment will be a lot more complicated today than it was yesterday."

"I'll pull up the modem and check it right now. I checked while I was waiting for the coffee. We'll need to get the coordinates about every twenty minutes all day today. We can't leave here until we know the GPS truck has moved so we're prepared to stay with them."

"Colonel,—I'm sorry—Albert. I just like to feel that I'm a soldier following orders leading up to battle. I can handle it, Colonel Albert. I feel confident about entering all the numbers in the spaces in the map picture. I can do that all day long."

"Well, good. You're going to have to. Our other complication is that we don't know the fucking route that the convoy will take. We need to be close by, but not visible. For that to happen, you will probably need to find a parallel route. If that seems impractical, because there are only country roads where we can't drive at a reasonable speed, or roads that go too far off in other directions, then we'll stay on the Interstate with them, but we'll have to be far enough behind or far enough ahead that they won't notice us. Did you get all that?"

"I did, Colonel Albert. We need to be right there with them, but not noticed by them. We could travel a couple miles behind the truck and stay at the speed limit. Nothing suspicious about that."

"Well, no one travels the speed limit on the Interstate, especially in Florida, for Chris' sakes. I think they'll go into Jacksonville to hook up with 10 west to I-75 north. Once through Atlanta, they'll go up to Chattanooga where they pick up 24 north to pick up their fucking I-40 West. They'll always take Interstate 40 when they possibly can."

Twenty minutes later, when they had finished their coffee and rolls, Albert lit up a cigarette and hit redial. Same coordinates.

Finally, forty minutes later, at about nine o'clock, Albert punched redial, again. Seeing the screen, he sat up with an intense look on his face. "They're moving, Henry. They're moving. We have to get going. We can't let the mother fuckers get away. Get your bag and let's go. I've got the equipment in this other bag. Just go."

With that, they were out the door and had thrown their bags in the trunk and had jumped into the car. Even Henry had moved at unfamiliar speed.

Once in the car, Albert said, "I'm taking I-95 south, okay, Henry?"

"Yeah. I think so. The truck is going west on I-40 from the base. Hold on. Now they're on I-95 south. They're ten miles ahead of us."

"That's okay for now. But we'll have to get closer in case they make a stop where we can operate. They can't go over 65 m.p.h. so I'll catch up.

"Let me hear from you, Henry. It's twenty minutes."

"Okay, Colonel. They're coming to the 295 junction to go around the city. Stay in your right lane. That's the only way they can go that makes sense. I'll redial. Okay. They're on it."

"Good work, Henry. Now we know that they're going to pick up I-75 north. I think we need to be ready for their first stop, which will be lunch, and fueling. I'm betting they'll stop around exit 73; after that slowdown when the traffic funnels into I-75 from 16 West coming from

Savannah. Everyone wants to get through that and north of the city before they think about stopping. That's a fucking mess.

"Henry. Look at that car ahead of us. Do you notice anything unusual about it?"

"It's kind of a drab color, you mean?" Henry offered.

"No, I mean the fact that there are three guys in the van all wearing cool shades. Three men in a vehicle? Who are they, fucking Boyz to Men? I don't think so. They're fucking agents. Wait a minute. We just got close enough to read U.S. Government on their plates. They might as well have a little flag on each side of the car. Jesus. Just look straight ahead when we pass them. Don't let them see that we're noticing them.

"I have a feeling we're going to see three trucks, in a row, coming up. Of course that's hard to tell with all the trucks on this route. We'll move on ahead and you look for other vehicles with three men in them, if you can see. Some of them will probably be in panel trucks, or have heavily tinted windows and you can't see. I don't know. Pull up the geocode on the truck."

"It's right ahead of us, Colonel. This is so exciting!"

"Never mind that, Henry. And for God's sake, don't look or point, if we pass one of them."

Within the half hour, they had passed the three silver-sided trucks that carried the nuclear missiles that were taken off an the submarine and were on their way to Amarillo, Texas. Well, not all of the missiles, if they had anything to say about it.

For nearly an hour they were in stop-and-go traffic, from thirty miles south of Atlanta, until they were north of the city. Henry continued to check the GPS tracker which showed the truck to be about five miles behind them, near as Henry could say. Albert told him to now check the coordinates every five minutes as they would have to stop within the next half hour.

At four-thirty in the afternoon the tracker indicated the same coordinates for the second consecutive time. The screen read +34.524661, -84.946289. Five minutes later, they were there. Three trucks were at one end of a large gas station/service-center with a food mart. "Remember that geocode, Henry," Albert said, excitedly. "That's the location that will be known around the world. Well, they might call it the Ground Zero of Georgia. More catchy.

"Look around here, Henry. This is perfect. Did you notice the mountainous country to the east for the last few miles? There can't be much development there. We're almost exactly between Atlanta and Chattanooga. Good news coverage, especially from Atlanta. This is a big service station but there's nothing else within sight. We have a perfect point of attack from the hill behind the station. We could be there for a while and be unobserved. The convoy vehicles, themselves, will be cover. It'll be a confusing scene. No passersby will know who's who.

"Let's wait it out and see how long they stay here," Albert said. "Oh, not long, apparently. One vehicle is already leaving. Gray was right when he said one agent will stay in each vehicle all the time. How many government vehicles are here? I see the three trucks and one, two, three, four vehicles that are definitely theirs. I'm taking pictures of the vehicles that are here."

Fifteen minutes later the last government vehicle had left the scene. "We were that close, Henry," Albert indicated the distance as an inch between his thumb and forefinger. "We were that close to a nuclear missile. Jesus H. Christ," he swore slowly, in awe.

"Let's get out of here." Albert said, suddenly. We'll head up into the hills, to the east. There's only one road over there that has any traffic. It's an area of small farms, with very little commercial interests. The only danger is being noticed as outsiders. Once we're in a vacated barn or shed, there won't be anything to see.

Get your ram's horn out, Henry. We're going to find a vacant shed; one where one can't hear your horn from the road, or the nearest building. That's a good test for privacy. Why the hell did you bring that thing, anyway? Never mind. Don't even answer that."

Chapter 31

“Thanks for pulling the evidence box, Lizzie. There was just the one carton?”

“Yes, Detective. I know there's usually more so I checked all around the area. Oh, and here are the dental records back from the ME's office, after they confirmed the identity. I heard that you recognized her from the computer image, and from ten years ago! That's amazing, sir. Can I get anything else for you right now?”

“No thanks, Liz. I don't think so. I appreciate that you were able to find the box back in those disorganized piles in that sorry excuse for an evidence storage area. I know we don't have the space for these cold cases like on the cop shows on TV—with every box found on the top shelf,” Detective Barnes said, smiling at the fiction.

“Okay, Pete. Come over here and I'll get you up to speed.”

His partner came over and squatted down to look at the dusty cardboard box on the floor next to Barnes' desk. Scrawled in Magic Marker on one end was “99-1276” on the first line, “MOORE, CATHERINE (CAT)” on a second line and “Missing, Presumed Dead,” on the third line, with the final identification on the bottom line: “COLD CASE.”

"I guess that's why there's only one box, Larry," Detective Pete commented, kneeling down to look at the delivery. "Without a body, there must have been little evidence, other than a few pictures and interviews." Opening up the flaps he peered into the contents and saw a lot of paper work. "Well, let's dig in and see what you've got."

"This was one of those really sickening cases, Pete. The girl was a freshman, had just come to school a few weeks before. Beautiful, full of promise. She went to her first college party. Most parents think that the worst-case scenario for their kids going to their first college party is that they'll drink. And she did. And it was illegal, at her age. Under-age drinking in Ohio can get you six month's jail time, max. Cat Moore ended up dead."

"You think this guy Arnstein is the perp. Any way she could have died accidentally of alcohol poisoning?"

"Nah, no way," Barnes said, dismissively. "She had a few beers, no doubt. I heard the boys were 'over-serving' her, but her friends at the party said they talked to her just before she left. She told them that she was going back to the dorm to call her boyfriend, like she had promised. They said she was a little tipsy. That's all. No way could she have been that functional and alert and had a lethal level of alcohol in her system. She wouldn't have been conscious."

"Do you know if she might have been drinking after the party? Detective Enright asked.

"Not according to this creep, Arnstein, who admitted to being with her after the party," Detective Barnes responded.

"You told me about this guy Arnstein, who was your main suspect. What's with that name—'Albert Arnstein?' I wonder what his parents were thinking sticking him with a name like that?"

"Good question. I remember asking him about his name," Barnes replied, looking off into space, trying to recall the details. "He said that his father was a professor of physics, somewhere. I can't remember. Anyway, his father did some kind of research with atomic energy and was a great admirer of Albert Einstein. He wanted that kind of greatness for his son and so he saddled him with that moniker. Parents can be pretty cruel, can't they?

"Anyway," Barnes went on, "this kid, Albert, said that he offered Cat a ride home after the party, had sex with her, mind you, and then dropped her off a couple blocks from her dorm. That was the last that anyone ever saw of her. I want to read back through all the files and refresh myself on his statements, and his contact information. I want you to read through the files, too, to learn the case. Here, why don't you read his statement?" The detective said, rifling through the paperwork and coming up with several manila folders.

"I pulled him in here a couple of times. I knew the bastard was lying but I couldn't prove it and I couldn't shake him. I went over his statement with him, pointing out the holes, but he never broke. Had eyes like ice. No warmth at all. Just answered my questions like we were talking about a missing dog, instead of a missing girl. Well, read his answers for yourself. See what you think. I'm just hoping the print on the purse clasp is his, if we can find the guy and can print him. A lot of ifs. I still say, if that print isn't Cat's, it belongs to her killer."

"What did a sweep of his car come up with?"

"Not a damn thing we could use. The problem was that he admitted the girl had been in his fucking car. I think we picked up a long blond hair or two. So what? There certainly wasn't any blood in the car, I can tell you that. We used luminal all over the damn car—the seats, the trunk, everywhere. There was nothing.

"The mother fucker even *produced* evidence. He showed us a blanket he kept in the trunk. Said he had laid it down on the ground when they parked alongside some road. No blood on that either. Used the luminal there, too.

"They both wanted to have sex, he claimed. Without a body, how can you refute it? I don't think *my* daughter would have wanted to have sex with the guy, but what do I know?"

Detective Peter Enright took the thick file, walked over to his desk, and laid it down.

"I think I'll need a cup of coffee, first," the younger detective remarked, crossing the room over to where a comparatively fresh pot had been brewed by the conscientious, Lizzie. Pouring himself a cup, he carried it back to his desk and sat down on his upholstered swivel chair. He picked up the file and started to read.

An hour later, Detective Enright looked up from his reading with a frown on his face. "Larry, I'm just reading the statement from Arnstein, and I see that you drove him over to where he said they parked after it had stopped raining that night. Do you remember that?

"Yeah. We went over to that ritzy residential street, not far from the campus. It's Sommerset Drive, I think, right? You've got it there in the statement."

"It *is* here in the statement," Detective Enright clarified, scanning the pages to read the down quickly. "When Arnstein first came in, voluntarily, to give a statement on the missing girl, he said that he didn't remember the street they had been on when he pulled over and they were making out in the car. Then they both felt the urge to go farther, and he took the blanket out of the trunk and they had sex on the blanket on the ground."

"Yeah, that sounds about like how I remember it. Why? What's wrong? Did I miss something? I couldn't contradict what street the guy said he was on. He showed me where they parked. I went back and looked around. There was nothing there to prove or disprove his statement."

"Okay," Detective Enright said, agreeing with his partner's conclusion at the time. "Here's the thing, Larry. I just had a flash-back to an incident from about ten years ago when I was working weekend nights as a waiter at that restaurant that's gone now, 'The Prime Minister.' Maybe you remember the place. It was a steak house; prime ribs, that kind of thing. I was working to help put myself through school. I lived here, but commuted to the community college in Cincinnati, every day. That's all I could afford.

"But that's beside the point. Reading this statement, I was thinking back to that time, to get a better feel for Arnstein's story and I remembered an incident from back then.

"This particular night, it had been raining, and there had been a couple of accidents due to the weather, so I was driving slowly. On Commercial Avenue, about midnight, after the rain had stopped, I had to brake suddenly when I came upon a parked Miata, sitting there with its lights off, partially on the roadway. I recall that it was a Miata because that was the kind of car that I wanted, but couldn't afford. I was driving my dad's Camry.

"Anyway, there wasn't a lot of traffic that night, but as it was dangerous for a car to be parked there, I thought there must be a problem. I stopped behind the gray sports car, keeping my headlights on to see something, and called out to see if they needed any help.

"There was no response at first. I think I called out again. Then a guy on the curb side of the car stood up in my beam and waved. I wasn't sure what he meant by that, so I stayed where I was, to see if he would come back to my car. He didn't. Then the guy sort of lifted another person into car on the passenger's side. I thought someone was sick or had been drinking. I waited another few seconds.

"The guy came around in front of his car and gave me the "okay" sign or something like that. Then he got in the car and waved me on while he started up his car.

"The point is, what jogged my memory was our conversation about this guy, Arnstein, and his father naming him after the physicist. Then, as I read Arnstein's statement it brought me back to that scene.

"It was the guy's license plate that stuck in my mind that I recalled just now. It was a vanity plate that read: E mc2. Energy equals mass times the speed of light, squared. *Einstein's Theory of Relativity.* I remember thinking, when I pulled up behind the Miata, what's this 'Einstein' doing parked on a slick road at midnight without his lights on? You know, like who's *this* idiot?

"Your Albert Arnstein wasn't making love to a girl on Sommerset Drive that night. He was dumping her dead body into his car on Commercial Avenue."

Chapter 32

"Let's just go down our punch list, as we'll call it," Albert said, to get order from the group. "We may be one day away from blowing away a large chunk of northeast Georgia. I want you to wrap your minds around that. We need to mentally prepare ourselves for what we're about to do.

"Henry, what the hell is that pile of pillow stuffing that you're sitting on? And I hope you're not planning on wearing those orange knee socks on the mission. Listen, this is not the time to be going off on some crazy fantasy. You have to take this seriously and be mentally here, with the rest of us, in these final hours."

Albert was meeting with his recruits in the 'living room' of the rusted trailer, working out the details of what he considered *his* seizure of the ultimate power; an atomic bomb. He still had no reason to trust Gray, an unknown quantity, or his two lackeys: one too dumb to think for himself and the other so damaged he was unstable. But he needed their help.

They had met again on this Sunday afternoon to prepare themselves for their final battle against the Evil United States Government. In their minds it was The Battle of Armageddon. The assault was anticipated for that week, perhaps the very next day. Albert felt wired. But what the hell was Henry doing, now? He could bring down the whole carefully-constructed scheme.

"I *am* taking this seriously, Colonel," Henry protested, churlishly. "I want to inspire us by the vision of the end times in the Book of Revelation. I'm the mighty angel, in the tenth chapter, who comes down from heaven, 'wrapped in a cloud, with a rainbow over his head, and his legs like pillars of fire.' This was the best I could do, obviously. I thought I was quite successful at getting at the essence of the scripture, if not the reality. It's meant to inspire us."

"Whatever." Albert pressed his fingers against his temples as if to ward off a headache, while closing his eyes. "Okay. Let's get back to the business at hand. I've jotted down the problems we needed to solve.

"Number one: 'Locate the trucks on the trip from Kings Bay while we remain out of sight.' Gray has taken care of that. He mounted a GPS tracker on one of the trucks. Henry and I were able to follow the geocode, or latitude and longitude positioning, of the shipment on its trip last week from Oak Ridge to the Kings Bay base, out to Amarillo, and then back to Oak Ridge. The system worked perfectly. Henry will be our intel guy on the location of the truck." Henry smiled, and appeared to dip a little into a bow. Albert cringed.

"Number two: 'Intercept the codes for the key pads that lock the trailers.' Gray?

"Bingo," Gray responded. "I've discovered that the john in back of the service area has a window that looks out where the tractor-trailers are parked outside before a trip. That's where the agents punch in the key pad numbers. The room will give me privacy, of course, as well as having a wide enough opening to see the key pads on the ends of the trailers in the area where the trailers will be parked. The binoculars give me easier-to-read numbers than are on my cell phone. I got the last codes. But some of the agents are very careful to conceal the pads as they enter their code. As every trailer has its own two-man team to enter two different codes, it won't be easy to intercept the two codes on the same trailer."

"Besides that, what if someone else is in the john when the agent goes out to the truck?" Albert asked.

"I've thought of that, Albert," Gray responded. "Then I go to Plan B. There's another window that is reasonably obscured by hose racks and shelving. I'll use that. And yes, I've tested that window, too. The odds are that the bathroom will be unoccupied and that would be better."

"Okay." Albert sounded unconvinced. "Well, it's up to you. You'll be sure and get the key pad codes, or the mission is off. I guess you know that. You'll contact us all with the codes. We'll all need it. Just in case." The 'case' that went unstated would be Gray being killed in a fire fight before he had a chance to punch in the codes.

"The next one is yours, too, Gray," Albert said, looking down at his notes. "Number three: Tamper with the exhaust manifold to release a minimum of 800 ppm of carbon monoxide into the vehicle cabins at a precise time when the trucks are stopped. Gray?"

"Bingo, again, but this one took me all week to work out and practically killed me in my own truck, testing the particles per million. Anyway, I have a lot of experience with IEDs in Afghanistan, right? So, obviously I've put that knowledge to good use in this effort.

"For this purpose, we needed a central control unit with remote-device selection information. Are you with me so far?"

There were a couple of uncertain nods.

"The remote control devices are connected over a bidirectional line to a telephone interface for receiving programming information. By making a particular selection of a displayed icon, a command can be decoded and sent via an infrared link to the charge I've set on the exhaust manifold of each vehicle.

"I've targeted the gaskets that fit between the engine head exhaust ports and the exhaust manifold. They will stay in place for the trip but will be blown out when I detonate a minute flare at that site. The gaskets are made of a heat-treated paper product that can easily be destroyed by the small explosion.

"Once those gaskets are compromised, lethal levels of carbon monoxide will immediately be released into the passenger compartments. We need to get up to a 1% concentration in the vehicles, when the level can kill a person in less than three minutes. That won't give them time to react. They'll be immediately overcome as soon as they're aware that there's a problem."

"If you're planning on setting these off when they get to the service center I've told you about, many of the agents will be out of the vehicles. You'll have to time the flares to go off when the vehicles and trucks are two minutes away from the service center. Have you placed them in all the vehicles? You know that all of the escorts don't necessarily stop at the same place. How are you controlling all of them?" Albert asked.

"Okay. First, I'm planning on all the gassings to take place just prior to the convoy's arrival at the service center, and I'm not talking about all the vehicles. I've set charges in the three trucks, of course, and the four vehicles that you photographed at the stop on their last trip. A couple of the vehicles are equipped for Fast Response Teams. They stay close enough to the trucks to keep them in view, so they'll be at the stop. That's fairly certain.

"I can't know where the other vehicles will be when the trucks pull into the service center, but any vehicles not there won't be aware of our activity until it's too late. We'll be already gone."

"If there are any at the service center who manage to get out of their vehicles before they're overcome, we'll have the advantage of surprise and we'll shoot to kill," Albert asserted.

"Your main responsibility at first, Gray, is to make sure the flares go off and destroy the gaskets. You've got seven remotes to worry about and set off as you see things developing. I'll be in command and oversee the operation with Henry.

"Dirk and Hubie will be in position behind the signs close to the station," Albert continued, confidently. "Dirk will have the compact tractor there. He knows how to operate it. You, Henry and I will be armed, across the street," Albert said, addressing Gray.

"That was number three: Secure equipment to take the bomb off the truck and put it on Gray's truck. Henry and I found an equipment rental place about a half hour away that has a small compact tractor with a utility attachment that can hold the bomb. Gray is going to rent the tractor as soon he can get down there after the convoy takes off from Oak Ridge. He has an alias he can use to prevent tracing it back to any of us.

"If we hit them with the gas and gunfire all at once we'll quickly create massive carnage and confusion. The gassing will serve a second purpose as a diversion. If they manage to react fast enough, they'll at first think they have some problem with their vehicles. When they get out of the vehicles to investigate, we'll start picking them off with our assault weapons with large-capacity clips. Eliminating or disabling them will allow us all the time we need to enter the code on the key pad.

"We'll cover Dirk from firepower they might have, as he drives the tractor over to the truck. We can roll the warhead onto the attachment from the semi-trailer and drop it onto Gray's truck. We'll have a tarp ready to cover up our "pay load." The tractor will be left behind. Be sure you don't leave anything else behind . . . except a few agents, of course." He smiled, cruelly.

"Number Four: Find a hideout," Albert had continued with his list. "Henry and I discovered an abandoned shed that is up in the hills and far enough away from the nearest inhabitant that we won't be observed or heard."

"Exit 305, that we've targeted, is almost midway between Atlanta and Chattanooga. Two weeks ago, on the same route, the trucks stopped at about 5:45 p.m. when they left Kings Bay at approximately nine a.m. and made their first shift change around Tifton. We're going to plan on a similar time frame but we're not going to assume *anything*. We'll be there by 3:00 p.m. with our equipment. That's earlier than they could possibly arrive. Then we'll get set up and wait it out.

"Gray, you and Dirk and Hubie will bring the assault weapons and magazines. I'll bring my own Glock and Henry has a little Colt piece of shit, so he needs a rifle and magazine. Henry and I will be back-up as we're not sharpshooters.

"I'm looking at five minutes to subdue the federal agents in the attack, get access to the cargo on the truck, load the bomb onto Gray's truck, and leave the area. No one will be on our trail for twenty minutes, at least. By the time the cops show up and figure out what happened, and mount any kind of chase, we'll be snug in our shed.

"As soon as Gray contacts us that the convoy leaves Oak Ridge for Kings Bay, we get everything together for departure the next day.

"Here are the pictures I took of the trucks and the vehicles at the service station. The other pictures give you an idea of the station, itself, and the immediate area around it. Gray, you already have a set of pictures you've used to identify the vehicles you've wired.

"The last pictures are of the shed, inside and out, and the land around it. That'll be where we bring the bomb. I'll be set up there with the computer to decode the encryption of the PAL box to arm the weapon.

"Gray, you and Dirk and Hubie will be going in your truck. Henry and I will take Henry's car, God help us. Someone at the station might have noticed my car last week so we'll be unnoticed in Henry's Plymouth. I'll check it out mechanically before we leave. It would be the height of absurdity if we miss out on the greatest heist of all time because our car broke down at Chicamauga, or some damn place.

"You guys will follow us to the shed. It's big enough for both the truck and the car. We'll need all four of you to be on the lookout for any pursuers, just in case. Put scopes on your rifles to take them out before they have a chance to move into a strategically feasible position.

"Everyone has to do his job *exactly* as I've outlined it and I won't tolerate any screw-ups or excuses. I don't need to tell you what the consequences will be for not handling your assignment.

"We'll hide out in the shed for as long as it takes me to decode the bomb. When I decode the encryption we'll set a timer for the explosion giving us enough time to get outside of the thirty-mile radius of total destruction. We'll meet again at Gray's trailers.

"Any questions? No? Well, this is it. There's no turning back. We're now past preparing for war. This *is* war; a just war against our oppressors. When we're together again we'll have won that war.

Chapter 33

The following morning Gray arrived for work well before the start of the work day. Pulling up to the security check-point station outside the Secure Transportation Building, the regular guard asked for his identification and Gray handed over his badge bearing the printed name of Mark Hunter, with his signature under his photo. The guard examined it and waved him through.

Gray used his key to unlock the building's door as he entered quietly, lost in his thoughts. Needing to turn on the lights, he knew that he had the service area to himself. Checking his watch, he estimated he would be there alone at least for another fifteen minutes.

The usually noisy garage was still. The air compressors, hammers, wrenches and all the motorized tools that would be soon be in use, were inert. The four lifts were down prior to the start of what was expected to be a typical work day. The residual odor of gasoline and motor oil were other indications of the brisk activity that would later ensue.

Gray thought about last week when he had worked on the targeted vehicles up on the lifts. It was fortunate that the manifolds were only visible under the engines and there would be no reason for any other mechanic to check on them anytime soon. There had been no reports of leaks.

As no one else was around, Gray used the opportunity to assess the situation and imagine where the other mechanics would be working that morning. Walking over to the work sheet, that had been posted the night before, he saw that several vehicles and the three trucks were scheduled for maintenance and trouble-shooting this morning. The one inescapable conclusion was that a trip was scheduled for today. The couriers presumably would be making the trip to Kings Bay to pick up another shipment of W88 warheads to deliver to Amarillo, Texas.

He felt himself flush at the realization that the clock was ticking. It was counting down to when he would have to perform his vital role to intercept two codes that would be entered on the keypad of one of the three trailers. Hopefully, there would be two agents assigned to the same truck who were both lax in following the security regulations and reveal the numbers of their codes.

Gray had been able to observe the couriers' security practices when they picked up their vehicles from the motor pool. The majority of the agents were very guarded in their actions and conversation regarding their work. They could be friendly and converse about other topics, but they'd never give away any details about their trips.

But there were a few who would occasionally break the rules and give out information about their jobs, like their destinations or their time schedule.

The emphasis the DOE placed on security was made apparent in the fact that the agents, themselves, were only advised of their destination just prior to leaving for the motor pool to pick up their vehicles.

Gray crossed over to the work bench, unzipped his duffel bag and reached down under a shirt to pull out the binoculars Albert had given him. Taking them into the washroom, he scanned the parking area with the glasses to confirm that the view was sufficient as he had noted in his earlier experiment.

A couple minutes later, as he came out of the washroom with the binoculars around his neck, he turned to walk toward the window that was behind the shelving: his fall-back vantage place.

"Hey, Hunter."

Gray stopped in mid step and jerked his head around to look at the speaker. "Jesus Christ, Bud! I didn't hear you come in! I was just in the washroom!"

"Yeah, I saw you come out. Relax—and what's with the binoculars? Somethin' goin' on outside?" Bud asked, innocently.

"Wha? Oh, no, nothin's going on. It's just that I've got tickets for the Smokies on my day off. I found my military "glass" and put them on to test looking at distances, to see if I should take them to the game." Gray felt himself flush again, and turned away, hoping that Bud wouldn't have noticed. Thankfully, Bud had picked up his newspaper and didn't seem to have any further interest in the binoculars. *I've got to get a hold of myself. Act like it's just another day. I could have blown everything right there.*

Gray continued walking over to the workbench and dropped the binoculars into his bag. He could retrieve them later, and put them on under his work clothes, for the few minutes he would need them.

By seven o'clock all of the mechanics had reported for work, put on their work coveralls and were ready for work. One of the mechanics had made the coffee and most everyone took a cup as they looked over the day's work sheet waiting for their assignments from Ron Draper, the service manager.

"Hey, Hunter!" Draper called out.

"What?! What's wrong?" Gray's voice was high-pitched and sharp.

"Nothin's wrong. I was just gonna say that you left your duffel bag on the bench. Jeez. Don't be so tense. By the way, while I have your attention, I'd like you to do the check list on the trucks this morning. We have word that the convoy is leaving at 9:30 this morning for a lengthy trip. Do a thorough job, okay?"

"Yeah, sure, Ron. I'll get on it right now," Gray responded, relieved to have something to do.

Gray started the maintenance program by first checking the oil readings and adding a quart to each cab to keep the level high enough for the powerful engines to perform at their best.

Next he checked the radiators and their overflow bottles, and topped off the radiators after they were tested for leaks and none were found.

In checking the tires, Gray had discovered that the tire pressure on the cabs and the trucks had fluctuated slightly and many were lower than their ideal inflation, probably from having been driven on the highway at high speeds for many hours the week before. With the help of one of the other mechanics to complete the task of adding air to all the tires, Gray then rechecked them to ensure that they had the same pressure.

Having driven the trucks up to the pumps, Gray had dispensed the diesel fuel to completely fill the dual fuel tanks on each truck. In addition, he had checked the fuel vents to be sure that wasps or other insects hadn't built nests there creating a blockage and, thereby, a misreading that the trucks were low on fuel.

Finally, he backed the trucks out of the service area to depress the brakes to check them for any vibrations or squealing, and had found that they were operating properly. He then parked the trailers in the most advantageous positions to be seen from the washroom window.

When he had completed his check list, he signed off on the work order for Ron and told one of the assistants to run the cabs through the wash. As he signed his name on the order, Albert's sarcastic words came back to him. "We wouldn't want you to sign off on anything that wasn't true," Albert had mocked him. *What he signed off on today was true,* he thought. *No one had asked him about the exhaust manifolds.*

With Gray's check list in hand, Ron examined the trucks to satisfy himself that they all checked out and were properly readied for a long road trip. Finished with the trucks, he went on to inspect all the other vehicles as the couriers started arriving to take possession of them.

Gray had picked up another cup of coffee when he spotted the agents walking out the back door to set the codes on the key pads on the trailers. *This was it: the moment of truth.* He had the binoculars on him already, having retrieved them when he saw the first courier approach the motor pool building.

Looking over the couriers he saw two agents who might not be so careful when they entered their codes.

Trying to look calm, Gray put down his cup and ambled over to the washroom. It was unoccupied. Good. Once inside he locked the door and pulled out the binoculars but didn't raise them to his eyes at first. He looked out the window without them, to take in the whole scene with his own eyes before he magnified any one thing. As he took in the group of six agents, he concentrated on the two agents he thought most likely to punch in the numbers without covering up the keypad. *Oh, shit! They were walking over to different trailers!*

He then lifted up the binoculars and focused on the back of the trailer where one of the more careless agents was chatting to his partner as he casually punched in his code without covering his movements with his other hand. As Gray watched, he read in his binoculars: 3-9-9-4. He got it! He had the one code. Now the agent stepped up to enter his code. But as he pointed his index finger to hit the numerals, his other hand came up and covered the key pad! *Son-of-a-bitch.*

Immediately, he scanned over to the other trailers. One pair of agents had already finished their coding. The men had stood very close to the pads when they each entered their codes and he couldn't have seen anything. *Another lost opportunity,* he thought, dismally.

His only hope now was the third pair of agents. Luckily, one of them was a rule-breaker. And, just as Gray had thought, this agent was not concentrating on his job and started punching in the numbers without covering the pad with his other hand. Gray saw the first number -6. The second number -8.

At that moment, the other agent put up his own hand, covering the keypad from his view, as he said something to the courier who had been improperly entering his code. Evidently, the second agent was admonishing the first agent for breaching security.

Was this even possible?! He had had three chances to get the codes for access to the warheads and had missed all three!

Gray's legs became weak enough to cause him to slide down the washroom wall and sit on the floor. He put his head in his hands, stunned and disbelieving. He couldn't move.

"Hey, Hunter! Aren't you finished in there?!" came through the door from one of the mechanics.

No, I'm not finished here. Not by a long shot. But don't worry, I'll be back and then I won't fail to finish what I've set out to do. They were just lucky this time.

Chapter 34

" **F**rom the beginning of this case, when we were first called out to the scene of the remains, I felt that we would be able to identify the skeleton and break the case," Detective Barnes declared to his young partner as the two were having a lunch-time sandwich at a downtown café. "It was so unlikely that Cat Moore's skeleton would have ever been found, it became our duty to identify her and seek justice for her."

"I don't know how providential it was, since it took ten years for someone to discover her remains," Detective Enright offered.

"Yeah, it took ten years but look how fortunate the timing was," Detective Barnes argued. "Think about it. Let's say the events that occurred at Miller's dairy farm had happened five years ago. The FBI wouldn't have had the computer imaging technology to animate a likeness that I could recognize. The clay sculptures are blank-looking without expressions, making recognition extremely.

"But more importantly, five years ago you were a county cop. You wouldn't have been a part of this investigation. But now, as a detective, reading the details in Arnstein's statement, you recalled that night when you stopped behind a car with that unique license plate and thought of the name "Einstein" and made the connection. Your story convinced me that we now have a slam-dunk case. And no one else on earth would be able to provide your damning testimony. That's providence, or luck, or fate. Whatever you want to call it."

"You could possibly nail Arnstein with just the print on the clasp, if it belongs to him," suggested the younger detective. "You had said that was conclusive."

"Well, we don't know if it is his print. Besides, even if it is, there are no guarantees that that evidence would hold up. A sharp-witted defense attorney could come up with six different scenarios to explain away his print. 'He reached into her purse for a tissue to wipe away her tears when she was upset about having sex with him,' Detective Barnes dramatically intoned, imitating the imaginary lawyer.

"I still think it's vital evidence when you put it together with the circumstantial evidence we have: the fact that he was the last person to be seen with her, and the statements of other female students that he had a temper and could be nasty if they discouraged his attentions.

"I got the impression from Arnstein that he didn't get along with his own family," Detective Barnes continued. "He had made some disparaging remarks about his father. When I had asked him about his name, he said that his father had cursed him by naming him after the physicist. He thought his father wanted him to grow up to be a genius, too.

"It was his father who bought him that little Miata sports car. That might have been his father's real curse. Undoubtedly, the father ordered those vanity plates for his son's car that read 'E mc2' that will be his undoing at long last," Detective Barnes concluded.

The detective folded his napkin carefully. "What I'd like to know is why. Why did he stop on the short drive back to her dorm and kill her alongside that road? That's what I want to ask him. My guess is he raped her and knew she'd report it. That's why he admitted to having sex with her—just in case we found the body early on and could test the semen.

"Well, let's get back to the station, and see if we can track down that murderer," the older detective said, finishing his cup of coffee. "We're a long way from wrapping this up. After all, he's been on the lam for ten years."

Two hours later, back in the detective's room, Detectives Barnes and Enright had re-read through all the records in Catherine Moore's file. Their review confirmed what they already knew; that the only address in the file for Albert Arnstein was the fraternity house, where he had lived as a student ten years earlier. When Cat had been reported missing, Arnstein had only been detained for questioning, as there was insufficient evidence to show probable cause for an arrest. His room had been searched, by his own consent, but the search had yielded nothing connected with the missing coed. There had never been any further investigation of Mr. Arnstein.

"We'll start with his fraternity," Detective Barnes told his partner, after they had finished with the files and discussed the lack of background information on the suspect. "Those groups are better than the FBI at tracking down people. They somehow manage to maintain an up-to-date mailing list of all their members to run them to ground for pledge requests. I can't imagine that our guy sends in contributions for house renovations, but they might still have his address.

"I can't believe a cold-blooded killer like him wouldn't have committed any other crimes since he left school, but the NCIC didn't have a record on him," Detective Enright commented, referring to the National Crime Information Center computer data base accessible to all law enforcement agencies. "I ran his name this morning, again, trying a couple of different spellings, just in case. No record."

"My guess is that he's not kept his nose clean but he just hasn't been caught yet," the older detective asserted.

"We should get some useful information from the fraternity house," Detective Barnes continued. "I just had another thought. Even if they don't have a current address for Albert, they should have his parents' names and the family's address where they lived when Albert was a student. Albert told us that his father was a 'well-known' scientist, and a professor. It shouldn't be too hard to run him down on a computer search if he's written anything for publication. And what scientist hasn't written something for publication?" he asked, rhetorically.

"One of the other problems we're undoubtedly going to have to deal with if we locate him is that he'll be living outside our jurisdiction," Detective Barnes said. "If we locate him in another state we'll need to enlist the help of local law enforcement to step in and assist us in serving subpoenas and a warrant.

"As you know, the Sixth Amendment guarantees that an accused goes on trial in front of a jury in the state or district where the crime has been committed.

"Best case scenario: we locate him, get his prints that turn out to be a match, and make an arrest. Then he's bound over to us for his trial back here in our county, and we turn the case over to the District Attorney for prosecution. That'll be my greatest pleasure. With our circumstantial evidence, and your eye-witness testimony, we'll get a conviction. Hopefully, the DA will seek the death penalty and the jury will grant it.

"Let's go over to Arnstein's fraternity house and see what we can find out," Detective Barnes said. "I know it's been ten years since the commission of the crime, but I still believe that every minute counts."

Chapter 35

O n Monday morning between 6:45 a.m. and 7:00 a.m., Gray and the other four mechanics and the two assistants who worked in the motor pool, arrived at the check point station. After they showed their photo security badges, they were waved through to the Secure Transportation Building parking lot. It had been a week since Gray's failed attempt at intercepting the keypad codes.

In the pre-dawn darkness, the first mechanic to arrive unlocked the four-bay garage and turned on the lights. After everyone arrived, they put on their navy blue coveralls and stood around for a few minutes, drinking coffee, and talked about last night's game. Finishing the morning ritual, they picked up their assignments for the day's work of prepping nine vehicles, including the three semi-tractor trailers, that would be driven on an extended trip leaving later that morning.

As usual, working from a maintenance check-list, Gray and the other mechanics went over each vehicle, carefully; checked all the systems and fluids, cleaned interiors and exteriors and pumped fuel. Also, as usual, the final inspection was done that was a part of their motor pool routine: checking for any signs of sabotage. None was found.

At 8:00 a.m., the twenty-seven federal agents, on duty today, gathered together for a pre-trip briefing in the meeting room of the courier section to receive instructions from Convoy Commander Berger, assigned to be in charge of this trip.

After a few preliminary remarks, the Commander announced that their destination that day would be the Kings Bay Naval Submarine Base near St. Marys, Georgia. That had been a forgone conclusion for most of the couriers, as they were all aware that many more warheads needing refitting in Amarillo. They assumed that this would be their regular weekly itinerary for at least the next month, unless an emergency intervened that would change the schedule.

Commander Berger consulted his notes. "We will be taking the same route as we have taken on our last two trips to the base: I-40 East to 26 East to I-95 South, taking Georgia exit 3 to highway 40 east to the base. The National Weather Bureau advises that the weather is expected to be clear on our route today. Some road work delays are anticipated on I-95 South between South Carolina exits 33 and 18. You can expect to encounter heavy seasonal traffic as well as the usual truck traffic on I-95 South.

"Our ETA at the base is 1800 hours. All of you have been on one or both of the last two trips so you all know what to expect. We'll be eating after we get to the base and staying overnight there. Tomorrow, after the loading of the shipment, we'll be leaving again for Amarillo at 09:30.

"We'll also be taking the same route from Kings Bay that we took on our most recent trips: I-95 south to 295 around Jacksonville, picking up I-10 West to I-75 North all the way up to Chattanooga, where we pick up 24 West up to Nashville, where we get on I-40 West that we take all the way to Amarillo.

"Prior trips with this routing have gone smoothly and there are several accommodating service areas to stop for refueling and food.

We might repeat on one or two of them. I'll be advising you on your radios when the trucks are pulling over for any reason.

"Okay, people, before I hand out your vehicle assignments, are there any questions?

"Oh, I almost forgot. There's a 40% chance of rain in Georgia, in the Atlanta area, most of the day tomorrow. No thunderstorms, just showers. If it's raining, we'll need to drive slowly when we get there, but I don't expect that we'll have to pull off. I'll update you on the radio when we get near the area.

"Any questions? No? Okay, then. Let's have a good safe trip. I'll see you all in Kings Bay."

Commander Berg then handed out the trip assignments, assigning three agents to each of the vehicles. The two Special Response Force (SRF) teams, and the two Quick Reaction Teams (QRT), were assigned to their specially-equipped armored vehicles.

After the Commander had released them, the agents dispersed to the locker room to get what they needed for five days on the road. The SRF agents, in addition to their personal belongings, had to get their tactical vests, or kits, as they were called when outfitted with ammunition magazines, smoke grenades, metal and plastic handcuffs, chemical lights, first-aid kit, portable radio and the ear microphone. When the agents had gotten their gear together, they drove their own cars over to the motor pool to sign for the government vehicles they were assigned for the trip.

At 9:00 a.m., most of the agents had arrived at the motor pool, were checking out their vehicles and loading in their possessions. Their next stop would be at the armory where all of the agents would pick up their military-style M-4 rifles and magazines. The guns were the shortened version of the more familiar M-16s. The M-4s fired three-round bursts and were effective, with sight mounts, up to 300 yards.

The SRF teams would also sign out additional weaponry and explosives for use in case of a theft of a nuclear weapon. If, such an unprecedented attack would occur, the teams were prepared go in pursuit to capture the attackers and recover the stolen nuclear material.

Before the vehicles left the motor pool area, six of the agents first had to go out back of the garage to enter their security codes in the keypads on the trailers.

George Newsome went over to the first trailer with Ernest Dodd. "I'm missing my kid's Little League game tonight," George commented as he punched in his code, 5-4-8-9, in front of Ernest. "He's getting to be quite a pitcher. I can't believe a kid his age can smoke 'em like he does."

"For Chris' sakes, George," Ernest chided, "you're not supposed to put in your code with someone else watching. Don't you ever follow the rules?" Ernest asked, like a scolding parent. "Now walk away, while I put in my code."

As George walked away, Ernest entered his code, 7-8-6-6. George didn't see it.

Inside, in the locked bathroom, Gray was writing down 5-4-8-9, and 7-8-6-6 as well as G 459 320, the number of the license plate of the trailer. *Got it. And from the two biggest ass holes in the courier section.* Sitting down on the floor again, but this time in relief, he pulled out his cell phone to text Albert. "the eggs are all counted. the bird's flying south."

At 9.30 a.m., silhouetted against the Cumberland Mountains, under a clear azure sky, a convoy of three silver tractor-trailers, nicknamed Alpha, Beta and Omega, and six vans pulled out of the parking lot at the east end of the Y-12 National Security Complex of the Department of Energy. At the end of the drive, they turned left onto Bear Creek Road taking it to Highway 95, and turned left again, continuing on 95 until they came to the entrance to Interstate 40 East. Merging with traffic, the government convoy blended in seamlessly with the stream of SUVs, vans, cars and trucks that were also headed east; to Knoxville, to the Smoky Mountains, or points beyond.

All of the convoy vehicles were unmarked to conceal their identities and purpose. To a sharp eye, the evidence of their ownership was there on their license plates, which bore the phrase, "U.S. Government" in small relief letters above the numbers.

As they traveled on the interstate, the escort vehicles started moving apart to facilitate their surveillance, and to escape notice by the public. Traveling at various rates of speed in front of and behind the trucks, they could maintain a view of the entire assault range of the three semi-tractor trailers.

It was like a game of chess played out on the highway with three eighteen-wheeler "kings" protected in the center with six other players defending by leading, following and circling.

As usual, the vehicles stayed in contact with one another on VHF radios, that operated like walkie-talkies with a range of only a few miles. At Operation Headquarters in Albuquerque, the SECOM (Secure Communication) division followed the convoy's progress on HF radios that operated by radio waves that bounced off the ionosphere and back to earth. AM/FM radios were in the dash boards of each vehicle, for entertainment for the many long hours spent on the road.

The three agents in the scout vehicle would hold a position well ahead of the big trucks to be able to pull off at weigh-in stations to get permission for the trucks to circumvent the scales. The agents in the scout car were the first ones to scan the landscape; detect any road hazards, in particular, or anything suspicious alongside the road. It was all the more challenging when the convoy traveled at night, often on unlit roads. They also were responsible for guiding the convoy vehicles off the roadway into parking and refueling areas for planned stops, or to quickly find roadside parking space for emergency stops.

The two black GMC vans were occupied by three-man Quick Reaction Teams. They traveled in any position during the convoy trip, but were usually in sight of the trucks as they acted as first responders if the shipment came under attack. In such an event, the QRT agents would hit the Klaxton alarm, immediately abandon their vehicles, and deploy towards the trucks with their weapons drawn and attempt to neutralize the attackers.

As they would be engaged in combat, it could be several minutes before they would be able to relay any information to the Tactical Commander in the trail vehicle. Without hearing from the QRT, but aware of the attack, the Tactical Commander would assume that the QRT members were all dead and would call in the other agents for assistance and information.

The SRF team of leader, Rob Woods, with Dana and Dave, were in the purple Ford Econoline E-350 van for the trip. The equally-equipped red E-350 van was assigned to SRF team leader, Owen Knight, with his team members, John McGinnis and Danny Greco. The two SRF vehicles were allowed to travel in any position at any distance from the shipment. At times they would move ahead of the shipment and drive back the opposite direction in their surveillance.

The TC and two other agents were in the trail vehicle. Not having a visual on the trucks, the TC relied on radio communication with the other agents. As appropriate, he would issue orders to both bring in reinforcements after an attack and salvage the cargo, or to deploy the SRF to go on the offensive against the terrorists.

As the morning wore on, the trucks had to slow down to carefully negotiate the tight curves and the un-shouldered sections of I-40 that snaked through the mountains west of Ashville. At times the roadway was hard against sheer limestone walls, and at other times the highway bordered on harrowing drop-offs into deep chasms. Once they cleared the mountains they picked up route 26, where the land leveled off.

In the purple van, after they were on route 26 for a while, Rob asked Dana, "What would you like to eat?" crediting that she might care more about what she ate than he or Dave.

"Oh, I guess a Salade Nicoise with a crisp Chardonnay. You know, the usual."

"Yeah, that's just what I meant, smart ass."

"I know. You meant what side window should we pull up to, and get a big bag of empty calories. Well, I'm going to suggest McDonald's. I actually had a pretty good Caesar salad with grilled chicken there last week. The chicken was warm, with grill marks on it; and not even the creepy fake ones. What was weird was that the salad was the same price with or without the chicken. Their math is a little fuzzy, but the salad was good.

"Okay," Rob agreed. "McDonald's it is. Dave and I won't have any problems finding something suited to our tastes. I'll go in and eat, take a little time, before I come back to sit shot gun. You can too, if you want, Dana. Is that okay, Dave?"

Yeah, sure. I'm not hungry. I'll run in, after you come out. Then I'll take over the wheel and Dana will be in the sleeper."

Through the afternoon they continued their trip without incident, merging onto I-95 some forty miles west of Charleston, and continued down to the St. Marys, Georgia, exit.

It was twenty minutes after six in the evening when the convoy turned into the Franklin Gate at the Kings Bay Naval Base, passing by the memorial of the 'sail' of the submarine, the USS George Bancroft that was displayed on the lawn, surrounded by trim landscaping and gardens. The vehicles continued through the sprawling acreage of the base, past several buildings and parking lots until they came to the port area. There, ahead of them, floating in the bay of the Cumberland Sound, was the USS Manatee, looking like a captured monster from the deep.

"Good timing, Dave" Dana commented, looking at her watch, as they into a parking space. "We have time to get in our rooms and throw a little cold water on our faces before we eat. This was a pretty easy day. Oh, that's right. I didn't have to drive, today."

"We'll all have enough driving for the next leg that's 1,400 miles to Amarillo," Rob said. We might be driving through a lot of rain tomorrow. We should all get a good night's sleep to be prepared for whatever we'll run into, on the road."

Chapter 36

" C ome here and look at this, Pete," Detective Barnes said as he motioned to his partner. Holding up an index card he had taken out of a large file box, he read aloud, 'Arnstein, Albert: Member, Class of 2000. Home Address: Mr. and Mrs. Harold Arnstein, 5234 S. Drexel Blvd., Chicago, Illinois 60615.' "Kind of makes the hairs on your arm stand up, doesn't it? It's the first connection we have to the whereabouts of this cold-blooded killer.

"This is the home where he lived or, perhaps, still lives in comfort, with his parents, near the University of Chicago. All very respectable. All, except for the fact that Albert couldn't take a beautiful young woman on a short car ride without strangling her, and stuffing her body under a tree."

Detective Barnes and Detective Enright were sitting in a basement storage room of the fraternity house where Albert Arnstein had been allowed to freely live out his four years of college.

"I'm not surprised that Albert hasn't made any contributions to his fraternity since he graduated," Detective Barnes mused. "The last date on this card is 2000. Of course, no one who lives in the house now knows anything about him. I think the best way to proceed is to go back to the station and do an Internet search on Harold Arnstein. We'll try Albert, too, but I would bet we'll have a hit on Harold, first."

An hour later, back at their respective desks, Detective Barnes sat in front of his computer and typed in a query on a search engine: "Harold Arnstein, physicist at the University of Chicago." Several results came up. As he checked through the dates on the summaries, he found one article, "How Can the Spherical Torus Concept Contribute to Fusion Energy Development?" that caught his attention.

"Gee, I wish I had time to read the whole article," Detective Barnes cracked to his partner. "This paper was written by a Harold Arnstein, employed by the Department of Energy, National Security Complex, Oak Ridge, Tennessee. How about that? This Internet sure makes our job a lot easier. I don't think there would be more than one Harold Arnstein, who's a physicist. At any rate, we're going to go with this. I didn't come up with anything on an 'Albert Arnstein,' not surprisingly."

"I think I'll hang around while you contact Professor Arnstein," Detective Enright suggested. "I have a feeling we'll soon be taking off for Oak Ridge, Tennessee."

Another Internet inquiry resulted in a phone number for a laboratory at the Oak Ridge complex. Detective Barnes composed his thoughts for a moment, and placed the call.

"I'd like to speak with Dr. Arnstein, please," the Detective asked of whoever answered the laboratory's phone. "This is Detective Laurence Barnes of the Butler County, Ohio, Police Department. I'm calling on official business. Thank you. I'll wait."

After a couple of minutes a gravely-voice came over the wires. "Detective Barnes? May I ask what this is all about? And why are you interrupting my work here at my laboratory?!" Dr. Arnstein demanded of his caller.

"Please excuse the inconvenience, Dr. Arnstein," Detective Barnes responded without sounding apologetic. "Let me ask you first if you have a son, Albert, who graduated from the university here in 2000."

"Why would you want to know that? What is the nature of your business?" Dr. Arnstein continued asking his questions, angrily.

"I'm calling on urgent business in reference to investigating the apparent murder of a young woman named Catherine Moore, who was reported missing in 1999, immediately after she was in the company of Albert Arnstein. Several days ago skeletal remains were found that have been positively identified as being those of the late Ms. Moore."

"I don't know anything about that, and I'm offended that you would contact me in relation to your inquiries," Dr. Arnstein said in clipped response.

"Dr. Arnstein, I need to discuss this matter with your son, and I would appreciate it if you would furnish me with his current address and phone numbers, where I can reach him."

"Detective, I don't want my family involved in your sordid business. I am a nuclear physicist here at the center of the development of nuclear energy. I'm not about to assist you with an investigation of the murder of some college girl of loose morals who got herself in trouble.

"There was no evidence ten years ago that my son had anything to do with this, so there certainly isn't any cause to disturb us now. You are not to contact me again concerning this. Not here or at my home. My wife would be horrified if she were to learn of your indecent request. She has very delicate nerves."

"I'm sorry to hear that, Doctor," the Detective broke in, "but I intend to pursue this matter with or without your help. And I must warn you that if you were to continue to hinder our investigation, you could see yourself facing an Obstruction of Justice charge."

"Don't threaten me, Detective. If you want to see my son, I'm sure you can find him. You'll have to excuse me now. I don't have any more time to waste on this matter. Good day." Dr. Arnstein terminated the conversation without waiting for any response.

"Well, Pete," Detective Barnes smiled at his partner after hanging up the phone. "I think we're pretty close to Albert Arnstein. I feel like I have more understanding into the attitude of old Albert years ago, as well. His father is worried more about his wife's nerves than that his son might have murdered someone.

"He wouldn't give me anything on Albert. Except that he didn't deny being his father. I guess it's back to the Internet, Pete. I'm sure we'll find Albert close by. Probably in Oak Ridge."

"I'm way ahead of you, Larry," Pete said, waving a sheet of computer paper. "When I heard your end of the conversation, I knew this guy was a lost cause. I pulled up the address and phone number of an Albert Arnstein right there in Oak Ridge. It's no more than a five-hour drive through Cincy, south to Lexington, and then down to Knoxville on I-75 most of the way.

"Good work, as usual, Pete." Looking at his watch he observed, "It's pretty late in the afternoon, now. Why don't we plan on leaving tomorrow morning? That'll give us a chance to scope out the area and get a handle on how to proceed. We'll need to bring in the local police on this, anyway. I'll bring the file for them."

"Yeah, sounds good," Detective Enright agreed. "Why don't I meet you at your place at about nine o'clock. Do you think the Professor will tip off our boy?"

"From his statements and his tone, I don't really think he gives a damn about Albert. He sounded a lot more concerned about himself and his wife. I think he figures if his son is in trouble, that's his problem. He doesn't want anything to do with it or him. Let's just hope he's around and we don't have to go looking for him."

Chapter 37

Albert stared hard at the text message on his cell phone. "the eggs are all counted. the bird's flying south." *He did it,* he thought. *Fucking Gray finally got it right after screwing it up last week.*

Albert was now in the position of having to rely on Gray and his followers to do their jobs to put his own plan into effect. It was hard to admit, even to himself, that he needed those idiots to pull off his brilliant scheme. But they would become disposable after the warhead was safely in his possession.

Still holding onto his cell phone, he waited five minutes until he called a familiar GPS modem number to retrieve a message that would be just as significant as Gray's message. Looking at the display on his screen, his lips curled back with perverse pleasure as he realized where the duffel bag and its owner must be at that moment. He knew that the coordinates were east of Oak Ridge. He'd wait another twenty minutes and call the modem again, to be sure they were on their way to Kings Bay. He wanted to make certain that she was going to be on the scene of the assault and the theft of the nuclear warhead.

It was her job to protect the nuclear weapons from being stolen. He wanted her to know how miserably she had failed and how easily he had triumphed. Oh, yes. She had to survive long enough to realize that she had brought this on herself. She had to know that she was the target.

After Gray and the three stooges helped him steal the bomb, he would take control of the operation. He wouldn't immediately reveal to the public his responsibility for the mass destruction. It would be more entertaining to sit by and watch the couriers' and the FBI's feeble efforts to investigate.

Muslim extremists would surely be blamed, and any Muslims in the area would be brought in for questioning. There wouldn't be any evidence to link *him* to the crime. At some point he would get the message to Dana that he was behind it all, and that her threats to him were the cause. Then he'd confront her and take out his revenge. She would be begging for her life this time around. But by the time he got through with her, she would be begging to die.

Right now, he had to contact the others to prepare for the assault. They would meet at the trailers this evening and arm themselves from Gray's arsenal of assault weapons and rocket launchers. Tomorrow morning they would leave for the exit north of Atlanta where the nuclear shipment trucks would stop. It would be their last stop.

He called the modem again. This time he checked the coordinates on his laptop. Then he checked the modem number on the truck. Why hadn't he just done that in the first place? The coordinates were the same, and further east on I-40. Game on.

At eight o'clock that evening, Albert and Henry drove out in the country to Gray's trailer to work out the final details of the plan, and to pack the vehicles. They would travel down to Georgia the next morning in two vehicles; Gray's truck and Henry's car. Gray had already loaded the truck with several M-16s with high-capacity 30-round magazines.

Albert had his laptop to decode the PAL box on the warhead. When the authorization code had been deciphered, Albert would set a timer and they'd drive back to the trailers to wait it out. The detonation would occur when they were safely home. The destruction should reach as far as Atlanta to the south and Chattanooga to the north.

"I never thought I'd see somethin' I did that would be shown on the TV," Hubie commented as they talked about the attack.

"CNN will be right there to cover it," Gray said, "if the television station's still there," he added.

"Let's just worry about pulling it off," Albert interjected, "before we worry about the media coverage. Let's go over our battle plan.

"We've all got ear pieces and mics for radio communication. Use them them so we know where you are and what's happening at all times. Don't do anything without telling me in your mic.

"Henry and I will be parked right off the exit to identify the vehicles and get the license plates. Then I'll radio Gray to set off the charge two minutes before the vehicles get to the service center. We don't want to knock out the agents before they get to the station, or give them a chance to park before they know something's wrong and can get out of the vehicles. The timing is critical. We'll time the drive from the exit to the station a few times to pick the exact mark on the pavement where the remotes should be activated.

"Gray will be behind trees across the street from the station to pick off one or more agents who may be able to crawl out of the trucks or vans after they pull in. Hubie and Dirk—you'll be behind the billboard next to the station to fire off rounds to help out Gray.

"After all the agents have been taken out, Dirk will drive the tractor from behind the billboard to the truck that has the license plate number G459 320, and wait for Gray. Write that fucking number on your arms so you don't go to the wrong trailer, for Chris' sakes.

"We'll all be at the trailer by then and Gray will drive his truck up right next to the shipment trailer. Then he'll enter the codes into the keypad. The door will be opened and four of us go up onto the trailer while Dirk operates the tractor and the utility scoop. We'll need to roll one of the tubes so that Dirk can pick it up and upend it to get out one of the warheads.

"This is something we won't be able to practice so be ready to help steer, or lift, or whatever we have to do to get the warhead onto the scoop. Then Dirk will drop the warhead onto the truck bed, and Hubie and Henry will be ready to cover it up with the tarp. I'll be there, in Henry's car, to lead us all to the shed up in the hills. Make sure that you drive carefully so you're not stopped by some fucking cop out to make his quota. I wouldn't want to hear Hubie's explanation for why there was a nuclear warhead in the back of the truck.

"Once in the shed, I'll connect my laptop with the port in the PAL box, and take it from there. The rest of you will be on the lookout for anyone who might come nosing around. Anyone does; don't ask questions. Just take them out. Use your sights to shoot from long range.

"I'll decode the box to arm the warhead and we'll get out of there. We'll probably all leave together, depending on what happens. You'll take my orders at all times. I want that clearly understood. Don't do anything without telling me and do everything I tell you to do.

"We leave here tomorrow morning at eleven o'clock. We'll stop for lunch at a truck stop just north of Chattanooga. They get new business all the time. No one will pay any attention to us. Wear non-descript clothes, without anything identifiable on your person. Henry, you're going to wear what you wore on our surveillance trip. You got that?"

"Yes, I remember. I still think it would be better if we dressed in disguise. I could get a few costumes together. I was thinking of false beards and overalls; to look Amish."

"Henry, for Chris' sakes, we've been over this. I don't want to see any unusual clothes or hear any accents or conversation about traveling as a sports team or some fucking thing. We don't want to attract any attention. Just keep your mouths shut. Talk about the weather, if you have to talk.

"We should get to the coordinates by two o'clock. Gray will go rent the tractor and attachment and bring it back on the truck and park it behind the billboard. Then we'll go over the timing and positions of everyone for when the convoy comes.

"Anyone want to say something?"

"It doesn't sound like you're taking any part in the action," Gray observed, to Albert.

"I'm only detonating the fucking warhead, not to mention that the whole thing is my idea," Albert countered testily. "What's your problem? You're the military genius here. I thought you'd enjoy blowing everyone away."

"I don't enjoy it. It's what's necessary," snarled Gray. "At the very least we'll have fifteen agents who could potentially make it outside the vehicles to draw their weapons; maybe more who come to the station. All five of us need to be ready to fire on them. That's one problem I have. The other is I just want to know what's going to happen after we detonate the bomb. You have something in mind?"

"Yeah, I've thought about it once or twice," Albert replied, snidely. "We're going to cool it right here for a few days while the FBI and the agents screw around. When the time is right, we'll put out an anonymous statement to help them figure out why the convoy was attacked. We'll include your grievances against the government and the military. Whatever you want. The country will be in total chaos. We'll just enjoy it for a while. Then we'll see." *You won't be around to worry about it, fool,* Albert thought to himself.

"Albert, are you sure no one will be able to track us to the shed or here? Dirk asked. "The agents could call for help, or something."

"There's no way," Albert said dismissively. "The agents at the station will either be dead or unconscious. We won't take time to check. If anyone else is in the station we need to take them out. It's impossible to predict everything that might happen, but if anyone comes after us, we'll shoot them. It's as simple as that.

"Okay, if that's all, let's turn in. Be prepared for whatever might happen," Albert finished.

Chapter 38

"The trucks are taking Exit 73 for a lunch break and shift change. Do you copy?" the disembodied voice asked over the VHF in the console. It was twelve noon.

Picking up the VHF mic, Dana keyed in and responded, "Mobile 7. Copy that."

"We'll get off at the same exit," Rob advised from the shotgun seat. "There's a little place with really good hotdogs. Is that okay for our stop and shift change?"

"Sure," Dana agreed. "Dave, did you hear the Command Vehicle say that the trucks are changing at exit 73?" Dana called back to the sleeper compartment. "Do you want to eat? Rob's into hot dogs. Are you there? We haven't heard from you for a while."

"Huh? Oh, sorry," Dave answered. "I was just reading this dumb book I brought along for my down time. Some of these authors really get off on explosions and mayhem. I'm just at the part where they're blowing up New York City. Of course, no one's around to stop them.

Anyway, I heard the transmission, and you. I had a big breakfast. I'll just use the restroom, get a snack and relieve Rob. I hope they have some decent coffee. I feel like I need a jolt before I drive."

*   *   *

"This is Exit 305, where we get off, Henry," Albert said, as pulled off the interstate onto a down ramp. "Hit the stop watch when I come to the stop sign at the highway. Just a minute, okay, now, hit it! And tell me when two minutes is up. Exactly two minutes. We need to find the spot where Gray should set off the remote charges that's two minutes travel time to when they'll pull into the gas station."

"Will do, Colonel Albert!" Henry replied, as they took the turn. "It's 27 seconds, now."

"Never mind telling me all the seconds, Henry. Just tell me when we hit two minutes. Do just what I say. Don't improvise."

Coming from the north, Albert had driven seven miles south to the next exit and had come back to duplicate the route the convoy vehicles would be taking. A light rain was falling on the windshield; just enough to need the intermittent wipers.

"Your god-damn wiper blades are squeaking!" Albert groused. "Does anything work right on this car? We don't need this fucking rain, either."

"You're just getting nervous, Colonel Albert," Henry said soothingly, after they pulled in the service center. "You'll do great when . . . two minutes!" he cried out, interrupting himself.

"Okay, this isn't any good. We've been here in the station at least thirty seconds. All of the agents would have had a chance to exit their vehicles. We have to add thirty seconds on to the time when we tell Gray to set off the charges. We're going to get back on the interstate going south, turn around and come back north and do this all over again. While we're here, can you see anything of those assholes, Dirk and Hubie, who are supposed to be hidden behind the billboard?"

"No, I don't see them. Do you want me to call out to them?"

"Hell no, Henry!" Albert said, cuffing him on the back of the head. "This is serious business! We're in a dangerous situation here. People will be shooting at us if they get the chance, unless we can take them out first. We don't want to attract attention or give away our positions to anyone! We need to be absolutely perfect in how we carry this off, if you want us to live. Now, just do as I say, okay?"

"I understand," Henry said, quietly. "Please don't be upset with me."

"All right, all right. Just do what I say from now on."

Fifteen minutes later the dark blue Plymouth Neon, traveling northbound, was coming to the same exit. This time, as Albert just started down the long ramp, he said to Henry, "Hit the stop watch now!" Then, at the bottom of the ramp, where the interstate passed overhead, he stopped to look for traffic. Seeing none, he turned right and continued northeast for half a block, and turned right again into the station and pulled up to a gas pump.

"Two minutes! We did it!" Henry called out excitedly, just as Albert had turned off the ignition.

"Okay, at the top of the ramp is the spot where the charges have to go off," Albert said. "With the carbon monoxide coming full-blast into the cabins for two minutes, that should take out most of the agents. They could take up to thirty seconds longer to get to the station, and it'll still work. Two minutes is the earliest they'll know something's wrong and open their doors. Some might be able to get out and Gray and the others will be ready to take them out from their hidden positions.

"Speaking of Gray, we have to go find him and see that he got the right tractor and attachment. If he's screwed up again, we're dead. But first, we've got to pump some gas so we aren't attracting attention just sitting here. The god-damned rain is getting worse, too."

"I'll get out and pump the gas," Henry offered, already getting out of the car.

After Henry had finished fueling and had tightened down the gas cap, he motioned to Albert, who drove off, and parked the car near the billboard. Exiting the car and looking to see that no one was around, he waved Henry over to follow him around the side of the billboard. Hubie and Dirk were standing there, soaking wet, looking miserable. Hubie looked even more pathetic hanging onto a bulging long black canvas bag.

"Where's Fordham?" Albert yelled, to be heard through the rain.

"He's gettin' the tractor, like you done tole him to," Dirk said defensively. "I just heard from 'im. He said he got it and he'll be here in twenty minutes."

"Okay!" Albert continued, yelling, "Let's get out of the rain, and dry off inside, for Chris' sakes! We've still got a couple of hours before the convoy vehicles get here. And bring the bag with you!"

In the front area of the large interior was a mini mart comprised of two aisles filled mostly with snack foods. Several coolers occupied an end wall. Behind a counter off to the right side, a young woman took money for purchased food and cash payments for gas and diesel. Behind her was shelving stocked with cigarette cartons and other tobacco products.

In back of the mini mart, on the left, was a small fast-food franchise. In the middle, at the rear of the space, was a free-standing station offering gourmet-brand coffee. Completing the back area, to the right, were the restrooms.

About a dozen people were now inside the center. A couple people were in the mini mart and several people were seated at the rear tables, eating hamburgers. Albert led his group to the back to the food service area and coffee set-up. As the four new arrivals paused near the dining space to look around at their options, Hubie was holding the black canvas bag on its end.

"Hubie, put the bag down the long way," Albert hissed, out of the side of his mouth. "or do you want to just tell everybody here that you've got a couple of M-16s with you?"

"No, I don't wanna tell 'em that," Hubie complained.

Albert, his eyes like slits and his jaw clenched, stepped even closer to Hubie to get in his face. "Go sit at that table in the far corner and put the fucking bag down next to the wall—the *long* way." Then turning to the others he said, "Henry, go with him and throw your jacket over the bag. Dirk, you and I will go to the counter and get a few hamburgers and something to drink."

"I don't want onions on mine!" Henry called back, on his way to the table. Albert shook his head, mumbling something inaudible, as he and Dirk walked over to the order station.

* * *

"Well, here comes the rain," John commented, unnecessarily, to Danny who was sitting in the shotgun seat. The rain was suddenly splashing the windshield in big splotches from a cloudburst. John turned on the wipers to a fast speed. "Good thing the traffic has eased up now that we're just a few miles out of Atlanta. Look at that dumb fuck passing us on the inside. He must be going eighty miles an hour. Where's the highway patrol when you need them?"

Just then the VHF radio crackled into life and a voice came on saying, "the trucks are pulling off at exit 227 to kick a tire. That's a five-minute stop."

"Mobile 8. Copy that," John responded into the VHF mic. "Who was that in the CC's vehicle? He has to tell us it'll take five minutes?" John asked.

"Sounded like George Newsome," Danny suggested. "How would you like to drive a run like this with George? That's way too long to hear about his amazing life and his importance in the Gulf War. Didn't he say that he was the Aide de Camp to Lieutenant General Waller?"

"Yeah. I think George took credit for the 'left hook' strategy that took the army behind the enemy forces of Iraq into Kuwait to end the war in four days."

"No, I think George always had the 'left and took what he could' strategy," Danny countered. "He's never around for the heavy lifting.

Anyway, we're four miles behind the shipment, so we should be okay for their five minute stop."

"In this rain, I'm only doing sixty," John said. "But look, you can see it's already lighter up ahead."

"Speaking of doing the heavy lifting, Danny, how are you coming with that patio you were putting in? Didn't you get a ton of bricks delivered?"

"A ton?" Danny asked, as if in disbelief. "There are only 300 bricks in a ton, John. That's enough bricks for like a 4'x 8' patio; hardly worth the effort. I got more like four tons of bricks and I'm still preparing the fucking base. You try leveling out clay mixed with rocks.

"I'm just lucky Maggie didn't want a garden there. I can cheat quite a bit with the sand that goes down first. Then the bricks go on top and you can level them in the sand. It should look good, but it's a lot of work. Maggie found the instructions in some magazine as a 'weekend project.' I've been on it for a month."

"Just don't mention it to Claire, if you see her," John said. "Our concrete pad is just fine. I hose it down a couple of times during the summer and she's happy. She doesn't need to get any ideas."

*　　*　　*

The rain had tapered off by four o'clock in the afternoon as Gray was sitting in his parked truck on an abandoned gravel drive across the street from the service center. Overgrown bushes along the drive screened his truck from the road. He had everything in place, ready to go: cell phone, remote controls, walkie-talkie radio with an ear piece, and two M-16 rifles, fitted with scopes and equipped each with several 30-round magazines.

"They should be a half-hour away," Albert's voice came over his ear piece. "Are you ready?"

Gray picked up his mic and answered, "Yeah, Albert, I'm ready. Don't worry about me, okay? You and Henry just do your jobs, to describe the vehicles, and catch their tags, so I can match them up with my remotes. There'll be some vehicles that don't have a charge installed, and some of the wired vehicles won't be stopping. Just stay there for five minutes after the trucks come off the ramp to give me a heads up. Dirk, Hubie and I can take care of any unwired vehicles once they get to the gas station."

"I'm way ahead of you," Albert said, snidely. "I've got a vantage point above the ramp where I can see them with the binoculars, just as they exit. I've got the plate numbers listed, but I'll recognize the vehicles before I can see the numbers."

Hubie and Dirk were sitting by the small tractor they had parked behind the billboard. They each had an M-16 rifle with eight 30-round magazines, apiece. In his ear piece Dirk heard Albert say, "We're within a half hour. Are you both ready?"

Dirk radioed back. "Yeah, I'm ready. Hubie is too. But I've got a little job to do first, inside the mini mart, like we talked about. Most of the customers have left. I'll take care of the rest in a few minutes."

At 5:25, Dirk bolted across the parking area and crashed into the mini mart with his M-16 rifle. Entering the store he leveled the gun and swept the area. Women's screams were heard by Hubie, outside, behind the billboard.

"Hands up! Everybody put your fucking hands up in the air where I can see them, and you won't get hurt!" Dirk ordered the few people in the store who all looked terror-stricken at the outburst.

"You! Shut up!" Dirk pointed the rifle at the woman who had screamed, who was now choking on her sobs. An older man, near her, put a hand on her shoulder to quiet her.

Looking back at the restaurant Dirk shouted, "You, behind the counter back there, come out with your hands up! And you with the fry basket! Everyone get the fuck out here, goddamn it, or I'll shoot, I swear to God!" Two young men and a grey-haired woman emerged from the restaurant with their arms up. Their hands were shaking.

Turning to the stricken young woman behind the counter, he barked, "Unlock the cash register or I'll blow your head off! C'mon! C'mon!"

Bug-eyed and shocked, the girl seemed frozen, but after a couple of seconds, she mechanically opened the cash register. Dirk swung around again with the barrel of the gun following his gaze. Everyone still had their hands up. The crying woman was now staring at the ceiling, talking to herself.

"Okay, one at a time, where I can see you, take out your cell phone and wallet and throw them on the floor. Everyone else keep your hands up.

"You, mother fucker!" he shouted to the older man in the mini mart. "We'll start with you. Throw them down!" The man complied. Dirk went around the room and each one, in turn, threw down his wallet and phone as instructed. Then he pointed his gun at the still-sobbing woman.

"Where's your phone and wallet, bitch?!"

"They're in my purse! My purse is over there on the floor!" the woman's voice rose, as she was now near hysteria. "Please don't kill me! I have three children! Please don't kill me!" she wailed, again.

Dirk leveled the rifle at her and fired three rounds into her, point blank. Hitting her in center mass, her body collapsed heavily against the coolers, breaking the glass.

Gasps came from the others. Without hesitation, Dirk swung around, and started firing from left to right until he had emptied his magazine, and the other five people were taken down in the hail of bullets that also hit the display cases and shelving.

The air became thick with the smell of gunfire. Boxes had tumbled from the shelves and cans rolled in the aisles. After a few seconds, it became eerily quiet. There was no more movement.

Dirk walked over to the cash register, having to step over the young clerk whose body was wedged in the narrow space between the counter and the cigarette cases. She still wore a look of terror on her face, with her eyes staring out sightlessly. Dirk went about his business of cleaning the bills out of the register.

Taking a plastic bag from the store's supply, he went around the room picking up the cell phones and wallets, putting everything in the bag. *Might as well make a little on the side*, he thought, as he made for the door.

*   *   *

Five minutes later, at 5:35 in the afternoon, a light grey van, with U.S. Government plates, took exit 305 off the interstate. Ernest Middleton was driving the scout car, and had contacted the Command vehicle that he would be checking out the exit for the trucks to follow. They had stopped here two weeks ago and found it was a good place for a dinner stop and shift change. Access and egress for the large rigs had been easy with the generous parking areas.

Ernest got to the stop sign at the bottom of the long curving ramp where he checked for traffic. Nothing was coming. He turned right to drive the short distance to the service center to wait for the trucks and the Command Vehicle. He wouldn't leave before he had made sure that they had safely arrived and that everything was okay.

That was his plan, but as he turned into the service center he couldn't keep his head up, and collapsed on the steering wheel while his foot was still on the gas pedal.

"Ernest, what the hell are you doing!? You're gonna hit that gas pump!" Toby shouted from the shotgun seat, shaking Ernest's right shoulder, to alert the nodding driver. No response. "Oh, my God!" Toby just managed to yank the steering wheel to the right to avoid hitting the pump and causing a conflagration. The van kept moving forward until it rammed into a concrete abutment and came to a stop.

Toby sat there trying to make sense out of things. He couldn't wake the sleeping Ernest. He felt like he could fall asleep, himself. Jerry, in the back, hadn't made a sound. Toby tried to resist trying to resist falling into a black hole that he felt himself sinking into, but he kept falling further. After a minute he finally relaxed into the darkness, as it swallowed him.

* * *

"All three agents in the light gray Ford have been neutralized. I think they're dead," Gray radioed Albert. "That was the scout car that's always first. Others will be here in a few minutes. Jesus Christ. They look like they all fell under a trance."

* * *

At 5:46 the Alpha tractor-trailer came down the exit to the stop sign, waited a moment to look for traffic, and seeing none, turned right. "What's was that?!" Mike called out from behind the wheel. "There was a popping sound under the hood! There's some smoke, too! Charlie, didn't you hear it?" Charlie sat silent, with his head down.

"What's the matter with you?! Wake up! We've got to get to the service station and get out of the cab! I think there's some kind of toxic gas in the cabin! We've got to get out! Charlie! Jerry!"

Pulling into the truck parking area and stopping, Mike opened his door and dropped down to the oily concrete, and fell over onto his left side. He lay there, too dizzy to move, gasping for air. After taking a few deep breaths, his head was cleared enough that he was able to get up on his knees. He rocked backward and forward several times until he had the momentum to start to crawl around the front of the cab. He had to get to the other side to open the door to save Charlie and Jerry.

Around on the passenger's side, he had to hold onto the side-view mirror for support, to lift one foot to get up on the step, and then the other. He was wobbly, but standing, with his hand on the door handle, when a shot rang out. The bullet whizzed into his brain and his body twisted and jerked in mid air, spinning around until he flopped heavily onto his back, on the concrete. Blood oozed out of the side of his head, pooling a little, and then it stopped.

Right then, the Beta truck pulled into the parking area on the left side of the Alpha truck. The driver, Billy Sheldon pointed at the first truck, "What's going on!?" he asked Jake, sitting shotgun. Jake had his head down. "Why is their cab door standing open? Get the guns!" he shouted back to Sean in the sleeper. No answer. Drawing his Sig-Sauer semiautomatic, Billy opened his door and stepped down. Suddenly, he felt so nauseous he had to sit down. He had slumped against the cab's front tire when a shot screamed past his head.

"Jesus Christ! We're under attack!" Rolling over to get to the safety of the front of the cab he looked around but didn't see anyone by the mini mart station. He looked over at the billboard to the right of the building. That's when he saw a long-haired bearded man with an M-16 come from behind the billboard.

From a seated position and feeling ill, Billy was still able to fire a round from his Sig. Unfortunately his shot went wide. He heard the bullet hit the billboard; and that was the last thing he heard. At that moment Hubie blasted a hole in Billy's chest. For a couple of seconds red blood spurted from the gaping wound and then stopped, leaving just a crimson puddle on his light blue shirt.

"Good shot, Hubie!" Gray said, excitedly into the shooter's ear piece. "That second truck! That's the one!"

"Dirk!" Gray shouted. "Drive the tractor around to the back of the truck! I'll be there in a minute!" Albert had just radioed that another truck and a government van following it, were starting down the ramp and he had to set off the remotes.

"Bingo!" Gray said aloud, for the fourth time, and "Again!" he said, as two more charges were set off, discharging blasts of carbon monoxide in the exiting tractor-trailer and the van.

As Gray had started up the truck and was moving to the end of the drive, he caught sight of the third tractor-trailer. He could make out that the driver was Ted Lambert. As Gray watched, he saw Ted look over at the parked trucks, with their cab doors open, and bring the truck to a stop in the roadway. Ted's door opened but he was no longer visible. Gray figured he must be on the step and using the open door for cover.

Gray turned off his ignition and picked up his M-16 from the back seat. He jumped out of the truck on the passenger's side and peered over the hood. The tractor trailer was still sitting there. Still, no Ted. He could see that the agent in the shotgun seat was slumped over against the window. He took a chance that Ted was similarly impaired and rushed the truck, firing at the space between the open door and the cab. He had fired several rounds before he saw Ted fall forward out of the cab and land on the roadway.

Gray ran back to his truck, got in and started across the street just as a dark gray van approached. The vehicle stopped at the station's driveway. Both front doors and the back door opened and three agents jumped out with their M-4 rifles, running around to the far side of their vehicle. *They heard the gunfire before they had been overcome with the gas,* Gray surmised.

Stopping the truck, Gray radioed Hubie and Dirk. "Three agents, armed with M-4s, on the other side of the dark grey van. Hubie, go around the back of the gas station to come out the other side where you can blindside them. Dirk, come around on this side. I'll drive my truck next to the van to give us cover. You go around the front of the vehicles and I'll go around the rear!"

Gray drove the truck across the street, keeping his head low and stopped his truck near the dark grey van. Several rounds were fired from behind the agents' van, hitting Gray's side door. Getting out of the passenger side, with his M-16, he waved Dirk over, signaling him to keep low. Gray stood up and returned fire in the direction of the van.

Gray caught a glimpse of Hubie coming around from the back of the station and fired several more rounds to keep the agents' attentions. More gunfire was returned from the agents, hitting Gray's mirror and side window. Dirk started moving around the front of the truck to get a better angle and fired several rounds. One of the agents screamed, "I've been hit!"

Gray then saw Hubie move closer to the van, firing rounds. Dirk moved around to the front of the agents' van, firing one round after another at the other side of the van until there was no more return fire coming from the agents. Gray stood up looking at Hubie and Dirk for confirmation that the three men had been taken out. Hubie nodded and started walking over to Gray.

Dirk went back behind the billboard and started up the rented tractor. Putting the front scoop in the 'up' position he was able to easily maneuver the machine around the billboard and drive it over to the back of the Beta truck.

"Albert! Where the hell are you?!" Gray bellowed over the walkie-talkie. "We've secured the station, and neutralized all the agents and I'm ready to open the door to the shipment. Do you think you and Henry could help us?"

"It was your idea for us to wait five minutes after the last truck! I haven't seen anyone else. You've got another vehicle that's wired. What about that one?"

"I'll just set it off," Gray responded. "We don't have time to fuck around. Someone in the gas station or an agent might have gotten off a call to 911. Just get over here."

"We'll be there in two minutes! Put in the codes. You can do that without our help," Albert had to add.

Gray went to his truck and picked up the last remote. Setting it off, he said, "Bingo!" one more time.

Calmly walking back to his companions by the truck, Gray flipped up the cover to the keypad. He was about to enter the codes when he saw movement out of the corner of his left eye. An agent from the dark van was moving along on his stomach around the back of the vehicle, towards Gray. Going to his truck, Gray picked up his rifle, raised it and pointed it at the unsuspecting agent.

Gray called out, "Hey, you! Where do you think you're going?" The courier stopped and rolled under the van. "Nice try," Gray sneered, as he fired several rounds under the van. Bending down, Gray saw the still-outstretched arm of the very dead courier.

Walking back to the Beta truck with its opened keypad, Gray entered the memorized codes, 5-4-8-9 and 7-8-6-6. "Open Sesame." Lifting the latch he was able to open the back doors of the trailer just as Albert and Henry drove up. Getting out of the car and joining the others, all five men stood there in awe of the sight of dark grey tubes stacked and tied down.

"C'mon, let's get a move on!" Gray exclaimed. "Did you see that sensor light go on in the trailer? You can bet that a silent alarm is going out alerting their headquarters that the doors are open. We've been here over seven minutes, already! Henry, cut the tie-downs with this," Gray said, reaching into the back of the truck and pulling out a large steel cutter. "This is specially made to cut heavy straps."

The ties gave way as Henry cut through with the over-sized shears. "Oh, good! Henry exclaimed. "Which one are we going to take?"

"How about the one on top?!" Gray scoffed.

While Dirk lowered the scoop, the other four men rolled one of the tubes enough to rest atop the attachment. Shifting the long tube down towards its open end, a warhead slid out landing just inside the door of the trailer. Not taking time to marvel at that accomplishment, Dirk dipped the scoop as the others rolled the warhead into the open trough and Dirk pulled the attachment up in the air and swung it around to the back of Gray's truck where he dropped the weapon neatly in the cargo space.

"Son of a bitch! Son of a bitch!" Gray repeated, joyfully, while Hubie and Henry cheered like kids watching the half back run in for a score.

"Henry and Hubie, get the tarp over the weapon and let's get the hell out of here!" Albert ordered. "Dirk, drive the tractor over behind the billboard. We'll just leave it here. Who the fuck cares? They can't trace it to us."

Hubie and Henry managed to get the large blue cover over the warhead and tied it down with some ropes that Gray had in the back of his cab for the purpose. "All set!" Henry said. "No one would know there's a bomb under this!" he boasted.

"Not unless you tell them, genius!" Gray groused. "The truck already looks suspicious with a bunch of bullet holes in the door and a shattered side mirror and window."

"Okay, get in the car, Henry, and let's take off!" Albert ordered. "Gray, you three just follow me. We'll be there in less than twenty minutes, without speeding. Everyone just look cool."

The old blue Neon and the dark green truck drove away from the scene of murder and mayhem, without a second glance. Twenty minutes later, on a narrow gravel road, they came to a couple of ruts that seemed to lead nowhere. The Plymouth stopped and waved the truck on ahead to turn onto those ruts. The two vehicles then bounced along the uneven terrain, past a stand of oak trees that had probably once encircled a farm house, until they came to a sagging, weathered shed. Henry jumped out of the car and walked over to the truck.

"This is the place! It's nice, isn't it? I'll just get the doors open and show it to you. You'll like it."

"Henry, you're not some fucking realtor!" Albert shouted through his open car window. "Just open the damn doors." Following instructions, Henry pulled back the two large barn doors that scraped over the tall grasses. The shed's interior was then made visible by the shafts of daylight that entered through the spaces left by several missing boards.

It was one room about twelve feet across by twenty feet deep that was open to the rafters with a hardened dirt floor. As Henry waved, Gray drove the truck inside and parked it near the end of the space and Albert followed and stopped, leaving several feet behind the truck. Everyone got out of the two vehicles without speaking. Even Henry seemed sobered by the occasion.

Finally Albert spoke. "All right. We don't have any time to waste. Other agents are going to arrive at the service center and send out the alarm. We need to get the tarp off and get that warhead off the truck so I can connect my laptop to its computer and try decoding its authorization to fire."

Gray, Hubie and Dirk obediently got up on the truck bed, tore off the tarp and rolled the cone-shaped weapon to the edge of the truck bed. Henry and Albert stood below to guide it down. Tipping the weapon off the steel bed, it fell only a foot before it landed heavily on its base. There was a shudder felt on the dirt floor as the eight hundred pounds made contact.

The five men stood back, gaping at it, as though it could blow up right then and there.

"Henry, get my laptop in the car," Albert ordered. "You can identify the parts of this PAL for me. The rest of you need to give us absolute silence. If I can't decode this, the most damage it can cause is if it falls over on someone's foot."

Henry had brought over the laptop and was pulling the wiring over to plug an end into the port in the PAL box. "It's a CAT F PAL," Henry said, matter-of-factly.

"You know that?!" asked Albert, in amazement. "What's that, in English?"

"It's a Category F, Permissive Action Link box," Henry said slowly. "It is activated by a 12-digit key. That's all there is to it." He looked at Albert as though he had told him how to open a can of peas.

"Twelve digits," repeated Albert. "I can do this. I can fucking do this."

Chapter 39

"This is good police work," Chief Croft said, looking up, after reading through the file Detective Barnes had furnished him. The two Ohio detectives had been in the Chief of Police's office in Oak Ridge, Tennessee, for the past hour and a half. They had met with the Chief to explain their need to apprehend of one of the residents of his jurisdiction, and to seek his office's assistance in that objective. After giving the Chief a summary of the case, the Chief scanned through the file, reading more carefully through significant portions of the record.

The Chief was a heavyset man of about sixty years of age, whose unlined round face was accented with clear blue eyes behind wire-rimmed glasses, and a grey clipped mustache. The man's corpulence attested to his sedentary administrative duties, while his darting eyes and deliberative speech gave evidence of his keen intellect.

"I'm particularly impressed with your own identification of the victim," the Chief said, addressing Detective Barnes. "I haven't seen, first-hand, the new FBI technology of three-dimensional computer imaging done from a skull. Amazing you could recognize her, when you never even knew her in life."

"Yeah. I was a hundred percent sure. Not officially, of course. But I wasn't surprised when the ME confirmed the identification with the dentals."

"So," the Chief went on, smoothing his mustache, "what you've got for evidence is a partial fingerprint on the clasp of the deceased' purse and a ten-year old recollection of Detective Enright, here, from when he was a teenager." The Chief's skepticism was thinly disguised.

Detective Barnes responded, "That's a fingerprint on an object thrown on top of a dead woman, and the indelible memory of a unique license plate, by a professional detective, that contradicts the suspect's statement. We wouldn't be down here unless we believed we had enough to detain the suspect for an interrogation, pursuant to an arrest."

"Of course he doesn't have to cooperate," Chief Croft said, warily. "At the very least, you'll need to get his fingerprint that's a match, to obtain a warrant, don't you think?"

"It's certainly an important piece of the case, I'd say," Detective Barnes agreed. "It would make the District Attorney happy if we had the forensics to back up the circumstantial."

"Well, if you want Mr. Arnstein for questioning, I'll send Officer Brady with you. Brady can bring him in to the station for you. Mr. Arnstein will undoubtedly lawyer up before he's willing to say anything. I see his father is the head of a laboratory at Y-12. The senior Mr. Arnstein will want to protect his reputation, and, hopefully, his son."

"At this point, let's just bring him in for questioning," Detective Barnes suggested. "I'm not planning on telling him about the print on the clasp. He might accept a cup of coffee or soda, where we can print him, so I wouldn't want to tip him off. He wouldn't think it possible that he left a print behind.

"I think we'll pick up on 'consciousness of guilt' by his demeanor after revealing to him that we found and identified the bones. He never expected that to happen. Anyway, I don't want to go back to Ohio without confronting him. Pete and I will go grab a bite to eat and come back. In case Albert's at work, I want to be sure to give him enough time to get home."

"Okay, fine. Just come back to the station and ask for Officer Brady," the Chief said, standing up and stepping out from behind his desk. "He'll be expecting you. And good luck, Detective Barnes, Detective Enright," he continued, shaking hands with both men. "It's an interesting case. If he's guilty, this would be a great conclusion. No department is willing to settle for a cold case."

An hour later, Detectives Barnes and Enright were seated in the squad car driven by Officer Brady. A few minutes into the ride, the officer pulled up and stopped in front of a three-story apartment building covered in the cemestos boards typical of its era. "This is it," Officer Brady announced. "This is the address you have. Let's go see."

"It looks pretty decrepit," Detective Enright observed. "I would have thought the son of a physicist, and named for Einstein, at that, would live in a place a little more upscale."

"I'm glad he lives in a dump, Pete," Detective Barnes commented. "Why don't you go around the side of the building and find the fire escape. I think we'd better cover any means of escape."

"Sure. I'll stay down here. Just call if you need me."

The front door was unlocked allowing the two lawmen to simply walk in. "Not much security, either," Detective Barnes noted. "Here are all the mailboxes in the foyer. Looks like we can find his apartment, easily enough.

"Right here," Detective Barnes pointed out. "Arnstein, 3B. Gives me the chills, to be honest. Ten years is a long time to let this guy run around enjoying his life. There's one other apartment on the third floor. 'De Salvo.' Let's go up and see what we can find."

Starting up the three flights of stairs, the policemen looked at one another, askance, as they smelled the stench of decay and foul air. At the top landing they saw the doors of the two apartments. There was no name on the first door. Walking down the hallway, the other door had a nameplate that read "H. De Salvo."

The two men walked back to the first door and Officer Brady stepped back to allow Detective Barnes access. The detective soundly rapped twice on the old warped door. "Police! Open up!" There was no response. "Police! Open up!"

They waited several seconds, listening at the door for the sounds of any movement. Hearing none, they walked back to the other door. Again, Officer Brady stepped back to allow Detective Barnes to knock on the door. "This is the police. Please open the door," he said, more politely, this time. No response.

"Well, we don't have exigent circumstances to break down Arnstein's door," Detective Barnes observed to the officer. "I certainly don't want any evidence we might find inside to be thrown out, as it was illegally obtained. I know we could lift prints in there, but they would never be admitted. We have to play this one strictly by the book, to make sure we get a conviction.

"Let's go, for now," he said, turning to walk down the stairs. "Detective Enright and I will come back and stake out the place until the suspect comes home. He has to come home, some time, and we'll be here. Then we'll contact the station and you can meet us back here."

"It's a shame this guy wasn't here," Officer Brady said when they got outside. "I was looking forward to his reaction in seeing you, outside his door, ten years after the fact."

"Hey, Pete!" the detective called, walking partway around the building. Detective Enright appeared, momentarily. "Not home?" he inquired.

"Nah," his partner answered. "We'll have to sit on the place; see if he comes back tonight. We'll get the car and wait here for a few hours. If he's still a no-show by midnight, say, we'll find a motel, get some sleep and come back tomorrow."

Chapter 40

"**S**on of a bitch!" Dana exclaimed to Dave. She was now in the shotgun seat and Dave was driving. They had just heard from SECOM over the HF that the Beta truck's doors had been opened and the truck hadn't responded to their calls.

She keyed the mic. "Mobile 6, Mobile 7, come in!" she said, calling the Convoy Commander's vehicle. "Mobile 6, can you read me?"

"Mobile 9, Mobile 7," she said over the mic, calling the TC in the trail car. "Negative contact with the CC, after hearing from SECOM that Beta's doors are open. We're responding to the trucks."

"Ten four, Mobile 7. Prepare to pursue."

"Mobile 7, Mobile 8," came over the VHF. "Ten mikes out." It was Owen calling Dana back, to let her know that he and his team were ten miles away from the trucks and they were on their way.

"Mobile 8, Mobile 7. Copy that."

"We're about eight miles away from Exit 305," Dave said to his team members. "We should get there before Owen."

"Vests on, Dana!" Rob said from the back. "Got your rifle?"

"Yeah, I'm ready!" she answered, excitedly.

Five miles down the interstate, the three of them noticed rippling blue mars lights. A state patrol car was parked along the side of the road close to a van in a ditch.

"It's Cliff's team," Dana advised, referring to one of the two QRTs. "They've pulled off into the ditch. It's clear that we're under attack! We'd better get a move on and be ready to kick some ass," she said, with a mix of excitement and determination.

"Try to call them, Dana," Rob said, from the back of the vehicle. "See if you can raise them."

"Mobile 2, Mobile 7, are you there?" Dana asked into the mic. There was no response. "Mobile 2, Mobile 7. Come in."

"I'll radio Hank, again," Dana said, with the mic still in her hand. "Mobile 9, Mobile 7. Cliff Hartnett's vehicle is disabled at the 300 mile marker. Negative contact. State trooper at the scene. We're proceeding to the trucks."

"Mobile 9, Mobile 7. Ten-four."

As they drove by the accident scene, a highway patrolman had just emerged from the agents' van and was approaching his fellow law officer. His face was drawn and serious.

"All three men are dead," Officer Melbourn advised the other state trooper. "And I don't think they died by crashing into the ditch. They appear to have been asphyxiated. They collapsed in their seats and have the discolored skin tone of oxygen deprivation. And get this, they're all government agents! Their badges say, 'National Nuclear Security Administration—Federal Agent.'"

"They're federal escorts for nuclear weapons," Officer Long observed. "We need to find out where the nuclear shipment is! I'm calling in a 10-33," Long advised, referring to an emergency. "And a 10-78," he continued, using the Georgia State Trooper code for needing assistance to work the case. "Let's start investigating for sabotage. If we find evidence of tampering, this becomes a situation involving terrorism. I have a feeling something really big is coming down!"

Since the call from SECOM, Dave had been driving the van at high speeds, realizing they were in a race against time. Arriving at the gas station, Dave brought the heavy vehicle up sharply next to the Beta truck that sat there with its back doors standing open, exposing its cargo of nuclear weapons!

The three agents jumped out of the van, with their rifles drawn, and ran to the back of the Beta truck. They could immediately see what had happened by looking at the tube that was rolled halfway out of the trailer. Dana gave voice to what they all knew. "The sons of bitches have stolen a warhead!"

"Check the doors on the other trucks," Rob instructed. Dave and Dana quickly went to the other trailers and answered back that they were still locked.

"They must have just left!" Dana said. "No one's come to check out all the gunfire. Although, there's nothing much here," she added, looking around at the undeveloped surrounding area.

"Let's check and see if anyone is still alive who can give us some answers." Rob ordered.

Walking to the front of the Beta truck's cab, Dana found the body of Billy Sheldon. "Billy's been shot dead," she called over to Rob. Looking in the truck she discovered the lifeless bodies of the other two agents. "Jake and Sean are dead in their seats. No wounds. They weren't killed by gunfire."

Dana called over to the two men from the scout car, "All three are dead in their seats here, too. No one was shot. I'll go check out the CC's vehicle."

On the driveway, next to the van, she found the bloodied bodies of two agents. "Nick and Adam were killed by gunfire," she called out. Then, seeing a shoe under the van, she bent down far enough so she could identify the agent: George Newsome. "George was shot in the face trying to fire on the attackers from under the van. It appears he was the last of this group to die," she added. "He died doing his job."

Rob and Dave had quickly inspected the other two tractor-trailers and found six more dead agents. "Most of them died in their vehicles without firing off a round," Rob concluded, after checking over the bodies. "Fifteen agents are dead, here. I don't know how they did this, but we just need to find them and the warhead!"

"Dana, call the TC and report this. Owen should be here in a couple of minutes, anyway. The TC will advise SECOM and they'll call in all available support; the local police, the state police, the FBI and NEST," he added, referring to the Nuclear Emergency Support Team of the Department of Energy.

As soon as Dana was off the radio with the TC, Owen and the other SRF members pulled up, and the three agents leaped out of the van. Scanning the scene, Owen looked at Rob and asked, "Have you cleared the mini mart?"

"No. We were just about to." Rob replied.

"Okay. Danny, stay outside to secure the area until Hank comes," Owen ordered, referring to Hank Burger, the TC. "The rest of us will do an entry of the mini mart."

The five agents quickly lined up at the mini mart's door, with Owen in the lead. Throwing open the door, Owen rushed forward and did a 'button hook' move, while holding his rifle butt pressed against his shoulder, with the barrel in the 'low ready' position. The other team members rapidly moved through the door, closely behind him, with their rifles held in the same position. Dana and Dave crossed the space to opposite corners as John and Rob came in, each one moving in different directions, keeping clear of the door and windows.

Seeing only lifeless bodies lying on the floor, the team looked to Owen for a hand signal on how to proceed. He motioned to the four agents to pair up to execute the same entry maneuver in each the smaller closed rooms, as they worked their way back. The last room to clear was the storeroom at the back of the restaurant.

Owen and Rob entered the last room. "Back here!" Owen called back to the others.

The other three SRF responded to the back storeroom to find Owen standing, with his rifle pointed at a young man, wearing a paper hat, who was cowering in a corner.

"Who are you?!" Owen demanded.

"My—my name is Jimmy," he squeaked. "Ji-Jimmy Hawser. I work here—in the restaurant. I'm just the fry cook," he whimpered. "Please don't hurt me!" He started blubbering.

"Okay, calm down, Jimmy. We're not going to hurt you. We're federal agents. Here, you can see my badge. What do you know about this?" Owen asked, cocking his head back toward the mini mart.

"A guy with a rifle came into the mart and shot up the place!" Jimmy cried out.

"Okay, Jimmy, just relax now. We're here to find whoever did this. You'll need to tell an authority everything you know about what happened here.

"Dana, go and see if there's a state trooper here, yet. We need someone who can question Mr. Hawser."

A minute later Dana reappeared, accompanied by a state trooper. "Mr. Hawser, this is Officer Harrison. He's going to take down your story. Tell him everything you saw and heard."

"Trooper Harrison," Owen said, "relay the information you obtain from Mr. Hawser to our Tactical Commander, Hank Burger. He'll be here directly, securing this area, and setting up a command post."

"Will do, Agent Knight." The lawman replied.

"Okay, Mr. Hawser, say and spell your full name for me," the SRF heard, as they departed the room.

The SRF agents, stepping outside, were relieved to see that Commander Berger had arrived. The TC was checking out the scene in the parking areas with several police officers. Ambulance sirens could be heard in the distance.

The TC approached the SRF teams. "State troopers radioed me that Cliff and his team were also found dead. Asphyxiation. The troopers alertly assumed it was an act of terrorism and their department has dropped a net over a fifty mile radius, setting up roadblocks on all the arterials, including the interstate, both north and south."

"I've been in contact with SECOM and they've called in NEST who should be operational out of Atlanta within a couple of hours. They'll be sending copters equipped with sensors to pick up on radioactivity. Oh, and some suits from the FBI are flying in from D.C. They'll be getting underfoot picking up spent shells and dusting," the Commander grimaced.

"I'll be getting the Beta truck moved off to the side and the Omega truck off the road after the ambulances take away the bodies," the Commander advised the team. "The county sheriff's department has arranged for the transport of the bodies to a local hospital morgue until dispositions can be made. I'll make notifications to our couriers' families. The local police will be making the notifications on the victims inside."

"Oh, Hank," Owen said, "There's a state trooper—Harrison—inside, talking to the one survivor of the attack. He's a fry cook who was hiding in a back storeroom when a gunman came in and killed six people in the mini mart. We've asked the trooper to inform you of his testimony."

"Okay, good. I'll radio you with any pertinent information we get from the survivor. I'll leave you to it now, Owen. Good luck to all of you."

Owen had the rapt attention of the other five SRF members as they gathered together. "The kid in the restaurant said the gunfire stopped just before six o'clock. We won't be far behind them.

"Look around for some clues as to where they went from here. We'll then take off and scour the surface streets in the target area. We have to assume the worse; that they'll try to detonate the warhead.

"They've killed eighteen federal agents and six civilians, in broad daylight. They managed to sabotage six government vehicles, and they knew both codes to unlock the trailer's doors to steal a warhead. It's obvious they've had some inside help. But we'll figure that out later.

"Right now, our job will be to do the ground search. As you know, our investigation space becomes a National Security Area, so inspect every building on your routing. Put on your blue jackets for I.D.," he added, referring to the DOE navy jackets with 'Federal Agent' in block yellow letters on the backs and the National Security Agent badge on the front.

"If people are around, ask them if they've seen any unfamiliar cars or trucks today. This gang didn't come from around here, as we know they have a direct connection to our operation back in Oak Ridge. One W88 warhead could have been transported in practically any kind of vehicle. Pay particular attention to abandoned buildings where the attackers could hide.

"As you know, it's a submarine warhead, but it does have a PAL box installed on it for its transfer to Amarillo. It's a CAT F, which requires 12 digits for detonation. There's no way they could have the combination. Of course, there's always the possibility they can work out the encryption, but that'll take time. I don't know what those odds might be, but I remember hearing that the biggest lottery winner had odds of over one in 135,000,000 and those numbers didn't have to be in any sequence.

"We've had some rain today, which could help us. Look for tire tracks going away from the scene. We'll do a fast sweep of the area and then take off in the vehicles and cover the 50-mile radius. I picked up a few local maps from the service station. I'll mark how we'll divide up the roads after our sweep of the station. Okay, let's move it!"

A minute later Dana, from behind the billboard, called Owen over to see what she had discovered there. "The rental company's name, address and phone number are all right here on this sticker," she said, pointing to the label on the tractor. "This must have been what they used to transfer the warhead from the trailer to their vehicle!"

"No doubt," Owen agreed. "And they would have needed to show some identification to rent it, but it seems unlikely that they used their real names and then just left this behind. You and your team stop by this business while you're driving, and see if you get a name, an address. The rental company is just down the road, not far from here."

After a few minutes, Owen called over the SRF team. "Dana found the tractor they rented to pick up the warhead and load it on a truck, I'm assuming. Did anyone find anything else?"

"Tire tracks leave out of the station to the north," Danny said. "Also, I found muddy truck tire tracks from the driveway across the street that came over to the station. That driveway is abandoned, so it must have been the attacker's truck. I don't think there are more than two vehicles, including the truck."

"Okay, good info. Anything else?" Owen asked of the group. "I've marked all the local maps with a highlighter. My team will cover the green area, and Rob, your team will cover the yellow area. I've told Dana that you should make a quick stop at the rental company in your area and see if there's something immediately useful."

"I can't believe these attackers could have pulled this off without someone seeing something. There are a lot of places to hide around here, though. Take the maps and start checking off the areas that you've searched. If you find something, radio the other SRF for backup. Okay, let's go!"

Back in the storeroom, Trooper Harrison had gotten his interview underway. He knew that the information might prove very useful if the agents found the missing warhead or could even help them in their search.

"Okay, Mr. Hawser, take it a step at a time. What happened first?" Trooper Harrison asked, calmly.

"I was here in the storage room gettin' some packages of buns for the dinner crowd. A woman screamed and I looked around the corner and saw this guy with a big rifle like they have in the army. He yelled for everyone to raise their hands. He didn't see me as I was behind the door, lookin' through the crack. I heard the man say that he wanted all three restaurant employees to come out, so I figured he dint know I was back here."

"What time was that?" Trooper Harrison asked.

"The gunman came into the mini mart about five-fifteen. I know, 'cause I wanted to have all the supplies set up by 5:30.

"Anyway, I decided to take my chances and hide behind the boxes. Then I heard 'im ask for everyone's cell phones and wallets. After that, he started shootin' up the place! I knew he had killed everybody with all those bullets. I just stayed here. After a few minutes I heard gunfire outside the station! I din't dare even move. I knew he'd kill me, too!" This last statement started him off crying, again.

"I din't hear any more gunfire after 6:00. I was about to come out and call for help when the federal agents burst in."

"What did the gunman look like? Did he seem foreign? Did he have an accent? What was he wearing?"

"When he came into the mini mart with the gun, I thought he was a guy I had seen earlier in the restaurant with some other guys." Jimmy replied.

"Tell me about that. How many were there? What did they look like? What did they do that was suspicious that you noticed them?"

"Well, I was back fryin' hamburgers, and when I brought a tray of them up front and put them under the heat lamps I noticed this rough-lookin' guy with another guy at the counter who was well-dressed and kind of sissy-looking. They looked really different from each other to be together, y' know what I mean? They weren't no foreigners—they were Americans. I didn't hear 'em say much. The tan guy was soakin' wet and the other guy was almost dry. They just caught my attention.

"The one guy, who I think was the gunman, was thirty-somethin' and muscular. Like a fighter. His hair was cut in a mullet style. He had a full mustache and tattoos on his arms. Words, I think."

"The man who was dry was scrawny, like he *never* exercised. He was real pale, with long curled hair, like a girl's. He didn't seem to like the tough guy. Stood apart from 'im. I looked to see who they were sittin' with, because they were so peculiar. There were two other guys at a table, waitin' fer their food. The ones at the table were both weird looking. One was soft and pudgy, with tufts of dark hair, and the other guy was skinny with long scraggly hair and beard. I guess I mostly noticed hair."

"Did you see them outside to see what kinds of vehicles they were driving?"

"No, we don't have no windows back here to the outside and I was too scared to come out."

"Do you think you could identify any of them if you saw them again?"

"I don't know about the others, but I think I'd know the shooter."

"Do you think he was wearing any kind of disguise, like a wig?"

"No," Jimmy said, defiantly. "You could tell it was his own hair. Everythin' fit together on him, y' know what I mean? Nothin' looked out of place, or fake."

"Did you know any people who were here at the time this group was here, other than those who were killed, of course."

"There were a couple people I've seen here before but I don't know 'em. Not their names or nothin'."

"Okay. You've done a good job. Just wait here while I check with Commander Berger and agents from the FBI, if they've arrived. You're a lucky man."

"Don't I know it? Thank you Jesus!" Jimmy raised his hands in the air. "The Lord saved me!"

Chapter 41

"Hold the flashlight closer and over to the left, Henry," Albert instructed, looking at the miniature keyboard on the PAL box. "Look at the fucking primitive conditions I have to put up with! Dim light, a dirt floor to sit on, stagnant air, and intense heat. Not to mention I have to decode an encrypted switch system on a mechanical device I've never seen before. And fucking Gray had the balls to say I wasn't doing my part!" Albert mocked Gray in a whining voice.

Henry leaned in close. "Shh! He might hear you, Colonel Albert!"

"Yeah, that'd break my heart. Henry, hold the light steady."

"Henry, are you sure there's no way to detonate the bomb without unlocking the PAL?" Albert asked.

"No, there isn't," Henry firmly stated. "It's impossible to bypass or reverse-engineer. PAL parts are located deep inside the warhead, and the outside of the sphere is tamper-resistant. If you did break through the covering to try to circumvent the detonation electronics, the PAL would disable or destroy the weapon."

"Henry, could you tell me something that I *can* do instead of what I *can't* do?" Albert asked, getting exasperated as he studied the Signal Generator on the weapon, in the small beam of the flashlight.

Henry peered over at the mechanism. "All you have to do is input digital signals into the Unique Signal Generator that you're looking at. Just put in the correct digits in the correct order."

"Yeah. That makes me feel a whole lot better. Look, there's no visible plaintext or cipher text, and that makes cryptanalysis nearly impossible. The design principle appears to be to control the detonator current. Along with the physical barrier, it's very secured. Why don't we just call the Commanding officer of the U.S. Nimitz, or whatever the hell was the name of that sub? He'll have the code."

"The *USS* Nimitz is an aircraft carrier, Colonel," Henry said, soberly. "This warhead came from a submarine named the USS Manatee."

"Thanks for the lesson in naval nomenclature."

"Henry, I just realized something—the code was set on this PAL controller, right?

"Of course."

"Do you have a nail file, a file of any kind?"

"Sure. I have a file on a pocket knife. Why? Are we still talking about the PAL?

"No. We're talking about manicures. Of course we're still talking about the PAL, for Chris' sakes! Henry, get me a pencil and give me your file. And hurry!"

A minute later Henry returned from the car with two pencils, and handed them to Albert, along with his pocket knife. Albert set about filing off the tips of the pencils on the keyboard of the PAL, the black dust settling over the keys.

"What are you doing?" Henry asked, warily.

"The code was set on these keys. I haven't touched them yet. Therefore, the only fingerprints on the keyboard were made when the code was set on the weapon. And a code was set only after it came off the *Manatee* submarine, since there aren't any PALs on naval warheads, when they're at sea.

"Look! You can see fingertip patterns on some of the numbers and not others," Albert said, excitedly. Only five numbers out of nine have been touched -1, 2, 4, 6, and 7."

"But it doesn't help you with the sequence, does it?" Henry asked, doubtfully.

"No. But I can apply logical sequencing decisions with the numbers that remain, minimizing incorrect input. Having only five numbers will decrease possible combinations by multiple millions. I'll use the software to come up with all the possible combinations.

"According to mathematical theories," Albert continued "we know that most codes start with either a 2 or a 4 and end with a 6, 7 or 9. That will limit the number of possible combinations, which will cut down on the hours it takes to go through the sixty million possibilities. I'll program the software with these further restrictions and we'll see what we come up with. This is the first time I've done this so I can't estimate what time I'll need.

"Right now I need to call that she-devil's modem for her location."

Having said that, Albert made the call and checked the coordinates on his map. "The bitch is still in this area, about a half-hour away, if she drove straight here. Of course, she doesn't know where to go as we didn't leave any clues, or any witnesses," he added, with a mirthless smile.

"How's it coming, Albert?" Gray called over from the back of the truck where the three of them were playing cards. "You want me to take a look at any of the wiring?

"I've got everything under control. As I understand it, your specialty was *disarming* weapons. I'll take care of the arming."

Chapter 42

D ana, Rob and Dave had stopped by the Rent-It-All equipment-rental business where the tractor had been leased.

After the agents identified themselves, the owner, Raymond Dunn was reluctantly responding to their questions. "All I kin tell you is that the feller signed the contract at 2:00 for the rental of the tractor and utility attachment and gave me I.D. that matched the name that he gave me—Gray Fordham—and a local address. I didn't check out the address, because he gave me cash for a half-day and a deposit of $100. And now, you federal agents are tellin' me that he used it to steal some kind of weapon? I never had my equipment rented to commit no crime before. I kin tell you that," the business owner asserted with confidence.

"Just answer our questions," Rob said, letting his annoyance show. "Save your explanations for the FBI. They'll be in contact with you, as might other law enforcement agencies. Now, tell us something that can help us locate this guy. Like,what he looked like, if you've ever seen him around here before, a description of his truck. Any useful information."

"I've never seen him before. I can tell you that. I guess you'd say he weren't a bad lookin' feller—about 35 years old, dark hair, fit-lookin' and clean. I think I'd probably recognize 'im again if you'd need me to say."

"Do you remember his truck?"

"Yeah, it was a Ford F-150, not too old. It was green, I think. Didn't pay much attention. One of my helpers put the tractor on the flat bed for 'im."

"Did he say anything, other than that he wanted to rent this piece of equipment?"

"No, not that I can recall. Look, I don't bother my customers with a lot of questions. It was a simple transaction."

"Yeah. Well, maybe in the future you'll ask a few more questions."

"What about my tractor? How do I get that back?" he called after the departing agent.

"Like I said, Mr. Dunn," Rob responded, over his shoulder, "the FBI will be in touch with you. Take it up with them. Not our call. It's evidence, now, so don't look for it to be returned anytime soon. Hold onto that contract with this guy's signature on it. We'll see you around," he said, getting back behind the wheel of the van.

Driving away, Rob said to Dana, "Okay, you're in charge of our route. Tell me where to go first to cover our area. We'll check out every building. Simple as that."

"Sure, Rob. Just drive up this road that we're on, Wilbur's Cross. There are houses up ahead. Right here, on your right. There are a few buildings."

Pulling the van up to the outbuildings alongside a two-story white frame house, the three agents got out, with their guns at 'low ready.' "Let's do the house first, check out who lives there and clear the house. Then we'll do the outbuildings," Rob directed.

Before they got to the front door of the house, a thin, rangy woman, with frizzy blond hair, wearing a T shirt and jeans, came running out of the house, with her hands up. "Please don't shoot!" she cried out. "What do y'all want? My husband's at work an' I got a coupla kids in there. Is it my boy? Did he do somethin' wrong?"

"Federal agents," Rob said, holding up his badge. "Responding to a national security emergency. We need to search your home and the other buildings here, in order to clear them. We won't be interfering with your family, if you'll cooperate. Now, let us get on with our business."

As the agents burst into the home with their M 4 rifles, a young girl and teenage boy skittered across the front room and stood, wide-eyed, flattened against the opposite wall. The three couriers, using their practiced technique of moving through the rooms in different directions, quickly searched each room on the first floor, in order. The children's mother had come into the house and had gone over to her children, shielding them.

"We're going upstairs, now," Rob said to the mother, in particular. "We'll be down in a few minutes."

Upstairs, the three entered each of the three small bedrooms, quickly checking out closets and the bathroom. Completing the tour they came down the stairs.

"Thank you, Ma'am," Rob said to the still-frightened woman who stood with her arms stretched out in front of her children. We'll just clear the garage and sheds and be on our way."

A few minutes later they had cleared the three buildings that contained equipment and vehicles, and finding nothing significant, they exited the last building and started walking over to the van, as the woman again ran out of her house.

"Everything okay, officers?"

"Yes, Ma'am. Sorry to have bothered you. Have a good day."

Getting into the van, Dana remarked, "I don't think she's having a good day."

"No, I 'spose not," agreed Rob. "But then, neither are we."

*   *   *

Owen led the way to the front door of the first trailer in the trailer park. In response to his knock, a disheveled woman, holding a can of beer, answered the door. "Whaddy ya want?" she asked with slurred speech.

"Federal agents," Owen said, showing his badge, "here on a matter of national security. Just step away from the door. We need to search your home."

"You got no damn business here. I ain't done nothin'," the woman responded, with her arm stretched out across the door opening to deny them entrance.

"Step aside, Ma'am, we're coming in." Owen ordered, matter-of-factly.

With that, Owen, with Danny and John close behind, eased past the woman who shouted after them, "Hey! You've got no cause to come bargin' into my place! I'm a free citizen and I've got my rights! Don't touch any of my stuff, you bastards!" This last protest was screamed in response to Owen opening a closed closet door.

Owen motioned his team to go right as he turned left, all of them with their M 4s in low-ready position. The agents had to pick their way through the trailer that was littered with garbage, soiled clothing, beer cans, empty liquor bottles and dirty dishes. They continued opening doors and scanning the space in the trailer until they had completed their inspection. Owen signaled the others that the trailer had been cleared.

As the three agents walked out the door, the woman shrieked at their backs, from the open doorway, "You govermint pigs! Don' ever come back! Ya' hear me?! Ya' hear me?! she repeated, glaring at the agents, who had ignored her. "Bastards!" she spat out. Finally, she turned to go inside, slamming the door behind her.

"I think we can split up for the rest of these units," Owen said, as they regrouped outside the next trailer in the row. "You two clear this one, and I'll do the next, then you leapfrog over and so on. We'll meet at the last one and get out of here."

"None too soon," groused John.

*   *   *

After Rob, Dana, and Dave had been driving for a couple of hours, they heard the helicopter overhead. Looking up, Dana could clearly see the unmarked grey and navy NEST Bell 412 copter with its red and white rotors, noisily hovering overhead at about 300 feet.

"You can even see the attached containers of gamma and neutron detectors," Dana said to her team, with her head against the window to get a better look. "It doesn't have the NEST initials on the side," she commented, "but at that altitude, it sure makes its presence known."

"They have to fly at that altitude to pick up on the man-made radiation source," Rob said. "The FAA gives their copters a higher control priority over airspace. Basically, they can fly anywhere with their call sign of 'FLYNET.' Since the area to be searched is restricted to a 50-mile radius, we might come across their Hot Spot Mobile van," he added, referring to a NEST mobile lab containing sensitive instruments to detect alpha, beta and gamma neutron radiation.

There were explosive ordnance disposal experts in the vans who could use one of several options to disable or destroy the bomb. They could enter a disarming code, wreck the bomb's wiring, or even surround a warhead with a multi-story height and width tent which would then be filled with special foam to contain the radioactive material, if the bomb were to explode in the process of disabling it.

"Here's the next house. Let's get out and clear it," Rob said, pulling the van up to another frame farm house. "We've only done about a fourth of our area so far. We need to find something and find it in a hurry. Owen says that he hasn't come up with anything yet, either, but I'd bet my life that that warhead and those murderous bastards are someplace on this map," he said, angrily, poking his finger at the unfolded paper. "SRF has to find that warhead. We've been training for this for too damn long to not come through, now."

Chapter 43

" Larry, that old white Mercedes Roadster there, in the parking lot, hasn't moved," Detective Enright commented to his partner. They had returned to the back of Albert's apartment building the morning after their late evening stake-out. "It was here when we arrived early last evening and it's still in the same place. There's no mass transportation around here for someone to get to work without a car," he continued.

"I know what you're thinking, Pete. Albert had a sports car in college. It's possible he would be interested in a car like that. It's not just an old car; it's a vintage model. I'd say it's from the 1960s, and it's in excellent condition. It must be owned by someone with a real interest in preserving antique cars. Well, let's run the tags and see if our friend is, indeed, the proud owner. You've got the laptop, Pete, why don't you pull up the record?"

Detective Enright entered the license plate number into the law enforcement database. "Well, lookee here. The owner is one Albert Arnstein, living at this address, with a landline phone number. It's a 1965 Mercedes-Benz 230-L Roadster and the VIN is included here.

The title was registered three years ago and there's no lien holder. There have been no moving violations."

"Okay, fine," Detective Barnes said, distractedly. "What I think we need to do now is go back to the station and get a forensics technician to come back here with us to lift any prints that may be on the driver's door handle. It's a long shot to get a clear print, but considering we lifted a ten-year old print on a purse clasp, I wouldn't bet against it."

An hour later, the two detectives in their car were followed to the apartment building by a van imprinted on the side with 'Oak Ridge Police Department' and the slogan, "A Protective Past—A Proactive Future." Arriving and stopping at the parking lot, an energetic young woman named Wendy hopped out of the police van, with a fingerprint kit in hand. The detectives walked her over to the Mercedes-Benz.

"You say this car isn't stolen?" Wendy asked the lead detective.

"No, it's not. We're trying to match a print found at a crime scene. Our investigation leads us to believe the car's owner is our perp," Detective Barnes answered.

Snapping on her latex gloves, Wendy first examined the distinctive discreet pull-out bar on the handle that engaged and disengaged the lock. Next, she dusted the driver's door handle and bar with the black magnetic powder and photographed the image of circles of curved lines that emerged. Then, she ripped off a strip of fingerprint tape. After pressing the tape on the handle she slowly and carefully lifted prints and transferred them to a clear plastic Kromekote card to take back to the laboratory.

Looking at the result, she said, "We're lucky the car has this bar that has to be firmly grasped to open and lock the car. It looks like we have two images. I can't tell you how clear they are until I get back to magnifying and light equipment at the lab. Then I'll compare it to the print that you brought with you. We'll see. Stop by the lab this afternoon. I'll have an answer for you."

"Thanks, Wendy," Detective Barnes said, smiling at her. After she drove off, he wiped off the blackened handle with a couple of tissues. "No sense tipping him off that he's being investigated," he commented to his younger counterpart.

"Now, what I think we should do, is find a local car repair shop that specializes in vintage cars," he continued. "Albert would need a special source for service and parts for an outdated vehicle. Let's check out yellow pages' listings on the internet to find places to check out. Someone who knows him, even as a customer, could give us some valuable information."

Stopping for coffee at a local restaurant, Detective Enright did a computer search and found the most likely repair shop for Albert's car under Automobile Services, Vintage: a repair shop named 'C.A.R.–Classic Automobile Repairs,' on a local street near downtown.

"We'll start there. Let's pay them a call," advised Detective Barnes.

At the C.A.R. shop, they introduced themselves to the owner, Doug Wilson, who appeared to be in shock when they asked him if he had any knowledge of a customer by the name of Albert Arnstein. "Customer? He *works* here, part time. Why are you asking about Albert? Did he do something? What's this all about?" he asked, without taking a breath.

"We're investigating a matter we'd just like to talk to him about. Are you expecting him to come in to work anytime soon?"

"No. I call him when we get a car in for restoration. That's his specialty. I take care of the regular maintenance and parts. I think he gets some support from his father, who's a big deal scientist up at Y-12, so he don't need to work full-time. He really knows his stuff, though. He refurbished his own Mercedes. Did a beautiful job on 'er."

"Did he tell you that he was planning on being away for a while at this time?" Detective Barnes inquired.

"No. Far as I know, he's around. I just haven't had the business, lately, to call 'im. Now, I've made an appointment for a '92 Jag to come in on Thursday. I might need 'im then. The owner just got the car. Wants it completely gone over."

"Okay, well, thanks for your help. No need to tell Albert that we were making inquiries. We'll contact him at his home."

Back in the car, Detective Barnes said, "Let's stop for a sandwich and then head over to the station and see what Wendy has for us."

Over lunch at a fast-food franchise, Detective Barnes went over their options. "If Wendy comes up with a good print, and we have a match, that would give us enough for an arrest. I think we should hang around for another day, at least through tomorrow, to see if Albert comes back. We've been in touch with the sergeant at home and nothing has popped that needs our immediate attention. I know we could leave surveillance up to the local force, but they aren't invested in this matter. I can't see going home with an arrest pending."

"No, I agree," his partner said. "His employer expects him to be around. He wouldn't be gone too long without his car. Let's try that neighbor, De Salvo, again this evening, and see if he or she has any information."

Back in the car, the two detectives headed over to the police station. Walking in, and identifying themselves to the sergeant on the desk, they were directed downstairs to the Crime Investigation Unit.

Once there, they asked to see Wendy, and stood waiting for only a minute before the cheerful young woman came out, and gave them her news. "They're only partials, Detectives; probably a thumb and index, but our Fingerprint Analyst thought one was a match. It has nine corresponding minutiae to your print. Of course, as you know, you should have a minimum of ten for evidence in court. The other print wasn't as clear. We found only three matching minutiae. Sorry about that."

"We just needed the one, Wendy. Thanks for the good work," Detective Barnes said. "We'll be in touch if there's anything else."

Returning to Albert's apartment building, the detectives resumed their watch. Detective Barnes parked the car down the street, but in view of the back lot and front walkway. By 5:30, several people had parked their cars in the lot, and walked into the building. At 6:00, the two officers got out of their car, walked down the block, climbed the three flights of stairs to the top landing and again knocked on both doors, with the same result as the last time.

"There are just the two tenants on this top floor. It's possible this H. de Salvo and Albert know each other well and they've gone someplace together." Detective Enright said.

"Could be. Let's go back downstairs and run all the tags in the parking lot and see which names we can match up with the building's residents; see if only this De Salvo's car is missing. We can get the full name from our search, using the last name and address. It's something to do while we wait, anyway.

"With the print match, we're not going anywhere," Detective Barnes asserted. "When that little piece of shit comes back we can cuff him and read him his rights."

Chapter 44

Albert was breaking out in a cold sweat as he labored to find the right combination of twelve numbers to arm the warhead. Almost like a person facing death, snapshots of his life flashed through his mind. He recalled the many times he had been abused: when he had wet the bed, when his parents didn't come to his big concert, when he got lost in the woods and was jeered by the Boy Scouts, when his father berated him, when his mother ignored him, when Cat was repulsed by him, and, most recently, when he was assaulted and threatened by the bitch who was even now hunting him down.

Everything was on the line this time. He had something to prove to all of them, and to himself. He was in the fight of his life. He saw everything that had happened to him thus far as preparing him for this moment. This would be the ultimate test of his intellect, of his worthiness to wield power, of his revenge against all of those who had mistreated him and kept him under their thumbs.

The numbers rolled down, a line at a time; dozens of them, and then hundreds of them, and then thousands of them, rolled down without arriving at the one unique combination of twelve numerals that would unlock a force greater than the Hiroshima bomb.

And then he heard a sound in the distance. The unmistakable whirr of the rotary blades of a helicopter. It was muted, but it sounded ominous: they were coming after them. Helicopters were emergency vehicles, not transportation.

"Did you hear that?" Gray shouted. "It sounds like more than one copter! They're not too close, but they're coming after us, and they're not the only ones! We left nine agents alive! They'll have called in all the national security resources—the FBI, Homeland Security, the works. They'll be combing the countryside to find us.

"Hubie and Dirk—we've got to go outside and take a look around. Then we'll take turns standing guard until we can get out of here."

"Albert! Haven't you come up with anything yet?! How long are you going to fuck around with that PAL? I thought you said you could come up with the combination with your software!"

"Look, Gray. If this had been easy, someone else would have done it before now, wouldn't they?! But no one ever has. And certainly no one else in *this* group could pull it off, or, would you like to try? Just do your job and I'll do mine, okay? I know I'm getting close. I've narrowed down the choices and have run through hundreds of thousands of combinations. It's just a matter of time. You just need to buy me some time."

Gray grabbed for his M-16, and a few magazines, and kicked the side of his truck. "We'll be outside, Albert!"

"Jesus Christ, Henry! That son-of-a-bitch could blow this whole thing. He's a loose cannon. When I set this thing, you and I are getting the hell out of here! Those three have got to stay here to protect the warhead to give us time to get away to a safe distance."

"They won't be able to come with us?" Henry asked, bewildered.

"Of course not! Use your head! We can't let the agents get to the warhead before it's detonated. They'll know how to disarm it, I'm sure. Maybe they even have ways to detect where it is. If they get here before I'm ready for them, it will be the end of our plans. We won't have gotten our revenge. *Your* revenge. We're entitled to strike back at the evil that we've endured for all these years. That's why we're here—why we're doing this.

"I told you that we could never trust Gray. You think for one second that he wouldn't leave *us* here if *he* could set the bomb? Of course he would! This is survival, my friend. Not some fucking game. Who do you want to stay with—me or Gray? That's your choice. You decide. I have to get back to this encryption. I can't spend any more time arguing."

As Albert got back to his program, he watched in fascination as more numbers flew by, clicking into more and more combinations, even with restricting the first digit to a 2 or a 4 and the last digit to a 6, or 7 with only ten numbers in between.

Suddenly, a green light came on as the numbers stuck in place in the small PAL controller computer: 4261 6442 1227. That was it! The number that only a couple of people in the government were privy to know. The number that Albert Arnstein now knew, that would arm the nuclear warhead. His father should only know what a genius his son had become, and in his father's field, no less. *He would be so proud;* he smiled wryly, to himself.

"Henry, look!"

Henry came over to look over Albert's shoulder at the green light on the PAL controller computer. His face cleared with recognition. "You broke the code and found the combination!"

"Son-of-a-bitch! I did it! I'm a genius! I've finally lived up to my fucking name. Quick, Henry! Give me your jacket to throw over this computer! The cover isn't light-tight. We can't let Gray know I've broken the code, or we're dead! You got that?! We're dead, and he stays alive. It's as simple as that. Who are you going to help?!"

"Well, you, of course," Henry said, sincerely. "You've helped me through everything. How can I leave you now? I'm just sorry that we can't help the others, too. Hubie seems real nice."

"Henry! For Chris' sakes! We're not talking about 'nice' here! We're talking about having this one chance to put down the worst kind of evil in the world! The kind of evil that robs people of all their freedoms—that denies people the recognition of their worth, of their God-given right to thrive in this world. It's us or it's them, Henry! And Gray is included in 'them,' I'm sorry, but that includes Hubie, too, and Dirk, as they've thrown in their lot with Gray.

"And, by the way, do you think Dirk had any problem slaughtering all the people in the convenience market? I don't think so! That's because it was them or him. That's what this comes down to. Dirk would take us out too, without blinking. Don't you get it?!"

"I get it, Albert. I just said Hubie is nice."

"Yeah? Well, fuck Hubie! Nice guys finish last.

"Henry, there's no time to lose. I've got to set this timer. "Here, I've attached it. Does this look right to you?"

"Yeah, make sure that wire is wound around the screw there, for contact. That looks good, Albert! What time are you setting it for?"

"Well, let's see, it's about ten o'clock. Jesus Christ, it's late! That would put it close to midnight for a detonation. Like the Doomsday Clock, Henry! You know, how they keep moving the minute hand, as a metaphor, to gauge the closeness of a global nuclear catastrophe? Well, this is it, isn't it?! I think it's now set at six minutes to midnight. Something like that. We're delivering on the forecast. I like the sound of that," he said, as he set the timer. "Their clock and our clock—synchronized, to set off a nuclear holocaust that will have global consequences at six minutes to midnight.

"Now, we gotta get out of here! And we've got to convince the others that they have to stay to protect the warhead. I've got an idea. Let's go outside and tell Gray that we're going. Just be cool and follow my lead, okay?"

Albert and Gray made their way to the double doors, and pulled them wide open.

"Hey! What the hell are you doing, Albert?!" Gray asked, in a hoarse angry whisper. "You're letting the light shine out here, giving away our location. Are you crazy?!"

"Jesus, get a grip. No one's around. Henry and I have to get the hell out of here, right now! There's no time to lose if you want me to finish the job."

"What do you mean; you and Henry have to get out of here?" Gray pronounced the words slowly with emphasis.

"Henry says I'm going to need a couple of tools—a clutch-head tip screwdriver and a web clamp. He'll go with me to select substitutes if we can't find these. We'll take a round-about route and watch out for any law enforcement. We'll just be an hour or so. I'm close to breaking the code. This isn't the time to be a hard ass, Gray. I know what I need and you don't. That's all there is to it. Just leave everything as it is. In fact, don't even go near it!"

"Not so fast, Albert. What do you need those tools for, anyway? You never said you needed any tools. What do you think you're trying to pull? You're not going anywhere unless we all go. You got that?"

Albert leaned against the shed and folded his arms. "You don't want us to go? Fine. That's the end of the plan, then. We'll all just go back to what we were doing like nothing ever happened. I thought you wanted to retaliate for all that you've been through." Then, looking at Hubie and Dirk, he said, "I thought you all had a pretty big stake in this. If some agents show up and we're all gone, they'll just take back the bomb. Is that what you want?

"I've never done this before, so I didn't know what I would need," he continued, trying to sound reasonable. "Henry said this clamp will separate and hold some wires out of the way while I work inside the bomb where part of the PAL is located. You can't even see them, for Chris' sakes. I can't hold them with my hands!"

"Gray, let 'em go," Dirk spoke up. "Shit, we didn't come this far to walk away without the damn thing blowin' up! We don't know what he needs. We just have to trust 'im."

"I don't trust him, but, you're right that we can't give up before we know that the bomb will detonate," Gray answered Dirk. "But I swear to God, Albert! You'd better not be screwing with us. I'll be your worst nightmare. I'll hunt you down more than the FBI will. You've got an hour and a half to get back here with every fucking thing you can think of, or we leave here and come after you."

"I can live with that," Albert said, calmly.

Chapter 45

It was 10:45 at night, five hours after the nuclear warhead had been stolen from the tractor-trailer at the convenient mart at Exit 305. Rob was driving the purple Econoline van; Dana was riding shotgun and Dave on the jump seat. They had been searching houses for four hours without picking up any clues, and the strain was beginning to show.

Dana had the passenger overhead light on, looking at maps. "We've been canvassing the area for about four hours and are only halfway through our area. We're in the dark in more ways than one," she complained. "No one we've talked to has seen any vehicles that seemed suspicious or unusual. Even *I* don't know what that means. We already know the truck is a Ford F-150, dark green and unmarked, like thousands of others. The exit, where the bomb was taken, services several small towns, so people could hardly be expected to know what trucks *do* belong and what trucks *don't* belong in the area. The warhead could have been easily concealed under a tarp—it's only three feet long, tip to base."

"Dana," Rob said, ending her litany, "the state police have cut off the escape routes on main highways and the Interstate. We're closing in on them and reducing their choices of getting away. They can't possibly know the code to arm the missile. We just need to stay cool and do our job."

"You're right, Rob," she said, sighing. "I'm just blowing off steam, out of frustration; not very professional. On a positive note, now we're searching houses on county roads where the only vehicles you see are those belonging to the relatively few people who live on them. People out in the country *would* know an unfamiliar truck. Someone will have seen something. We just have to keep clearing buildings as quickly and as thoroughly as we can. Like you say, the more we do, the closer we're getting to them."

"Here's another house, on your left, Rob, kinda set back," Dave said.

The three agents looked up at the weathered brick Georgian style farmhouse, with iron fixtures lighting the doorway. Climbing the steps up to the deep furnished porch, they rang the bell. Showing their badges, they were shown into the home by a young couple, who had both responded to the door.

"I heard your van drive up," the wife said, excitedly. "My neighbor had called and told me that you were searching all the homes in our county, I guess. I just wanted to ask if you could be quiet upstairs where our two small children are sleeping. They would be terrified to wake up and see y'all. Also, I wanted to tell you about something I saw earlier this evening. It could be helpful."

"All right, ma'am," Rob said. "Agent Knowles will look upstairs and try not to wake the children. Agent Witkowski and I will clear the downstairs, and then we'll take your statement."

"Okay, sure," she said, looking uncertainly at the agents with their M-4 rifles. The three strangers' appearances were made even more menacing by their dark padded helmets fitted with night goggles; their bulky ballistic vests and their outer tactical vests with multiple flapped pockets for tactical equipment.

The shaken couple backed up and sat down, together, on the living room sofa. They remained there, holding hands, and not speaking, while the agents finished conducting their search and returned to the front room. Dana came down the stairs and joined the team. The couple stood up in place.

"Okay, ma'am, what did you see you think we should know about?" Rob asked.

"Well," the wife started, "I spent the day canning tomatoes and beans and forgot to go down and get the mail until real late. I was about to fix supper when I remembered. Anyway, when I got down to the mailbox, a little after six o'clock, a truck passed by, followed by a car."

"Was there something unusual about them?" Rob prompted, to get to the point.

"Yes. They were going slowly so I got a good look, although I tried not to stare, because of what I saw. They both passed by me, going east, so I was close to the drivers' sides. The front of the truck had been hit by gunfire! There were bullet holes all over the driver's door, and window, and the side mirror had been hit. It had to have been a violent shoot-out, so I didn't want these people to know I took any notice of them. I saw just the truck driver in profile, but I don't think I've seen him before. There were three men in the truck; two men in the car, but I didn't look at the others, at all. I was pretty shocked by the sight of the truck.

"What make and color was the truck, and the car? Did you see anything they had on the bed of the truck?" Rob asked, intently.

"The truck was a dark green Ford F-150. We've got the same model. They did have something on the bed that was covered up with a bright blue plastic tarp. The car was an older model sedan; dark blue, I think. I didn't pay much attention to the car."

"Where did they go after they drove by?" Rob asked quickly, his brow furrowed.

"Like I said, they were going east. I could see the two vehicles just until they got to the top of the next hill and then they disappeared from sight."

"Are there any abandoned buildings down that way?" Dana asked.

The wife looked at her husband, as she responded. "There's the old Carmichael place, right, Ed? The house has been torn down, but I think there's an outbuilding, or maybe two."

"That's right, Binnie," her husband agreed. "It's set far back, on the north side of the road. It'd be hard to see even in the daytime, though. You couldn't see it at all at night. It's about three miles down the road and there's a circle of old oak trees where the house used to stand. Do you want me to take you down there? You'll pass only a couple of farm houses along the way. There's nothing nearby that property."

"No, thank you, Mr.—?"

"Taylor—Ed and Bonita Taylor."

"Well, thanks," Rob said. "You've both been a lot of help. We'll be on our way. Good night."

After stepping off the porch, all three agents ran back to the van. Once inside, Dana said, "I'll radio Owen's team; see if they're on the road now. "Mobile 8, Mobile 7."

"Mobile 7, Mobile 8. Go ahead."

"We're outside a farmhouse on County Y, about ten mikes east of 411. We've received intel on suspects reported to be in the area. Over."

"Mobile 7, copy that. Stay where you are. We're ten minutes away."

"Ten four."

"I'm switching off the head lights and brake lights," Rob commented. "We'll use our NVD goggles to drive," he said, referring to the Night Vision Devices that would absorb what little illumination there was from the sporadic moonlight, to make objects visible in a bright green color. I'll open my window to listen for the SRF.

In a few minutes, they heard a vehicle coming down the road from the west. Looking behind their van, they could make out the other SRF van, which then pulled up next to them, as they were parked just off the road. Rob, Dana and Dave got out of their van.

The three arrivals quickly and quietly got out of their van, and joined the first team. Owen, who had been driving, walked over to Rob's team. "What intel did you get?"

Rob spoke in a low voice, but with urgency. "The homeowner in this farmhouse we just cleared, reported seeing a dark green truck, followed by a car that passed by their place a little after 6:00 this evening. The truck had been shot up on the driver's side. They advised us of an abandoned property—a shed hidden behind a circle of oak trees, about three miles east of here, on this road.

"Our van will lead," Owen said. "At the two-and-a-half mile point, slow down to a crawl to check for any set-back buildings or signs of an exit off the road. When we see an indication of the right location, we'll stop and I'll notify SECOM. Good work. It sounds like the break we were looking for."

The two vans started slowly driving down the narrow graveled road. Several minutes later, Owne's van pulled off the road and came to a stop. Dana peered through the windshield and pointed to something off the driver's side. "I just saw a light flicker through the branches of those trees in the distance, over there on the right! I'll get out and take a closer look."

Jumping out of the van, Dana met up with Owen, looking at some flattened weeds just off the road. "There are at least two sets of tire tracks in the damp ground," Owen advised, from his kneeling position. "The grass is still fresh, like it's been driven over recently."

"I can make out the circle of trees the Taylors told us about, but not a building," Dana said. "Could be hidden by the trees. There's the amber light, again, I saw a minute ago." she pointed out to Owen, across the field.

"Okay," Owen acknowledged. "We'll go in for an assault. I'll go back and notify SECOM for reinforcements." As they stood looking at the trees for more signs of activity, the other SRF members joined them.

"We'll work our way down, in our usual formation," Owen instructed, referring to the spacing of fifteen feet apart, "until we get a visual on the building, then look for my signals to spread out and circle the place. There are clouds crossing over the moon, but we should get some good moonlight tonight to see by with our NVDs. Rob, you'll be the point man."

The six agents, with their rifles in the low-ready position, started moving ahead, stealthily, following the tire tracks, as Rob led the way. It was very dark, now, as clouds covered the moon, but the light in the trees, appearing as neon green, could be glimpsed, from time to time, in a stationary place.

As the teams approached the oak trees, Owen paused. The light became steady as they now had a sight line past the trees to its location. Making eye contact with the other five team members, in turn, he touched his nose with his left index finger, and then brought his left hand forward to indicate the direction he wanted each agent to move. They would be spread out from this point.

Moving by the trees, Owen paused, turned, and made a cutting motion across his throat with his left hand, palm down, indicating that they were approaching a dangerous area. They all crouched down, moving more slowly ahead, with John and Danny looking on the left; Dave and Rob, on the right, while Dana stayed at the back, in the trail position, frequently checking behind the group, but seeing nothing.

After traveling twenty yards further, Owen signaled for Dave and Rob to separate from the group, continuing to their right, through the trees, to approach the yet-unseen building on that side. The other four

SRF continued ahead for about thirty yards until they could see past the trees. Clouds over the moon prevented them from making out a building, yet.

Owen signaled for Danny and John to separate out to the left, moving forward, and he and Dana would move straight ahead. As they approached where they assumed the shed was, they would be executing a flanking maneuver, attacking the building from two angles and from straight on, to maximize their positions against the target.

Just then the clouds moved past the moon. The agents saw a misty an outline of an old, sagging shed that was located about a hundred yards ahead, slightly off to the right. Owen signaled for everyone to keep down and keep moving in the same directions they were now headed. The amber light was steady, as there were no more trees between the agents and the shed.

All that could be heard was a high-pitched chorus of crickets. All that could be seen was the roofline of the shed, while the lower part remained in shadow. There were no vehicles by the shed.

Dana and Owen slowly crept closer to their target. Now, they were maybe fifty yards from the shed, and could no longer see the flanking agents. The moonlight seemed brighter and even some stars shone as pinpoints of light over the scene.

Owen had just turned his head slightly towards Dana, to get her position, when the crack of a rifle splintered the silence. Owen cried out, and fell to the ground. Dana, seeing him go down, moved closer, to see him holding his right arm with his left hand.

"Jesus! I've been hit!" he said, grimacing in pain.

"Roll over, to your left!" she ordered Owen. "There're some rocks there! Roll over behind them!" I've got you covered while you wrap your arm."

She got down low and moved back from him as they heard more gunfire, and another bullet whizzed by her ear. Lying on the ground, now, Dana peered around some weeds and made out a form in the shadow of the building. She fired off several rounds at the OPFOR. She could now distinguish that gunfire was coming from the other two agents' positions.

She saw one guy by the shed go down. She looked over at Owen. He had wrapped his arm and was still holding onto his rifle, but wasn't firing. She moved a little closer to see how he was doing.

Seeing her, he said, "It's still bleeding. I haven't been able to stop it."

She came over to him. "Hold your other hand tightly over the site and don't move!" Dana ordered. Reaching into her tactical vest, she took out some ointment and rubbed some on his arm. Looking at the site of the bleeding, she said, "The bullet went through a fleshy part. That's good. "Hold your arm up!" she ordered.

Reaching again in her pockets, she took out a small knife, which she used to slice through the fabric at the hem of her pants and ripped the material up past her knee. Repeating her cut, a couple of inches away at the hem, she tore the material again and yanked off a strip of the fabric from her pants.

She held up Owen's right arm, and wrapped the strip of fabric around his arm above the wound, and tied it off tightly. Then, taking a pen out of one of her pockets, she tied it over the bandage and gave the pen a turn, tightening the crude tourniquet.

She could see that his eyes were closed now as he slumped back. "Owen, the bleeding seems to be stopped, but you've lost quite a bit of blood. Can you hear me?"

"I can hear you, Dana. I'm going to make it. Just let me rest here for a minute."

*   *   *

"Hubie, good shot!" Dirk said, from around the corner of the shed. "You took one of them down! Good thing you heard them creeping up here, man. There are like, half a dozen of them against the three of us, but we have a building and they don't!"

His last words were drowned out by the repeat of gunfire coming from where Owen had been struck by one of Hubie's bullets.

"Hubie!" Dirk called out his friend's name, as the latter crumpled over, his head hitting the ground. "Hubie!" Dirk called, again, reaching around and pulling Hubie's head up by grabbing his shirt collar. But the eyes that he saw were not looking at him. They would never look at anything again.

"Hubie!" Dirk keened. "I'll get the bastards who did this to you!" He fired off repeated shots, spraying the area where he heard gunfire, from left to right. Gray rushed out of the shed from where he had been firing between the gaps in the boards. He followed Dirk's lead and sprayed across the area. Seeing Hubie dead, he cursed the attackers, and unloaded.

*   *   *

Gunfire and smoke now filled the air from all directions. Dana could tell that there was more than one gunman firing from the shed; someone else had joined the original shooter. It was impossible to tell how many there were, as she couldn't see them. How in hell had they seen the agents? They must have been looking for them and saw them when the moon first cleared.

Dana finished off her magazine and put in another. She could see flashes of gunfire from the far side of the shed, coming from Dave's and Rob's rifles. She couldn't see Danny and John, but thought she could distinguish rounds from their direction.

Owen sat up, behind the largest rock. "I think you stopped the bleeding, Dana. I'm feeling stronger." For just a moment he squeezed her hand, weakly.

Releasing her hand, he leaned out from behind the rock and, seeing another OPFOR, fired off several rounds. He was rewarded with the yelp of one of his targets. More gunfire came from the flanks, as the agents on both sides had moved up, hearing the hit.

*   *   *

"Take that, you bastards!" Gray yelled, as he fired in the direction of the majority of the gunfire. He emptied a magazine and inserted another. Firing at the blaze of gunfire on his right, he was rewarded by the shout by a man who had been hit. Hopefully he had killed him.

Gray allowed himself to think about what was happening. *Thanks to Albert, the three of them had been left, outnumbered. They had been tricked,* he knew. *Probably the warhead had been set and Albert and Henry had left to be safe. He had to live through this,* he thought. *He had to retaliate against Albert, who had left them to fight for their lives.* He fired off several rounds, and then headed to the doors to get back inside where he could continue shooting between the spaces in the boards.

*   *   *

Owen and Dana heard one of their own cry out on the left flank—either John or Danny. As Dana loaded and fired off several rounds to cover her two comrades, she could make out John, firing off his rifle, and running towards the shed. Owen saw it, too and stood up and fired at the shed, then fell back down.

More screams were heard, coming from the shed. Dana and Owen moved from behind he rocks and crawled forward. Owen then had to drop down, to clear his head.

Gunfire was still heard coming from their right flank. As Dana and Owen looked in that direction, they could see flashes from Rob's and

Dave's rifles, less than twenty yards from the shed. After that burst they saw or heard no more return fire from the shed.

Owen signaled Dana to hold her fire, to listen. After a minute, the other agents stopped firing, as well. All was quiet. Dana kept low, but cautiously started moving towards the shed. Owen followed, slowly. She looked over and could make out John, near the shed.

John motioned that the OPFOR by the shed were down. As he got to the shed and found the fallen bodies, he sent a round into the brain of each of them, doing a 'dead check,' referring to the practice of shooting the assumed dead in the head.

Owen motioned that there must be others in the shed. Rob and Dave had now made an appearance from the right. As the five agents approached the building, Owen signaled with his hand, that they were still in danger. Still, nothing was heard from within. They couldn't fire, as there may have been hostages.

John walked over to Owen and said, in a low voice, "Danny was hit in the leg. He's wrapping it to stop the bleeding. He's said he's okay.

"Dana, go check on Danny," Owen said, hoarsely. "We don't want to lose him." Dana nodded, and turned to hurry back towards where Danny had gone down.

Owen motioned for the agents to converge in front of the two large doors that were closed. John, Dave and Rob prepared to rush in, to clear the area, prepared to fire at the interior in three different directions. Owen pulled on one of the old handles, and the door swung out.

The three agents quickly moved in, followed by Owen, with their guns in low-ready position. The light inside the shed illuminated a dark truck at the opposite end. But, in the front of the shed, on the dirt floor, with a piece of clothing covering the box on its base, sat the M-88 warhead, its cone pointing menacingly towards the roof. Although they expected to see it, the materializing of the bomb seemed surreal.

Rushing past it, the four agents moved through the space, in different directions. They didn't see anyone, at first. When John got to the driver's side of the truck, he heard a choking sound and looked down. "Over here!" he called to the others.

The other four agents quickly responded to John's location, to find a man they all recognized, gagging on his own blood. "Where are the others, mother-fucker?" Rob said, coldly, as he grabbed the man's shirt front, pulling him up to a seated position.

"Gone. Com—in' back," the man they knew as Mark Hunter said, in a gurgling whisper.

"Is that bomb set?" Rob demanded, more than asked.

"I don't . . ."

"You don't what, shit head?" Owen had edged past Dave and John. But Mark's eyes had glazed over and he knew he was now talking to a corpse.

"Get that rag off the PAL controller!" Owen ordered anyone who could get to the warhead first. "And bring the lantern over so we can see the damn thing."

As Dave brought the light over to the warhead, Rob opened the cover of the computer and looked down at the keyboard. A green light was on. It was armed. Attached to the computer was a timer. It was set for 11:54.

"What's the time?!" Owen asked, even as he was lifting up his own sleeve to look at his watch.

"It's almost 11:15," Rob was the first to answer. "We have thirty-nine minutes!" he added.

Just then, Dana and Danny came limping into the shed. Danny had his right arm over Dana's shoulder while she had her left arm around his waist. On his right leg was tied a bloody green cloth that matched Owen's tourniquet. "I've called for the ambulances," she said.

"Okay," Owen said. "Danny, it's good to see you, man. The warhead is armed and set to go off in thirty-nine minutes," he said calmly, to the two of them.

"Rob, call SECOM," Owen ordered. "They'll contact the Launch Control Center or the Manatee's Weapons Officer and Commander, or NEST or whoever else has the disarming code for this weapon. John, read me off the number on the weapon."

"It's W-1241," John answered. "Did you get that, Rob? W-1241."

"I'm calling them," Rob said. A pause followed. "Sir, Owen has been hit. I'm calling to tell you that we've taken down the attackers who were here in a shed on County Y and we have the warhead. It's armed and set to go off in 36 minutes. The launch code is 4261 6442 1227. The number of the weapon is W-1241. We need the code to disarm. We're standing by."

Several minutes passed. The agents spent the time checking the identities of the killers who had been able to pull this off, at first—to steal a nuclear weapon, arm it to detonate to kill thousands. The incident and the explosion probably would have had a devastating effect on the economy of the United States.

And they might yet be successful, if SECOM didn't call back with the disarming code. The agents had to just wait there to finish their assignment.

"Hubert Strange," John read the name off one of the dead man's driver's license. "He lived at a rural address in Anderson County. The other guy is Dirk Black, with the same rural address. Mark Hunter has an address in Oak Ridge.

"How was that maniac able to get an FBI clearance? That's what I'd like to know," John said, in disgust. "We're going to have that investigated! If we can't trust the people who got security clearance from the DOE, we can't trust anyone."

"We've got twenty-seven minutes," Owen reported. "What's taking SECOM so long? What's the hold-up? The whole SRF is here, sweating it out, for Chris' sakes."

Five minutes later, Rob's phone rang. "Yeah!" he said, answering. He nodded to the others in answer to their pained, unspoken expressions, questioning if SECOM was on the other end.

"Okay, I've got it." He repeated, "7227 2446 1624. This is the reverse of the launch code. Hold on. We're going to try it.

"John, enter the code. Did you get it? Okay, okay," he said in response to John's incredulous look. "We're entering the code," Rob said to SECOM, over the phone.

John's hands were shaking a little over the keyboard, but he carefully punched in the code SECOM had given them. "There's no response!" he called out to Rob, to relay to SECOM. "The green light is still on!"

"Hold on, John! Rob responded. "Okay, got it," he said into the phone. "SECOM says, don't press any other numbers! Just wait!" Rob ordered John.

There was absolute silence in the shed. There were already twenty-six people dead and two more people were wounded in the attackers' efforts to steal and detonate this warhead. Northeast Georgia would be obliterated if this code didn't work.

There were sixteen minutes left on the warhead's timer. The staring, stone-faced group of six then heard the whirring sound of the computer's hard drive calculating. Then it stopped. Then the drive started whirring again. Dana sank down against the wall, in exhaustion.

To the astonishment of everyone, a red light came on. No one had to be told what that meant. The SRF members all blew out their held breaths, loudly, then smiled and grasped each others' hands and slapped each others' backs.

"Sonofabitch, we're good!" John shouted, echoing everyone's feelings of relief at the outcome.

As they stood there with the disabled warhead at the center of their circle, the beating of rotors could be plainly heard overhead, and the rhythmic thrum was getting louder.

All the SRF agents, who were able, moved outside, raising their arms and waving them in the air, like people who were being rescued from a deserted island. The two NEST helicopters were hovering above the group, preparing to land in the field, near the shed.

The W-88 warhead, now rendered harmless, was sitting on the dirt floor of the old shed; just an assemblage of Uranium, Plutonium, Tritrium and Deuterium explosives, protected by heat shields, and lenses, inside a cone-shaped canister. It would be picked up and returned to the trailer, to complete its trip to the Pantex plant in Amarillo, Texas, for re-fitting.

Its human protectors had won the day. All had survived, although two needed to be treated in the hospital. Ambulance sirens could now be heard in the distance, for the second time that day.

Citizens in half of the United States were asleep; and those in the other half soon would be, all content in the knowledge that they would wake up in the same world they had gone to sleep knowing.

Chapter 46

"What is it, officer? Is there a problem?" Albert pleasantly asked the unsmiling Georgia state patrolman, who was shining a flashlight in their car. Along with the rest of the northbound traffic, they had been stopped at a temporary checkpoint on the interstate, just north of Dalton.

"License and registration, please." Henry, in the passenger seat, was fumbling in the glove compartment and brought out a stack of papers, dropping several until he found the right documents to hand to Albert, who gave them to the trooper.

Leaning into the open window the officer addressed Henry. "Is this your car, sir?"

"Yes, that's right. My friend and I are taking turns driving," Henry responded, nervously. Albert shot him a look.

"Your license, please," the officer asked of Albert, who took out his driver's license from his wallet, and handed it to the trooper.

"Where are you coming from this evening?"

"We were in Atlanta," Albert replied, smoothly. "Just walking around. And we had dinner. We're on our way home, now," he added, taking back his license from the trooper.

"You have to take turns, driving from Atlanta?"

"My friend meant 'taking turns' for the day. He drove down and I'm driving home," Albert responded, looking over at Henry, for confirmation. Henry rapidly nodded several times.

"Please pop your trunk, sir."

Albert found the latch, with some effort, and the patrolman walked around to the rear of the car. Henry, now noticeably shaking, turned to Albert. "He doesn't believe us, Albert!" he said in a high-pitched whisper.

"Henry!" Albert hissed. "Suck it up and pull yourself together. He's just trying to intimidate us, and you're falling for it. There's nothing in the car, damn it."

"What about the guns?" Henry's voice was in the upper register and rising.

"They're registered, and we have permits. Besides, they're tucked under the front seats and he won't search the car, unless you get hysterical and give him cause."

They heard the sound of the trunk being closed. Albert cuffed Henry's arm, as a reminder, then took a deep breath, and straightened up in his seat.

Back at Albert's open window, the patrolman asked, "Were you doing some work in Atlanta? I notice you have a laptop on the back seat."

"No, officer, I wasn't doing any work. I normally keep my laptop with me, to check my e-mail, and Facebook; that kind of thing."

The state trooper shone the flashlight into the car again, for several seconds, moving the beam back and forth between the two men. Henry had become strangely calm and gazed evenly into the light.

"All right. You can move along. Have a good evening."

Driving off, Henry sank back in his seat. "Oh, my God! Albert! That was a close one! He suspected us of something! That was good what you said about walking around, and checking e-mail and everything. I'm glad I wasn't driving, to answer all his questions."

They drove a little further, and Albert checked the clock on the dashboard. "Do you see the time, Henry? It's eleven fifty-four, on this clock! Six minutes to midnight! Shouldn't we be *hearing* something? I know we're over fifty miles away, but I think something's wrong!"

Albert kept checking the time, every few seconds, for the next several minutes.

"Change to another station, Henry! Why isn't there any news about the bomb being detonated?! It's midnight! It should have gone off six minutes ago! I knew we couldn't trust Gray and those other two. Either they discovered the bomb was set and changed the timer to get away, or the DOE agents somehow found the shed. Which is it?!"

A few minutes later, picking up an Atlanta station, they heard the first report of the armed robbery and killing of twenty people, including fifteen federal agents, at a convenience center and gas station at Georgia exit 305 on the I-75. State and federal law enforcement personnel had been called to the horrific scene and were investigating.

"What about the fucking warhead?!" Albert shouted. "Didn't they notice a nuclear warhead was missing and would probably be exploding any time now? What's the matter with these incompetent reporters? This is the biggest news story ever, in this miserable state! They talked about it like it happened all the time! No one has ever been able to pull this off before!"

"We have to reach Gray to find out what the hell happened. Give him a call, Henry. Tell him we were in an accident, or something. I don't give a fuck what you say. Just find out about the warhead! This is fucking unbelievable!" he spat out the last words as he pounded his fist on the steering wheel. "Twenty people were killed, blah, blah, blah," Albert mimicked the newsman, in a comic sing-song manner.

"There's no answer, Albert," Henry said, quietly. "It's going to his voice mail. Should I leave a message?"

"No! Are you crazy?!" Albert grabbed the phone out of Henry's hand and hit the 'off' button. "We don't know who has the phone, now, do we? We could find ourselves asking some FBI agent if the bomb is still set to go off! Don't ever call Gray or the others, again, until we find out what happened. Let's just get home, stay low, and keep an ear to the ground."

An hour later, Albert pulled the car into their apartment building parking lot. Both men got out of the car, stiffly, and stretched. Albert opened the back door and reached under his seat for his Glock, and picked up his laptop and binoculars off the seat.

As he closed the door, he felt a cold, hard object jabbed against the small of his back, as a man behind him on his right said, "I'll take those," and grabbed his things, pushing him forwards against the car.

"What the hell?" he croaked, as his arms were roughly pulled behind him and handcuffs were snapped on. He could see Henry on the other side of the car, with his mouth open, staring in disbelief.

A low, raspy voice spoke close to Albert's left ear, "You're under arrest for the murder of Katherine Moore. You have the right to remain silent. Anything you say can, and will be used against you in a court of law. You have the right to speak to an attorney, and to have an attorney present during any questioning. If you can't afford a lawyer, one will be provided for you at the government's expense."

Albert had managed to turn far enough to look into the tired, reddened eyes of his old nemesis, who, years ago, had spent months trying to destroy him. "Detective Barnes. Don't you ever give up?" was all he said.

Chapter 47

The two NEST helicopters had settled down on the grassy field by the old farm building. Immediately, two teams of eight nuclear experts each, comprised of chemists, scientists, technicians and engineers, had jumped out and dashed into the shed to inspect the warhead. Their first undertaking was to make sure that the bomb had been disarmed and then, to determine whether the arming mechanism had been damaged. In order to confirm the latter, scientists performed a number of tests, the most critical of which was an x-ray of the canister to see that the component parts, wiring and the PAL were still intact and functional.

The property was becoming overrun with emergency and other official vehicles that had rushed to the scene, arriving as a procession of lights and sirens screaming through the dark, slumbering countryside.

In addition to medical people, dozens of investigative personnel had been sent to the location by SECOM to untangle the events of the previous eight hours, in the aftermath of the agents' armed assault against the terrorists who had killed twenty-three people, to steal a nuclear bomb. It was the first such theft in history. Now, three of the assailants were dead; two were missing; and the warhead had been safely recovered and disarmed to prevent a catastrophe, the extent of which could only be imagined.

Several ambulances were among the first to arrive at the scene of the fire fight. Paramedics jumped out of the first one, pushing two gurneys to transport the surviving gunshot victims to the hospital emergency room.

Dana had gotten blankets from the back of the vans to keep Owen and Danny warm, as the two men sat on the ground, leaning against the shed. They had remained conscious and responsive, though weak and in need of medical care.

Checking on their tourniquets, Dana had satisfied herself that they hadn't started bleeding again, and seemed stabilized for the time being. When she looked at Owen's bandaging, he had attempted to make light of the situation, saying, "I like the ballpoint pen tied on top, Dana. Nice touch. The nurse at the hospital can use it for her charting."

Danny had looked over and said, "She did a helluva job—a lot better than I did when you got bit by the copperhead. Now that I think of it, you're a real pain in the ass. That's twice in the last three months that you've had to be saved!"

"Fortunately, the paramedics are here," Dana announced. "I can't say I'll miss nursing either one of you."

The EMTs had trotted over to them and were about to lift the two agents up onto the gurneys, and to wrap blood pressure cuffs on them.

"I'll see you later, at the hospital," Dana said, waving them off.

The EMTs who got out of the other ambulances had no reason to hurry as they were there to collect the three dead bodies of Mark Hunter, Hubert Strange and Dirk Black; to transport their remains to the hospital morgue. The medical examiner would conduct an examination and complete the death certificates.

Six FBI agents, who had been conducting their investigation at the convenience store, had arrived on the scene in their two black vans, right after the ambulances. As SRF leader, Owen Knight, had been taken to the hospital, the investigators sought out team leader, Rob Woods, to assist them in their inquiries.

Their line of questioning began with the couriers' intel regarding the attackers who had been killed, and any intel they had on the missing attackers. Rob advised them that it appeared that Mark Hunter, a motor pool mechanic, was their inside man. He couldn't resist asking how the FBI had approved Hunter for security clearance after their year-long investigation.

Hunter must have been able to spy on the agents when they entered their codes on the keypads for the trailer doors. No, he didn't believe that the two agents who had the code for the trip, George Newsome and Ernest Dodd, had been in on the scheme. In fact, as the scout car was the first vehicle at the service station, Ernest had been one of the first agents to die there, of asphyxiation. There was evidence that George had died while firing at the attackers.

Hunter must also have sabotaged the vehicles and the trucks, to release whatever toxic gas into the cabins. It appeared that he was the "Gray Fordham" who had rented the tractor and utility attachment.

As for his two cohorts who had been killed today, no one had ever seen or heard of them. As he was dying, Mark Hunter had told the agents that "others had gone and would be back." He died before he said anything else. Of course, the "others" hadn't been seen.

The eye witness Rob had talked to, a Mrs. Bonita Taylor, who lived three miles back on County Y, had said that there were three men in the truck and two men in the car, following. She could not provide a description of the car, other than it was dark blue, and an older model.

As Rob had no other information that the FBI didn't have, they thanked him for his help and dismissed him. *There was nothing more he could add,* he thought. *It was their job to conduct the investigation, but the couriers had a big stake in the outcome.*

*   *   *

A half hour later, Dana walked through the glass doors of the Emergency entrance, looking like *she* should be receiving immediate treatment, with her torn and bloody clothing. She was amused at how it must look, especially as she was carrying her designer duffel bag with fresh clothes to change into after she had a chance to clean up.

Showing her badge, she inquired at the desk, and was directed back towards the room where Owen was being treated. Walking down the dull beige hallway, which smelled and looked antiseptic, she came to his room number and found the door, ajar. Soundly rapping on it, she called out, "It's Dana. May I come in?" There was a short pause before Owen answered.

"Sure, come in." As she walked inside, she saw him pulling himself up against his pillow and smoothing his sheet.

"Jesus, you look like hell!" he said, as she got closer.

"Thanks. It's nice to see you, too. You must be feeling better, anyway, to be so blunt. So, what have they told you about your arm?"

"Apparently, the bullet hit a few veins, but not an artery, before it exited. Your 'Bic' tourniquet did the job in stopping the bleeding. That 45 millimeter cartridge really chews up tissue, you know. They want me to stay until the morning, just to see if there's any more damage or infection. I'll be fine."

"I'm glad to hear it. Listen, I brought in my case with a change of clothes," she said, lifting up the brown bag. "I'm going to use your bathroom, and make myself presentable, okay?"

"Yeah, sure. That's the least I can do for you," he smiled.

Five minutes later she came back out, flushed and excited. She had changed into clean clothes and her long blond hair was down, falling around her shoulders.

"I found something in my bag!"

"I see that. You look great."

"No, I mean I discovered something that was planted by the terrorists! I was feeling the bottom of my case for a hairbrush to fix my hair, and I felt a hard lump under the lining. I cut the seam and pulled this out!" She held up the black plastic case. "It's a GPS tracker! Think about that, for a second. Someone had access to my duffel bag that's *never out of my possession*, and followed me! Could it be one of the agents who's behind this whole scheme? Who else could get at my bag, and for long enough to neatly sew back the lining, for God's sake?!"

"What about Mark Hunter?" Owen asked, now concerned. "We know he got the keypad code; was able to sabotage the vehicles. Had you ever left your bag in the motor pool area?"

"No. I always put the bag in the back of the van, on that shelf, when I get in. I never set it down for more than a second. Besides, my vehicle wasn't tampered with, to release the poisonous gas—carbon monoxide, I guess it was. But there is some connection . . ." her voice trailed off, as she looked off, thinking.

"Like, how did they know where our agents would stop and at what time?" she mused, after a moment. "They were there waiting for those particular vehicles to stop: the scout car, the QRTs, and the trucks. All those vehicles were sabotaged to release the carbon monoxide just when they pulled into the station."

"Cliff Harnett and his team died from the CO 2 out on the Interstate, several minutes before they could have arrived at the gas station," he said.

"They were the last to be asphyxiated," she countered. "The terrorists had what they wanted by then: they had probably already made off with the warhead. They must have had timer controls attached to the explosives, or whatever, in the exhaust systems, and set them off when the vehicles arrived. They didn't want Cliff to get to the gas station. But how did they know that we would even stop there?"

"We stopped there two weeks ago," Owen said, soberly. "You weren't on that trip."

"Was it the same time?"

"No. It was later when we stopped there yesterday, because the rain had slowed us down."

"They couldn't have followed us for the last three trips, because we would have spotted them. They must have followed the route of trucks with GPS trackers, like the one planted in my bag. Well, they'd need just one tracker, as the trucks stay together. Mark Hunter would have known that. But they couldn't have *known* we would stop at that service station, as we didn't even know that until an hour before—unless they were working with one of our agents."

"But they were set up to attack the shipment before they could have been tipped off," Owen argued. "Mark Hunter signed the rental contract for the tractor at 2:00."

"That's right!" she exclaimed. "And the scout car didn't arrive there until after 5:30. But *I'm* still tied into this because we know they tracked me on a shipment route. That's the only time I have my duffel bag with me. They'll have to check out the purple van. Maybe there was a malfunction, and the gas was set to be released, but wasn't."

"Maybe, but *why you?*" he asked. "Did Mark Hunter have some grudge against you?"

"No, I barely knew him. But *someone* evidently had a big grudge against me. And remember, there are still two unidentified terrorists out there. I'm going to find out *who* had targeted me and that should lead me to the missing pair."

"*You?* It's the FBI's job to investigate, following our recapture of the warhead, Dana. We did our job, and damn well, I might add. The FBI has the resources and the authority to track down any guilty parties and turn them over to Justice for prosecution."

"Yeah? Well, no one has targeted the empty suits at the FBI: these people have targeted *me*. And I'm not going to sit by while the Bureaus' investigation grinds on, and their procedures are followed at a snail's pace. This is *personal* and I'm the best one to figure out who's after me. I'm sure there are some other clues I've missed. Someone was able to come that close to me and my personal things. I'm ready to return the favor."

Chapter 48

"**A**ren't you a little out of your jurisdiction, Detective?" Albert asked with a smirk, after he had been taken to an interview room at the local police station, and seated at a table.

"It's called judicial comity, Albert," Detective Barnes responded.

"Judicial comedy? I don't see anything funny about this," Albert replied, with a scornful snigger.

"Comity, with a 't'—it's a legal term. It means that the courts of one state show respect and courtesy to the courts of another state. We cooperate with one another in the pursuit of justice. You'll be hearing a lot of legal terms from now on, Albert."

"So it's legal to drag someone to a police station in the middle of the night to question him about an imaginary crime from ten years ago? What about the Statute of Limitations? I've heard of that," Albert said, smugly, sitting back on the chair, and folding his arms.

"There's no Statute of Limitations for murder. You really do have a lot to learn, Albert. And Detective Enright and I are sorry it's so late. It's pretty late for us, too, since we've been sitting in a car waiting for you for two days and nights. What have you been up to? Where have you been?"

"I don't have to answer your questions, Detective. That was the first thing you said to me, remember? That's a law I know."

"Okay, Albert. We'll play it your way. But we're going to stay here whether or not you say anything. Detective Enright and I have plenty of things to say. But I don't want to be heartless. We'll get you a nice hot cup of coffee, that'll help keep you awake. What do you use in your coffee, if you're willing to answer."

"Oh, there's the comedy," Albert smirked. "I drink it black. Can I smoke here, or is that against the law?"

"It is. But we'll make you a deal. You answer all our questions, and we'll have a guard take you outside for a cigarette."

"I have nothing to say. I don't *have* any answers. I don't know what happened to a girl who ran away from school ten years ago. I don't need an attorney, because I haven't done anything illegal and you can't prove that I did. This is just harassment."

"Detective Enright, would you mind getting the matron to bring us all coffee?" Detective Barnes said to his partner, and then turned back towards Albert.

"I told you that you have the *right* to an attorney, but it takes up to 72 hours for one to be assigned to your case, after you have shown evidence to a judge that you cannot afford one and he agrees to assign an attorney, at the tax payer's expense. I thought your father could hire an attorney for you. We'll allow you to call your parents—one phone call, you know. You'll need representation for your arraignment in the morning. If you don't have one, by then, you will have a temporary public defender to represent you in your plea."

"What, in God's name, am I being arraigned for? This is outrageous!"

"We found Cat, Albert. That is, we found what's left of her body that you stuffed under a tree in the woods, out in the country."

Albert visibly blanched and his jaw went slack. Blinking, as though to clear away something he hadn't seen clearly, he refocused on the detective and swallowed hard, but remained silent.

Detective Barnes allowed the corners of his mouth to curl up in a small smile. "I guess you didn't expect that, did you Albert? You didn't expect that a farmer's dog would catch the scent of the old bones while exploring the woods and lead his master to discover your dirty deed. Well, that's what happened."

"Here's your coffee, Albert. It looks like you need it," Detective Enright said, acknowledging the matron bringing in three Styrofoam cups on a tray, with powdered creamer and sugar. The two detectives helped themselves to a cup, and casually stirred in the whitener. Albert helped himself to the third cup and took a sip, keeping his eyes down. After taking two more sips, he looked up at the detectives and tightened his jaw.

"I was just surprised, Albert said, defensively. "I hadn't even thought about that girl in years. And now to hear that she *did* die. It was just a shock. Wait a minute—how do you know it was that girl, Cat, whose bones you found? You can't be sure of that, after all this time."

"You really *are* behind in your knowledge of criminal procedures," Detective Barnes said, shaking his head, as though in amazement. "Forensic science has come a long way. There are many tests and analyses that are done on human remains. You might have heard of bodies being identified through dental records? Cat's records gave us positive I.D., in addition to other forensics.

"Fine," Albert sniffed. "It has nothing more to do with me than it did ten years ago when she was just a missing person. I dropped her off near her dorm and that's the last I saw of her. If you know now that she was murdered, you should be off trying to find her killer."

"We *have* found her killer." Detective Barnes said, grimly. "You can confess right now, or we can go through the process that will cost Cat's family and your family, grief, time and money. Why drag it out? Do the right thing. Tell us what happened. How it all went down."

"I told you, I haven't done anything wrong, so I have nothing to confess. There's no point in going over this same old ground again," Albert said, defiantly, then loudly sighed in exasperation.

"I see you're done with your coffee, Albert," Detective Enright commented. "I'll get the matron, to get you another cup, or would you like a soft drink?" The detective opened the interview room door and waved to get someone's attention.

"I don't need anything else. I'd just like to go home, now, if you don't mind."

"We do mind, Albert," Detective Barnes answered. "We mind a great deal. You're staying here, as our guest. As I said, you'll be arraigned in the morning and you can make your plea, then."

The matron came in and removed the tray and cups, wearing her plastic gloves. Detective Enright followed her out into the hallway, and returned to the room after a few moments.

"I think you might want to call your father, now, Albert and ask for his help getting a lawyer. You're in a lot of trouble, here. If the judge is willing to even consider bail for you, it's going to be a lot more money than *you* have."

"You can't bully me! I have no reason, or any intention to call my father in the middle of the night to tell him about your rantings."

"You know, Albert," Detective Enright began, putting his elbows on the table, and steepling his hands. "We've actually met before." Albert furrowed his brow, scowling at the younger policeman. "I'm sure you'll remember the occasion, as I recall it for you. It was late, on a rainy night in September some ten years ago, on Commercial Avenue, near your college."

"Yeah, I've heard that one, 'It was a dark and stormy night,' Albert said, smirking.

"I had stopped behind a car parked partly on the road," the detective went on, without notice of the interruption. "My lights picked up a young man, who I saw putting his companion into the passenger's seat. This young man waved me off, like there was nothing wrong.

"Looking into this case and learning that you were named after Albert Einstein, sparked by memory of something that I had seen that night. I remembered an unusual license plate that read, 'E MC 2,'—Einstein's theory of relativity. And come to find out, that was *your* license plate. And when we apprehended you tonight, I *recognized you* from when you looked into my headlight beam, and waved me off.

"So think back to that evening, as I have, when I remembered that I saw *you*. I was driving my dad's Toyota Camry and drove on past you. That might help jog your memory. Do you remember seeing *me now*, Albert?"

Albert had been sitting upright at the start of the detective's story. As the detective continued talking, his body sank back in his seat and seemed to shrink, as the color drained from his face. His eyes stared off into space, as though no longer seeing anything there in the room.

"One more thing, Albert," Detective Barnes said, allowing himself another slight smile. "You shouldn't have opened Cat's purse to take out her wallet, to make it look like a robbery, and then toss the purse on top of the body. We were able to lift a nice clear print off the metal clasp. And thanks for the fingerprints you just left on your coffee cup. I'm pretty sure one of them will match our earlier print, aren't you?"

Albert had now covered his face with his hands, and took several deep breaths through his fingers. Taking away his hands he said in a low hoarse voice, "I think I'll call my father, now. You set me up, but you won't get away with this. I'll have my Dad's lawyer take care of you. If it's the last thing I do, I'll be getting out of here," he added.

Chapter 49

Three days after the attack, Dana had returned home from Amarillo and was sitting in her living room, looking out the window, gathering her thoughts. It was the first chance she'd had to reflect on the deaths of her fellow agents, the theft and recovery of the warhead, and the fact that there were two terrorists still at large. It had been a sensational international news story, carried wall to wall on cable, since the morning after the attack. The agents who had foiled the plot, and killed the terrorists, were being hailed as heroes.

But the news coverage hadn't delved into the emotional toll taken on those involved. The courier group had been decimated, but the survivors had to stay focused on their job, despite the tragic loss of so many coworkers. There would be numerous funerals, and some time set aside for mourning, but then, the agents would have to return to their duties. Additional couriers would be hired, from a list of those who had completed their training, and things were expected to go back to normal.

Dana had called her parents and sister to reassure them that she was fine, to tell them what she could about the situation, and to comment on both the accurate and misleading aspects of the news stories. Her parents had tried to sound casual about the fire fight that Dana had been in, but couldn't hide their concern. She reminded them that she had been well trained to go on counter-offensive attacks. She admitted that there were still two terrorists at large, as had been reported, but didn't elaborate with any details of her own.

She had gone over the same general information with her neighbor, Nancy, who had rushed over when she saw Dana return home from Texas. In their conversation, Nancy had made a perceptive remark when she said, "I guess we don't know *who* the terrorists are. They don't always fit the profiles."

Nancy was right, Dana thought. Of course, staying "under the radar," would be expected of any intelligent terrorist. All of the 9/11 hijackers had lived and trained in the United States, obtaining pilot's licenses in small flight schools. Not one of them had ever attracted enough negative notice to bring them to the attention of the authorities.

The DOE couriers, who were specially trained to detect threatening persons, had not observed anything suspect about Mark Hunter. Since the attack, it had been learned that Hunter had done five military tours in the Middle East; and in a dark and twisted bit of irony, that he had specialized in Explosive Ordinance Disposal. The FBI was now investigating his alternate life as "Gray Fordham."

When the sabotaged DOE vehicles and trucks had been inspected a GPS tracker had been found under one of the trucks. That came as no surprise to Dana; or the fact that it was exactly like the one in her bag. Unfortunately, they were not the type that required a service contract, so it would be very difficult to trace the purchaser, and wouldn't reveal much if it wasn't one of the escaped co-conspirators.

The inspection of the vehicles had also led to the discovery of the small, timed charges that had destroyed the cardboard gaskets on the exhaust manifolds in the three vans and the three trucks. There was no such devise found in Dana's purple van.

The fact that the same model GPS tracker that had been planted in the truck, had been planted in her duffel bag, confirmed to Dana that she was still a target. Since her van hadn't been sabotaged, she concluded that she had been singled out for reasons other than being a member of an SRF team. She didn't think that the tracker had been there very long. She had rifled in her bag, no more than a month ago, when she couldn't find her sewing kit. She should have noticed the tracker, then.

So, who had she angered to the point that he would retaliate by attacking the convoy and taking a nuclear weapon?! *Someone who was insane*, she thought; someone who had demonized her, that they would include *her* in their plot. It did seem unlikely that she would be so important to anyone, sane or demented. Unlikely, but not impossible.

She remembered that the fictional detective, Sherlock Holmes, had said, "When you have eliminated the impossible, whatever remains, however improbable, must be the truth."

The only angry confrontation she could think of was with that guy in the white Mercedes, whom she had fought with after the sculling match. But he couldn't have followed her with the GPS in her duffel bag, as she didn't have the bag with her at the regatta.

But what about her car? Outside, in her carport, as she looked at her green Escape, sitting there exposed and unattended all night, she realized it would be easy enough for someone to attach a GPS tracker some place accessible from the exterior. She walked around the small SUV, wondering where to start. The high wheel wells seemed the most obvious choices, given the need for the tracker to pick up satellite signals.

Starting on the driver's side, she felt under the front well. Nothing there. Walking back, she felt under the back well. Nothing there, either. Maybe these places were *too* obvious. She stepped around the back of the car and felt under the rear passenger well. Nothing. Coming to the front, the last wheel well, she felt carefully, inch by inch, and then, her fingers found something. She bent down to improve her torque, got a good grip on the box with both hands, and pulled out what she already knew it had to be: a GPS tracker. It was different from the other ones that had been found. This one might have a service contract on it that would make it traceable. She'd contact the carrier.

Back in the house, she thought about the incidents that had brought that man to her attention. There were several contacts she and her neighbors had had with this man. She took out a sheet of paper to make up a list. She needed to remember all the sightings, incidents and what was said, and by whom, and put everything in chronological order, with as many dates as she could. Then she would review the evidence and proceed from there. She felt the excitement build as she thought of her plan. She was on to something. She knew it.

1. Mid-June—I walked into the mall. Noticed a guy with a limp behind me. Ran into him again in the children's dept. of Belk's. As I passed by him, I caught his eye, but he didn't smile. Creepy looking.

2. End of June—Nancy told me, after I came back from Arkansas, that late one night she had seen a man, who walked with a 'hitch in his step,' who seemed to have come from my back yard. Later, Peanut sniffed all over my house! Had he picked up the guy's scent?

3. Same day—I cleaned the house and found my duffel bag on top of my shoes in the closet. Had it been moved?

4. July 1—Nancy reported neighbor, Gladys Elwood, had seen a vintage white Mercedes, parked by her house, one morning and at night.

5. July 8—sculling match where I confronted the same guy. I knew he was following me that day. I saw his car—it was the Mercedes Gladys had described. He said some really strange things: that

we had a connection, that he had special powers and could control me. He tried to drag me to his car—When I broke his nose, he swore he'd kill me! Finally, he wouldn't give me his name, but said I'd find out some day! Like he would become famous? Infamous?

As she read over her list, it was solid evidence of someone who had preyed on her. But it was a leap from that to killing people and stealing a bomb. *But not impossible*—she thought back to her Sherlock Holmes maxim.

He could have easily broken into her house by means of the loose lock on the back door, when she was out of the house. If he had put the tracker in her duffel bag, he would have known that she was a federal agent working as a nuclear courier. How he was connected with the others, who wouldn't have the same motive concerning her, she couldn't imagine.

First thing to do was to contact the GPS cell phone carrier, and get the subscriber's name. The carrier would cooperate with a federal courier, in the aftermath of the terrorist attack, particularly.

* * *

An hour later, she was in the offices of the world-wide carrier. She explained to a service representative, that she was investigating the recent theft of the warhead, and handed over the tracker, saying that she needed the name of the person who had taken out its service contract.

After a few minutes, the young man who had gone back to a desk, had brought out the result of his search; the person who had bought the GPS tracker a month ago, and had set up the cell phone service, was an Albert Arnstein. He gave Dana the man's address and phone number. Dana noted that the address was a ten minutes' drive from her house.

Thanking the employee for his efficient service, she left the office, her mind spinning. This jerk was named 'Albert Arnstein?' Like, after the nuclear physicist? That association had to have some tie-in with the attack and theft of a nuclear weapon, though she couldn't imagine what, really.

Newly energized, and feeling hot on the trail, she now had to take the next step: she would drive over to his address. Then what? She wasn't sure. First, she had to see where he lived, get her bearings.

She had all the proof she needed to convince *herself* of this guy's guilt as a co-conspirator with Mark Hunter and the others. *But was it enough for a court of law?* she wondered. She could at least get him on a charge of stalking her. But so what? This man was a *deranged terrorist*. She had to make a plan to investigate him, properly. Take his picture to show to the fry cook at the convenience mart, for instance.

She was so angry at being a part of his diabolical scheme that she wanted to just confront him with her evidence and tell him it was over. She had to get the name of the other accomplice, too. They both had to be turned over to the authorities. Right now, she'd just check out his residence. See if his car was there, maybe catch sight of him.

A half hour later, she drove up to a war-era cemestos apartment building, with the address she had for Albert Arnstein. *Not surprising that it's a dump*, she thought. She went to the end of the block to drive around to the back of his building to see if his car was parked there.

When she turned the corner, on the next street she passed a parked car with two men in it.

What the hell? Was the FBI here already? No, this car had Ohio plates. Oh. She suddenly figured out who they were. She could identify two men in a brown sedan with government tags, slouched in seats that had been pushed back all the way: they were detectives sitting on a stake-out.

Driving into the apartment building parking lot, she didn't see what she was looking for—Albert Arnstein's vintage Mercedes. What a coincidence. Two cops on a stake-out nearby, and the terrorist wasn't here, but could be expected to arrive.

What did the cops have on this guy? This was getting very interesting. She decided to drive back around and approach their car with her badge. See what they'd be willing to tell her. Maybe they could work together.

Parking within a few spaces of the detectives, she walked over to their car, holding up her badge. The detective in the driver's seat put down his window.

"Excuse me," she began. "Federal Agent Dana Knowles. Nuclear courier with the DOE. I'm pursuing a suspect, Albert Arnstein, in connection with the recent attack, in Georgia, that's been in the news, and—"

The startled detective stopped her with, "Uh, Agent Knowles, is it? I'm Detective Lawrence Barnes and this is my partner, Peter Enright. We're from the Sheriff's Department, Butler County, Ohio, Homicide Division. We know Albert Arnstein. We arrested him a few days ago on a murder charge. He got out on bail, yesterday. We were just hanging around before we left town, to have a word with him; but it looks like he's gone, for now.

"You're looking for Albert in connection with the rampage in Georgia that's all over the news?! Agent Knowles, why don't you come and have a cup of coffee with us? I promise you that it'll be worth everyone's time. We have a lot to talk about."

Chapter 50

"You look a lot like her," Detective Barnes was saying, "Cat Moore. That's why Albert thought you and he had a connection. He probably fixated on you because you reminded him of the highpoint of his life, when he got away with murder. But I have to say that I'm shocked to hear he's wanted as a terrorist. Those people were slaughtered, indiscriminately, and the bomb that was stolen was set to detonate! Jesus Christ!"

The two detectives and Dana had been sitting in a coffee shop for the past hour, talking about Albert Arnstein; sharing information.

"I don't know what role Albert played in the plot," Dana said. "But I knew he was involved, when I linked him to the GPS trackers that were used in the scheme. It doesn't matter who actually pulled the triggers or set off the gas, as you know. They'll all guilty of *every single murder*, as well as the theft and attempt to detonate the bomb to kill thousands more.

"As I told you, until I found the trackers, I hadn't known Albert was a real threat. I had had only that one encounter with him, after discovering he had been stalking me. I had never seen that level of rage, though. After he took a swing at me, and I took him down with a few punches of my own, and broke his nose, he swore he'd kill me. But that's usually just an expression. I thought that was the end of it. It never occurred to me that he was anything more than a creep who had to be taught a lesson.

"I mean, he was irrational, but I didn't realize he was a psycho. Thinking back, I remembered that he said some really strange things like, 'he could control me with special powers.' I told him that he was sick and should get some help. I thought that was the last time I'd see him."

Detective Barnes said, "You showed him that he didn't have any power over you, and he couldn't tolerate that. Apparently, he sought the ultimate revenge and show of power."

"So he stole a nuclear bomb to detonate?!" Dana offered. "How crazy is he?! The dozens of killings, and the attempt to exterminate thousands of people, go way beyond even a psycho's revenge against one person. It looks to me like he's seeking revenge against the whole world."

"I think he's further descended into madness," Detective Barnes offered.

"You said he told you his father was cold and controlling," Dana went on. "Maybe Albert was unloved and even abused when he was a child. Probably was, from the icy look in his eyes. But who cares?! The point is, he has become a monster with no regard for human life, and he must be stopped! He needs to be found and arrested before he kills again, or tries to attack another shipment.

"I want to see him stand trial for those acts of terrorism—murdering my fellow agents and stealing a weapon from our shipment.

"And I'm pissed off if I was even a tiny, incidental factor in his bloody plans! I hope to God he didn't twist my rejection of him as some kind of symbol of how everyone rejects him; so he should kill as many people as possible! I think he was even the ringleader, given the fact that he was able to get away to safety and the others were left to fight for their lives."

"You're not responsible for setting off this maniac," Detective Barnes said."

"What *you are* responsible for is tracking him down. You got on his trail before anyone else. And it's a good thing we met up with you, because I think we can fill in the rest of the picture for you. We met Albert's last accomplice."

"What? How do you know that?"

"As we told you when we sat down, we arrested him three nights ago for the murder of Cat Moore. He had come home late with another man, a Henry de Salvo. We just took down his name as being present at the time of the arrest. He lives in the apartment next to Albert's."

"We heard about the horrific events in Georgia the next morning," Detective Enright added. "But we didn't connect Albert and this de Salvo guy with that."

"How did Albert get bail?" Dana asked.

Detective Barnes shook his head in disgust, and replied, "His father's attorney argued some bull shit. That the crime was ten years ago, there was minimal and, possibly, coerced evidence, he was no flight risk leaving the country as he didn't have a passport, and yadda, yadda. The attorney got him bail for 100k, which Albert's old man paid. Pete and I didn't see Albert after the arraignment. We wanted to emphasize, you might say, the importance of his showing up for the next court date that will be in Ohio."

"Did your witness make the car?" Detective Enright asked. "When we picked up Albert, he was driving Henry's car, a dark blue Plymouth, about fifteen years old, I'd guess. They stopped manufacturing the damn things *ten* years ago."

"Yeah, we got a general description. And that fits de Salvo's car.

"What I need to do *right now*," Dana said, emphatically, "is to put the screws to this de Salvo guy and find out where Albert is. I know I should be running this up the chain of command; bring in the FBI. But right now, I'm up against it. These two are the most wanted criminals in the world. I can't let them slip through my fingers. I've got to get some intel while I'm here at the scene. Then I'll inform the FBI."

"We'll go with you to talk to de Salvo," Detective Barnes offered. "We've don't have any jurisdiction in your matter, but we're both looking for Albert."

Twenty minutes later they met at the back of Albert's apartment building. "There's his car—de Salvo's," Detective Enright clarified. "This guy, de Salvo, seems a little strange, Dana. I'm not sure he's all there."

"I don't think any of them could have been sane, to do what they did," she responded.

The three of them took the stairs, and, getting to the top, they first went to Albert's door and knocked. Detective Barnes called out, "police!" There was no answer, as they had assumed.

Walking down the hall, they came to Henry's door, and Dana rapped several times. Detective Barnes called out, "Police, open up!"

Seconds later, the door was opened by the man the two detectives recognized as Henry de Salvo. But now he was wearing a sheet, possibly, tied at the waist with a rope. He stood, open-mouthed, as they had seen him the other night, as he gaped at each of them, in turn. "Did you want to see me?" he asked, in a high squeak.

"You're Henry de Salvo?" Dana asked. Henry nodded, uncertainly. "I'm Federal Agent Dana Knowles. I'm with the National Nuclear Security Administration." Henry backed up and leaned against the wall. His face had gone ashen. "We're here to question you about the murder of twenty-three people, including eighteen federal agents, and the theft and attempt to detonate a nuclear weapon, which was government property."

Dana hadn't finished her sentence before Henry had collapsed on the floor. Bending down, she saw that the man was out cold. After a couple minutes, Detective Enright got down and lightly slapped Henry's face, to bring him around.

"You're arresting me?" Henry said, as soon as he was conscious. Not waiting for an answer, he went on, breathlessly, "I might have known! Do you know what I opened to, in the Bible this morning? Not the Ten Commandments, but where Jesus is asked by a man which Commandments he must keep. Jesus said, 'You shall not kill. You shall not steal. You shall not bear false witness. Those are the most important Commandments.' And now here you are. And I have to keep those Commandments."

"Yes, Mr. de Salvo, those are Commandments we all must keep," Dana agreed, "and I'm glad to hear you say that. I have a few questions I want you to answer, truthfully, about those very subjects.

"You met Detective Barnes and Detective Enright the other night, do you remember?

"Yes, they took Albert away."

"That's right. Then Albert was released, on bail, before he goes on trial for murdering a girl ten years ago. Do you know where Albert is now? I'm looking for him, to question him regarding the terrorist charges I'm talking to you about."

"Albert's not a terrorist! He's my neighbor, and my friend!" Albert protested.

"All right. Do you know where your friend is?" Dana persisted.

"I can't bear false witness," Henry answered in a small voice. "Yes, I think I know where he is. I don't know if he's there at this minute," he clarified. "But I know where he's staying, for now. Promise you won't hurt him. He's been good to me."

"Okay, Mr. de Salvo. Just tell me where he is," she said, calmly.

"Please—call me Henry. I'll have to take you there. It's way out in the country off an unmarked road. He's staying in Gray's trailer. Do you know Gray, too?" he asked, as though of social interest.

"Gray Fordham is an alias of Mark Hunter, their inside man in the motor pool," Dana explained to the detectives.

"I heard a Mark Hunter was killed in the shoot-out!" Henry said. "I didn't know that was Gray! Oh, this is all terrible! We didn't restore power to the righteous and defeat the evil military complex!"

"Is that what you thought you were doing?" Dana asked. "Defeating evil?! What was so evil about the people in the convenience mart? Or the agents, who were doing their jobs?!" Her blood pressure was rising, heating her face. "Or the people in several communities around who were sleeping in their beds, who would have died in the explosion?!"

"Albert said they were evil because they had power over us and kept us from being who we were meant to be. I had been fired from my job at the weapons plant at Y-12. Albert was threatened by one of the agents who had said she would kill him. He needed to teach her a lesson about how powerful he was. Gray was angry about all the explosives that had killed so many soldiers in the war. Hubie and Dirk were friends of Gray's from my church, The Temple of Bountiful Salvation. That's how we knew each other. I introduced them to Albert."

"Did Albert plan the attack?" Dana asked.

"Yes. Albert's very smart. He thought of the GPS trackers to follow the convoy. I helped by reading the maps. Gray wired the vehicles to set off the gas. But Albert was the one who was able to decode the lock on the warhead. I helped a little with that. I had more knowledge about how the PAL was wired to the bomb."

The detectives and Dana looked from one to another, in bewilderment, at his apparent pride.

"Well, okay, Albert. We appreciate that you've us the details of the attack. We'll all be going to the station, later, until we can make arrangements with the FBI, who'll want to talk with you. Right now, we need you to take us out to the trailers to find Albert."

"Sure. You want me to drive and you can follow?"

"No, Henry," Dana said. "You're being detained, pending arrest. You'll sit in the back seat of the detectives' car and direct us to where Albert is hiding. Change into some regular clothes and then we'll be on our way."

"Okay, Albert tells me to do that, too. I hope he won't be too mad at me that I'm bringing you to the trailers, but I had to tell the truth. Albert always told me I should follow the scriptures that I found so he should understand."

Chapter 51

Dana was getting angrier by the mile, as she followed the detectives' car back into the hills on their way to apprehend Albert. After learning about Albert's history, she was outraged that he had almost gotten away with another deadly crime.

Albert had finally been charged with the ten-year old murder of the college student, Cat Moore, thanks to Detective Barnes' dogged persistence. The crime had been a senseless one. The victim had been young and naïve. She had trusted that she was safe within the universe of a college campus and with her fellow students. When a casual acquaintance had offered her a ride to her dorm to get out of the rain, she hadn't hesitated; and she had paid for that decision with her life.

Dana could see that Cat had no reason to think Albert was dangerous, but what was her excuse? She was a mature woman; a professional security agent, trained to detect anyone who was a threat. She had seen him as just a nut case, a nuisance; certainly not a psychopathic killer.

Albert and his accomplices hadn't fit the ethnic, extremist profile of terrorism, yet they had committed terrorist acts, and probably acts of treason, as they had attempted to make war against their government.

And they had almost gotten away with their scheme. They had stolen the weapon, and had decoded the security controls. But they hadn't gotten away from the couriers. The agents had systematically hunted them down, killed them, had taken back the weapon and had it disarmed. In all, eighteen agents had been killed, and two more agents were injured in the final showdown. They all could have lost their lives in the fire fight, but they were prepared to make that sacrifice.

Albert had sacrificed his accomplices. Now she was going after him. She was the one person who could connect him to the crime, and she, like Detective Barnes, was determined to make him pay and bring him to justice. She had notified the FBI of her intent, was giving them directions and would keep in touch to apprise them of the situation as it developed.

They had now been driving over twenty minutes. *Where, in God's name are we going?* she wondered. Maybe that weird Henry was leading them on a wild goose chase, but how long could he do that? More likely he had lost focus and they'd missed a turn, or something.

Henry didn't seem to have a firm grasp on reality, although she didn't think he was violent; if she could trust her judgment anymore. He was like a child. He thought they were all part of some bible story of good conquering evil. Too bad for him that he had been on the wrong side in that battle.

Henry foolishly admired Albert and considered him a friend, but she doubted that Albert felt the same way about Henry. Psychopaths weren't capable of empathy or friendship. They were only nice and charming to be able to use people for their own benefit.

Surely they'd get there soon. She was getting anxious to confront Albert and get this over with. *He should be surprised to see me,* she smiled to herself.

*   *   *

"Henry, are you sure we're still going the right way?" Detective Barnes asked for the second time in their trip. "If you're trying to get us lost to protect Albert, it won't work. We're going to be driving around here until we find him. I'll tell you that, right now."

"Yes, Sir. This is the way," Henry responded, with certainty. "See, we're just coming to the collapsed shed. I'll start looking for the split pine tree where we turn next. We're about fifteen minutes away.

"Albert won't be happy to see all of us. He wanted to be alone back here. When you let him come home from jail, he just stopped by to tell me that he'd be at Gray's trailer for awhile and not to contact him. He'd call me."

"Listen, Henry," Detective Barnes said. "This might not have a good ending. We're going to ask Albert to come peacefully, that there's no way out. At this point, he has no good options. The only way Albert could be in any more trouble is if he refuses to give himself up. We don't want this to turn ugly, but that's what will happen if he resists. Do you understand?"

"Sure," Henry responded. "I don't want Albert to get into any more trouble. It's for his own good to turn himself in and come with us. He can give a good explanation for everything that we did."

"You'll both be given an opportunity to tell your sides of the story to the FBI agents, who will be arriving at the trailers, and taking both of you into custody," Detective Enright added.

"That sounds fair," Henry said. "I'll tell Albert that. He can be very persuasive when he's trying to bring other people around to his point of view. You can tell he's very intelligent. He's always given me good advice and helped me with my problems.

"There's the pine tree split by lightning!" Henry said, delightedly. "We're almost there. I'll be glad to get this over with. So will Albert."

*   *   *

Albert had been in the cramped trailer long enough now to feel the flimsy walls closing in on him. Fortunately, the place had a TV so he could follow the news coverage, which had been very unsatisfactory to this point. He hadn't heard one reporter who was impressed with the superior intelligence it took to steal a warhead, and break its locking code.

And who the fuck was this eyewitness who said there were two more accomplices? They hadn't had contact with anyone—unless it was that woman with the apron on, out by the road. They should have shot her. That was a mistake; never leave any witnesses. Fortunately, she couldn't have gotten a good look at him, and there was nothing to tie him to the attack, anyway.

He had been smart in getting the hell away from the shed after he set the timer. Too bad for Gray, and the others, getting caught. Looks like they weren't the marksmen they thought they were. What pissed him off was, why couldn't have protected the bomb for another half hour so it would have detonated. One more lousy half hour. If they couldn't have done that, what was the point of it all, for Chris'sakes?

At least he was here, and safe, to plan his getaway. His old man had coughed up the do-re-mi to spring him from jail; but he could thank his mother's weak constitution for that. She had taken to her bed, when her only son had been arrested for murder. He knew she was just worried about the publicity so she had convinced his father to pay his bail. Now he just had to wait for the old man to make the arrangements and finance his disappearance, once and for all.

Barnes thought he had him nailed after the bones were found. That's when he concocted the so-called evidence. A print left on the purse? Impossible. And you could drive a truck through the holes in Enright's story. He remembered a license plate and a stranger from ten years ago? I don't think so. Easy enough to get his license plate from the DMV. Just his luck, that for once they weren't totally inept.

Anyway, he wasn't going to stick around and count on his attorney to get him off, as easy as it should be. You didn't want to trust your life to some fucking morons on a jury, either.

He was going to get far away from here, as fast as he could, even though he hadn't taken care of all his business. That Knowles bitch had survived. He should have made sure her vehicle had been gassed. He really screwed up there. Of course he hadn't expected the hapless agents would ever find the shed, but that must have been because the farm woman had ratted them out.

The only person in the world who knew he had planned the attack was Henry, and Henry would never turn him in. He couldn't wait to hear from his father and get out of here and get this whole messy business behind him.

What the hell is that?! He heard the sound of cars approaching, their tires crunching the small pebbles of the gravel road. Looking out of one of the small trailer windows, he couldn't believe his eyes. One grey sedan that he recognized as Detective Barnes' had pulled up close to the trailer and a lime green Escape had parked behind it. *The lime green Escape driven by her?! What was happening here?!* He ran and got an M-16 from the corner and inserted a 30-round magazine.

Albert had the gun in his hands, and was aiming it out the window. He saw Henry in the back seat of the detective's car! Henry had turned him in and brought the people who wanted to see him dead! How could this have happened?!

Dana, jumped out of her car, and crept down behind the parked Mercedes, as the detectives exited their vehicle, keeping the hand-cuffed Henry with them, and joined her, with their weapons drawn.

"I'm going to try to negotiate with Albert," she said to the others. "Henry, you may have a chance to try to convince him that he has no other choice, but to come peacefully."

"Yes, sure. I think he'll listen to me."

"Henry, what the fuck are you doing here with these people?!" Albert hollered out the window.

"I knew he would be surprised to see me," Henry said to Dana. "And I was afraid that he'd be angry. Looks like I was right."

"How could you do this to me?! These people are here to kill me!" Albert yelled, again.

"They don't want to hurt you, Albert!" Henry hollered back.

"Let me go in, Agent Knowles," Henry said. "He's been mad at me before but he would never hurt me. I know if I can talk to him, in private, I can convince him to do the right thing, that it'll be best for him."

"I want to talk to Henry, alone!" Albert called back out the window.

"No way, Henry," Dana said. "You're in our custody and we have to protect you. You're a witness. If Albert has the chance, he'll kill you, too. I'm sorry, I know you want to help, but that's not the way."

"Albert!" Dana called out. "Henry has nothing to do with our being here! I found the two trackers that you planted to follow me and I got your name from the service contract on one! I know you planned the attack! It's all over! Give yourself up, you piece of shit!"

"Just let me talk to Henry! I have nothing to say to you!"

"There's nothing to talk about! We'll just sit here and wait for the FBI," Dana yelled back.

Suddenly, Henry stood up, ran around the front of the car, towards the trailer, managing to jump up the steps to the doorway as the detectives and Dana started after him. Shots rang out, coming from the trailer as bullets hit the sedan's front window, shattering it.

"Henry!" Dana cried, crouching down, again. "Come back!"

As soon as Henry got to the top step, Albert opened the door, and grabbed Henry, pulling him inside the trailer. Henry, breathing heavily from his run, had been thrown off balance by the movement and fell against the opposite wall, and sank down to the floor.

"How could you sell me out?! Albert hissed. What deal did you make with them? That's what I'd like to know!"

"Albert, you've got it all wrong. Let me catch my breath and we'll talk."

"You've got one minute. Talk."

"Okay. Here's what happened. About an hour ago, Detective Barnes and Detective Enright and Agent Knowles came to see me in my apartment. They're all very nice, I should tell you at the start."

"Henry, cut the bullshit! They're not *nice*. Just tell me what they know and they better not have heard it from you!"

"Okay, Albert, just hear me out, without getting mad. They know that we planned the attack on the nuclear weapons convoy."

"They don't *know* a god-damned thing, unless you told them, Henry! There's no way they can connect us with that! They already killed Gray, Hubie and Dirk. You want them to kill us, too?! I can't believe that you brought them here! Now we're going to have to shoot our way out!"

"No. Listen, Albert! I didn't tell them anything, except that I had opened the Bible and found the Commandments not to kill, steal or tell a lie. They call it 'false witness' in the Bible, but"—

"Shut up, Henry! Just shut the fuck up! So you told Detective Barnes, who has spent ten years trying to frame me for a murder, and Agent Knowles, who wants to kill me on sight for no reason, that I'm responsible for the attack on the convoy and stealing the warhead!"

"No, Albert! I swear! They told *me* that they have proof that we were behind it all. Well, we are! Why would they say that—how could they have even come to my apartment if they didn't have proof. I know we had good reasons for what we did. That's what we'll tell the FBI. That's who's going to meet us here, so we can tell them our side of the story. That's what Detective Barnes said."

"How naïve are you, Henry?! You just signed our death warrants. They don't care about our *sides of the story*. They're the evil authority that has tortured us our whole lives and now you want to hand me over to them as a present. Well, I'm not going. I have a way out of here and I'm going to take it! And you can go screw yourself!"

"Albert!" Dana called out. "The FBI is on their way! They'll be here any minute. Let Henry come back out. You have no reason to hold him! He's tried to help you!"

"Fuck you! Fuck all of you!" Albert shouted out from inside the trailer. "He's not going anywhere, bitch!"

Albert fired a shot out the window and just had time to duck down, as a barrage of bullets sprayed through the window where he had just been. Meanwhile, Henry had fallen down and was trying to get under a piece of furniture, shrieking in terror.

Albert got in the window once more, getting ready to fire off more rounds, when two more bullets flew past his head causing him to sink to the floor, out of sight. "Hold your fire! We're coming out!" he yelled from under the window.

A minute later, the trailer door opened and the three law enforcers saw only Henry stagger through the door unsteadily, his mouth contorted, and his reddened eyes were tearing, squinting to try to see Agent Knowles and the policemen. In a high-pitched, wavering voice he kept repeating, "When I am afraid, I will put my trust in thee! I will trust in thee!"

Albert stood directly behind him, holding Henry close, as a shield. "You're going to have to shoot him first!" Albert screamed. "Go ahead; just shoot a hand-cuffed man in cold blood! I dare you!" he taunted. Albert nudged Henry down a step and then had to grab him and pull him back, as Henry had started to topple forward. "Stand up, Henry, for Chris' sakes!"

"Either shoot Henry right now, or let us get out of here!" Albert called out, from behind the frightened hostage.

"You're making a big mistake, Albert!" Dana yelled back. "Use your head and give up while you still can, without getting hurt! I'm giving you fair warning! Let Henry go and drop your weapon! You're a smart guy!

You know you don't stand a chance here! You can still save yourself! None of us wants more bloodshed!"

Albert knocked Henry forward with the muzzle of his Glock, down to the last step. "You can't shoot me while I'm holding Henry, Agent Dana Knowles! You can only shoot me if the bullet passes through Henry first so, go ahead, why don't you shoot Henry?! You can get two for one!"

"All right, we'll have to do it your way, Albert!" Dana said with resignation. "Henry, do you see how Albert is giving you up to save himself? Well, I want to save you, instead. I've given Albert every opportunity. Do you see that?" Henry shut his eyes tightly and nodded. "Okay, work with me here, Henry. When I say 'Now!' just put your head down, okay?"

"Don't do anything she says, Henry!" Albert ordered. "I'll blow a hole through you, if you try to help her out!"

"Now!" Dana cried.

Henry put his head down, turning away with his eyes still shut. A single shot rang out. Albert stood frozen for a split second, just staring at her. But only one cold eye was staring at her. The other eye was gone, leaving in its place a bloody dark hole, as the bullet tore through and entered his brain, just before his lifeless body sank to the ground.

"Oh, my God!" Henry cried out, running forward to safety, to be with the agent.

Dana went towards him, and put a hand on his shoulder. "I warned him, Henry. I gave him a choice, and he chose to sacrifice you. Just like he sacrificed the others back at the shed in Georgia.

We'll stay here, now, and wait for the ambulance to come for Albert's body. The agents from the FBI will be here soon, too. They'll take you into custody for questioning. You just tell the FBI everything you can of Albert's plan, and how you went about executing it. That's all the good you can do, now."

"That was a hell of a shot, Dana." Detective Enright had walked over and shook her hand. You handled this situation very skillfully. It couldn't have had a good outcome as Albert saw it."

"If you need any back-up for your actions with the DOE and the FBI, just let us know, Detective Barnes added. "They should all be proud of you. You did as well as anyone could. You got Henry to trust you, and you saved him from Albert."

"Thanks, Detective. I appreciate your words. The Bureau's people should be here soon. I was able to give the agents directions as we went. And I had kept my phone on while it all went down, so they can judge my actions for themselves. Anyway, now that I've stopped Albert from hurting anyone else, I'll take my chances with the FBI."

Epilogue

After Albert was killed, two FBI agents visited Harold and Judith Arnstein to explain the circumstances of their son's death. At the news, Mrs. Arnstein collapsed. Dr. Arnstein expressed shock and disbelief that Albert could have had anything to do with the terrorists in Georgia and, besides, wasn't Albert under arrest for the murder of some college girl at the time of the attack?

The next day the physicist went to court to get back his $100,000 in bail money, and then made arrangements to bury his son. Mrs. Arnstein regained her composure and arranged for a sit-down luncheon featuring quiche and fresh fruit salad, following the funeral.

*　　*　　*

Six months after the assault on the nuclear convoy and theft of the W-88 warhead, the matter of *The United States of America vs. Henry Martin de Silva*, 10-2435, was decided in the U.S. District Court, Eastern District of Tennessee.

For weeks there had been legal wrangling over the charges and the jurisdiction. There were several complicated issues facing state and federal courts involving the following facts: All of those involved in the attack had been residents of Tennessee; the crime had been planned in Tennessee, and the government vehicles were sabotaged there. But the murders of the eighteen federal employees and the five civilians were committed in Georgia, with all the civilians being Georgian residents; and, finally, the theft of the nuclear weapon and the attempt to detonate it, occurred in Georgia.

Other issues were controversial and had to be adjudicated: it was argued that the murders of the agents and the theft of the bomb were acts of domestic terrorism, as defined by the U.S.A. Patriot Act, as it was a "calculated use of violence (or threat) against civilians in order to obtain goals that are political or religious or ideological in nature." Due to the fact that federal agents were murdered and a nuclear bomb was stolen, it was argued that it was a crime of treason, as it was an "attack of war waged against the United States government . . ."

Georgia wanted the state trial in its county courthouse to prosecute for the civilian murders of its citizens. This would have proven detrimental to Henry, as he was pleading 'innocent by reason of insanity,' through his public defender. Georgia was one of the few states that offered a "guilty, but mentally ill" verdict, which would have sent Henry to a state prison for life, following treatment.

Tennessee allowed for a verdict of "not guilty by reason of insanity," an affirmative defense that read: "a person is not responsible for criminal conduct, if at the time of such conduct as a result of mental disease or defect, he lacks substantial capacity either to appreciate the criminality of this conduct or to conform his conduct to the conformity of the law." Henry's attorney would have to convince the jury that Henry's mental functioning complied with the legal definition of insanity. The defense was rarely successful.

In the end, all of the crimes were prosecuted in federal court, as the authoritative federal law read, "If a crime was committed as part of another federal crime, the case would appear before a federal court."

Hence, on February 10, 2011, Henry was brought before the District Court in Knoxville on charges of twenty three counts of conspiracy to commit murder; of which eighteen counts were conspiracy to commit murder against federal agents; various acts of domestic terrorism; and the theft of a nuclear weapon, that was government property, with the intent to do violence against a civilian population.

Henry was represented by a Federal Public Defender in the case. The attorney, Phillip Warner, became convinced of the viability of the insanity defense after his first conversation with Henry in jail, where he was awaiting trial. In researching his client's background the attorney learned of Henry's past drug use, including Ecstasy, which paved the way to prove his defense of diminished capacity.

At trial, Attorney Warner put three psychiatrists on the stand who testified to the drug's effect of destroying certain brain cells. After discontinuing the drug, the brain cells don't reconnect normally, causing paranoia, anxiety, confusion, and other psychological problems.

Henry's parents, Anthony and Rosa de Salvo, tearfully testified that Henry had been a "wonderful boy who had gotten in with a bad crowd in high school." He had reformed and became very religious, but had gotten in with another bad crowd, now that he was forty-two. On the stand, they occasionally caught Henry's eye and he would wave, in response.

Henry's pastor, Brother Bob, testified for the defense, to explain how Henry had opened the bible at random, as he was led by the 'Spirit.' Many of the passages from the Old Testament, in particular, depicted acts of vengeance taken against those who had done wrong. Henry's friend Albert told him that the Spirit wanted him to seek the Lord's vengeance against the people at Y-12, who had wronged them both.

After closing arguments, the jury convened to deliberate. After an hour and a half they brought in the verdict that Henry was "not guilty by reason of insanity." Henry smiled broadly and thanked the jury. He was then transferred to a mental institution where he will stay in treatment for the foreseeable future.

*   *   *

Dana's pursuit and fatal shooting of Albert was determined to be justified by the Department of Professional Accountability of the DOE and the FBI after their reviews of the circumstances. In the end, she was commended for taking the initiative to apprehend Albert, in light of his continual efforts to flee and avoid capture and prosecution.

In the aftermath of the attack, Dana thought back to the time when she had been frustrated by the long hours spent in training, without seeing any action. She would never again doubt the value of the repeated exercises, as they had fully prepared the agents to be successful to take down the terrorists and prevent incalculable harm to the country as a whole.

The attack had also been a turning point in her personal life. Having proven to herself that she had been up to the ultimate challenge, she felt she had earned the right to move into a career that would offer her a more balanced and fulfilling lifestyle.

At the time that Henry was being relocated to a mental institution, Dana was relocating to Chicago, where she had taken a position with the Homeland Security Administration. She would be a Personnel Security Specialist, investigating backgrounds of those who would work in highly-sensitive positions in national security. Her two years of college, her military experience and her two years as a nuclear courier had qualified her for a GS 11 level salary to enable her to live comfortably. She had also enrolled in night school at a downtown university, taking courses towards a degree in terrorist studies.

And, as things turned out, Dana didn't make the move to Chicago by herself. She and Owen had gotten together after the attack, spending many hours talking about this experience, their views on many subjects, their life's goals and finally, their feelings for each other. With Dana finding the right job for her in Chicago, Owen was glad for the opportunity to move back to his hometown and reconnect with his family. He soon landed a job in charge of security management of a large investment firm on LaSalle Street. It meant a thirty percent increase in income, for a forty-hour work week. His parents and brother, Pete, were very proud of him.

As for the courier service, newly-trained agents were brought in as replacements for the fallen members, but life didn't get back to normal. There would never be anything 'normal' again for this group of courageous security specialists, who had avoided the worst nuclear disaster in the history of the world, and many of them had paid with their lives. Thousands from the surrounding communities attended the memorial service that honored all the agents who had been killed in the line of duty that day in August, at a truck stop in Georgia.

In the aftermath of the attack and near nuclear catastrophe, there had been a shift in the country's psyche regarding the face of terrorism. Most people came to realize that terrorists could no longer be narrowly defined as only those ideologues that belonged to a certain foreign ethnic group, and believed in certain extremist religious causes and principles. Terrorists could be native-born individuals, with irrational grievances against the government, or sociopaths with a grudge against society. Terrorism could spring from any radicalization, of whatever form or rubric.

In addition, a consensus was building to properly identify and treat those with mental illness; including members of the military who suffered from post-traumatic stress syndrome, to offer them a pathway to better mental health and a fulfilling life.

Debates continued regarding the rationale of stockpiling, there being 23,360 nuclear weapons in the world, at the time of the attack. And there was much public discussion about the hundreds of locations holding nuclear weapons or weapons-grade material, with no binding global standards of securing them. Even military leaders were becoming more serious about the need to reduce the numbers of weapons through arms treaties between countries. Hopefully, the numbers would continue to go down and the security of those that remained would be improved.

But in Oak Ridge, Tennessee, twenty-seven federal agents had proven to the world that the greatest deterrent to a nuclear weapon being stolen and used against a population was the human factor. When all the safeguards had been overcome by the terrorists, only the agents' skill and determination had prevented a nuclear disaster.

It gave a lot of people a sense of well-being and security, while for others there had come a new awareness of the grave consequences of the remote, yet possible, event of another theft of a nuclear weapon that could be detonated.

A year after the attack, one nuclear reality remained unchanged: The Doomsday Clock was still set at Six Minutes to Midnight.

Acknowledgements

The writing of this book was complicated by the fact that the whole subject of nuclear weaponry, and their safeguards, is not widely known or understood; certainly not by me, prior to undertaking this project. Also, many of the particulars in this area are classified information.

In approaching this subject with a high degree of authenticity, without straying into a prohibited area accidentally, I relied on my friend, Bill Harris, a former federal agent, who worked as a nuclear courier for seventeen years. He was invaluable in describing the para-military maneuvers, the firearms and their use, as well as the general training, duties and responsibilities of the brave and dedicated people who work as couriers for the Department of Energy.

I would like to thank Carolyn Carlson, my sister-in-law, who acted as a proofreader/editor throughout the project. I relied on her for her enthusiasm, and her insightful responses to the story line and the characters' actions and conversations. She gave me a lot of advice and little criticism. I waited for her reaction to every chapter, to consider her suggested rewrites, before finalizing each one.

I thank my daughter-in-law, Chanin Peyton, who inspired me to keep going, and offered her proofreading skills on the chapters I sent her.

I especially thank my husband, Jim, who steadfastly encouraged me with his comments and support; and who never begrudged me the enormous amount of time I needed to work in isolation and without interruption.

Finally, I want to thank many relatives and friends, who won't be named here, but who will recognize themselves, for always showing an interest in my efforts and cheering me on to finish.

Edwards Brothers,Inc!
Thorofare, NJ 08086
13 April, 2011
BA2011103